Where There's Smoke

Cathy Cole

First published by Fireborn Publishing March 2017
This edition published by Inglenook Press 2019.

Copyright © Cathy Cole 2016

Cover Art by: Mnsartstudionew

ISBN-13 978-1-9160439-0-9 (PRINT)
ISBN-13 978-1-9160439-1-6 (EBOOK)

ACKNOWLEDGMENT

From conception to final draft, a lot of people have helped in the creation of this novel.

On the technical side, I'd like to thank: Joe McKnight, Station commander, Command and Control Systems Manager, Northern Ireland Fire & Rescue Service, who answered my early enquiries and treated me like a "real author." Then, when the book began to evolve, my go-to guy was my brother, Rory Dumigan, a dedicated firefighter who has spawned a family of firefighters. What they do on a daily basis takes my breath away.

To all the firefighters and emergency services out there, you deserve so much more — in payment and in a public's grateful thanks.

I also want to thank my beta readers. A book, like a human being, goes through many stages in its life. If you have the right people around you then your story can only grow into something amazing. Beta readers rock! So, thank you Carrie, Nadine, Mairi (R.I.P), Linda (Firefly), and Paul McAteer, plus Mywriterscircle.com and the Absolute Write forum. This book would never have got to this stage without you all.

Special thanks go to my amazing editor, Jamie Rose. I shall endeavour to keep killing off those IBP's.

On a more personal level, I want to thank my husband Paul, who put up with last-minute meals and an absent wife. To my children, Kristopher and Patrick — and Ciara, who has my undying love for giving us our gorgeous granddaughter, Séarlait. Life would be nothing without you all.

This book is dedicated to my sister, Oonagh McDermott and my father, William Dumigan.

I miss you guys, always and forever.

PROLOGUE

Death approached, not with a scream but a whimper, as six-year-old Lucy Hamilton's thumb slipped from her mouth. She sat up in bed and peered into the darkness, wondering what had awakened her.

Outside, the wind whistled and shrieked, and she shivered as the branches of the old oak tree tapped against her window, like brittle knuckles rapping for entry. She reached for her Barbie but found the bed beside her empty.

Taking a deep breath, Lucy slipped from the covers, legs trembling beneath her bright-pink nightdress. Determined not to cry, she held tightly to the mattress with one hand, while the other groped shadows until she found the smooth curve of a plastic leg. With a relieved sigh, she clasped the doll to her chest and clambered back into bed.

A loud thump came from the direction of her parents' room and Lucy froze. She heard a cry, quickly muffled, then a thud. She waited, but the sound wasn't repeated. "It's okay, Barbie," she said, her arm tightening around the doll. "There's nothing to be afraid of." She lowered her head, nuzzling the doll's fine blonde hair.

The wind eased, silence descending once more over the house. Safe and warm, with Barbie to keep her company, Lucy was lulled by its gentle whisper. Her eyelids drooped.

"Little bird?"

Lucy bolted upright. "Who's there?"

The answer was a laugh — a laugh so cracked that her skin shrank in protest, shrivelling until it felt much too tight for her bones.

"Daddy?"

Even as she asked the question, Lucy knew it wasn't. She held Barbie close.

"Mu-Mummy?"

The figure advanced and Lucy's nose crinkled in disgust. No, not Mummy either. The bed dipped and a large shadowy face appeared.

Lucy began to cry.

"Ssshhh," the voice soothed, "I won't hurt you."

Lucy didn't believe him. She opened her mouth to scream, but found it blocked when a heavy hand descended.

"I've brought you flowers. Roses. You like roses, don't you?" The voice hardened and the pressure on her mouth increased. "Don't you?"

Terrified, Lucy nodded. She couldn't breathe. Her nose was full of snot, but she couldn't stop crying. Crazed with fear and frantic for air, she struggled to throw her attacker off, but he was too strong, easily subduing her with a forearm across her chest.

"My little birds are usually fast asleep when I visit," he said. "They never get to see my roses, to appreciate the time and effort I put into them. It makes you special. However, it leaves me with a bit of a problem."

The forearm on her chest lifted and Lucy heard him fumble in his pocket. "Luckily, I came prepared."

There was a sweet, sickly scent just before the cloth covered her face and the pressure on her mouth eased. Lucy was quick to take advantage. Voice released, she screamed in shock and pain.

"Daddeeeeeeee... Mummeeeeeee."

There was no answer. The only sound Lucy heard as darkness reached out to claim her, was the unrelenting tapping of the bony limbs on glass, and the first faint crackle of fire.

CHAPTER ONE

Seven years later

Firefighter Jo Woods checked her air gauge: one hundred bar. Not good.

"Gonna be tight," her teammate Dave said as he crested the staircase behind her.

Jo agreed. Turnaround time was ninety bar, but they were close. She could feel it. "Exit'll be quicker."

They stepped into the smoke-filled hallway. Jo dropped to a squat, sinking to the neutral plane below the smoke.

Dave followed suit. "And if we hit a snag?"

"We won't." Retreating wasn't an option. Five-year-old Emma Forbes and her parents were relying on them.

The odds were against them, Jo knew. They had been briefed on entry. Four rooms upstairs — a bathroom and three bedrooms. Chances were they'd have time to search one — two, if they were lucky. She peered up the hallway. It didn't look like the fates were on their side. Visibility was almost zero. For all she knew, her next step would send her hurtling into thin air.

"Move it, Woods."

Jo hoisted the bulky hose, took a deep breath and a leap of faith. Her boot found solid ground. A half-step later, she located the first room. The door was ajar. A quick glance was enough to confirm it was the bathroom. Unlikely the family would be there, but they entered anyway, doing a primary search.

Clear.

No time for disappointment. Jo forged ahead, panting and sweating in her heavy fire kit. One down, three to go. The next door was closed tightly, the one beside it open and spewing smoke. She groaned. *Can things get any worse?* The neutral plane shrank beneath the added smoke.

She waited for Dave to signal retreat. Prepared herself. When he didn't, she moved into place. While he tested the back of the door for heat, she listened to the sound of the fire inside.

She heard the usual mixture of crackles and pops, and... Alert, she listened closer. There was something else, something above the fire's normal voice.

"Jo?" Dave was pressing for an answer. Her adrenaline spiked. The noise could be anything — or nothing. It was a judgement call. She gave Dave the thumbs up.

It was a go.

Jo pushed the door open and Dave sent a pulse of water fog into the room. She shut the door, letting the water droplets take effect. They waited a beat then repeated the process.

Time ticked by. Jo tapped Dave's shoulder. "I'll do this one," she shouted. "You do next door."

Dave stared at her, clearly unhappy with splitting up. It wasn't procedure. However, they both knew it was their only option if they wanted to save the family. With a reluctant nod, he moved up the hallway.

Jo checked her air; eighty bar. It would be close.

"Out! Out!" Dave reappeared, voice urgent. "Boss says the building's about to go."

Instinctively, Jo looked up. A useless action. The light on her helmet couldn't penetrate the dense smoke. She assessed their exits — stairs and front bedroom window. Both were accessible — just.

"Out!" Dave said again. He tugged her arm.

All her training told her to leave, but Jo's conscience wouldn't let her. She turned back to the door. Thick fingers of smoke scrabbled over the engraved plaque — *Emma's Room.* She knew it was hopeless. Yet, she didn't move.

"*Now, Jo!*"

She nodded, but as Dave moved away, Jo darted through the open doorway.

Darkness engulfed her. A blistering cloud of smoke surrounded her. She ducked lower, the muscles in her thighs protesting. Jo closed the door against the hose and checked behind it.

Nothing.

Jo refused to be discouraged. Emma hadn't made it this far. That was all. At the back of her mind was the knowledge that children hid from fire. They huddled in the most obscure places, believing that if they couldn't see the fire, then the fire couldn't see them.

She moved farther into the room. Clusters of fiery embers appeared, glowing like bullseyes in the dark. She stamped on those closest, putting them out.

The valves in her facemask clicked in pace with her laboured breathing. Around her, the air seared and crackled. Sweat poured down her brow and into her eyes, making them sting. Jo's hands became her eyes as she searched on, in, under, and behind every piece of furniture she could find. She tossed cleared items out of her way.

She didn't dare look at her air gauge. Although only seconds had passed, Jo knew she was running out of time. She forced herself to slow down, to control her breathing.

She scanned the room for any sign of life. Distorted shapes appeared then disappeared just as quickly. Smoke was an impenetrable barrier — especially when searching for someone as tiny as a child, yet something drove her on. If there was the slightest chance, she had to take it.

She heard something and moved forward, straining to hear. Was it a moan? A hiss? The noise came again. Jo tilted her head, trying to decipher the sound.

"Emma?"

A flicker on the edge of her vision alerted her. She turned. An ominous glow sparked then grew.

Jo stood transfixed as a lake of flames appeared. *Dammit.* Her desperate efforts must have fanned an ember. One of the bullseyes had reignited. The flames leapt, shooting up the walls and across the ceiling.

Time to leave.

As if to confirm her decision, Jo's gauge beeped a warning. The low-pressure whistle sounded. Ten minutes of air left. Fear had a stranglehold on her chest. Her heart accelerated, as did her breathing. At this rate, her air wouldn't last five minutes, never mind ten. She had to get out and she had to get out *now.*

Jo stepped back. Her training kicked in. She moved slowly, sweeping and tapping the floor with the heel of each foot. At the same time, she waved her hands to the front and sides. The firefighter shuffle — a movement so deeply ingrained that she did it automatically, checking that the floor was secure and no obstacle blocked her path.

Had she deviated from the line she'd taken on entry? When she'd called out, turned towards the flames, had she moved? If so, she was up the proverbial creek — and not just without a paddle. This time she was missing the whole damn boat.

Her Bodyguard pulsed again. A long continuous beep sounded. Jo looked down. The illuminated display showed a running man.

Recall.

Nausea coiled in her stomach. *This is bad.* The valves in her facemask clicked faster and faster. The urge to run was overwhelming. Hand shaking, she pressed the button to acknowledge Recall. She pressed it again, held it to say she was coming out. Outside, one of the crew would be blowing the whistle, sounding the evacuation alert — not that it would do her any good. Nothing would if she didn't haul ass.

Sweat pooled beneath her heavy gear. Jo ignored it. *Where is the exit?* She strained to see through the smoke. *Surely I didn't come this far?* Panic grew. Had she missed it? Passed it in the darkness?

Just when she thought she'd never find the way out, Jo spotted the outline of the bedroom door. The fire hose still propped it open. She sighed with relief. *Maybe I'll make it after—*

There was a time lapse between the sound of the explosion and the window shattering. The world fell silent, a deathly quiet punctuated only by the furious pounding of her heart. Jo found herself on the floor, curled in a ball, hands covering her head. She jumped to her feet. With the window broken, air had been released into the room. *And if there's one thing fire loves...*

Time returned to normal. A wave of fire hurtled towards the window, seeking escape. Jo, standing next to the door, was lifted with it. In that instant two things happened. The smoke parted, swept sideways like curtains on the stage, and she finally found Emma Forbes.

The image seared into her brain. Disbelief mixed with horror. The little girl lay atop her burning bed, surrounded by a thick spread of roses. Dark hair fanned her unnaturally pale cheeks, hands clasped over her small chest in an obscene caricature of Sleeping Beauty.

A second later the image was devoured by the rapacious flames, just as Jo herself was propelled through the doorway on a searing punch of air.

CHAPTER TWO

"Are you fecking deaf, Woods? You were told to get your ass out of there. Jay-sus, if you die and I don't get to put you on report, I'll bring you back just to fecking kill you myself."

Her station commander's husky voice pulled Jo back to consciousness. She opened her eyes, blinked in the harsh sunlight, and realised she was on the grass outside the Forbes's house. "You do, Boss," she croaked, "and I'll haunt you to the end of your days." She tried to rise.

"Stay down." He pushed her back with his beefy hand. "Women!" A cigarette appeared between his fleshy lips. "Never do what you fecking tell them" — his hands shook as he lit the tip, drawing his dark brows together —" unless you've changed your mind, then they'll do it till the cows come home." Bill Simmons glared at Jo before stomping off, puffing furiously.

"What were you thinking, Jo?" Dave took his place, his voice, like hers, raw with smoke. "You... *We* could have been killed." He tapped his foot while the paramedic checked Jo's vitals, making no comment when she refused to roll up her sleeve. Instead, she insisted the pressure cuff go over her shirtsleeve.

Dave waved the man off as he made to do the same to him. "Look. I don't know how things worked in your last place, Jo, but here, we don't like heroes." His green eyes hardened. "Heroics are apt to get you killed. Understand?"

Jo nodded, knowing the only reason she was alive was because he, too, had disobeyed orders.

He seemed to relent. "You okay?"

"What happened?"

"Gas heater in the kid's bedroom exploded."

Jo could have kicked herself. Venting gas. That was the sound she'd heard, the one she'd had trouble deciphering.

"Guess the parents put it there for extra heat," Dave said. "Sure did that all right."

Memory returned, propelling Jo upright. "Oh my God, Dave. Did you see her?"

"Who?"

"The little girl, Emma Forbes."

"She was long gone before we got there, Jo. Her parents, too. Nothing we could do."

"But did you *see* her?" She grabbed his arm. "The roses?"

Dave winced as her fingers bit deep into his skin. "Roses? No. What—?"

"Hey, does she have to go to hospital?"

At the sound of the boss's voice, Jo dropped her hand.

"She should..." The paramedic seemed to shrink as Bill's huge figure advanced, his scrawny neck disappearing beneath the sweaty collar of his shirt. "Observation and all that."

One look convinced him to change his mind.

"No... No, sir. Not if she's feeling okay."

Bill swivelled towards Jo, who nodded. "Good. Won't have to waste time with the fecking roster then. You're good for the rest of the day, yes?"

Jo knew the question was rhetorical, but she nodded anyway, trying not to grimace as every bone in her body protested.

*****

Lips twisting in disgust, I watched the firefighters scuttling back and forth in their desperate effort to dampen the last of the smouldering embers. So eager. Pathetic in their black and yellow fire-kits — like a swarm of ineffectual bumblebees buzzing round a long-dead flower.

My contempt grew and anger began to ferment deep in my belly, stirring the already volatile gastric juices contained there. Oh yes, they were so eager now — now, when it was too late, when life had stilled within those seared and blackened walls, freeing Emma from her tortured existence.

I did that. Pride at the thought, but not so much as to be sinful. I wasn't the one who had sinned, not this time. My eyes followed the scurrying bumblebees and hatred gnawed. Where were they when Emma had needed their help? Any fool could have seen that life had become intolerable for the child, a cage from which she'd yearned to be freed. Yet they'd hesitated. Why?

"Isn't it obvious?" the voice I heard only inside my head said. *"Emma's story wasn't salacious enough — no guts and glory, no do-or-die, or rags to riches to splash across the front page. Money and power, that's the only thing that counts."*

Was it really that simple? Sadness crushed me. Would I be the only one to truly mourn Emma? Talk about ironic.

While I took some measure of pride in my work, I took no joy in the act. Yes, I had freed Emma, but she had paid dearly for her freedom — a bill I knew only too well. Pain and grief threatened to smother me, but I forced myself to move beyond the emotions, just as Emma had moved beyond this plane. No one could hurt her now. The thought calmed me. Emma was safe. This world and its horrors no longer had the power to corrupt her. I had seen her pain and I had cauterized it. She was safe. For a second, I was assailed by doubt. *Isn't she?*

When the familiar acid rose, I greeted it as I would an old friend, smoothing and rubbing my hand over my swollen belly. There was no room for doubt. My mission was defined, precise. No uncertainty or error could be allowed to intrude. I had been chosen because I was the only one who could see, could understand — a gift not given to many.

"*More like you're the only one willing to do what needs to be done,*" the voice said.

I pondered that. The voice made sense. People were basically lazy, unwilling to get involved. Involved? I snorted. "Couldn't be bothered, more like."

"*Not like you.*"

"No, not like me," I agreed. I wasn't one to shirk my duty — never had been, never would be. I subdued the memory threatening to break free, unwilling to re-open that old wound. Yet it festered. The proof? The constant caustic sea in my belly. "It's my duty to free all the little birds."

The voice was silent, but that was fine. My moment of uncertainty had passed as swiftly as it had come. I had a task to perform, a very important task.

"Freeing all the little birds," I murmured.

"*And there are so many of them.*" The voice was back.

I smiled. "Yes, so *very* many."

*****

The journey home, in marked contrast to the one out, was spent in silence. Jo sat in the back of the fire engine, lost in thought. Each jolt in the road sent waves of pain through her body and yet, inside, she felt curiously numb.

When they reached the depot, the six-man crew, covered in soot and bleary-eyed — and not just from the smoke — wrapped up their gear, leaving it ready for its next outing, all without their usual banter.

They filed into the duty room where they had their second debriefing, the first having taken place at the scene, not that Jo had been in any fit state to take part. She wasn't now, either. With the same calm detachment she'd shown since the explosion, she filled out her report.

Although they would have to wait for Shaunessy, the arson investigator, to confirm, the consensus was accidental fire — the point of origin having been the parents' room adjacent to the little girl's. It looked like the father, who by all accounts was a drunkard, had fallen asleep on the small sofa there with a lit cigarette in his hand.

"Bastard!" Don Flanders spat, fleshy jowls quivering in indignation. "If the man had spent less on drink and more on buying a new sofa, this whole tragedy might have been averted."

"Yeah, pity we can't force people to get rid of their cheap furniture. It's bloody toxic when it burns," Dave agreed as they all got up.

Jo followed the rest of Red Watch up the stairs to the rec room. Usually after a turn-out, they congregated in the galley. Adrenaline worked up a hunger that had nothing to do with food and everything to do with the need for human contact. To talk, to eat, to share the mundane, ultimately to prove they were alive — at least for now.

Not today.

Jonjo Maguire, or Wart, as he was affectionately known to the guys on Red Watch — the nickname standing for "worrywart" and not the skin affliction — headed straight for the gym, flexing his muscles.

Pat Meehan, after a hesitant look to see what the others were doing, followed Wart, scampering at his heels like an overeager puppy.

"I need some fresh air," Flanders said, pulling on his jacket. "What about you, darlin'? Wanna come?" He leered at Jo, who ignored him. She smiled tiredly at Geoff Davis, their watch commander, who pressed a sympathetic hand to her shoulder as he passed. His cadaverous face was etched with sorrow as he settled his lean frame into an armchair and grabbed a book from the nearby table. He lowered his head and perused the pages in silence, creating a barrier between him and any conversation.

Jo decided she was in no mood for company either. She escaped downstairs to the showers where she stood beneath the steaming water, arms at her sides, not moving. Sapped of energy, she let the spray do the work, washing away the sweat and grime but not the memories. She stared straight ahead at the hastily constructed wall blocking off the men's shower area. The odour of fresh paint was strong enough to catch her throat. Mourne Lough Fire Station had been coerced into joining the twenty-first century with her arrival. Her smile was wry. At least they'd made an effort, unlike some she could name.

Her smile faded. The numbness was wearing off. She could no longer avoid the memory of the fire, the family they had been unable to save. There was a gnawing ache in her belly. She felt sick but knew it had nothing to do with the sour stink of paint. Without warning, the tears she'd held at bay for so long exploded, wrenched from deep inside her. She began to keen, rocking backwards and forwards, arms now locked around her middle.

Bowing her head, Jo squeezed her eyes shut. It didn't help. Behind her lids, forever embedded in her subconscious, was that last, surreal image of Emma Forbes. *Could I have been mistaken? Did I see the child lying on a bed of roses?* Paper roses, judging by the way they were burning. *Or did I dream the whole thing?*

When the paroxysm passed, Jo un-braided her hair and squirted shampoo into the palm of one hand, working the lather through her long tresses. She rinsed and repeated the process in an effort to dispel the acrid smell of death and smoke — and guilt — that had leached into her pores.

In the end, she conceded defeat, resting her head against the tiles. She searched the aching contours of her body, seeking out new bumps and bruises marring her already blemished skin. A tender spot at her waist held her attention. Like a child unaware of the consequences, she prodded it, welcoming the pain, relishing the way it covered the growing ache in her heart and the awful truth that she could no longer avoid after seeing Emma Forbes.

It had been no dream. In fact, if she were right, it was her worst nightmare come to life.

It's happening again.

CHAPTER THREE

Dave was in the locker room as Jo exited the shower, his six foot four frame perched awkwardly on one of the narrow wooden benches.

"Hurts, does it?" he asked, seeing her wince.

"Yup." Jo dropped her wet hair towel and shampoo onto the seat. Not only did she ache all over, but her head was thumping from the force of her crying, and she knew her eyes were swollen and red. She pretended to search for something in her locker.

"I think it was your dismount that was the problem, 'cause your double summersault out that bedroom door was spot on." Dave's voice turned serious. "Jo? You said something back at the ambulance..." He rubbed a hand over the dark stubble mottling his jaw. "It's been bugging me. Something about roses?" He waited.

Jo sighed. She didn't want to talk about the roses — not now, not ever, if she could help it. She wanted — needed — time to think, to compose herself. Inwardly, she groaned. *Who am I kidding?* A thousand lifetimes wouldn't be enough to overcome the horror of seeing Emma Forbes laid out like some awful sacrifice. Never mind what it might mean for her, if what she surmised was correct.

Feeling unbelievably weary, she closed her locker, sinking to the bench beside Dave. "The little girl, Emma Forbes... She was... covered in roses. Paper roses."

Dave laughed. "What?" He threw his hands up in apology when Jo glared at him. "I'm sorry, but honestly, the way you were carrying on, I thought it was something serious."

"It *is* serious."

"You were only in the room for a few minutes, Jo. You and I both know that smoke and adrenaline can confuse your perceptions, make you see things that aren't there. It was probably a flowery duvet cover that, in all the confusion, you—"

"I know what I saw, Dave."

"You had a bad knock on the head. I know you didn't let on to the paramedic, but don't forget that I was the one who carried you out of the building."

Reminded she owed him her life, Jo bit back the sharp retort hovering on the tip of her tongue, but she wondered whether he would have mentioned the knock on the head if she were a man. *Or are only women prone to such delicate sensibilities?*

She kept her voice even. "It wasn't an illusion caused by a bump on the head, nor was it the result of smoke inhalation or any of that crap. That little girl was covered in paper flowers and she didn't put them there herself."

The laughter drained from Dave's face. For a second he was silent, as if stunned by her suggestion. "Maybe they were a school project?" he offered. "She could have been playing with them and fell asleep before the fire?"

"Not the way they were arranged. It was too deliberate. They had to have been put there when she was already unconscious."

"You're not suggesting one of the parents?"

Jo wasn't, but not willing to say why, she shrugged. "Maybe."

"Judging by the father's reputation, he would have been well out of it long before the fire took hold. So, the mother?"

Again, Jo shrugged. She could tell Dave was humouring her, which increased her irritation.

Her lack of response seemed to inflame him. "Jesus, Jo! You're saying this is arson? That a twenty-three-year-old housewife has bamboozled our

whole watch—of specially trained men, I might add."
He stared at her as if hoping she'd change her mind.

When she remained silent, he stood. "Give me a break."

Jo couldn't blame him for his scepticism. She had seen Emma Forbes with her own eyes and she was still having trouble believing it. She felt tears start and blinked them away. They kept coming, and with them, a wave of depression that threatened to swamp her. *I can't go through this again. I can't. It's too damn hard.*

Dave seemed to sense her distress. Anger forgotten, he sat beside her and put an arm around her shoulder, saying, "What's up, Jo? This isn't like you."

Before Jo could reply, there was a commotion outside. A string of curses filled the air and a second later the door to the locker room swung open.

"Eh... hiya, guys." Jim Tumilty, the recently deposed newbie with Jo's arrival angled his lean frame through the doorway, his ferret eyes sizing up the situation with a sly smile. "Oy. Oy."

"Tumilty." Dave dropped his arm, rising. "I thought you were off-duty?"

"Got some cheap booze I need to offload." Tumilty tried to peer round Dave's broad shoulders. "You interested?"

"Not for me, mate."

"Me neither." Jo stood, trying to appear casual as she sauntered from behind Dave. She bristled at the knowing look Tumilty threw her.

"Your loss." Tumilty winked, not in the least bit perturbed. "I'll have some cigs later. I'll give you a shout back then, shall I?" Without waiting for an answer, he exited the room as quickly as he had entered.

"That guy's been here five weeks," Dave said, "and already he's tried to sell me two dozen fir trees, a suite of furniture, and a litter of cats." He winked. "You'd think the cats, at least, would have been hurt, falling off the back of that damn lorry."

Jo smiled, glad of the change of subject. For a moment there, she had been tempted to confide in him, maybe more than was wise this early in their friendship. "You think that's bad? He offered me a year's supply of toilet paper. I told him I live in a two bedroom flat. Where the hell would I put that much?"

Dave laughed then grew solemn. "You going to tell the boss what you think you saw?"

"Not 'think'," Jo corrected. "What I *did* see."

Dave, about to argue, shrugged and headed for the door. "Guess you have to do what you have to do." He paused in the doorway. "Good luck."

"I'll need it," Jo said softly to his retreating back, "more than you'll ever know."

*****

Jim Tumilty held his breath, counting to fifty after Jo's footsteps disappeared up the stairs. He unfurled from his hiding place — a small closet next to the locker room — and glared at the brush on the floor. Years of work almost destroyed in one careless moment. He cursed, kicking out, dispatching the offending article to the farthest reaches of the cupboard, uncaring now of any noise it might make.

As he slipped from his hiding place, he allowed himself a quick grin. The little he'd overheard had proved interesting.

Very interesting indeed.

CHAPTER FOUR

Jo climbed the stairs to the boss's office. This was supposed to be a new start, yet here she was, not a month into the job, about to complicate matters... again.

Most people considered Mourne Lough a comedown from her last post at fire HQ in Lisburn. Jo didn't. She found the smaller unit a plus. For starters, there was only one pump. Still four watches, comprising of seven, or in the case of hers, eight men—unlike Lisburn, which had boasted fourteen men to a watch. Twenty-eight full-time men to get to know—and avoid in equal measure.

Being the newbie wasn't a lot of fun, though, and neither was being the sole woman. Then again, she reminded herself, she hadn't joined up to have fun. Her mind flicked to Don Flanders and she grimaced. The guy was a Neanderthal. It was a wonder his knuckles didn't scrape the ground when he walked. Every station she'd served in had one — a man who thought women weren't cut out for the job. Jo rolled her shoulders. She felt a showdown with "Mr Bloody-minded Flanders" approaching, and at this precise moment in time, she was looking forward to it. That was more than she could say for the showdown she knew lay ahead with the boss.

She topped the stairs and moved past the gym where Wart and Pat Meehan were working out. Her thoughts returned to her Lisburn days and her friend, Mavis. What she wouldn't give for a bracing dose of Mavis's calm, practical, good sense right now. Nervous as she was, Jo smiled. She knew what Mavis would say, and *how* she'd say it. "*If in doubt, better sorted out.*"

Mavis was full of little aphorisms like that. She was also the reason Jo was in Mourne Lough. Jo's smile slipped. Mavis wouldn't be happy when a copy of the notes from this meeting came across her desk — and they would. As secretary to the chief fire officer — the head honcho himself — everything went through Mavis.

Great. Damned if I do, damned if I don't.

She slowed as she approached the boss's door. She took a deep breath, then a second and a third, working up the nerve to knock. Her head began to spin. "Don't be a wimp," she berated herself. The boss finding her in a crumpled heap in the hallway wouldn't help her case, and the thought of the ribbing she'd take from the guys — Flanders, in particular — was enough to dispel the cloud of stars hovering on the edge of her vision. She rapped at the door.

"Come in."

Even couched in the soft southern burr of his homeland, Bill Simmons's welcome sounded more like "piss off" than anything else.

"Can I have a minute, Boss?"

"I said 'come in', didn't I?" A butt was dispatched to the ashtray. Another took its place between yellow-stained fingers.

The fire station was a non-smoking zone, but no one had the nerve to remind Bill, and Jo wasn't going to upset the status quo. Not about that, anyway. She took a seat.

Bill held up a hand to say he'd be a minute. Jo surveyed his office while she waited. A smoky pall covered the walls and ceiling. Wispy ears of paper dotted every available surface, overspill from the bulging filing cabinets squatting to her left. Her gaze returned to the desk. It too was cluttered, the dark wood scored and pitted, heavy with dust. That's why the photo stood out, the area around it pristine. Intrigued, she tipped her chair for a better look.

It was a family portrait — the boss with who she assumed were his wife and son — no daughter-in-law, she noted — and three grinning cherubs.

Grandchildren? And is the crusty old goat actually smiling?

"What's on your mind, Woods?"

Jo hurriedly settled her chair back in place. "I wanted to talk to you about the Forbes fire."

"Apology accepted."

Jo looked suitably contrite before getting to the real reason she was there. "Any reports in?"

"Jay-sus, give us a chance. This isn't the great metropolis, you know," Bill said, in reference to her last post in Lisburn. "Our wheels grind a tad slower here. Although," he gave her a self-satisfied grin, "we can be speedy when we want to be." He nodded to the phone. "That was Peterson from SOCO. First sight has him leaning towards accidental. Has to wait on the coroner, of course."

"And Shaunessy?" Jo asked, mentioning the arson investigator, called in after any fatality. "I saw him in here earlier. Did he have his initial findings?"

"Why are you so interested?" Bill asked, eyes alert. "Something you want to share?"

Jo wondered how much he knew, but his face gave nothing away. She decided to jump right in. "I don't think the Forbes fire was accidental."

"Oh, you don't, do you? And would you be having a reason for this belief of yours?"

"When I entered the child's room, I saw..." She swallowed. This was harder than she'd thought.

"Spit it out, for feck sake, Woods. Jay-sus, a man could grow grey here."

"Roses." It exploded from her, and in the silence left behind, Jo understood how incongruous the word had sounded. She wasn't surprised when he laughed.

"Roses?" Jay-sus, Woods, that fall must'a scrambled your brains more than I thought."

Jo evaded any mention of her injury. "I'm telling you, Boss. The girl was covered in flowers and she didn't put them there herself. I think she was murdered."

"What?" Bill shot upright in his chair. "Holy Mary, Mother of... But... But..." he blustered. "This is Mourne Lough. Things like that don't happen here."

It wasn't a question, but Jo took it as such. "They happen everywhere, Boss."

Bill glared at her. "It was dark in there, Woods, lots of smoke, hard to see anything."

Jo had a feeling of déjà vu. "I know what I saw," she repeated, voice firm.

"You had a nasty bang on the head," Bill continued as if she hadn't spoken. "Maybe I should have ordered you to the hospital?"

"I was fine, even the paramedic said so." Jo hurried on. "Emma Forbes was covered in roses." She enunciated each word. "And. She. Didn't. Put. Them. There. Herself."

Distracted, Bill stubbed out his cigarette. He glared at Jo when he noticed what he'd done, as if it were her fault. He rescued another from his endless supply and took a draw with a beatific expression, which darkened when he looked at her. "Why didn't you say all this at the debriefing?"

Jo debated how to answer without lying outright. When he didn't press her, she realised he knew more than he was letting on.

"Leave it with me. I'll have a word with Peterson and ask him to take a closer look."

"But—"

"I said, leave it with me."

And with that, Jo had to be content.

CHAPTER FIVE

"You want a lift?"

Jo, lost in thought, hadn't heard the car approach. She bent to the open passenger window, smiling when she caught sight of a familiar face. "Dave."

"Your carriage awaits, madam." His green eyes twinkled up at her.

Jo was tempted. After her encounter with Bill, she could do with a friendly shoulder to cry on. However, time and experience had taught her that friendly shoulders came with a price attached, especially if they were married.

"Thanks, but you'll be stuck for hours." She nodded towards the main street and the thick ruby necklace of brake lights winking in the distance. "Walking's quicker, which is why I left my car at home this morning."

Dave eyed the shadowy stairway snaking through the warren of houses that had sprung up seemingly overnight. "They may be quicker, but I doubt they're the best place to be this time of night. Come on. Jump in. I can afford the time and the petrol. You look beat."

Too tired to argue, Jo opened the door and slid inside. "Thanks."

"Tough day." It wasn't a question. "How'd it go with the boss?"

Jo filled him in.

"Yeah, no one gives a dressing down like he does, huh?"

He'd obviously never met Mavis. Jo would put her money on her friend, any time. Maybe she should introduce the boss and Mavis. She pictured it for a minute — two old goats butting heads — then discarded the idea. If she was wrong about the boss knowing more than he was letting on, she didn't intend to give him any additional ammo.

The car was warm and she relaxed into her seat. Her eyes grew heavy. Silence reigned until they reached her turn off.

"That's the plats," Dave said, nodding to a flash of green on their left, "where the orphanage barbecue is this weekend."

"Uh-huh." Jo wished he hadn't reminded her.

Minutes later, he pulled to a stop. "Here we go." He glanced around. "Looks like a nice place."

"Liar," she said without rancour. The six separate apartment blocks stood in an incomplete square, two to the left, two to the right and two at the back, each one containing four flats. She lived in the back block, which butted onto an empty field — the only other green area left in Mourne Lough apart from the plats, although not for long, the way the town was growing.

"Okay, they're a bit bleak."

"Just a bit," Jo agreed. They weren't the most attractive edifices, but they were close to work and that's what mattered. Light shone from the two downstairs flats in her block. In comparison, the two upper windows — hers and her neighbour, Ethel Reilly's — lay in complete darkness. She held back a sigh, thinking of the unpacked boxes waiting for her inside.

"Why don't you come home with me, have a bite to eat?" Dave offered. "Fran won't mind."

Jo wanted to, yet she was reluctant to be drawn into her teammate's life — make small talk with people she didn't know. She cringed at the notion. "Thanks, but I—"

Dave put the car in reverse. "You're coming and that's final."

Too tired to fight and, if she were honest, not as averse to the idea as she'd let on, Jo didn't argue.

She leaned back in her seat and closed her eyes.

*****

"We're here." Dave woke her.

"Huh?" Jo rubbed her eyes and looked around, disorientated.

Dave unhooked his seatbelt and leant over to do the same to Jo's when she didn't move. "Come on. Fran's dying to meet you."

Jo got out of the car. Dave's house was huge. Her whole block of flats could sit comfortably between Dave's house and his next-door neighbours with room to spare. It made her uncomfortable and she cursed the tiredness that had precipitated this visit before she was ready. Maybe she should have—

Too late. Dave opened the front door. "Fran?"

Warm air drifted outwards and with it, the delicious smell of cooking. The aroma engulfed Jo, held her. From inside came the sound of running feet.

"Dave, you're home." A woman stood silhouetted in the light. A long dress skimmed her dainty ankles. Her elfin face was raised for a kiss, like a scene from a romantic film. "I was getting worried."

"Long story," Dave said. He pecked her cheek. "I've brought a friend home for tea."

"Oh!" Like a rabbit caught in the headlights of a car, the woman started backwards.

Jo, wide-awake and feeling like a third wheel on a bicycle, held out her hand. "Nice to meet you, Fran, I'm Jo. Don't worry if you haven't enough to go around. I can—"

"I won't hear of it." The woman regained her poise and took Jo's hand. "I always cook far too much, as Dave knows." Her smile transformed her

26

plain features and made the furrows on her brow dance. "Please, come in. It's great to finally meet you. Dave has told me so much about you."

Jo wished Dave had been as forthcoming with her. "Well, if you're sure." She stepped inside. A huge chandelier stabbed flawless prisms in her direction and it took a moment for her eyes to adjust. When they did, she spied a long hallway decorated in a delightful shade of apricot. Huge pictures in ornate frames lined the path between the front door and the kitchen to which Fran directed her. The smell of cooked meat grew stronger, making her stomach rumble.

"Jenny!" Fran shouted, "Daddy's home."

"I'll get her, love."

Dave squeezed Fran's waist in an intimate gesture that made Jo's heart contract. She quashed the brief pang of envy.

"Don't you girls be talking about me while I'm gone," Dave said before charging up the stairs, shouting, "Jenny Wren? Jenny Wren, I'm coming to get you."

An answering giggle sounded, childish and light. The pang in Jo's heart deepened. *I shouldn't have come. This is a mistake.*

Fran was an unstoppable force, propelling her towards the kitchen. "Sit yourself down," she said, motioning to a huge, mahogany table set for three. She didn't miss a beat, going to a drawer, lifting out a set of cutlery. "Here you go. Dinner won't be a minute."

"Can I help?"

Fran seemed shocked by the idea. "Don't be silly. You're our guest." She plucked an apron from the back of the door, putting it on before moving to the oven. She hunkered down and opened the steel beast. "Almost done," she said, checking the contents. "Can I get you a glass of wine?"

Jo nodded, hoping her desperation didn't show. She hated polite conversation, was terrible at it. She accepted the glass and clutched it to her chest like the last available raft on a sinking ship.

Where the hell is Dave? She took a swift gulp.

Fran seemed equally nervous. "Do you like chicken, Jo? I'm so stupid. I never thought to ask. Because if you don't, I can—"

Jo reassured her she did.

"And I've peas, carrots, and roast potatoes. Is that okay?"

"More than okay," Jo said, her mouth watering. "It sounds fantastic, Fran." She smiled, hoping to put the woman at ease.

It appeared to work. Fran moved closer. "Did something happen today, Jo? I heard the Forbes—" From overhead came the thunderous pounding of footsteps towards the stairs. Fran stiffened and, for an instant, looked frightened. "Please don't tell Dave I asked."

Before Jo could speak, Fran darted towards the cooker. She checked the pots, looking busy. "Dinner won't be a minute," she said, hostess mask back in place. Puzzled, Jo listened to the light-hearted giggles of father and daughter coming down the hall. Her eyes followed Fran as she dished out the meal.

What on earth was that about?

CHAPTER SIX

Beep! Beep! Beep!

Jo lashed out at the alarm clock. Typical Sod's Law, she'd just dropped off an hour before the damn thing had started to screech. Her flailing arm found its mark and the clock disappeared beneath its cardboard perch. It continued to beep.

"Damn and blast!" Jo swung her legs out of bed, wincing as muscles and bruises screamed in complaint, but they were nothing compared to the pain in her head. "Shouldn't have had that last beer," she muttered as she groped around socks, knickers and God knew what else, until she found the alarm button, switching it off.

Silence left its own noise and it reverberated inside her head with a stomach-churning intensity. She massaged her temples and tried to keep her head steady as she foraged inside the mangled box for fresh underwear. She found some, pulled them on, and grabbed her work trousers and a long-sleeved T-shirt from the nearby chair. Last beer be dammed, she shouldn't have had any of them. But the glass of wine at Dave's, plus the one or two after, awoke a thirst in her that had demanded relief.

Did I do the right thing? It sure had felt like it at one o'clock this morning when she'd made the phone call, buoyant with the false bravado of alcohol and the belief that nothing was beyond her. In the harsh glare of morning, she wasn't so sure Mavis would agree with her.

Determined not to think about Mavis or the brief, painful phone conversation they'd shared in the early hours, Jo plaited her hair, shoving the singed ends into a rubber band. What was done was done. There was no going back now. She went to the kitchen, switched on the kettle and rescued a cup from the cluttered heap in the sink. She tossed in a teabag and groped for the aspirin, swallowing two dry.

When the kettle boiled, she made her tea and took a swift gulp. The tea un-furred her mouth but did nothing to silence the army of men inside her head, battering at her skull with what felt like hammers.

She should unpack. She surveyed the clutter of boxes lining the floor and countertops and tried not to think of the Everest awaiting her in the other rooms. She should — if she believed she might actually stay this time.

*****

Jo shut her front door and eyed the lift. She'd spent her first five hours in her new home trapped in that metal contraption and nothing short of an act of God would make her repeat the experience — and even God's participation was debatable. She turned towards the stairs.

"Ms Woods? Jo?"

Jo swung around, grimacing as the men in her head toiled once more. She squinted and spied a mop, followed by the diminutive figure of her next-door neighbour, Ethel Reilly.

"I'm glad I caught you," the old woman said, a determined look on her parchment face. "My Liam's taking me away this weekend..."

She said that as if it were an everyday occurrence, but Jo had lived there a month and this was the first time "my Liam" had been mentioned in the same breath as an outing. She pinned an interested look on her face and waited for the old dear to continue.

"My son," Ethel Reilly added unnecessarily. "He's taking me somewhere fancy. Going to treat me, he said."

"Sounds nice, Mrs R," Jo said, wondering what it had to do with her.

"It's just... I do the hallway floors Mondays, Thursdays, and Saturdays. I don't mind. I like to keep busy," she added, as if Jo were about to argue, "but seeing as my Liam is whisking me away..."

"No problem," Jo said, relieved. For a moment, she thought she'd be asked to water plants or something — not a good idea for someone once accused of killing plastic ivy.

"Good. Good. There's one other thing."

Jo hid her impatience. Mrs R was a nice woman, but this relationship business took time and energy — time and energy she didn't have to spare, especially if, as she surmised after her encounter with the boss, the chances of her staying here were getting slimmer by the minute.

Ethel Reilly hesitated as if picking up on her reluctance. "I don't want to be a nuisance."

Jo felt guilty. The old dear was lonely. It wouldn't hurt to spend a few more moments with her. "It's okay, Mrs R. What's up?"

"It's just... There's been a spate of burglaries. I've seen someone myself skulking outside late at night — youngsters, no doubt. I don't know," she said. "My Liam would never have scared old folks half to death; sad how times change. It's down to the parents, I say." She gave the mop a vigorous shake. "Spare the rod and all that — not that my Liam ever needed it. But, I thought, seeing as you're a policewoman, you might—"

"Fireman."

"Pardon me?" The pink scalp tilted, swivelled in Jo's direction, like an eagle spotting fresh prey.

"I'm a fireman. *Woman,* or to be more precise —
a firefighter." Jo wilted under the bead-like eyes,
feeling like she had made the wrong career choice.

"Oh."

Judging by the disappointment in her voice,
Mrs R agreed with her.

"But I'd be glad to help in any way I can," Jo
said.

"A firefighter, you say? Hmm, there *is*
something. Come." She waved a gnarled knuckle and
like an obedient child, Jo followed Mrs R into her flat.
A spotless interior reeked of freshly applied lemon
polish, which almost — but not quite — hid the
musty smell of old age. Dainty cloths covered the tiny
two-seater sofa and matching chair, lacy edges
pressed to within an inch of their lives and "my Liam"
hung from every wall, immobilized forever in varying
stages of awkward, pimpled development.

*No wonder he doesn't come home too often, if
this was what he has to face.* Jo suppressed a grin.

"Here it is." Ethel Reilly sank to her knees with
a groan. "It has been playing up this last wee while."

It was a gas fireplace, as ancient a contraption
as Jo had ever seen outside a museum. "Where did
you get this, Mrs R?"

"From my Liam, a present. Gorgeous, isn't it?"

Gorgeous wasn't the first word to spring to
mind, but seeing the pride etched on the wizened
face, Jo tempered her words. "It is indeed, a real
antique." She held out a hand to help the old woman
rise. "When did you last get it checked?" It was a
reflex question, but judging by the affronted
expression she was thrown, Mrs R wasn't going to
take kindly to her suggestion of a gas engineer
checking out her precious present. She changed
tack. "I'm sure your Liam would agree that, gorgeous
as it is, this is well past its best. There's no way he'd
want to put you in any danger."

She'd said the right thing.

"You're right, of course. I must mention it to him this weekend. Thanks, love." The woman's eyes, which had narrowed dangerously, were now doe-like. "Would—?"

Before Jo could be offered the vile-tasting tea she'd endured on previous visits, she made a show of looking at her watch. "Oh dear, is that the time?" She made her escape.

Eight thirty. If she took the car, she would have time to make a quick detour before her shift started at nine.

CHAPTER SEVEN

Even though she knew what to expect, Jo caught her breath as she rounded the corner. It was no longer a home, no longer even a house. The structure and people who'd made it that were gone.

The roof of number three Elm Tree Drive lay deep inside the ruins of charred bricks, its timbers devoured. Spears of soot, thick and rough as if drawn by a child's careless hand, arched upwards from empty apertures, now enclosed in hardboard. Jo shuddered. She shouldn't have come. There was nothing to learn here.

She moved up the water-sodden path, drawn to the ruined façade, even as her mind was drawn backwards. She relieved those last terror-filled moments, which she now accepted could have been her last.

She flinched as if she could smell the odour of burning flesh, although safe behind her mask, she had been spared that horror. She only wished she had been spared the awful sight of Emma Forbes's body, laid out like a sacrifice atop the once-pretty bedspread.

Jo's knees buckled as a roaring emptiness, reminiscent of the moment of the explosion, filled her mind. A siren's call — teasing, tantalising — it promised ease, relief from the pain in her body, the anvil in her head, and the desperate emptiness living in her chest. She ached to take it up on its offer, to dive headfirst into its empty embrace, if only for a while.

"Can I help you?"

"Huh?" Jo shook her head in an effort to clear it. A woman stood before her. Mid-twenties, Jo guessed. It was hard to tell, because the face was crumpled and swollen from many hours crying, but the hand clutching the mobile phone was unwrinkled and well-manicured, the hovering digit bony. A natural blonde, Jo decided, seeing the fair eyebrows arch as the question was repeated, this time colder, sharper.

"Can I help you, miss?"

Time to speak before the woman called the cops on her. "Are you the Forbes's next-door neighbour, Mrs Parsons?"

"Who's asking?" The woman lowered the phone and eyed Jo, taking in the mangled fringe — one a scissor-wielding two-year-old would be proud of — and the thick braid, which in comparison, looked relatively untouched. Her gaze dropped to the dark trousers and long sleeved navy T-shirt with its distinctive logo, understanding dawning. "Oh." Her chocolate eyes muddied with fresh tears. "I'm so sorry. You're one of the firefighters from last night, aren't you?"

Jo held out her hand. "Jo Woods. I was wondering if I could have a few minutes of your time."

"I don't know, I—" The phone in her hand bleeped. "Damn. Low battery."

"I can come back later."

"No, no, it's okay. Come on through." Angela Parsons opened the side gate between the two houses. "This way." She stepped through her front door and gestured for Jo to follow as she hurried down the hallway to a bright, airy kitchen. She plugged the phone into its charger. "Don't mind me. It's just been that kind of day."

"I guess it has." Jo looked around her. The kitchen could have come straight from a magazine spread, except for the dishes littering the sink and a fridge obscured by photos and pink reminder slips interspaced with childish drawings.

"Can I get you something? Tea? Coffee?"

Jo, ready to refuse, caught the heady aroma of fresh-percolated coffee. "Coffee sounds great."

"It's good stuff. Kept me going, that's for sure." Her face twisted with grief. "I'm sorry." A hanky appeared. She dabbed at her swollen eyes.

Jo patted the woman's shoulder, feeling awkward. *Should I say something? And if so, what?* In an agony of indecision, she kept patting, and the woman kept crying. Just as Jo was ready to slit her wrists with the nearest fridge magnet, Angela Parsons straightened, composing herself.

"Let me get you that coffee."

"Thanks." Jo waited until she had the cup in her hand. "Did you know the Forbes well, Mrs Parsons?"

"Please. You're wearing what's left of my mascara. I think you can call me Angela." She gave a wan smile, waving Jo to a chair. "And yes, Tanya and I went to school together, married around the same time, even had our kids within weeks of one another, although I married a man from Mourne Lough."

Jo detected a hint of censure. "You didn't like Mr Forbes?"

"Steven? It's not that... Oh, I don't want to speak ill of the dead." She moved towards the fridge. "You want milk?"

Jo shook her head and tried another approach. "With children the same age, you must have known Emma well?"

Suspicion and pain darkened the reddened eyes. "Why all the questions? The other firefighter didn't ask so many."

Other firefighter? "I'm sorry." Jo held up a hand in apology. "I don't mean to be insensitive. It's... Well, I'm the one who found Emma, and I don't know... She was so young... Hadn't lived at all. I guess I wanted to talk to someone who knew her. I know that must sound odd."

"Not at all." Angela caressed one of the crayon drawings on the fridge door before returning to sit beside Jo. "Mike, my husband... he won't mention their names, but I..." Her hanky rose, dabbed. "To tell you the truth, I'd welcome a chance to talk about them."

According to Angela Parsons, Tanya Forbes had been a good mother and a good friend. Her husband, Steven, or "The Thug", as Angela referred to him — Jo did like the woman — was a different kettle of fish.

"I saw bruises on Tanya, Emma too, these last few months." Angela's voice pulsed with anger. "How anybody could hurt that wee angel is beyond me. Not that I think he should have hit Tanya, either," she hurried to add. "But I felt she had a choice, you know? Emma didn't. It makes me so mad. Tanya should have stood up for her daughter, protected her from The Thug, don't you think?"

"I've never been in that situation, thank God. I don't know how I'd react, what I'd do."

"But you'd *do* something. Jesus, most people would do something, but not Tanya. Oh no, not Tanya. She sat there and took it. Worse, she made excuses for the toe-rag, lied for him."

Jo knew Angela wasn't angry at Tanya. She was angry at herself for not speaking up. Jo understood only too well how regret ate at a person. "Don't do this to yourself, Angela. Tanya made her choices. We might not agree with them, but they were her choices to make."

The fire died out of Angela's eyes and she sank back in her seat. "I know."

When Jo left almost an hour later, she had learned more than she'd ever wanted to know about the Forbes. The knowledge left a bad taste in her mouth. What haunted her most, though, was the realisation that she didn't know nearly enough about one of her teammates. Why was someone else snooping about, asking questions?

*****

"You're late."

Dave met Jo at the fire station door. "Don't worry. Porter hung back." He gestured to a beefy man in the middle of a yawn, testing the equipment at the back of one of the pumps.

As if aware of their scrutiny, the man raised his sleepy lids. With a smile of pure relief, Porter ambled towards them. "Ready to relieve me?" he asked Jo, trying to restrain yet another yawn.

Jo nodded. The fire service roster ran to a precise schedule. While there were seven men to a watch — eight in Red Watch's case — only six were on call at any one time. So, if someone was late — like she was — or sick, then one of the men on the previous shift had to hang back until either the person on duty arrived or another was called in to take their place.

"Thanks, Porter," she said. "I owe you one."

"Whatever." Porter waved, looking happy to be going home.

Jo added her name and the time to the roll call before resuming the task Porter had vacated.

"What's up?" Dave sidled over. "You sleep in? Too well fed after Fran's dinner, I'll bet."

Jo forced a smile. "Yeah, I'm not used to home cooking. Microwave dinners for one are the height of my culinary skills." She told him about Mrs Reilly and her dodgy fireplace, hoping he'd assume that's what had made her late.

"Ah, the perks of living next to a firefighter — always on hand to give free advice, day or night." He winked. "Fran said to tell you you're welcome to dinner anytime."

"Uh-huh." Still mulling over what Angela Parsons had told her, Jo finished at the pump and went to check the daily work schedule to see what she was supposed to do next.

Dave followed. "Is something wrong?"

Jo, realised she had been rude. "No, nothing's wrong. Tell Fran I appreciate the offer. I really do. I just have a few things on my mind. That's all."

"Anything I can help with?"

Jo shook her head. She had confirmed her suspicions with Angela Parsons. That was all she could do for now. The rest was up to Mavis. Once she'd told her about this latest development, Mavis would have to take her seriously about everything else.

CHAPTER EIGHT

Mavis Tidy suited her name — tidy by name and by nature. She was a dumpy woman who wouldn't have minded being five foot nothing if her legs had been four foot something, but the Lord had blessed her with a round figure, short torso, and even shorter legs. At the age of fifty-eight, Mavis had given up hoping for more.

She made the best of what she had. She kept her long grey hair wound in a neat bun, which made her look like the granny in the Tweetie Pie cartoon. The tiny glasses she wore served to emphasise the illusion. This benign exterior only fooled people for a short time.

As Mavis locked her car and made her way into Fire Service Headquarters in Lisburn, she brooded over the phone call she had received in the early hours — a call that had kept her awake and pacing until it was time to dress for work.

She knew Josephine had been drinking. It wasn't that Josephine had slurred her words or even seemed drunk. Mavis's ears were just well trained. A lush of a husband in her youth had seen to that. Age, she decided, brought its own bounty — in wisdom. A bounty the girl on the reception desk, even deep into her dotage, would never attain.

"What on earth is the brigade coming to?" she muttered, as Rochelle — or Chantelle — continued to file her nails, oblivious to her approach.

"Ahem!"

The receptionist dropped her nail file, face reddening. "Go-good Morning, Ms Tidy."

Mavis hitched her glasses up the bridge of her nose and ignored the greeting. Her thoughts returned to her friend as she made her way to her office. When

Josephine had joined up five years ago, Mavis had taken her under her wing. There had been something about the girl, a vulnerability that didn't match the tough exterior she'd exuded and an honesty that was both refreshing and frustrating.

It had been easy to uncover her past, not quite so easy to get Josephine to tell her story herself. Eventually, though, she had, and Mavis admitted to an inordinate amount of pride the child had chosen her to confide in. They'd become close, close enough that when things turned... delicate, Mavis had felt able to voice her idea for a transfer, knowing that without it, Josephine's time in the brigade was limited.

"*You need a town, Josephine,*" was how she'd put it. "*A town where life is so slow you have to go backwards to go forwards.*"

Mavis fired up the coffee machine. The transfer had seemed a good idea at the time. *Did I make a mistake?* She sat at her desk and flicked through the post, her mind focused on Josephine and her request. She knew that to aid her friend — to start all this nonsense again — would lead to more heartbreak. Yet, she couldn't ignore her friend's plea.

Mavis prayed Josephine wouldn't find what she was looking for when she checked out the family today. It was a forlorn hope. In today's society, abuse was the norm rather than the rarity.

She had a choice, she decided, getting up to pour herself a cup from the newly filled pot. Trust Josephine's instincts and do as her friend had asked or inform her boss, the chief fire officer. Either way, it could end Josephine's career, as it had almost ended it before.

Mavis took a long swallow of coffee and sat down. She lifted the phone. She had never been wrong about a person yet, and at her age, she wasn't about to start. Although, she wasn't sure Josephine would appreciate the first phone call she was about to make.

CHAPTER NINE

Jo was glad she'd had a few weeks with Red Watch before yesterday's ill-fated turn-out. If not, she might have decided the guys were always this sullen.

It never ceased to amaze her how diverse their job was. Yesterday, they'd attempted the rescue of a family, a life or — in the Forbes's case — death situation. Today, their main task was to liberate a reluctant cat. *Gotta love this job.*

She eyed Geoff as he lowered the ladder, his face pinched and tight, and resisted the urge to give Mick O'Leary a hug as his jokes fell like stones into the mine of each man's grief.

"Hey, if you were good old Terrance here," Micko said, cowlick straining to attention as he patted the rescued cat, "wouldn't you want to escape from her?" He gestured to the anxious woman berating a hapless Dave, oblivious to the fact her feline friend was safe. "I know in his place I'd have shot up the nearest tree, too."

"Shut the fuck up, Micko." Don Flanders kept his voice low so the cat owner couldn't hear, but the menace in the tone was unmistakable.

Micko retreated, clutching the tabby to his chest. The frightened animal, hoisted from his favourite perch, hissed, and scratched in an effort to free itself. "Ow!" Micko dropped the squirming cat and held his hands to his face. "You bloody bas—"

"Now, now Micko," Pat Meehan said, seeing the others grin. "That's the best laugh you've given us all day."

It was near the end of their shift, and for Jo, it couldn't come soon enough. Thank God, the day had contained nothing more stressful than a trapped cat and an easily brought-under-control gorse fire, because her mind wasn't on the job. It was focused on the boss, wondering what he was doing about her allegation. She winced as she eased herself into the back of the pump.

Dave clambered in next to her. "You okay?" he asked.

"Never better."

Dave, reading her expression, didn't press the matter.

*****

With forty minutes to make up, Jo didn't leave with the others. She knew Porter had covered for her, but as a newbie, it was a matter of principle that she complete her full shift. Plus, she wanted a quiet word with the boss. Twenty-four hours had passed since she'd voiced her suspicions. Surely, he would have something by now.

After parading off duty, she covered for a guy on Blue Watch who had an errand to run, then made her way to the boss's office. This time it took only one deep breath before she rapped confidently on the door. The worst had happened — at least she hoped it had. *What else is there to fear?*

"You just missed him."

Jo jumped. "Tumilty? What are you doing here?" She eyed the lanky figure, both annoyed and puzzled by his presence. Their shifts were taxing enough — four days on, four off, starting with two days commencing at nine am and ending at six pm, followed by two nightly stints of six pm to nine am. They were strenuous hours, downtime greedily hoarded in order to wind down and forget the carnage they viewed on a daily basis. To see Tumilty here on one of his leave days left Jo resentful and mystified. Did the guy have no home life?

"Those cigarettes I was telling you about...?"

"I don't smoke."

Tumilty edged closer. "No harm in trying." He gave Jo an ingratiating grin. "What did you want the boss for?"

"Wanted to explain why I was late today," Jo said, "No biggie." She waited.

When Tumilty didn't ask the obvious, Jo's mind flicked to her conversation with Angela Parsons and her mention of another firefighter asking questions. She'd pegged Angela as an astute woman. After all, she'd seen Steven Forbes for the bully he was. Jo didn't think she would confuse a firefighter with anyone from SOCO — the Scene of Crime Officers. And Shaunessy, the only other fire personnel who should have been at the fire site, was so gaunt as to appear half starved, surely something Angela would have mentioned in passing.

Could Tumilty be the guy Angela had talked to? And if so, why was he sniffing around?

Tumilty was giving nothing away. "You going to Murdock's?" he asked, mentioning the pub situated across the street from the station.

"I thought I'd give it a miss and have an early night."

"You have a lot of those, don't ya?" It was said without inflection. "Don't you know it makes for better relations if you socialise?" Then, as if realising he was speaking out of character, Tumilty's features changed, lips sliding into a sneer. "Just saying." He turned to go. "Words of advice are free — for now."

Jo watched him leave, feeling in need of a shower. The guy made her skin crawl, but he was right about one thing. She had been here over a month. Maybe it was time to take the lads up on their offer, build a few bridges? And if she happened to ferret out a little information along the way? Well, so much the better. First, though, she needed to phone Mavis, then she'd brave the lion's den.

*****

Jim Tumilty signalled his companion to silence and backed him into the galley. He held the door closed and listened for Jo's footsteps to descend the stairs. He waited until they'd faded into the distance before he spoke.

"Damn! I think she knows something."

His companion paled. "How?"

"Don't ask me." Tumilty's brow furled in concentration as he tried to recall the conversation he'd just had with Jo. It was nothing she'd said. There had just been something in her eyes.

"But I *am* asking you." The other man moved closer, dwarfing the smaller man. "Seems to me you don't sound all that surprised, Tumilty." The name was sneered. "What the fuck's going on?"

"Nothing." Tumilty tried not to show his unease. "We proceed as planned."

"How can we? You've just told me she knows. That could be dangerous — for her and for us."

With a strength and speed that amazed him, the other man moved and Tumilty felt a hand at his throat. He was lifted, propelled against the wall. Even as he fought for breath, his eyes narrowed slyly. "Maybe, maybe not," he managed to gasp.

The grip on his throat slackened. "What the fuck does *that* mean?"

Taking advantage of his opponent's confusion, Tumilty peeled the fingers away one by one. "Just what I say." He put distance between them. "Whether she knows or not is immaterial. You've got your job. I've got mine." He let that sink in. "We both have our reasons for doing this. You want to stop?"

At his words, the big man deflated. "No. But I don't like it." He turned to leave. "I don't like it one little bit."

"You don't have to like it," Tumilty said, rubbing his throat. "You just have to do what you're bloody well told."

CHAPTER TEN

After staring at the door to Murdock's bar for over a minute, Jo wondered if maybe she did have a problem after all, and if so, was there was a name for it? She tried a few in her mind. *Dooritis? Dooraphobia?*

No, they wouldn't call it something that concise, she decided at last. If there was a name for it — and she was pretty sure there was — it would be something oblique, probably in Latin so plebs like her couldn't understand and would have to spend a fortune in psychiatrist fees to find out.

Information and bonding, she reminded herself and took a deep breath. *Think of it as practice for the barbecue this weekend.* Then she would have no choice but to mingle. The idea depressed her. All she wanted to do was go home, slip straight into bed, and... *And what? Sleep?*

"What the hell. A drink might be just what I need." She pushed open the door.

At her entrance, all conversation stopped. Jo tossed her singed braid over her shoulder, fighting the urge to run as the silence lingered, like the scent of a newly formed fart.

She gritted her teeth and attempted to appear confident, striding towards the bar where Dave was in the process of ordering a drink. "My round," she said. "A thank you — and an apology for being such a moody cow," she added when he made no move to take her offer.

"In that case, I'll have a scotch." Dave flicked a glance over his shoulder and said in a louder voice, "A double, seeing as you're buying, Woods."

The tables erupted behind him, orders coming thick and fast.

"Mine's a double, too."

"A quadruple for me," someone else chipped in.

Wart, for once, looked happy. He tapped his glass and mouthed "*vodka*".

"If you're in a giving mood, I kinda fancy tits and ass," a voice said in the background.

Jo waved for silence. "Give them what they want," she told the barman, grabbing an open bottle of Bud. "But as for Pete's order..." She eyed the barman's bum, straining over the seat of his jeans as he bent to the cooler. "I'll leave that up to you. What you guys do in private has nothing to do with me."

Pete Murphy tipped his glass and looked sheepish at the guffaws that followed.

"Seamus doesn't have everything we want," Don Flanders said and jumped to his feet, barring Jo's way. "I'm not as desperate as Pete. I need a *real* woman." He clutched his groin. "You up to filling the hole, darlin'?"

What is this guy's problem? Jo knew the others were watching, waiting to see how she'd react. She had to handle this now or she was sunk. *It's definitely showtime.*

She conjured a smile. "What have you in mind, Don? You got an itch you can't scratch?" She rested a hand provocatively over his fly. "Maybe I can help?"

Flanders, not believing his luck, nodded. "Oh, baby, can you ever."

Jo let her hand hover over his groin a second or two more before she raised her knee and smacked it upwards with such force that the rest of the bar gasped. "How's that, baby? Itch gone?"

Geoff gave an inelegant snort that crumpled his face like crepe paper. "Yup, that will do it every time." His skeletal hands clapped against his pint. The others joined in.

"You've got balls, lass," Bill said from the smog-filled end of the bar, cigarette dangling between nicotine-stained fingers. "But as you've found out, they can be your strength or your downfall." His gaze moved to the prostrate Flanders, bushy brows rising. "Be sure you know which is which."

*****

The boss's veiled warning followed Jo home. She hadn't managed to speak to him, and she didn't think that was by accident. The closest she'd come was the tail-end of his ashy scent as he bypassed her en route to his taxi.

Later, standing at her bedroom window staring out at a landscape that wasn't home, Jo felt disheartened. She hadn't been able to talk to Mavis, either, and leaving a message hadn't satisfied her need to get things sorted. Now the boss was avoiding her. *Maybe I should pack up and go, not wait to be pushed?* Not that she'd have much packing to do, she thought glumly, surveying the wall of cardboard reflected behind her in the glare of smooth glass.

From the flat below, a child cried, a plaintive howl that echoed her own hopelessness. Through tear-filled eyes, the twinkling town lights in the distance sharpened, elongated until they appeared spear-like, the barrage directed straight at her heart. For an instant, the sensation was so strong, so acute, that Jo placed a hand over her chest, stricken to the core.

She had failed. Failed not only Emma Forbes and her family, but all those she was certain would come after them.

Unnerved at the way her thoughts were going, Jo snapped the curtains closed. As she undressed for bed, she couldn't escape the realisation that maybe the boss was right. *Maybe this time I bit off more than I can chew?*

*****

I cursed as the curtains swung closed, returning the night to darkness. Once again, I was alone, on the outside, looking in.

"Fucking story of my life!"

Envy brought bile to the back of my throat, and along with the surge of acid, the memories came — the memories I'd tried for so long to suppress. This time, I was powerless against their furious onslaught.

I was transported to the past — four children shivering in the snow, eyes glued to a blackened windowpane, behind which Mother's pitiful cries could be heard.

Rising... Rising... Falling... Falling...

We preferred it when she screamed. Not that we wanted her to be hurt, but at least then we knew she was still alive. In the long spaces between screams, we held our breath. Silence was the enemy. The devil hid in the silence, waiting to take possession of Mother's wicked soul — or so Father told us. Father knew a lot about the devil, knew he had to beat the wickedness out of Mother to keep her safe.

I wasn't sure I believed Father. Me? Yes, I was wicked. I could understand him thrashing me, although I doubted he'd ever beat the devil out of me. Deep down I suspected that the more he beat me, the larger the devil inside me grew. As for Mother? I wavered on that score. I had never seen her commit an evil act, but part of me — the part consumed by Satan — wondered why she didn't protect the little ones when Father turned his drunken might on them.

"Mother must have been really naughty this time," Amy said through chattering teeth.

We had lost track of time, but surely even Mother couldn't stand much more. Marge, ever the

51

bossy-boots, tried to rally the younger ones. "You sit there," she ordered, pointing six-year-old Serena in my direction.

Serena, green icicles of snot hanging beneath her snub nose, rushed to comply.

Amy crawled in next. At five, she was the baby of the family, although "family" wasn't a word we used much anymore. Father had seen to that, like he was seeing to Mother.

Over twenty years had passed and I could still feel them crouched there, trembling beneath my racing heart. I squeezed my eyes shut, fought to escape the memory. But like the snow surrounding us that night, soaking our nightclothes and sending aching, cramping waves of pain up our thin bodies, it was unavoidable.

"C'mon in, Marge," I heard myself say in my ten-year-old voice, opening my arms, "there's plenty of room. Jump in before you catch your death of cold."

I heard an answering thrill on the air. It lingered for an instant before it faded, lost forever in the past. Arms splayed wide, I found myself in the present, alone once more — alone and cold in the dark.

The familiar bite of anger was swiftly followed by the hollow emptiness of despair. "Goddamn you, Jo Woods!" I glared at the darkened flat. "Goddamn you for dredging up these old memories."

"You must rise above the memories. You cannot let the past intrude on your present — or your future."

"I know."

I didn't know why Jo had this effect on me. From the moment I'd met her, I'd felt this connection, a connection I'd only experienced before with my family. Now she was shutting me out.

"Why, Jo? Why let me in if you're only going to shut me out again? Damn yo—" I muffled the curse, afraid the other watcher would hear. Didn't she know I was trying to help? Couldn't she see?

Another, more desperate thought... Was I always destined to toil alone, to have no one to confide in, to share my pain with? A frisson accompanied the thought, making the fine hairs on my body dance. It took me a moment to recognize the emotion.

Fear.

Twenty years since I'd last experienced it and the second it reared its head, I felt ten years old again. Why did her opinion matter so damn much?

I formed a picture of Jo. I would be the first to admit the fire brigade uniform wasn't complimentary to the female form, but Jo took it to extremes, wearing long sleeved T-shirts and oversized trousers.

She did the same with her glorious hair, scraping it back from her face, restraining it in that bloody awful plait. Why did she hide her beauty? On the heels of that observation came another. What else was she hiding? Because she was definitely hiding something. I didn't know why I was so sure. Maybe it took one to know one.

I grinned. "Secrets, Ms. Woods?"

"You like secrets, don't you?"

I smiled. "Yes. Yes, I do." Secrets were my forte. Secrets, once found, brought power. And that, I thought gleefully, meant power over her. But there was something about her, a familiarity that tugged at the recently stirred pages of my memory, making me feel uneasy. The hairs on my arm receded, the others following suit until, once more, I stood alone, cold and shivering in the dark.

CHAPTER ELEVEN

Jo slept restlessly, her dreams full of dark thoughts and even deeper regrets. She woke early and spent the twilight hours drinking coffee and wondering which box to open first.

Morning brought no clear answer.

The child downstairs became more vocal with each passing hour, its voice rough and harsh with tears. Jo felt sympathy for the mother, because as tough as this was to listen to, it had to be a hell of a lot harder to live with.

She prowled the flat, the profusion of caffeine leaving her wired, and waiting for Mavis to return her call exacerbating the condition. In the end, she switched on her laptop and scrolled through her documents until she found a file marked "Names". She clicked it open.

A list of children's names appeared, along with their ages and addresses — a list too long for comfort, more so when she added Emma Forbes and her parents.

Jo had no need to read the contents, each line was imprinted in her mind, especially the two names near the top — Jade and Jason Magill, six months old.

Death by asphyxiation — 17th May 2006. *Twins.* A double loss for those left behind and so young that it made Jo's heart ache. She imagined them alive, giggling on a changing mat, chubby legs waving in the air, proud parents looking on — a fanciful notion, since only the mother's name was listed. At twenty one, she had been too young to die, too, but was there ever a good age, particularly when their deaths could have been prevented?

Reluctant to follow that path, Jo hit Save, then Copy before closing the file. Next, she logged into her e-mail account and composed a short note to Mavis, explaining again how she'd verified her suspicions about the Forbes. "Time" — she wrote — "to check the others against the Social Service At Risk Register."

Before she lost her nerve, she pasted the names to the bottom and pressed Send. It was the coward's way out, but she was in no mood for one of Mavis's lectures. Afterwards, she made a half-hearted effort to empty a few boxes, which only managed to transfer the contents of one box to another.

Jo surveyed the mess, hands on hips. "Bugger it to hell and back!"

She opted to quit while she was ahead — which showed what an optimist she was — and go explore this new town of hers. She knew she was avoiding the inevitable. The boxes would still be there on her return, as would her decision to unpack or not — with all that entailed. Jo wasn't stupid. She knew her inability to unpack represented more than an unwillingness to settle down or even mere laziness. She wouldn't go as far to say the boxes held her deepest darkest secrets, but they came close.

Something had changed last night. She didn't know what exactly, but somewhere between her showdown with Flanders and the odd sensation in her flat with its resulting sense of failure, she had come to a decision. She just hadn't known it until she'd seen the names in the file today.

She grabbed her coat from the back of the door. She couldn't — wouldn't — experience another Emma Forbes, not if there was the slightest chance she could prevent it. To do that, though, she needed help, and therein lay the problem. She had Mavis, of course, but she wasn't sure Mavis would be enough. She needed someone on the ground, here in Mourne

Lough, and, more importantly, someone she could trust.

Jo stopped short. Involve others? Trust them? She couldn't believe she was even considering it. And yet her mind immediately jumped to her teammates. She trusted them with her life — in their job you had to — but did she dare trust them with her secrets?

"You won't be trust-trusting them," she told herself. "They're a means to an end. That's all."

Shame washed over her. The guys on Red Watch were more than teammates. Dave had saved her life, invited her to his home, introduced her to his family. Geoff, her watch commander, was like a mentor to her, and Wart, Pat, and Micko were affable blokes, but Flanders and Tumilty? Right there were two reasons why she shouldn't trust too easily.

A means to an end, Jo reminded herself, uncertainty giving way to determination. With that settled, she planned her exit like a military manoeuvre. She waited until Mrs R went to replenish the vinegar solution she was using so diligently and pungently on the lone hallway window before making her escape.

It wasn't that she didn't like Mrs R. She did. That was the problem. In the end, it didn't matter what she decided. Whether she stayed or not was out of her hands, dependent on the boss and what he discovered. The old girl was lonely enough without Jo befriending her, then leaving.

She was staying, Jo reminded herself as she crept down the stairs, to stop any more deaths and to prove or disprove her theory. Or, if she wanted to be pedantic, for Mavis to do so. Attachments, of any kind, were not on her agenda.

Squashing how mean she felt, Jo sneaked down the last few steps, sighing with relief when she reached the front door without discovery.

"You're the new tenant, aren't you?"

Startled, Jo swung round. A waif of a girl stood in the open doorway to her right, with short black hair cut in a severe bob framing wan features. Before she could decide between fight and flight, the girl spoke again.

"I wanted to apologise."

"Apologise?" This Jo had to hear. "For what?"

"Emily's been up all night. You must have heard her."

Jo made a dismissive gesture. *Heard her? Is she being funny? The child could have been heard all the way to Lisburn.*

"She's teething, you see." Brown eyes lowered then shot up again. "We haven't been introduced. My name's Mary. Mary... Quinn."

That was a lie for a start, Jo thought, hearing the hesitation, unwillingly intrigued.

"Jo Woods." She offered her hand, felt it taken in a bony grip. She eyed the slender figure, noted the dark circles shadowing the toffee-coloured eyes. Crying child — or something else?

"Nice to meet you, Jo. I'm really sorry, Emily's usually a good baby. It's just—"

"Teething." Jo smiled, liking this nervous, anorexic girl-woman. "Don't worry. It will pass."

"Oh, you have kids?"

The pale face lit up and Jo was loath to disappoint her. She swallowed a dart of pain and formed her lips into a smile. "No, but I have a niece and nephew, and as the only aunt, I was roped into a lot of babysitting. A lot," she added with passion.

Mary laughed, the harsh features softening. "Thanks."

"For what?"

"For being so nice." Then, as if she'd said more than she'd meant, she ducked into her flat and closed the door.

"Scaring the neighbours?"

Jo, her mind puzzling over Mary's abrupt departure, turned. "Hmm?"

A man stood in the doorway of the flat opposite, head skimming the top of the doorframe. He pulled a denim jacket over what, even in her confusion, Jo noted were broad shoulders. *So, this is my other downstairs neighbour.* Today was turning into a right "meet and greet."

"I'm not surprised with a face like that," the man said. He locked his door then deposited the key in his coat pocket.

"What?" Jo's mouth dropped open.

"Ooh, and that one, too. It could curdle milk, that could." He held up his hands, index fingers making the shape of a cross, as if warding off an evil spirit. "You might want to work on that." He gave Jo a cheeky grin.

"Why you—" But she was talking to empty air. The denim-clad figure was past her and out the front door. She heard him whistling down the pathway. "Of all the..." Fuming, Jo followed him and not even to herself would she admit she eyed his tightly clad backside the whole way down the steps.

*****

Mary Quinn watched from her bedroom window as her two neighbours disappeared. They made a striking couple, she thought, the spark between them obvious and uncomfortable to watch. Or maybe that was guilt talking? After all, spying on them through the peephole in her front door and from her bedroom window wasn't the nicest thing to do.

She groaned as she rose from the rickety chair, stretching to work out the kinks in her aching body. She yawned. She was tired — beyond tired. Emily's constant crying was wearing her down and the fear she was doing something wrong — that she was responsible for her child's distress — was, at times, too much to bear.

Moments like these she wished for someone to share the burden with, someone to look after her the way she imagined the guy across the hall would look after Jo Woods, given half a chance. Mary fingered her shorn hair, the new bob strange to the touch. *What am I thinking?* She might be young but she wasn't that naïve — not any more.

And yet, as if conjured from her mind, her mobile chimed. Mary stood motionless. No one had this number except Emily's doctor, in case of emergency. Her heart raced. Had he discovered something during their last visit, something more than teething? The mobile chimed again. With a feeling of dread, Mary picked it up. The display said *unknown caller* and her heart expanded against her ribs. *It can't be, can it?*

From the bedroom, Emily, as if sensing her mother's distress, began to cry. Still clutching the phone, Mary rushed to her side. "Sshh," she crooned, "Mummy's here. I won't let anything happen to you."

But there was no power to her voice and no truth to her words and the child, as children often do, picked up on it. The little face contorted, mouth opening in a protracted scream. The ringing phone seemed to mimic the child's frustration.

Mary lifted the baby from the crib and rocked her back and forth. "It's okay, sweetheart." She pressed her head to the sweaty curls. "It's gonna be okay." The frightened shake in her voice gave lie to her words.

Emily burped, spewing forth a mouthful of foamy milk.

"Was that what was bothering you, sweetheart?" Mary tenderly wiped the smiling lips, grinning back at her in return. "That's mummy's clever girl." The phone was silent, but she knew the respite would be short-lived.

She was right.

No sooner had she settled Emily into her cot than the phone rang again. Quickly, she answered it, moving to the living room to avoid waking the sleeping child.

"H-hello?"

"Fucking keep me waiting! You do that again and I'll rip your tongue out, bitch! Be hard to talk with no tongue, dontcha think? But at least then I'll know the reason why you're not talking to me."

Mary's heart settled around her knees. She nodded, too afraid to speak. *Dear Lord, he found me.*

"I don't hear you."

A wave of desperation engulfed Mary. "I'm sorry, Thomas. I... I won't do it again." The apology was automatic.

"You'd better not. What the fuck did you think you were doing? Thinking you could escape me, run away, steal my kid? You think I'm stupid, that I couldn't find you?"

"No, Thomas, I—"

"Don't go there, bitch. Don't ever fuck with me." Anger roughened the voice, sharpened the edges to needle-like rigidity.

In the room that for a short time had become her haven, Mary flinched.

"Didn't I tell you I'd always find you, that you'd never get away from me? There's only one way to escape me, Mary, *my love*." The endearment was snarled. "Tell me what it is, if you're not too thick to remember?"

Mary complied, the freedom of the last few months disappearing with every syllable. "Death, Thomas."

"Till death do us part? That's what the priest said, remember? We made a vow, you and me, an oath before God. That's sacred, that is. I kept my part. Why'd you break yours? Why?"

"I'm sorry, Thomas." Again, the apology was automatic, learned the hard way over the long torturous months of their marriage. "I—"

"Shut it!" Menace laced his voice. "Why do you wind me up this way, Mary? Why can't you ever learn?" He didn't wait for an answer, never had. "You gotta be punished. You know that, and you know how much I hate doing that."

Mary didn't. In fact, she thought he rather enjoyed it.

CHAPTER TWELVE

Mourne Lough exceeded Jo's expectations, although, having none to start with helped. She did admit to a certain fascination as she was bombarded by smiling faces and cheery greetings. In one case, she'd even been offered a doffed hat.

Either she'd landed slap bang in Stepford or this was the rural Ireland she'd heard about. It was so different from Belfast, where she'd grown up, or her last post in Lisburn where people avoided eye contact and, if given the chance, walked through you rather than around you.

Suspicion gave way to enjoyment, and yet, amid the throng of cheerful passers-by, Jo felt, if not alone, then lonely, and if she were honest, scared. She had lied when she'd said her teammates were a means to an end. In the short time she'd been here, they had come to mean a lot more than that to her and it terrified her.

She liked this town, she admitted. She wanted to build a new life here, get to know the guys on her watch — the guys like Porter and Pete Murphy on Blue Watch — meet their wives and girlfriends. She even wanted to meet "my Liam" — and that was saying something.

Trust didn't come easy to Jo. A new life meant letting go of the past, saying goodbye to her ghosts.

Am I ready? Can I do it?

Jo waited for the pain to strike.

And waited.

Wow. She found a bench and sat down to contemplate the enormity of this revelation. "Wow," she said again, this time out loud. "Looks like I have some unpacking to do after all."

Her decision to stay left her strangely at peace. She had tried running. It hadn't worked. Something told her it never would. Time to stand and fight, and this town, she knew, was the place to do it.

Buoyant with the discovery, she made her way to the station in plenty of time for her six o'clock shift and was pulled rudely back to earth.

"Boss wants to see you."

Flanders, eyes narrowed with spite that told Jo he hadn't forgotten nor forgiven her put-down in the bar, greeted her at the station door. "Guess you musta' blotted your copybook, huh?"

Jo ignored him and tried to hold on to her good mood as she took the stairs two at a time. She arrived at the boss's door out of breath and cautioning herself not to expect too much. Caught up, her Dooritis, for once, deserted her.

Her rap was answered immediately.

"Come in."

"Flanders said you wanted to see me?"

"Sit." Bill fanned the thick pile of papers in front of him.

Jo's heart dropped. It didn't take a brain surgeon to know the boss had done his homework. She clasped her hands in her lap and waited for the axe to fall.

"I checked your theory, Woods, and talked to Shaunessy and the SOCO guys," Bill said. "As we assumed, the fire originated in the parents' bedroom — couch first to go, then the drapes. With the general state of upstairs — papers, clothes lying about, poor housekeeping, *and* high fire loading, it was a fecking accident waiting to happen." He held up a hand as Jo went to speak. "As to your assertion that the victims" — his eyes flashed to the photo on his desk, lingered for an instant on the faces of his grandchildren — "were murdered, the coroner disagrees with you." He lifted the top page from the pile and began to read. "Death occurred as the result of smoke inhalation. Blood pigment saturated to sixty, seventy per cent with carbon monoxide," he quoted. "That seems pretty damn conclusive to me."

It did to Jo, too. Anything up to ten per cent was considered normal, especially when atmospheric pollution or smoking was taken into consideration. Levels over fifty per cent were more than enough to account for death, which meant the Forbes's had been alive at the time of the fire.

Jo had an explanation. "That wouldn't preclude drugging. If the family were drugged before the fire, their—"

Bill pulled a blue folder from his top drawer — her personnel file. "Sure, you'll be telling me next you went to medical school." He opened the file, pretended to read. "Funny, it doesn't say that here. Although," he impaled Jo with a steely glare, "the last few pages make for interesting reading."

Jo clasped her hands tighter. She knew what was coming.

"I've been made to look like a fecking ass, thanks to you," Bill said.

The fact he was breathing like a donkey, his voice hawing like a demented mule, didn't seem to strike him as funny and, at this point, Jo wasn't inclined to point out the similarities.

"I went to bat for you, Woods," he bellowed. "Called in a favour. And what do I find?" He slapped a beefy fist on the pristine pages, creasing them.

That was too easy.

"Fecking right," Bill exploded. "Seems this isn't the first time you've come across a *murder* like this. Care to enlighten me why you didn't tell me all this at the start?" Jo shrugged.

Bad move.

"Don't you dare fecking shrug at me." Bill sucked on his cigarette, taking it down to its tip in his agitation. "I'm guessing here, but has this anything to do with why you were transferred from your last place?"

"I asked for this transfer," Jo said. The fact she'd jumped before she was pushed was nobody's business but her own.

"Well, I'm letting you know right here, right now," he warned, "that as good as you are, you start this murder horseshit with me and you're outta here."

Jo couldn't let that go. "It's not horseshit, Boss. Emma Forbes and her family were murdered, just like the others."

"Others?" Bill was apoplectic with rage. "There are no *others*, 'cept in your fecking head." He made a visible effort to calm, but a vein pulsed at his temple. "It would take a mind greater than both of ours combined to do what you're suggesting — fooling not only us but the SOCO guys and at least a couple of coroners. Yours, I'm guessing, is a few golf clubs short of a set, but let me tell you, mine's fine — fires on all cylinders. Evidence!" he roared, striking the table again, making Jo jump. "That's the only thing you bring me, not any of these wacko theories — none of this 'I saw' shite or 'they were drugged, Boss' shite." His lifted his other fist. "Evidence!" It fell, hitting the desk with the force of a guillotine, cutting Jo's hopes in two. "Cold, hard, fecking evidence. Understand?"

Jo nodded. "Loud and clear, Boss." She pushed back her seat. Disappointed as she was, she felt a faint ray of hope. He hadn't sacked her. She backed out of the room before he changed his mind.

CHAPTER THIRTEEN

No sooner had Jo left Bill's office than the turn-out alarm sounded.

"What we got?" she asked Dave, both of them suited and in the pump.

"RTC."

Jo's heart sank. This was their second road traffic collision this week. "Any other info?"

"Two cars. No word on casualties."

Within minutes, they'd arrived at the scene. One car lay on its side, pressed against a steep grass verge, and the other upright, pointed in the wrong direction on the far side of the road. The air smelled of scorched rubber and a faint tang of metal. A lone indicator light flicked on and off.

"Yes." Pat punched the air. "We beat the police."

"Shut it, Meehan, and get the cones," Flanders said. Sirens sounded behind them, "We need to cordon off."

Geoff, the officer in charge, did a quick three-hundred-sixty-degree survey while the rest of the crew unloaded the RTC equipment and rolled out the hose. "Let's speed this up," he said on his return. "Light's fading. Pat, perimeter search. Jo, set up the equipment. Tumilty, help me stabilize this vehicle." He nodded to the car on its side. "Dave, you're on this casualty. Flanders, you take the guy across the road. Stay with them until the ambulance arrives."

Jo caught a glimpse of the occupant trapped in the toppled car as she passed — just the eyes, wide and fearful. A moments' inattention, a split-second decision and the lives of these two motorists had changed, maybe forever, depending on their injuries. All it took was a single instant, Jo knew, to change the course of your whole life. It had happened to her, last November while on a routine turn-out — if any turn-out could be called routine. The house was supposed to have been empty, the occupants on holiday. It hadn't been until they were on scene that things had changed, for the worst.

"Persons reported," the controller had informed Jo, voice clipped, impartial. "Two adults, three children — youngest eighteen months, oldest four. Neighbour spotted the family late last night."

"Damn!"

New urgency had infused the pump. With the house occupied, every second counted.

Jo had been in first. Shades of the Forbes's fire, the house had been well ablaze. Unlike the Forbes's fire, she hadn't made it as far as the bedroom.

From the foot of the damaged staircase, she'd spied the little boy. He'd lain in the upstairs landing, curled on his side as if asleep. His open eyes had told Jo they'd arrived too late. Then she'd seen the roses — an incongruous sight amid the smoke and ash, like thick droplets of blood, marking the child's last resting place. Unbelieving, she'd moved closer just as the kitchen had exploded.

The blast had destroyed everything in its path. Luckily for Jo, she had only been attempting to find a way up the stairs when it had blown or she would have been killed outright.

Things had unravelled the moment she'd mentioned the roses. Her Lisburn teammates had laughed, and unable to put into words the look of pleading she'd imagined in the child's dead eyes, Jo hadn't been able to blame them.

The little boy had haunted Jo's dreams. Night after night he'd visited, demanding she catch his killer, punish him. She'd dreaded going to sleep, had lived in a constant state of anxiety. She had been offered leave — the option to visit the brigade counsellor couched in more stringent terms. He had been easy to fool — her slow realisation that smoke may have been a factor and with the victims so young... Yeah, he'd been easy to convince. It had been Mavis who'd been the problem, but then, Mavis knew the whole story.

In the end, the autopsy showed the Thompsons died of smoke inhalation. The fire — as in the Forbes case — had been classified accidental. Yet, from the second Jo had seen those roses, she'd known something was terribly wrong.

She'd dug deeper. In the five years since she'd joined the brigade, there had been twenty fatal house fires involving children, an increase of eighty per cent on the previous five years. Of the twenty, only three had been classed as arson. However, the marked increase concerned Jo. With little more than that and a gut feeling, she'd investigated further.

What she'd found had staggered her. Of the twenty original fires, fifteen families were — as one obnoxious individual had put it — "the dregs of society". What he'd meant, in his quaint, Flanderish way, had been that the families had been classed as dysfunctional — single parents or in the Thompsons' case, as she'd later found out, on the verge of becoming so. Drug addicts and alcoholics, and, in seven cases, physical and/or sexual abuse had been suspected.

Two or three families she could have put down to coincidence or the sad state of society today, but fifteen? There had to be a link.

With that sliver of a connection in mind, she'd pressed on.

Her mind continued to wander as she worked on the equipment. *Why leave roses at the scene, take a chance — no matter how slim — that they might be discovered?* Jo felt a dart of excitement. The roses were important to the killer. *Why? Are they symbolic? A sign of remorse? Part of—*

"Earth to Woods. Helloooo."

Jo jumped, recalled to the present. "Sorry, Pat, what did you say?"

"Soft and hard protection. We're ready to extricate the second casualty."

Second casualty? Jo looked behind her. The car on the wrong side of the road now sat on the hard shoulder. An ambulance, lights blazing, disappeared into the darkness. A second ambulance, lights flashing, hurtled towards her. *Jesus, how long have I been distracted?*

"Here." She handed Pat the soft cover that protected the driver from debris.

Pat didn't move. "What's with you today, Jo? You're off your game. If Flanders notices..." He checked over his shoulder.

Jo grabbed the hard protection. "He won't. Thanks, Pat."

Pat looked like he wanted to say more. In the end, he flicked a salute and said, "Don't mention it," before scurrying off.

Jo tempered her excitement. Realising the roses were important to the killer was well and good, but the last time she'd investigated this guy, she'd ended up here, in Mourne Lough, with the threat of dismissal hanging over her head. This was Mavis's backwater town, where Jo was supposed to behave herself, stop making waves, and she'd intended to — until the Forbes fire, that was. When Angela Parsons had mentioned Steven Forbes and his temper, alarm bells rang. Another angry, abusive parent linked to a fire with paper roses and a dead child. *It has to be more than a coincidence.*

However, Jo didn't think the parents were involved, a fact borne out when the Thompsons' social worker had told Jo the family had been in a car accident the day before their deaths. The parents' injuries were severe enough to question their ability to murder their children. Although, she'd argued, how much effort did it take to drug one adult and three small children before setting fire to a house?

Jo wanted to scream. She had too many questions and not enough answers. For instance, if the parents weren't involved, then who else could get close enough to administer the drug? It had to be someone in a position of trust — a bottle of wine or a few beers for the parents, treats for the kids — doctored, of course. The thought made Jo physically ill. This guy was one sick bastard — or woman, she corrected. Drugging was a female trait. Men preferred up close and personal — guns, knives — the bloodier the better.

One thing she knew for sure was that a definite pattern was emerging. She ticked off the similarities — the marked increase of fire fatalities involving families in crisis, all with young children; the roses she'd noted on not one, not two, but three occasions; and lastly, the fact that every fire had been deemed accidental.

The last point concerned her the most. All those fires ruled accidental? Luck or something else?

"Jesus Christ, Woods, you gonna use that, or are you gonna stare at your navel all day?"

Flanders' caustic tone cut through Jo's musings. The guys were huddled around the car, preparing to cut the roof off, police and ambulance crews at the ready. She could hear Dave in the back seat, reassuring the driver. He — or she, Jo couldn't tell with the soft protection covering them like a blue hijab — was moaning softly.

Time to focus. She moved into place, holding the hard protection while Flanders used the cutting gear to remove the roof. It lifted off in one piece and was consigned to the equipment dump. The ambulance crew did a quick assessment then gave Geoff the thumbs up. Red Watch moved into place as the support board was slid in behind the driver. It would take all hands for the final move. They each found a handhold then took a firm grip.

"On my count," Dave said, taking charge of the driver's head. "One... two... three."

They wrestled the support board from the car and brought it to the casualty handling area. The ambulance guys took over.

"Job well done," Jo said, smiling at Dave.

He didn't smile back. "Still got the clean-up to do."

"Gloomy Gus. Take time to enjoy the little things, Dave." She put a hand on his shoulder. "Not often we have a positive result. This is a good day."

He shook her hand off. "If you say so."

Before she could ask what was wrong, someone punched her arm. "Move it, Woods."

"Ow." Jo turned, but the culprit was gone and the guys were heading en masse to the pump without her. She followed, footsteps slow. *What was that about?* She rubbed her arm, mind slipping back to Bill. He'd hit the nail on the head when he'd said whoever was doing this was clever. In fact, if the killer was as smart as Jo suspected, he possessed not only a full set of golf clubs, but a hell of a lot more cylinders than Bill could ever hope to own. The Forbes were only his third mistake. Either they'd arrived too quickly or he'd messed up somehow. Jo figured the former. He'd miscalculated this time, the bastard.

Her enthusiasm died. *Mistake?* Emma Forbes had been five years old, her parents in their twenties. They weren't a mistake, even if Steven Forbes had deserved to be strung up. They had been people with their whole lives in front of them and this guy — and Jo, drugging aside, was sure he was a guy — had taken that from them.

If she forgot that, she was no better than he was.

But that set her thinking. Clever equated with skill, but the skill to cover a murder with a fire and make it look like a botched arson attempt took a certain type of expertise.

The type only a firefighter knows.

Jo tried to quash the idea. It couldn't be. Firefighters saved lives, not took them. Yet, the more she thought about it, the more sense it made. Who was more trusted than a firefighter? Who else could stage it so they were never caught?

A firefighter, that's who.

Someone here?

Jo stared at her teammates, aghast. That was jumping the gun a bit, she told herself. Just because it might be a firefighter didn't mean it was someone on her watch. It could be someone on Blue Watch, someone retired, a trainee, a firefighter wannabe.

Yet her mind refused to let it go.

CHAPTER FOURTEEN

"Bastards!"

Jim Tumilty cursed as they returned from their fifth hoax call of the evening. "Little butt-wipes. Don't they know they're putting people's lives at risk with their stupid pranks? What if there'd been a real fire while we were out? What then?"

"At least we're not getting petrol bombed or pelted with stones like they are in Belfast," Geoff said. He wasted no time heaving himself into his bed with a tired grunt.

It was twelve thirty, not quite halfway through their shift, and they were all shattered.

"Not yet," Dave said. "But give them time. They're quick learners round here."

No one laughed, Jo least of all. Miserable, she trailed behind the others. Her initial excitement at finding what she'd hoped was the missing link had given way to dejection. She had opened Pandora's box and unable to call Mavis at another ungodly hour, it would be a long time before she could close it again.

Whilst she'd been oblivious to the others' coolness at the RTC and later turn-outs, it was unavoidable now, tension palpable in the tight confines of the dorm. Dave avoided her eyes, and Pat darted furtive nods of support when he felt himself unnoticed. *What is going on?*

Flanders was milking it, whatever *it* was, for all he was worth. Piggy eyes alight with mischief, he stripped to his boxers and stood in front of her, stomach levitating above flabby thighs. "Nite, nite, darlin'." He scratched his hairy navel, paused and raised a hand to his mouth. "Oops, not exactly PC. Sorry."

Jo scowled but refused to rise to his taunts.

"PMS," Flanders imparted loudly to Pat, who gave a nervous giggle as he clambered into his cot.

The sleeping area was snug, eight beds clumped together — space and luxury not a design consideration. Jo tugged off her pullover and tried to ignore Flanders. It was hard. All these years avoiding people and the second she'd let her guard down... *Bam!*

Flanders she could understand. He was still smarting over their showdown, but the others? Their silence spoke volumes. And yet, she really thought she'd connected with the guys last night, built a rapport.

Clad in trousers and a long-sleeved shirt, Jo threw herself on the covers. *Screw them.* She'd go back to her first instincts, treat them as a means to an end, nothing more. She turned her head to the wall and tried to convince herself she meant it.

Coughs and sniffs permeated the air, interspaced with the occasional fart, but otherwise, the room was silent — a heavy, oppressive silence.

"I hear they go all moody, psycho shit, if you're not careful," Flanders said to no one in particular. He tried to hum the theme song to Psycho but gave up. "But I guess we gotta make allowances. You think she'll make allowances for my wet dreams, if I sleepwank, er... Sorry, darlin', walk?"

"Enough!" Geoff rolled out of bed. "This needs sorted." He moved to stand in front of Jo's cot. "The boss had Evans in his office all day, questioning your sanity." He motioned Dave forwards. "Now me," he said, glaring at the others, sitting on the edge of their beds enjoying the show, "I think you're as sane as the rest of us, but if we're going to get any sleep tonight, you'd better speak up."

Jo sat up, both gratified by his words and terrified about how to proceed.

"Dave?" she asked, playing for time.

Dave looked embarrassed. "I'm sorry, Jo. It's true. The old boy hauled me over the coals, asked if I thought you were up to the job, if maybe you had... problems."

"She's got problems all right." Flanders elbowed his way forwards. "I'm guessing of the female persuasion." His eyes lingered on Jo's stomach.

Jo took comfort from the fact that nobody laughed, although Jim Tumilty gave her a greasy smirk. It hardened her resolve. "What exactly did the boss say, Dave?"

"That you'd done this before — made something out of nothing." He hitched his shoulders to convey these were Bill's words, not his. "He said it was to do with your past?" He waited.

Jo ached to speak up, hated the deceit, but some things were too personal, too painful to say out loud. Aware she could be talking to a killer, she chose her words with care. It was obvious they knew she didn't consider Emma Forbes's death an accident. But did they know why? The *real* reason why?

"The only thing this has to do with my past," she said at last, "is I've seen something similar to the Forbes's fire before."

"What's to see?" Pat said sadly. "Fire burns. Fire kills."

"Not like this," Jo said before she could stop herself. And yet, at the back of her mind was the realisation that Pat, at least, was in the dark. *Or is he playing dumb?*

"What does *that* mean?" Tumilty said. "You saying there's a psycho's out there, killing kids and leaving a pretty trail of roses to mark his patch?"

The fact Tumilty knew the real story didn't surprise Jo, especially after her encounter with Angela Parsons. She'd never liked him — his sly

75

ferret face, the twist of his head he affected when brokering one of his deals. He gave her the creeps. Yet, deep down, she knew looks didn't factor into this kind of evil. She may as well say the boss was the culprit. He had the expertise — more than Tumilty, more than any of them. For a moment, her mind took flight.

"Roses? Who said anything about roses?" Pat said in the background. "No one tells me anything."

"Shut it, Pat," Flanders said. He rounded on Jo. "You're the psycho, Woods." Looking ridiculous in his stripy boxers but obviously determined not to let the situation get away from him, he placed his fists on his hips and glared at her. "Relatives need closure. You're extending their grief with this murder theory of yours."

Jo ignored him. *Closure. That would tie things up nice and neat, wouldn't it?* Flanders was her second choice after Tumilty.

"It's more than a theory." She looked at Geoff and Dave, wanting them to understand. "I have proof — or I will soon," she amended quickly, thinking of Mavis. It was still a bit of a stretch. All Mavis would be able to tell her for definite was whether Emma Forbes and the others were on the Social Services Register. While that would confirm they all fitted the same pattern, it wouldn't prove conclusively there was a killer at work. Still, once she got Mavis to check if any of the guys were stationed close to the other fires, she would have another string to her bow. She sensed them wavering. "In a few days, I'll be able to—" She broke off. *What? Tell them which one of them is a killer?*

Like a shark sensing blood, Flanders attacked. "Able to do what? String a sentence together?" Face suffused with red, he turned to the others. "I always said females had no place here. They're too irrational, scared of their own shadow most times."

"If in doubt, better sorted out," Geoff said, sounding to Jo's ears remarkably like Mavis.

"What the fuck does that mean?" Flanders advanced, ready for a fight.

Geoff wasn't intimidated. "It's our job to be sure, Don. Every time we go on a turn-out, we clear up a mess, usually caused by someone's carelessness. We cut and scoop human remains like they're slabs of beef and every time" — he swivelled to encompass the others — "every time, we ask ourselves why? Why did this happen? What could have been done to prevent it? What could we have done to prevent it? And sometimes, like now, we have a chance to say 'this doesn't feel right'" — he tapped his chest — "in here. Is there any man who would argue with that?" He pinned the group with a look and even Flanders blushed.

"Whatever Jo is doing, she isn't doing it to cause trouble. I think we know her well enough to know that. And whether she's right or wrong, she has the right to speak out. There's the bell."

He was gone before the others realised the alarm was sounding.

*****

Later, at the station, Jo came across Geoff ensconced in his favourite chair, book in hand. "Thanks, Geoff."

"For what? I only told the truth."

Jo left it at that, grateful that at least one person was on her side. But as she climbed into her bed, she couldn't escape the insidious thought: *Why? Why did Geoff defend me? Does he really believe me or is he playing a clever game, throwing me off the scent by siding with me?*

*****

For the second time in as many days, fear poked its head out of my past, bared its teeth and spewed its rancid breath over my skin. The second encounter tasted no better than the first, especially when mixed with the battery acid in my stomach, but at least this time the memories failed to materialise. What did was a whole host of questions.

Did Jo really know something? If so, what? And how much?

"Of course she knows something, you moron. She said she had proof."

"Not quite." Correcting the voice helped me feel in control. "She said she *may* have proof *soon.*"

"Oh, that's so much better. Don't be dense. She knows about the roses. She's told other people about them." The voice hardened. *"The roses are* our *secret. Ours!"*

I, too, felt violated. The roses were personal — an integral, intimate part of my ritual. Strangely, though, the thought of Jo knowing about them didn't bother me nearly as much it did the voice.

"That's because I'm not thinking with my dick. Get bothered. This is a disaster. She could ruin everything."

Sometimes I hated the voice. "She's fishing. She knows nothing, and even if she did, no one believes her. They're humouring her. Didn't you hear them? She's got a track record for doing stuff like this. Trust me. She's no threat to us."

"And the proof she says she's going to get?"

"She's lying. There *is* no proof. I'm far too clever for that. That's why I use the roses. They burn along with any other sliver of evidence I may have left behind. *May* have left behind," I emphasised for the voice. "Everything burns. There is nothing left to tie us to the any of the scenes."

"*So you say. You have allowed yourself to be seduced by Jo Woods. She has a hold on you, a hold I don't understand. It makes you weak.*"

I didn't want to admit the voice had a point. I swallowed a glass of milk, hoping to neutralise the acid in my stomach. It didn't work. I couldn't escape the acid any more than I could this strange connection with Jo. It felt so real, like she was supposed to be part of this — part of me.

"*Get your mind out of your pants.*"

"It's nothing to do with that. I—"

"*If your mission is to succeed, you need to remove yourself from all physical temptation.*"

"I have. I—"

"*Physical isn't always sex. Your loneliness blinds you. You need to understand that you're never alone, as long as you have me.*"

"I know, but sometimes I need... more."

"*More?*"

How to explain something I didn't understand myself? I didn't want to hurt the voice. It was my saviour. It had been with me as long as I could remember — had kept me sane in those lonely, terrible years. I wouldn't have survived without it. The voice had saved me from the devil more than Father's beatings ever could. It had shown me my calling. I owed it everything.

"*Then listen to me. You need to deal with Jo Woods — now, before she destroys everything you've worked for.*"

I met the voice halfway. "I'll watch her. If she becomes a problem, then I'll deal with her."

"*Will you?*"

The doubt in the voice was understandable, but it still grated. "Yes. Yes, I will." It was an easy answer because I knew I was right about Jo. She was on my side, even if she didn't know it yet. Our connection was too strong for her to ignore. Joy overwhelmed me. I wasn't alone any more. Watching her would only bring her closer to me.

"And if it doesn't."

This time there was no hesitation in my reply. "Then I shall free her, just like the others."

CHAPTER FIFTEEN

The next morning, five minutes after she'd finished her shift and the second she was alone, Jo phoned Mavis. She ignored the soft clucking sound Mavis made when she voiced her new request.

"Oh, Josephine."

"Don't!" Jo said, hating the pity she heard in Mavis's voice. "It makes sense. Only a firefighter could get away with it for so long." When there was no further objection, she forged on. "I need you to compile a list of the men working here, see if a name pops up in conjunction with any of the fires I emailed you."

"Josephine I—"

Jo cut her off. "I saw Emma Forbes with my own two eyes, Mavis. I saw her *and* the roses! It was the Thompson fire all over again. You gonna tell me she's a figment of my imagination, too?"

"Of course not. It's just..." Mavis hesitated.

Jo knew what Mavis was thinking. Any witness other than Jo herself would have been better — preferable, in fact.

"Are you sure you didn't see what you wanted to see, Josephine?" Mavis said at last.

Jo was fed up with people asking her that. Next, Mavis would question how much smoke she had inhaled. Good job she hadn't mentioned the bump on the head. "I guess you're going to have to trust me, Mavis."

Silence hummed between them, and in those few seconds, fear did a quick tango up Jo's spine. Last night it was possible she had let a killer know she was on to him. If Mavis didn't come through for her—

She kept her voice steady. "What can it hurt, Mavis?" she wheedled. "No one will know if I'm wrong, but what if I'm right?"

"Okay," Mavis said at last. "I'm not happy about it," she grumbled, "but I will do it."

Jo decided to change the subject. "What about Emma Forbes? Did you find out if she was on the register? And the others, were they—?"

"I'm still looking into it. It's not easy getting those sorts of records, you know."

Jo was reluctant to push, but she was desperate for answers and she was confident Mavis would confirm her suspicions. It was the only thing all the fires had in common. The children were, in some way, involved with Social Services. "Something tells me this guy's been plying his trade a lot longer than the last five years," she said. "I think we should expand the search to say... the last ten to fifteen years."

"Oh, no problem, I'll get onto it right away. It's not like I have anything else to do."

"Are you okay, Mavis?" Jo asked. Mavis sounded more brusque than usual. Maybe she was asking too much of her friend? "This won't get you into trouble, will it?"

"Ha! I'd like to think I was cleverer than that," Mavis said. "I'll email you the second I get anything, but after this, that's it. This madness has to end, Josephine. This is no way to live."

"I agree," Jo said. She could almost hear the surprise on the other end of the phone, was surprised herself. This Stepford town had a lot to answer for. "To tell the truth, Mavis," she said, "it's not living at all. But this is something I have to do, and you know why." She waited a beat. "I promise you. I promise you," she repeated, half-believing it herself, "if this doesn't pan out, I will let it go. Just

help me this one last time. Can you do that for me?"
The silence lingered, seemed to go on forever.

"Always, honey." A deep sigh. "Always."

*****

Mavis put the phone down, feeling the weight of every one of her fifty-eight years. She had lied to Josephine. Shame warred with pride. The girl was quick, though. Her request to search further back mirrored Mavis's actions after reading Josephine's email.

Compiling the data had been a heartbreaking task, more so when she saw the same pattern emerging that Josephine had. Mavis rested her hand on the thick folder at her side. So much anguish contained in these stark, innocuous pages. *And so much more to come*, she thought. If she was right, this would destroy Josephine.

*****

Jo was too fired-up to sleep, any lingering tiredness from her busy night shift disappearing during her conversation with Mavis. When she found herself, for the umpteenth time, checking her inbox for Mavis's email, she knew she had to get out of the flat before she drove herself crazy.

The sound of Mary's baby crying downstairs gave her an idea. What better way to get rid of her nervous energy than to take Emily for a brisk walk? Plus, it would give Mary a couple of hours sleep, which by the look of her, she was in desperate need of.

Mind made up, she changed into jeans and a jumper and slipped down the stairs, rapping on Mary's door.

"I'm so sorry, Jo," Mary said before Jo could speak. "I know you worked late last night and need to sleep, but I've tried everything. Honestly, I have," she said as if she didn't expect Jo to believe her. "Emily just won't stop crying."

"I know." Jo smiled at the child sitting in her baby walker, cheeks rosy, eyes and nose swollen and dripping with mucus. "Are you going somewhere?" she asked Mary, spying the two bulky suitcases leaning against the hall wall.

"Er. No... Yeah... Maybe." Mary looked flustered.

Jo decided not to pry. "Right. Where's Miss Emily's pram?" She lifted the toddler, feeling the sweaty body shudder against hers. "And I'll need a change of clothes."

When Mary didn't move, Jo touched her shoulder. "Mary?"

Mary flinched, then tried to cover the action. "Sorry. What did you say? Pram? Clothes?"

"Yes. Emily and I are going for a walk, aren't we darling?"

The baby cooed.

"Oh, but I can't let you—"

"Yes, you can," Jo said firmly. She sat on the couch with the fractious child, stripped off the sweat-sodden Babygro and put on a fresh nappy. "I'm off today, so it's no bother," she lied. "Now, clothes?"

"Clothes? Yes... er..." Mary looked around, spied a table drowning in laundry.

Jo watched in concern as Mary shuffled towards the table and bent in an awkward manner to pick an outfit. "Are you okay, Mary?" It looked like the girl was in pain.

Mary straightened, quickly hitching down the sleeve of her nightgown, but not before Jo glimpsed the vivid bruises marring the creamy skin.

"I'm fine!" A wave of crimson washed the pale cheeks. "I'm sorry, Jo. I didn't mean to snap." Mary handed Jo the clothes, close to tears. "I'm just so tired," she said, and with that the dam burst. "I don't know which end of me is up anymore," she sobbed.

She looked so forlorn, like a child herself. Jo ached to give her a hug, but she knew from Mary's earlier reaction the overture wouldn't be appreciated. "It's tough being a new mother," she said as she dressed the baby, "the toughest job there is. No sleep, no time to call your own. It's natural to be upset."

What wasn't natural was Mary's cowed behaviour, but now wasn't the time to delve into that. Jo settled the baby in her pram. Mary needed sleep. That was all she could give her, for now.

*****

Mary slid into bed. Exhausted as she was, she knew she wouldn't sleep. Every time she closed her eyes, she saw Thomas's face, twisted with hate and anger, huge fists raised to "pound some sense into her" — for her own good, of course.

After his phone call, she had wasted no time, flight as instinctive as breathing. She'd packed in a frenzy, desperate to get away. When someone had knocked on the door, she had known before she'd answered it that he had come to make good on his threat to punish her.

She touched her ribcage, grimaced. It hurt to breathe. Had he broken something this time? Outside, she heard Jo say something to Emily and the child's answering giggle. She was surprised at a sudden urge to confide in her neighbour. Embarrassment and shame held her back. She'd never have the courage to tell the confident, beautiful Jo how much of a scaredy-cat she was. She didn't have the courage to tell anyone what a failure she had become.

Scared to talk, scared to run, she thought sleepily. She slipped into a healing slumber with the final thought — *but more scared not to.*

CHAPTER SIXTEEN

The safety flooring in the park was effective, Jo decided, as a chubby boy launched himself from his swing and landed without so much as a squeal of complaint, not that she was ready to put it to the test. When Emily woke in time for a quick swoop down the slide, Jo cradled the child in her lap and put the brakes on early. It was a toss-up who'd enjoyed it most.

A nappy change later and they'd made their way to a café Jo had visited the day before. Once there, she gauged Emily's age as over six months and under a year. She ordered mashed potato with carrots and gravy — innocuous at any age — and a coffee for herself.

When Emily's food arrived, she scooped a spoonful, automatically checking it wasn't too hot, before offering the spoon to the child — a well-remembered action and a habit as old as time itself.

Watching Emily in her high chair wasn't as painful as Jo had expected. In fact, as she spooned and re-spooned the mashed goop into the greedy bird-like mouth, she felt a part of her heal; a part she'd thought would be raw forever.

"Jay-sus, Woods! You kept this little tyke quiet."

Startled, Jo looked up and met the boss's quizzical gaze. She watched in amazement as he tickled Emily under the chin.

"I... No, this is... er, my neighbour's child," she said at last.

"Uh-huh." Bill didn't sound convinced. Before he could speak again, a little blonde girl about three years old appeared at his side.

"Granpa. Granpa." She tugged his coat until she got his attention. "Can I have nice cream? Nanny says I hafta wait until after my dinner." The rosebud mouth pouted.

The bushy brows that instilled such fear at the fire station looked positively benevolent as they alighted on the fairy-like child. "Now, Sara, you know Nanny's right but," he scooped the sullen child into his arms, "don't worry. You can have ice cream for dessert." He winked and the child giggled.

"Now, Bill, dontcha be givin' in to that chile."

A stout lady appeared at his side, clutching the hands of identical twin boys, older than the little girl, but not by much. "You'll be spoilin' her," she said, her southern Irish accent more pronounced than her husband's. "Howya." She turned to Jo, her currant-bun eyes disappearing into chubby cheeks as she smiled. "I'm Marian, Bill's wife — for my sorrows," she said on a bellow of laughter. "You must be the newbie?"

She pronounced it noobee, but her good humour was infectious. Jo smiled and held out her hand. "Jo Woods. Nice to meet you, Mrs Simmons."

"Away wit ya. It's Marian. And dis is Simon and Bill Junior." She nodded to the two boys, who smiled shyly. Sara, the obvious leader, wound a finger through her grandfather's hair and said. "Hungrmy."

"Okay, pet." Without so much as a goodbye, Bill turned and threaded his way up the restaurant, the boys traipsing behind.

"Putty! He's pure putty in that chile's hands." Marian shook her head with good-natured humour. "So, how ya finding this wee town of ours?" Her eyes, for all their lack of guile, were astute, probing. "It can be a bit of a culture shock, can't it?" She didn't wait for an answer. "I have to say your presence has shook the station up a bit." She laughed. "'Bout time, if you ask me."

Jo grinned, liking the woman. "I can handle it."

"I'm sure you can. Well, t'was nice to meetcha,

Jo." She turned to leave, then stopped. "Are you going to the barbecue on Saturday?"

Jo nodded. The boss had made it clear that attendance was mandatory for those off shift.

"Here..." Marian reached into her handbag and pulled out a fistful of tickets. "In case you want to bring someone." She winked, before bustling off to join her family.

Jo looked at the tickets. *Who on earth could I give them to?* Apart from the guys at the station, she didn't know many people. She shoved the tickets into her pocket and wiped Emily's sleepy face. "Time to go home, darling." She gathered their things and, deep in thought, made her way back to the apartment.

"You bore her to sleep, too?" hunky downstairs neighbour said, bare-chested, spliff in one hand and sprawled in an old deckchair outside the flats. He nodded to the sleeping child.

"Don't you ever work?" Jo tried not to stare. *Didn't the man feel the cold?*

"I do, when the muse calls. Mind you," he said with a lazy grin, "that's not often."

"Oh, you!" Good mood spoilt, Jo pushed the pram through the front door, into the foyer.

Mary opened the door at the first knock, smiling when she saw the sleeping baby. "I don't know how to thank you, Jo."

"It was my pleasure," Jo said, blinking in surprise. Gone was the nervous woman with pasty skin and shadowed eyes of a few hours before. She reassessed her original estimation. Mary couldn't be more than eighteen years old.

"Don't leave," she said as Mary tried to disappear into her flat, searching for a reason to keep her. Inspiration struck. "We're having a barbecue this Saturday. I've got tickets." She patted her pockets. "It's in the plats." She nodded towards the playing field a short distance from their flats.

"Would you and Emily like to come?" She found the tickets Marian had given her and held out two.

Mary looked torn.

"Go on. It will be a distraction." Jo couldn't believe how much she wanted Mary to say yes. "Emily will love it and so will you."

"A distraction?" Mary repeated, a strange look on her face. "Thanks, Jo." She took the tickets. "Just what I need."

"Me, too," a voice said behind Jo. "Sounds like a fun day. Am I invited?"

Jo tried to ignore the shiver skimming up her spine. She turned to face hunky downstairs neighbour. "Do what you want. You pay your money and you can come, same as everybody else."

She strode off, unwilling to admit, even to herself, that she was no longer dreading Saturday.

CHAPTER SEVENTEEN

Two o'clock found Jo standing outside three Elmtree Drive again. She told herself it wasn't that she wanted to see Angela Parsons — after all, friendships weren't her thing — but she couldn't help a dart of disappointment when she saw the Parsons' driveway empty.

"You a reporter?"

The high-pitched voice came from her right and sounded eager. Jo turned to see a small woman with a wrinkled face and gimlet gaze, peering over the stubby hedge next to her. *This woman could put Mrs R, to shame*, she thought. "Er... N—" She wasn't allowed to finish.

"I'm Mrs Seaton. You can take my picture if you want." The elderly lady posed, lips twisted in a moribund grin. "I knew them, you know. I could tell you stories. Why don't you come with me into the conservatory?"

Before Jo could object, the woman grabbed her arm over the hedge and frogmarched her towards a small gate separating the two properties. With an iron grip that belied her age, she steered Jo up the pristine garden.

"We've just got it done, you know," she said misinterpreting Jo's stunned look, her voice full of pride and plums. "I can tell you all about it, if you want?"

Jo wasn't sure if she meant the conservatory or the wilting trees, cut to uniform length. She had no chance to ask.

"Sit." She was motioned to an overstuffed chair. "Excuse me whilst I get us some iced tea."

Iced tea. Jo felt like she'd fallen into an episode of *Keeping Up Appearances* as Mrs Seaton — or should that be Mrs Bucket? — bustled off.

She re-appeared immediately, as if she'd had the tea waiting and set the tray, complete with little doilies, on the wicker table. Shrunken muscles strained as she lifted the enormous cut-glass jug. "Just what we need for this weather, don't you think, dear?" Once again, she didn't wait for an answer, pouring a generous helping into two tall glasses, which, like the jug, were obviously Waterford crystal.

Jo accepted her glass, holding it with both hands. "Mrs Seaton, I—"

"The stories I could tell," Mrs Seaton said. "Not that I wish to speak ill of the dead." The avid glint in her eyes belied her words. She took a hefty swallow of her drink, then waited for Jo to follow suit.

Jo complied but gasped as something potent hit the back of her throat. She coughed. *Iced tea isn't meant to contain alcohol, is it?* "So, Mrs" — she remembered at the last minute not to say Bucket — "Seaton, what can you tell me about the Forbes?"

*****

Jo rolled home an hour later with the makings of a headache and an overwhelming urge to jump in the shower and scrub herself clean.

Hard as it was to believe, Mrs Seaton put even Flanders and Tumilty to shame. Petty and smallminded, she had shown no remorse at the death of her neighbours, the Forbes, no grief for the young lives so tragically lost.

Jo felt no pang of conscience for letting her believe she was a reporter. After all, she *had* tried to explain. Mrs Seaton hadn't given her a chance. And she wasn't going to lose any sleep over the old vulture thinking a photographer was coming round the next day to take photos of her and her new conservatory.

Her mood wasn't improved when she spied her cheeky male neighbour still sprawled half-naked in his deck chair in front of the flats. Joint clasped in one hand, he was taking full advantage of the unseasonably warm May.

"Disposition not improved, I see." He greeted Jo with a lopsided grin.

Jo frowned — or tried to. The iced tea had caused partial paralysis.

Downstairs neighbour was undeterred. He took a long draw of his spliff, held the smoke in for an age, then said, "You do know life is meant to be enjoyed, don't you?" He waited, seemingly interested in her answer.

Jo ignored him, but he was thicker-skinned and better looking than Flanders.

"Honestly, you look like you've a poker shoved up your bum half the time."

"That's rich, coming from you," Jo retorted. "You seem to be enjoying yourself enough for the rest of us." She eyed the joint, what was left of her eyebrows rising.

"Jealous?" His grin grew.

"Oooh..." Jo was momentarily at a loss for words.

"Oh, go on," he tapped his seat, "join me."

Jo would rather have a Brazilian wax, followed by having her eyebrows plucked, and she told him so.

"Can't vouch for the Brazilian, but those scrawny brows of yours could do with some help." He laughed at her look of outrage and waved his joint amicably. "Lighten up. Frowning gives you lines, dontcha know." When Jo glared at him, he said, "Have it your way." He leaned to his left, grabbed a glistening bottle of Bud from a packed cool bag and prised the lid off. "If good old wacky's not your thing, how 'bout one of these?" He waved the bottle.

Jo eyed it greedily. The iced tea had made her thirsty, but not thirsty enough to sit down with a dopehead. Although it was pretty hot...

"I've been keeping them on ice."

Those were the magic words. Without a word, Jo grabbed the bottle and lifted it to her mouth. Immediately, she got brain freeze. Brain freeze and iced tea. To her fevered mind, it had a perfect symmetry. She giggled, an alien girly sound. *What the hell did Bucket put in my "tea"?*

Yummy downstairs neighbour was still talking. He had a great mouth, Jo decided, hanging onto the front door for support, even as she drowned the thought in another swallow. *And cheekbones.* Bloody Sod's Law at work again. Men didn't need beautiful, tapered, cheekbones, not when they had eyes the colour of caramel and just about as tasty looking.

"What do you say?"

"Say?" Jo shook her head, puzzled. Obviously, he expected an answer, but she was damned if she knew what the question was.

Downstairs neighbour was giving nothing away. He took another long draw on his cigarette, waiting. The silence became embarrassing. She had to say something.

"Er... I agree, yes?" A safe bet. *Men prefer affirmatives over negatives. Didn't they?*

He looked surprised, but recovered swiftly. "Good-oh." He rose to his full height — *pretty impressive* — stubbed out his joint and lifted the ashtray. He handed Jo the cool bag full of clinking bottles and folded his seat, tucking it under his arm. "First on the right," he said when Jo didn't move. "Here." He jostled open the main door, waved her forwards. "This way."

Oh bugger! She'd agreed to go into his flat. At least she hoped that was all she had agreed to. "After you," she said, trying to appear composed.

His flat wasn't at all what she expected. Similar to hers, a narrow hallway led to the kitchen on the right, toilet on the left, and three doors at the far end — living room and two bedrooms. One of the bedroom doors was ajar and Jo caught a glimpse of a computer atop a sturdy wooden desk. It was a beast of a machine with reams of paper stacked meticulously on either side. In his work, dopehead was a neat freak. Intrigued, she edged closer.

"This way."

The door slammed closed, the one next to it opened. Jo, about to apologise for being nosy, caught her breath. "Oh, wow!"

"You like?"

Do I ever. To her immediate left sat a leather couch, cream and lush enough to swallow her whole. It was a perfect foil for the lemon walls and leafy plants, artistically displayed in enormous earthenware vases. She wasn't going near those, not with her killing touch. A huge ornate marble fire surround enclosed a state-of-the-art gas fire insert, which, Jo knew, would give out realistic flames and, unlike Mrs R's, wouldn't asphyxiate the occupant in his sleep. "It's okay, I suppose."

Eyes bright with laugher he flicked a switch to engage discreet lighting.

Jo, iced tea wearing off, decided that now was a good idea to exchange names. "Jo Woods." She held out her hand.

Hunky neighbour took it in a firm grasp, palm below, palm above. Her skin tingled.

"Ian Cooper. Friends call me Coop."

Jo ignored the offer, disengaging her hand. "Nice to meet you, Ian." Uncomfortable under his scrutiny and all too aware of his semi-naked body, she lifted the bottle of Bud to her lips, draining it.

"You want another?"

She shouldn't. She was on duty later. "Thanks." Jo held out the empty bottle. That damned iced tea had a lot to answer for.

Coop took the bottle and retrieved his bag from her shoulder. "There you go." He handed her a fresh one, along with a bottle opener. "I'm just gonna put the rest of these in the fridge."

Jo twisted the cap off her Bud and watched him go. He really did have a nice ass. She blushed, turned to assess the room. If she got rid of a few boxes, threw on a bit of paint, and spent a fortune on accessories, would her flat look this good? She took a swift drink. *Not in my wildest dreams.*

"You get it open okay?" Coop filled the doorway, one lean hip cocked against the doorframe. In the soft light, his fair hair appeared golden. His hazel eyes, in contrast, looked dark and full of danger.

"Huh?" For a moment, Jo was confused, then she glanced at the bottle. It no longer appealed. "Yeah. Thanks. But I've... gotta go."

"Go?"

Was it her imagination or did he sound disappointed? "Yeah, I have to go to work."

She edged past him. "Thanks for the drink." She handed him the bottle and escaped out the door, running up the stairs. She glanced at her watch. Three thirty. She started work at six. At this point, she needed coffee — lots and lots of coffee and maybe an hour's sleep. But before she did any of that, she needed a shower, and not because of the repulsive Mrs Bucket. This was going to be a cold, mind-numbing, lust-abating shower.

*****

In the flat below, Ian Cooper listened to Jo's footsteps above his head. With a heavy heart, he walked to the kitchen and poured her drink down the drain.

It wasn't meant to be like this.

He hadn't expected to like her, to feel protective of her in her obviously drunken state. Neither had he expected the sadness he'd detected in those glorious blue eyes — a sadness he'd thought belonged solely to him. He cursed and dropped the empty bottle in the bin. He wasn't cut out for this shit.

Coop left the kitchen, made his way down the hallway and opened the bedroom door Jo had been so interested in earlier. He settled himself in front of the computer and began to type. Coop couldn't let himself be distracted. He had one purpose in life now and no one — *no one* — was going to stop him.

*****

I was incandescent with rage, but interspersed with the rage was the tiniest whiff of panic. She had been spying on me.

Jo had. The bitch! How dare she!

I was oblivious to the double standard, aware only that she made me feel things I didn't want to feel. Foremost was the sensation I was losing control — of the situation, of myself.

My fault. I had become complacent, wishful. For so long I had toiled alone, with none to guide or hinder me. My mission — my freeing of the little birds — was a solitary quest, lonely at times, but the rewards more than made up for that.

And yet, this connection I felt to Jo had me questioning everything.

"You cannot let her derail your mission. It's too important."

I agreed with the voice. My mission was everything. Evil could not be allowed to flourish. The innocent *had* to be saved. No one, not even Jo, would be permitted to interfere.

"Especially not Jo," the voice said.

The voice knew me too well. Jo was a danger to me, for reasons I had yet to fathom. She needed careful watching.

"You said that last time. You also promised you'd deal with her if she became a problem."

"And I meant it. I'm just not sure she's that much of a problem — yet."

"So, for now you'll do what? Keep an eye on her? Close surveillance? You'll enjoy that."

"That's not why I'm doing it." I kept my voice low so the figure ahead wouldn't hear. "It's not about enjoyment."

"But if a little comes your way?"

I ignored the voice. I had no time for its petty innuendo. Serious work lay ahead. Jo had to be contained. I shook at how close she had come to undoing all my good work.

Careful planning had been my saviour. As accustomed, I had done my usual follow through, checking with the neighbours that no sign of suspicion had fallen on my act, the same thing I had done on numerous occasions. Only this time a chance remark from that busybody Sheila Seaton, of all people, had alerted me to the fact that Jo was checking up on me.

Me!

My fingers curled into fists. Was this the proof Jo had spoken of? If so, I had little to fear. Foolish, foolish Jo. Sheila Seaton knew nothing, except how to gossip. Still, I couldn't let this situation continue. It was time to take back the advantage, make my presence felt. I still hadn't found out Jo's secret, but I figured a little scaremongering would suffice. I grinned, good humour restored. That would take her down a notch or two.

Oh yes, fear, if it was to be enjoyed, should be a two-way game. After all, what fun was it to play alone?

"Let the games begin." I laughed out loud. The thrill of finally having someone to share my quest with making me forget about the watcher.

Leaves stirred above my head as if rocked by my humour. Spooked, the crouched figure ahead jumped, head jerking at the sound.

"Amateur!" I studied the watcher, no longer amused by his ineffectual attempts to blend in. Not my concern, I decided.

Not yet.

There was no reason to stay, yet I lingered, unable to tear myself away.

We shared something, Jo Woods and I. What, I didn't know yet, but it was enough to make me wait until she left the flat and follow her to her place of work.

I didn't stop there.

I spent the night next to her, shoulder-to-shoulder, hip-to-hip. I basked in the rare pleasure of her smile, laughed at her dry, biting wit. And when darkness fell, I crawled into a bed next to her, close enough to hear the gentle rasp of her breathing, to see the steady rise and fall of her breasts beneath the thin blanket. And in the darkness, I smiled.

I could touch her now. Touch her so she would never know she'd been touched, caress that long, sinuous body, the braided hair, the way I'd done a thousand times in my dreams.

If I wanted, I could close my hand around her throat, stop the threat in its tracks once and for all.

Common sense prevailed and I did none of these things. I tucked my hand under my pillow and watched her sleep until my own eyelids grew heavy.

Soon.

It was like a lullaby.

Soon.

CHAPTER EIGHTEEN

Jo fell into her own bed at nine thirty the next morning. Stripped to her underwear and long-sleeved T-shirt, she slid between the cool sheets with a sigh. Unlike Tuesday night with its endless hoax turnouts, last night's shift had been quiet — workwise. Her interaction with her teammates hadn't gone quite as well.

"You haven't been answering my calls?" Dave had greeted her, face grim. "Why didn't you tell me, Jo? I thought we were friends?"

"I—" If she'd thought bringing everything out in the open would make things easier, she had been mistaken.

"You trust me enough to save your skinny behind, but not enough to tell me there's a homicidal maniac on the loose? Goddamn it, Jo!" He'd punched the door of his locker.

"It's not that I don't trust you, Dave, It's just—"

"Just what?" He'd glared at her. "If you *trust* me so much, then why keep it a secret?"

"I needed to be sure, Dave. I almost lost my job over this once before. I couldn't afford to do it again, not without a damn good reason. I needed evidence." Then she'd gotten angry. "You think you're the first person to tell me I'd inhaled too much smoke or the bump on my head might have addled my brain?"

"You still could have told me." The anger had gone from his voice, but not the hurt.

"I know, but what could I have said? That I thought a serial killer was at work and Emma Forbes was just the last in a long line of victims? Come on, Dave. You said it yourself. I'd been knocked out. What would your reply have been?"

"That you were out of your tiny, cotton-picking mind."

"See?"

"I suppose." He'd rubbed the rough stubble on his chin and dropped to the wooden bench. "But you could have warned me."

"I know. I should have." Jo had sat beside him. "I'm sorry, but I had a hard time believing it myself. Saying it out loud? Well..." She'd played with the brittle end of her braid, "It makes it real — too real, if you know what I mean?"

"I guess. But, Jo, are you certain? Do you really believe there's someone here in Mourne Lough killing kids?"

Jo had nodded and wished she could tell him why she was so sure, but until Mavis got back to her, she hadn't dared. It wasn't fair to voice her suspicions until she had something concrete.

As if he'd read her mind, Dave had said, "And you've evidence to support this theory of yours?"

Jo wouldn't lie to him. "Not yet, but I will," she said before he could speak.

"Goddamn!" Dave had slapped the bench. "I can't believe it."

"Believe it," Jo had replied. "But we're going to get him." It had been a promise.

"Darn tootin'." He'd eyed her. "You're still holding out on me, though, aren't you?" Jo had avoided his gaze.

"I knew it." He'd rose, had begun to pace. "What aren't you telling me?"

Jo had managed to dodge his question with the arrival of the others, but the respite, she knew, wouldn't last. The other guys, apart from Geoff and Flanders, had been easier to placate, a re-run of what she'd already told them had been sufficient to shut them up. Geoff had been harder to hoodwink. He'd been concerned, something Jo wasn't used to, and as a result, she'd found it harder to field his queries. As for Flanders, he liked to stir the shit, so she'd let him get on with it.

Dave had been great, running interference. It had been nice, Jo admitted, to have people on her side for once.

The main part of their night had been spent playing poker, followed by a few hours at the pool table, which had seen Micko attempt to perform a handstand atop the green baize. The hospital had reported he'd be fit and ready for work on Monday, no matter what he'd said to the contrary. They'd hit their beds by ten.

Jo, like most firefighters worth their salt, had perfected the art of immediate slumber, hundreds of turn-outs leaving her with the ability to sleep at the drop of a hat. For some reason, though, that skill had escaped her last night. Every time she'd come close to dropping off, she'd started awake, heart pounding, mouth dry, like she had been in the midst of a bad nightmare.

She put the strange aberration down to three things: having imparted her secret — or as much as she was willing to share — she was now open to the consequences. Sleeping in a room with five guys, none of whom were related to her — and one of whom was Flanders — was enough to put any sane woman on her guard. And the frightening, inescapable fact that she could, in effect, be turning her back on a killer.

Now, safe in her flat, Jo snuggled beneath her covers and was soon fast sleep. What felt like moments later, the phone woke her out of a confused, erotic dream, in which Ian Cooper played a starring role. She was going to kill whoever was on the other end, she decided furiously, punching the answer button.

"They didn't believe you, did they?"

Jo bolted upright, dream forgotten. "Wh... Who is this?"

"They think you're some kind of nut, don't they? And you think *I'm* some kind of nut. There's a kinda poetic justice in that, don't you think?"

There was a bark of laughter that made Jo's skin crawl. "Who *is* this?" she asked again, but she had no need of an answer. She knew.

"I guess you could say you're looking for me."

Jo pulled herself up in the bed, wide-awake. She strained to hear if she recognised the voice and cursed her sleep-addled brain. *What am I missing?* What little nuances in his voice had she been oblivious to while still half asleep?

"I don't know what you mean," she said, playing for time.

The harsh laugh repeated, letting Jo know the caller was aware of her stalling tactics. "Why are you doing this?" she asked, not expecting an answer.

She got one, of sorts.

"That's for you to find out. Find the 'why', and you get the 'who'. Find the 'what', and you get the 'where'. But you're late to the game, Jo. Can you find me before I disappear again?" The voice changed, turned reflective. "You are the only one who sees what I'm doing. Who understands."

The voice, pitched low and devoid of emotion made identification impossible, but she would swear it was a man's voice. His last comment registered. *Understands?* Jo's stomach churned, the urge to vomit overwhelming. She wanted nothing more than to hang up, but she had to keep him talking. He might let something slip, some weakness she could exploit. "What is it you're doing?"

"Freeing the little birds," the voice said, as if it should be obvious.

"Birds!" Jo was trembling, but whether from horror or disgust she couldn't tell. "You're killing children, you psycho!" The second the words were out, she knew she had made a mistake.

There was a hiss at the other end of the phone. "I thought you understood."

Jo struggled to remain calm. "I do. I do understand." She looked for her tape recorder, saw the boxes and bewailed the fact she hadn't unpacked when she'd had the chance. She had to keep him on the line. "Tell me more." She fell to her knees, hunting through the first box she found. This was her chance, all the corroboration she needed. If she could get his voice on tape, Mavis, the boss... All of them would have to believe her. Frantic, she tossed spent lotion bottles and odds and ends of make-up on the floor. *Wrong box! Where the hell is the tape recorder?*

"You don't understand," the voice said, rising. "I thought you did, but you don't."

Jo knew this was her last chance. She was losing him yet she couldn't stop the words forming. "What's to understand? You killed Emma Forbes, murdered her parents. She was five years old! How could you do that? What did they do to you?"

The speaker sighed. "You're not the one. I thought you understood, but you don't. You led me on." Anger edged the voice, as if it were Jo's fault.

"Fuck you." Jo crumpled to the floor, knowing it was useless. "Fuck you, you psycho, I'm going to get you. You hear me?" she screamed down the phone. "I'm going to get you, and you're going to pay for what you've done."

The only sound was the hollow echo of his laughter then the dull tone of a broken line.

CHAPTER NINETEEN

The alarm shrilled at eleven, but Jo had no need of it. She sat on the edge of her bed, tape recorder clasped in both hands. She didn't know who she was angrier at — the killer for daring to call her or herself for not being quick enough to get his voice on tape. She stood, the sight of her freshly pressed uniform depressing her further.

The Forbes funeral was today.

She began to dress. She might be edging closer to the killer's identity, might have him worried enough to call her on the phone, but that didn't change a damn thing. Emma Forbes and her parents were still dead. The others she only knew as names on a computer file were still dead. And if she didn't stop this monster, more would follow.

Jo cinched her belt tight, the leather biting deeply into the raw flesh at her waist. Like a penitent donning a hair shirt, she welcomed the pain. It kept her focused. She clipped her tie to her shirt and picked up the navy-blue jacket, buttoning the shiny brass buttons. Lastly, she donned her cap and looked in the mirror.

Before her stood a firefighter — tall, shoulders erect, jaw tilted at just the right angle, perfect, except for the tears slipping down her cheeks.

Mrs R was nowhere in evidence as Jo left the flat. She heaved a sigh of relief and descended the stairs. At the bottom, she paused, squared her shoulders, and checked that her hat was on straight, before stepping outside.

"For you." Coop slouched against the wall, close to where he'd sat the afternoon before, a rose in one hand.

What the hell? Her recollection of yesterday was hazy but surely she hadn't—?

"I thought you might want it," he said, holding the rose out, "for the coffin."

Air hit Jo's lungs. "Thanks. But how—"

"It's a small town, Jo. News like that..." He lifted his shoulders. "Let's just say that bad news travels fast."

The deep cadence of his voice reminded Jo of her dream and she blushed. "Wh-what a lovely thought, Ian. Thank you."

"No need to sound so surprised, and you can call me Coop, you know. I won't bite."

It wasn't that Jo thought he would, just that she might enjoy it if he did. She hid her feelings behind a wan smile. "Thank you... Coop."

"See? That was painless, wasn't it? Better than a Brazilian wax any day."

Jo agreed but was damned if she'd say so. "I've got one scheduled for later. I'll let you know."

His laughter followed her down the road and warmed Jo in the cold hours ahead.

CHAPTER TWENTY

"I'm glad that's over." Micko took off his hat and ran his fingers through his hair. Immediately his cowlick pinged to attention.

It was another balmy day, and the others followed suit, hair sticky with sweat, all except Geoff who had no hair to speak of. His pinking dome glistened with moisture and he dabbed at it with his hanky. Jo tucked her hat under her arm and watched solemnly as the cortege moved out of sight, the tiny white casket sheltered protectively between the two large oak coffins, Coop's rose a tiny red beacon atop it.

Her gaze flicked to Dave. He looked shell-shocked. His daughter, Jenny, had been best friends with Emma Forbes. He'd known the family well. She took his hand, squeezed it.

Dave, his eyes focused on Fran and Jenny standing with the other mourners, gave an answering squeeze before leaving to comfort his family. Geoff took his place. A widower, he was no stranger to death — first with his wife, then, Jo had heard, with his eldest son, Gavin. Looking at his face, she knew grief never went away and kids never grew up. They just — if you were lucky — got older.

Micko had twin girls, six months old. As he told what was obviously a ribald joke, his eyes held the shattered look of a parent who realises death — no matter how ardently sheltered from — hovers like a spectre in the wings.

There was a quick flurry of laughter, but Jo took no offense. Laughter was their safety valve, opened in times of immense pressure. Everyone here today had their coping mechanism. A few thumbed their nose at fate, believed themselves invincible.

Others waited, frightened by every cough or sneeze for the inevitable to happen. The lucky ones went home, hugged their loved ones and told them — while they had the chance — how much they loved them.

People who dealt with death — firefighters, police, ambulance service — knew those chances were all too fleeting. There was always something — a fire, a car, a gun, and here in Ireland, a bomb, to take it all away from you. They used their macabre kind of humour to mask their fear so they could continue to do their job — the job they loved and hated in equal measure.

*****

They congregated in Murdock's and this time Jo had no objection to going. Oblivion had sounded pretty good to her. She was also hoping she might recognise her late-night caller's voice, especially if he drank enough to drop his guard.

"Hey, Wart, you been eating lasagne again?" Micko said. "What do you think, guys? He getting flabby?"

The others, in varying degrees of intoxication, babbled their agreement.

"Oh yeah. Nic won't love you anymore," Tumilty joked, referring to Wart's long-time girlfriend.

"I still say big muscles, little weenie." This, of course, came from Flanders, belly holding his trousers up, his arm propped against the bar, holding *him* up.

"Oh, give him a break," Pat Meehan said. "That's not what will make Nic run. It's the lack of a ring. Ten years!" He rolled his eyes. "Come on."

The others were surprised into peals of laughter at his daring. "Hey, Wart," Micko shouted over the roar of the others, "looks like your lap dog has grown teeth."

Wart glared at Pat as if the family pet had turned on him. He sucked in his stomach, flexed his impressive upper body muscles and declared, "Marriage is a waste of money. Long-term never works out."

"How much longer do you need?"

"More than he's got," Don said with a smirk.

"Life's too short," Wart said, becoming maudlin. "Say I buy her a ring, spend all that cash. We could be divorced next week. She could be killed tomorrow."

"Is that a plan?" Micko snorted into his beer. "If so, make sure the life insurance is up to date."

"Is yours?" Wart asked, looking at the bandage on Micko's arm, courtesy of his stunt on the pool table the night before. "'Cause you'd better have Accidental Damage included."

They settled down, huddled round their table, flicking peanuts at a group of men in suits, who, not sharing their grief, refused to leave.

"Dickheads," Pat said. It took two attempts to get the word out. His face reddened when the others sniggered. "I'm jus' shaying." More laughter.

"Music. We need music." Tumilty jumped to his feet and went to the jukebox.

"Hey, Jo," Pat said over the crescendo of drums filling the air, well past drunk and on his way to garrulous, shyness forgotten. "Wot did you do before you joined the brigade? I wanna know," he said when the others jeered. "You don't mind, do you?" he asked.

Jo was just delighted they were speaking to her. "'Course I don't mind, Pat." She straightened her neck, looked downwards as if peering over a pair of spectacles. "I used to be a teacher. Pre-school. Pretty scary, huh?"

Dave, not long arrived, slapped his knee, green eyes twinkling. "I can see it. By God, I can see it."

The others cheered and laughed, trying to outdo one another.

"Please, Miss, I need to go to the loo." Micko raised his hand, swiftly followed by Pat.

"I need to go too, Miss. Pleeeze."

"What about you, Dave?" Jo asked in an effort to shift the attention off her and realising this was the perfect opportunity to find out more about the guys in her watch. While she didn't think Dave was involved, she couldn't forget he was the only person who could have told the others about the roses — never mind his meeting with the boss, which he'd rushed to share with everybody but her.

If Dave felt uncomfortable, he wasn't showing it. "I was a paperboy when I was twelve. Does that count?" He raised his glass. "Joined the brigade straight out of college," he said with pride.

"A real veteran." Micko lifted his pint with exaggerated care and clinked glasses with Dave. "Good job we won't have to put up with you much longer. Give the rest of us buggers a chance."

"Huh?" Jo looked puzzled.

"Didn't he tell you?" Geoff said, "Dave's on the fast track. Won't be long before he's crew commander in his own station." He raised his glass to Dave in salute.

Dave looked embarrassed. "Hey, Mick, tell us what you did before you joined up?"

"You'll never believe me."

"Try us," Geoff said.

Micko snorted, inhaled beer through his nose, and sneezed. "I was a gravedigger." He ran a sleeve over his face. "My uncle got me the job," he said as the group descended into paroxysms of laughter, "the summer after my A Levels. It was just for a few months. I only did it once or twice." He back-pedalled as the laughter grew. "Give me a break, guys. I needed the money. It wasn't as if I enjoyed it. What about you, Geoff?" He turned to the older guy in desperation.

Geoff, who looked mellower than Jo had ever seen before, gestured to Thomas, the barman, for another round before he answered. Over the cheer that elicited, he said, "Bit boring, I'm afraid. I was a lecturer at Queens University. English Lit, don't you know."

"Lit what?" Wart asked, joining Flanders, flicking peanuts at the suits. "I'm a fire starter... you're a fire starter." He hummed the popular tune, breaking off to punch the air when the suits left, throwing affronted looks in their direction. "Yeeha!" He high-fived Flanders. "Wot about you, mate? What did you do? Done? Did." He slapped his head and groaned.

Flanders grew bashful. A sight the others, even in their inebriation, noted and zeroed in on.

"Go on, Flanders. Tell us."

Jo watched her team-mates closely, ears attuned to the sound of their voices. She tried to stay detached, focused on finding out as much as she could, but in the face of Don's embarrassment and the others' good humour, she couldn't help smiling, as eager as the rest to know why Flanders was so reticent.

"You'd better tell them, lad," Geoff said. "They'll only find out if you don't."

Flanders acknowledged the truth of his words with a nod. "Okay. Okay. I was a Cub Scout leader. Not a word," he warned Micko. "The wife had a good job at the time. I was waiting to get into the brigade, and it looked good on my résumé, "he said, daring them to argue.

"So that's why you've no kids. Had your fill of them." Micko guffawed.

Jo caught a glimpse of pain in Flanders eyes, a deep-seated grief the others seemed oblivious to. "What about you, Wart?" she said, shifting the focus from Flanders, feeling sorry for the guy.

Wart squirmed, flexed his muscles. "Who started this conversation, anyway? Micko, a joke please."

"Not a chance, mate." Flanders motioned Thomas for another drink. "If I had to tell, you have to tell." He left the bar and placed his beefy fists on the table in front of Wart. "Come on. Fess up." All eyes settled on Wart.

"It's no big deal." Wart flexed his muscles again then took a deep breath. "I was... a gentleman's tailor. It's an important position," he said irritated as the table dissolved into hysterics. "Takes skill."

"Well, at least you've the hands for it." Micko sniggered.

It was true. For a muscular man, Wart possessed very small hands, more like a child's than an adult's.

"What is it they say?" Pat said, voice coy. "Little hands, little dick."

"Nic's got no complaints."

"Yeah, 'cept it's been ten years and you haven't married her yet. Maybe she's not waiting on your proposal. Maybe you have asked and she turned you down — for obvious reasons."

Wart made a rude gesture with his middle finger. "And what was it you did, Pat?"

Pat held up his hands. In comparison to Wart's, they were huge, blunt fingers tipped with ragged nails edged in dirt. "Guess?"

"A gypsy or a mechanic," Micko said.

"Got it in two."

"A mechanic?" Micko sounded amazed. "That's a good job. Why did you leave?"

"A difference of opinion with the boss and his wife."

"They didn't like you?" Micko, in his inebriation, couldn't understand why the others snorted.

"She did. He didn't."

"Oh."

"You're quiet, Jim." Jo eyed Tumilty and tried not to let her suspicion show. "You going to tell us what did before you joined up? Go on," she said when it looked like he wouldn't answer. "It can't be any worse than those two."

"I've done a bit of everything."

That Jo could believe. She listened intently to his voice.

"I've travelled the world, done missionary work in Africa..."

That she didn't believe for an instant.

"Sailed the Nile, worked my way through Australia, New Zealand, and America."

"Doing what?" someone asked.

"This and that. Experiencing life. But I have to tell you," his bony elbow landed unsteadily on the table, "that in all my travels, in all the jobs I've done — and let me tell you, some of them have been the dregs. This," Tumilty flapped his hand, "this has been the best experience of my life."

Jo was flummoxed. He sounded serious and, she hated to admit, nothing like her late-night caller.

*****

She'd learned nothing. Jo made her way home, stumbling up the steep steps to her flat. Not a damn thing. No familiar voice, no furtive glances. Nothing had raised her antennae. The guys were what they appeared — nice people. Even Flanders had been less obnoxious than usual, which raised another problem. Until she found the killer, she couldn't afford to like them, to let down her guard.

There was always White, Blue, and Green Watch, she supposed. It could be one of them.

Please, please, let it be one of them.

*****

The night had grown cold. Thick evening mist shrouded the landscape and clawed chill fingers through the air. I was oblivious to the ambient temperature. I had the memories of the day to warm me.

She had looked so shattered!

Tenderly I traced the memory of her face, the fingers of my mind hovering over Jo's grief-etched features as the coffins appeared, the tears in those glorious blue eyes that she tried so hard to hide.

So much pain. Poor, poor, Jo.

And yet, while her grief was strong, it wasn't as potent as her thirst for revenge. Like this was personal for her. The thought made me frown. That's exactly how it seemed — personal.

Instead of frightening me, the idea made me shiver with anticipation. I was no longer alone. I wanted to stand and shout aloud to the world, tell everyone the beauty of what I'd done. But I knew the time wasn't right. Last night had proven that. I had forgiven her. She needed time to understand. And she would, I was confident. No, the time wasn't right yet.

Not yet.

But soon.

My mind returned to our phone call. It had started so well. Jo's sleep-laden voice was husky enough to send a thrill coursing through my body. For once, the acid in my stomach had stilled, calmed by the mere sound of her voice.

"Is it the acid in your stomach you're talking about or the storm in your loins?"

"Don't. You don't understand." I didn't want the voice to bring me down. I wanted to savour this victory. I *needed* to savour this victory. "She enjoyed my banter. I know she did, even though I know she'd deny it if asked. My stubborn, stubborn, Jo."

"Easy supposition, seeing as you're never going to ask her."

I continued with the memory, acting as if the voice hadn't spoken. My opening had been hilarious. "They think you're some kind of nut, and you think I'm some kind of nut." I smiled now, remembering. We were two of a kind and she knew it. My little riddle had been quite clever, too, although Jo didn't seem to agree. "Find the why, and you get the who. Find the what, and you get the where." If only she knew how true that was.

I confess I'd lost my temper, something I rarely did, but I was man enough to admit when I was wrong. She needed time to appreciate my plan, to appreciate me. She'd lost her temper, too — a most unladylike display.

As a gentleman, I would take the blame for that, too. Taunting her that she was late to the game and how she wouldn't find me before I disappeared again was a tad harsh. But she needed to be told. She was making a habit of being late. Impatience raced through me. *Where the hell is she?*

Just as I thought I must have missed her, she appeared at the top of the steps, stumbling drunkenly, not realising she was on the level ground. I smothered a laugh. The pages of my mind stirred once more. I flicked through them, needing to know why she felt so familiar, why this was so personal for her.

As if aware of my gaze, she lurched to a stop and looked in my direction. I held my breath in dismay. For the first time, I felt the chill fingers of night air on my skin. Had I given myself away?

"Close surveillance. Not so nice when you're on the other side of it, huh?"

I shushed the voice. This was serious. If Jo saw me here, it was all over. I waited, my belly full of acid, for her yell of discovery. When nothing was forthcoming, I peered closer and discovered she wasn't looking at me at all. She was staring at the idiot hiding in his usual spot in the trees ahead.

The guy was starting to annoy me. I didn't give a shit what his problem was, but whatever was going on with him and the girl in the downstairs flat, he'd better sort it soon — or I was gonna sort it for him.

I swept my gaze back to Jo's swaying figure, and I greedily assessed her body. The open jacket gave me a tantalising glimpse — the gentle swell of her breasts, a hint of a slender waist encased by a thick belt. Then, as if in answer to my unspoken plea, the wind picked up, moulding the black slacks against her slim legs. For one brief moment, her body was outlined, open to my gaze. My groin tightened and my body strained forwards as if I could bridge the distance between us with my lust.

"Close surveil—"

"Shut it." I had no time for the voice. My mind, my body, focused on Jo and the picture she made against the dark backdrop of the night.

The moment, like all good moments, didn't last. She shivered, gathered her jacket around her, hugging her chest for warmth. She'd stood like this at the funeral. The thought consoled me. Her eyes, like mine, searched past the twin oak caskets to the tiny white coffin in the middle. But while she flinched as it came into view I had felt only satisfaction.

Emma Forbes was safe, at peace, in a place where no one could ever hurt her again.

I had freed her.

I had!

The sense of accomplishment made me feel invincible, restored my good humour.

"Sleep well, Emma, my little bird," I whispered to the frozen sky. "Don't worry. You won't be lonely for long. I'll have more playmates for you soon. But," my eyes followed the staggering figure, "I must deal with this little birdie first, if she's not to spoil our plans."

CHAPTER TWENTY-ONE

When Jo stumbled and almost fell for the third time in a row, she figured there was a distinct possibility she might be a tad tipsy. Not drunk like the guys, but not exactly sober, either.

However, when she spent the next fifteen minutes trying to open the outer door of the flat with her car keys, she had to accept that she may have drank more than she'd realised. "And then some." A giggle escaped and she quickly smothered the sound with her hand. Wouldn't do to wake the neighbo—

"Need a hand?"

Jo cursed under her breath as the door swung open to reveal Coop. *Of all the...* "No fank..." She caught herself then formed the words with deliberate care. "No thank you." She brushed past him into the foyer with as much dignity as she could muster. "I'm fine."

"I can see that." Coop followed her unsteady progress through the hallway.

Jo stuck her tongue out at him. Childish, she knew, but he brought out the worst in her. And what did he know? She reached the stairs, began to climb. She was fine. She could handle her dri... At that precise moment, her feet chose to go east while the rest of her attempted to go north.

"Whoa there. Let me give you a hand."

Before Jo could object, he encircled her waist, the feeling of his warm arm much too reminiscent of her dream the night before for her liking. "I don't need your help."

Coop made a show of looking behind her. "I see you've still got that poker up your ass."

Jo glared at him. "Better than being spaced out all the time." She was proud of that one. In fact, after the session she'd just put in, she was proud she could speak at all. She knocked his hand away.

"Not so fast. You can't insult a man and expect to get away with it."

"Can and vill." Jo licked her lips. "Will."

Coop stepped up a stair. Jo could smell the clean, tangy scent of soap on his skin. Nervous, she licked her lips again.

"That's incredibly sexy, you know."

"What is?"

"That." His hand came up to trace her mouth.

"Oh!" Jo stepped back, shocked by the dart of electricity caused by his touch. Then, as if their bodies were magnetised, she found herself propelled forwards, pressed against his chest, staring up into eyes darkened to ochre with passion. *Oh boy!* Was all she managed before he lowered his lips.

His kiss was soft and tender, almost dream lover-like. The thought no longer scared her.

Coop was the first to pull away. "You're drunk."

"Yup." Jo wished he'd stop swaying. "And proud of it."

His laugh sounded surprised and extremely sexy. It brought her to her senses. *What the hell am I doing? This isn't like going into a burning room in search of a child. This is much, much more dangerous.* "Er... I have to... go."

"Okay." But Coop made no attempt to release her. He smiled as she tried to walk backwards up the stairs — no mean feat, given her condition.

"Don't laugh at me!" Jo wrenched herself free, tripped up another step.

"Far be it for me to laugh at a lady," Coop said, but he kept coming.

"Where are you going?" Jo put a hand out to stop him.

"Making sure you get home okay." Coop matched her step for step, although it had to be said his were a lot steadier.

"I'm home now," Jo said with relief when they reached the upper hallway and her front door. "You can go."

"Not before I do this — in case I never get another chance." Coop pulled her to him.

He burnt a brand into Jo's back with his hand, kindling a fire in her belly with his lips. She melted, dissolving against him.

"Goodnight."

He was gone, a cheeky grin her last image.

Jo couldn't move. She listened to his footsteps skipping down the stairs. His front door opened then closed with an embarrassing finality. Stunned, she remained where she was. *What just happened? Did Coop kiss me or am I dreaming again?* She touched her mouth, remembered the feel of his lips on hers. Her heart skipped a beat. Oh boy, she was in trouble if she could no longer tell dream from reality.

"No more drink for you, my girl," she said as she opened the door to her flat — with the right key this time.

*****

Dream. Reality. Kiss. Dream. Reality. Kiss. Dreamrealitykiss. The words were a neon kaleidoscope — fitting together, then drifting apart. Jo's mind spun with dizzying images of laughing hazel eyes and a firm body pressed tightly against hers. Over and over again, as if caught in some cosmic loop, she experienced the feel of Coop's lips on hers, and in her sleep, she moaned. Yet even in the depths of slumber common sense prevailed. She had to wake up, stop this madness before it went any further.

Her mobile shrilled and the kaleidoscope shattered. "Hello," Jo croaked, trying to shake off the last remnants of the dream.

"Bill's grandchildren are cute, don't you think?"

The words, so out of context, didn't make sense at first.

"Did you know their mother ran out on them, just upped and buggered off? Nice, huh?" The voice dripped false concern. "Pity she won't be here to see them 'freed', but I don't think I can wait that long, do you?"

Jo bolted upright, dream forgotten. She groped for the recorder sitting next to her, held it to the earpiece and clicked it on in one smooth movement. "Bill?" she asked, but her mind had made the connection — Bill Simmons, her boss. Nausea coiled in Jo's stomach as she recalled the twin boys and adorable little girl she'd met the day before. "Bill who?" she said, playing for time.

The line hummed with silence, mocking her pathetic attempts at subterfuge.

"What do you mean you can't wait?" Jo said, desperate to provoke a response, any response. "What are you going to do?"

A puff of air, which may have been a laugh, was followed by more silence.

Jo's frustration grew. "Damn it. Talk to me."

"Sad day today, wasn't it?"

The change of subject confused her. "What?"

"The funeral." Amusement laced the voice. "They say only the good die young, spared the sorrows of this world. That's how it should be, don't you think?"

Jo couldn't answer. She was calculating how much time she had, how much time the boss and his grandkids had. Were they already drugged? Her eyes searched for the green glow of the alarm clock: 3:15 am. Safe to assume the boss and his family were unconscious by now, a meticulously set fire spewing toxic fumes.

She hesitated, torn — stay on the line to get the corroboration she needed or try to stop another fatality before it happened.

In the end, there was no choice.

Jo broke the connection and dialled 9-9-9. She got as far as the second digit before she realised she didn't know the boss's address.

"Shit!" She snapped the phone closed, and for an endless second sat motionless, aware people could be dying while she procrastinated. The answer when it came was so simple she wondered why she hadn't thought of it first. She opened her phone, found the number.

"Dave?"

"Yeah?" His voice sounded slurred, heavy with sleep.

"Where does the boss live?"

"Huh? Who is this?"

"I need his address, Dave. *Now!*"

"Is that you, Jo?" Dave sounded more alert. "What's going on? What do you need Bill's address for?"

There was no time to explain, but Jo knew Dave wouldn't give her the address without a damn good reason. "I received a phone call tonight — from the killer. He told me the boss's grandkids are next. They are living with him, aren't they?' she asked, wanting to make sure.

"How'd you—"

Jo cut him off. "So they are."

"Brendan moved back about a week ago. He said Eleanor was on holidays, but I had my doubts." Dave sounded wide-awake now. "Jesus Christ!"

"The address, Dave."

"It's 212 Briar Hill. But you don't think—?"

"Phone it in, Dave. This guy is capable of anything. I'm on my way."

"Wait."

Jo heard the rustle of covers, and in the background, Fran's voice asking what was wrong.

"It will be faster if I go, Jo. I know the area. You phone it in." He gave her Bill's address again. "Meet me there." He reeled off directions.

"Okay." Jo made a note of the address. "But make it quick, Dave. This guy doesn't hang about."

Jo cut the call and immediately redialled the emergency number, asking for the fire brigade and giving Bill's address. She knew the tele-printer in Lisburn would crank into action, sending orders to the nearest station — in this case Mourne Lough. When the guys on Green Watch got this address, it would be all hands to the pumps.

Jo dressed quickly, grabbed her car keys, and ran down the steps she'd fallen up so happily a few hours before.

She shouldn't be driving, and in normal circumstances, she'd never consider getting behind the wheel with even a hint of alcohol on her breath. But these weren't normal circumstances and losing her licence would be a small price to pay if she could save the boss and his family.

CHAPTER TWENTY-TWO

It took Jo a while to find Bill's house. After a few frustrating wrong turns, she finally spied the signpost. She didn't slow, taking the corner into the quiet cul-de-sac on a squeal of tyres.

Number 212 Briar Hill sat at the end, the house, like the rest of the street, in total darkness. *Where is Dave?* He should be here, rousing the boss and his family or at least the neighbours, in case the fire spread.

She screeched to a stop, didn't take the time to switch off the engine or close the car door. Heart racing, she leaped out and ran up the cobbled drive

"Boss! Boss!" She hammered on the front door.

When there was no reply, she banged louder then realised the futility of her actions. If they were drugged, they wouldn't be able to answer. She hadn't much time. She moved to the huge window. At her feet, ornamental stones edged a pretty flower display. She lifted the biggest rock she could find and hurled it at the window. The double-glazing bounced it back at her. Undeterred, she picked the stone up again and hammered on the glass. "Break, damn you. Break!" *Where the hell are Dave and Green Watch?*

The glass finally gave with a soft tinkle followed by the harsh shriek of an alarm. Jo kicked glass out of the way and clambered inside. She moved towards the front door and the large hallway leading to the stairs. *Am I too late?* She couldn't smell any smoke, but she knew that was no guarantee. In a house this size, a slow-burning fire, even in a contained environment such as a closed room, could at this moment be belching out enough toxic smoke to kill a small army.

"Boss!" She took the stairs two at a time. "Boss!"

Her voice was lost in the wail of the burglar alarm and the scream of an approaching fire engine.

"Woods! What the feck are you doing in my house?"

Bill Simmons, dressed in a pair of pyjama bottoms, appeared at the top of the stairs, a bat clenched in both hands.

At the sight of him Jo skidded to a stop, confused. He wasn't unconscious. "Fire, Boss. There's a fire."

Bill lowered the club. "If there is, Woods, it must be the smallest fire in Christendom for I can't bleedin' smell it. Can you?"

Jo had to admit she couldn't. But there *had* to be one. She scanned the darkened hallway, sniffing the air. Nothing.

"Bill?" Marian appeared behind her husband, white nightgown billowing like a ship in full sail. The two little boys were sheltered protectively at her side, the little girl hanging like a limpet to her neck. All three were crying.

Jo's heart dropped into her shoes.

"It's okay, Marian." Bill waved her back. "False alarm. I'll deal with it." He strode forward and took Jo roughly by the arm, propelling her down the stairs.

Dave met them at the bottom. "I'm sorry, Jo, I had a bit of an accident on the way over." He held a hand to his head, which was dripping blood. The guys from Green Watch stood behind him, eyes avid, watching the spectacle unfold.

Bill ignored them but his displeasure was evident, as was his stranglehold on Jo's arm. He punched in his code, switching off the alarm. Blessed silence followed.

A man Jo vaguely recognised stepped forward. "You okay, Boss?"

"Just fecking grand, John. You?"

The firefighter raised a slight smile. "No problems then?" His eyes searched the floors above.

"Not if you don't count that bloody great hole in my window."

"We'll get that boarded up for tonight, Boss." John threw Jo a probing look, before retreating outside, taking his men with him.

Dave, to give him his due, stood his ground. "Boss, I—"

"It's okay, Dave. Leave it." Jo shook her head. No sense both them getting a rollicking. "I'll call you later."

"Well, if you're sure?"

"She's sure," Bill said.

"Right, then." Dave, in the face of Bill's barely restrained anger, chose the better part of valour and retreated.

"You, come with me."

With her arm held in a vice-like grip, Jo had no option but to comply. She let herself be led down a short hallway into a massive kitchen. Once there, Bill let go of her arm.

"I need a drink." He opened a cabinet and took out a bottle of whisky and a glass. "You, judging by the fumes coming off you, have had more than enough."

Jo squirmed, rubbing her arm. "I'm not drunk, Boss." It was true. Between the dream and the events of the last hour, any vestige of drink and its effects were gone. She was completely, painfully sober.

"That's a matter for debate," Bill said, pouring himself a generous measure, taking a swift gulp. "Jesus, Mary and sweet... You know how much that window's gonna cost?"

Jo shook her head and he glared at her. "Well you will, 'cause it's coming out of your pocket, you hear?"

Jo nodded, feeling the beginning of a headache start.

"You want to tell me why you broke into my house tonight and brought all your friends with you?"

"Hoax call, Boss."

"To my house?"

"Yes."

"And you fell for it?" He sounded amazed. "For feck's sake, Woods, you know better than that."

"Bill, remember your blood pressure," Marian admonished from the doorway. "And think about it. Jo hasn't been here long enough to know this is our address, now has she?"

"She knew enough to shout 'Boss' as she stormed up our fecking stairs," Bill said, but the heat was gone from his voice.

"And didn't the doctor tell you to go easy on this stuff?" Marian took the glass from his hand and poured the contents down the sink. "Sit down and I'll make us a nice cup of tea." She included Jo in the invitation.

Jo sat, trying not to smile as the boss threw himself into a chair like a recalcitrant child, casting wistful glances at the whisky bottle.

"Not that bloody green concoction, Marian? I bleedin' *hate* that stuff."

CHAPTER TWENTY-THREE

Coop was sitting outside the flats — shirt off, jeans slung low on lean hips — as Jo got out of her car. She restrained a sigh. *Where is the rain when I need it?* She didn't want to see anyone today. In fact, if she hadn't run out of coffee, she'd planned to never leave her flat again.

Coop didn't seem any happier to see her. Sprawled in an old deck chair, hands cradling a bottle of beer, he muttered something suspiciously like a curse as she approached.

"I thought you liked the harder stuff," Jo said, doing her best not to stare at his taut, delectable midriff.

"Then you thought wrong." Coop took a swig of beer.

"Ooh, who rattled your cage? Is this what happens when you run out of wacky backy? At least with a Brazilian, I can take it or leave it."

There was no answering quip, just a flicker of an emotion Jo couldn't define and a huge, cartoonlike burp.

"'Scuze me," Coop said, not sounding in the least bit apologetic.

"I'm not sure I can. You're pretty snippy today."

"I wasn't talking about... Oh, just forget it!" Coop finished his bottle, reached for another.

Jo hovered, unsure whether to leave or not. She didn't know Coop well, but this abrasive humour seemed out of character. She owed him one, she reminded herself. He had been nice to her yesterday, giving her the rose for Emma's coffin. And last night he'd... Embarrassed, she quashed any memory of the kiss. "You okay, Coop?"

"Just fine and dandy. You?" He didn't look up. "I suppose you want one?"

Jo didn't. In fact, after last night's fiasco, she planned to swear off drink forever. But something told her Coop needed a friend right now.

"Seeing as you're asking so nicely." She perched on the front doorstep and held out her hand.

"So," Coop said, waiting until she'd taken her first sip, "heard you had a bit of fun last night?"

Jo grimaced. Bloody small towns! Nothing got around quicker than someone else's screw-up — except maybe bad news. "You heard?"

"Yup."

There was consolation in the fact she had raised a smile. It almost made up for the way her stomach heaved as fresh beer landed on top of last nights' fermented hops. "It was fun all right." Jo braced herself. "Go on. Get it out of your system."

"What?" Coop raised his eyes, the picture of innocence. "I wasn't going to say anything except I'm glad it was a false alarm and no one got hurt."

Jo looked at him, surprised. His voice contained a brooding quality she had never heard before. "You sure you're okay, Coop?"

"You do a great job, you know," he said, not answering her question. "I really admire what you and your friends do. Forget about last night." He waved a hand. "Better to go and not be needed, than not bother at all, right?" He drained his beer in one gulp then grabbed another.

Jo knew better than to comment on his drinking. After all, who was she to talk? Since she'd come to Mourne Lough, she'd drunk more than some small countries did in an entire year — or at least that's the way her head felt today.

"Well, thanks a lot. It's nice to be appreciated." She raised her bottle, wondering what was going on with him.

"But... how do you deal with it? The deaths? The ones you can't save?"

Jo didn't trot out the standard reply. She had a feeling Coop needed an honest answer. "As best we can. It helps to think of the ones we *do* save. You know, the people who are living and breathing, loving and crying right at this moment because of us. Me?" she said with a wry smile. "I like to think of the young people we've saved, the families they might have some day, children who have no idea how close they came to not existing. That's what helps me."

"I was married once," Coop said so softly Jo had to strain to hear. "Had kids an' all."

Jo tried to hide her shock. She waited, not saying a word.

"I've never told anyone that before." Coop lifted his beer, took a long drink.

"Why not?"

"'Cause they're dead." He placed a hand over his eyes, swallowing hard. "Burnt to death! And there was nothing I could do. Nothing. Not one bloody thing. Can you imagine how that feels?" His face twisted in pain and grief. "When you go into those young people's houses, speak of them as if they mean something to you, can you honestly comprehend what it's like to stand and watch everything you love, everything you've ever wanted, go up in flames?" His eyes were haunted by images only he could see.

"Yes, I can," Jo said, reaching out, touching his shoulder.

"No. You *can't*."

Coop swept her hand away with such force that Jo fell off the step, dropping her drink. The bottle shattered, beer spilling like blood onto the dry concrete.

"Shit!" Coop leapt from his seat, immediately contrite. "I'm so sorry, Jo. Are you okay?"

"I'm fine." Jo stood up, brushing spilt beer from her jeans. "Really," she said when he continued to hover, "I'm fine."

"Here," he motioned to his seat. "Sit down. Are you hurt anywhere?"

Jo didn't want to sit. She wanted to go to her flat, make herself a cup of coffee — the stronger the better — crawl into bed and pretend the last forty-eight hours, the last month, the last bloody seven years had never happened.

"It's their anniversary today," Coop said, by way of apology. "It's exactly five years ago today."

"Oh, Coop." Anger forgotten, Jo put her arms around him and this time he didn't reject her. He buried his head in her neck, holding on to her as if she were the only thing anchoring him in his sea of misery. Beneath her hands, Jo felt him trying to control his sobs, his naked skin pulsing under her touch, and she was aroused. Immediately, she was disgusted with herself. *What kind of person am I?* Here was a guy in need and she was lusting after him. Couldn't stoop much lower than that.

"It will get easier, Coop," she said, blocking out any carnal thoughts. "Time really does heal. The pain never goes away, but trust me, it does get easier. I promise."

Coop shuddered in her arms, fighting to regain his composure. He raised his head and whatever he saw on her face calmed him. "You do understand, don't you?"

"More than you can imagine," Jo said.

"I'm sorry about all this." Coop sat back down, his face pale.

"Don't be." Jo lowered herself to the step. Much like her first beer, any hope she had for a quiet day trickled away. Resigned, she held out her hand for another. "Why don't you tell me about them?"

Coop needed no urging. "We were too young, although you couldn't tell us that at the time. Stubborn, the pair of us. We were in love, and love conquers all, doesn't it? Mind you, Julie had stubborn down to an art form. Wouldn't take my name, insisted on keeping her maiden one. Said she wasn't going to be called after a barrel maker." His smile was wistful. "Then she told me she was pregnant. It was time to grow up fast." He snorted, an unhappy sound. "When they told us it was twins... Shit! I still remember the cold feeling it gave me, standing in that cubicle, the sonar beeping with its two heartbeats." He wiped a hand over his face. "I don't mind telling you I was scared, scared so bad I wanted to run and never look back."

"But you didn't? You stayed and made a go of it?"

"Aye, we tried. I got a job with more money, but it meant longer hours away from home. That didn't help. Julie found it tough looking after the twins alone. The arguments... Half of the time I was glad to get away," Coop admitted. "I took my time coming home. They say the fire started around four in the morning, smouldering for a while before taking hold." He rubbed his nose, fingered the twisted bump in the middle. "That's where I got this from. The neighbour — he wouldn't let me in — said it was too late. Jesus! They died, and I wasn't there." He looked at Jo, his expression tortured.

Jo couldn't help herself. She hugged him close and this time there was no desire involved. "I'm so, so sorry, Coop."

"They would be five and a half now, in school, becoming independent, developing their own personalities — or so I'm told." This time the smile never made it past his lips. "The funeral yesterday — that girl, Emma Forbes — brought it all back. I moved here to get away from the memories and now

I'm right back where I started. I may as well have stayed in Belfast."

"Belfast?" Something stirred at the back of Jo's mind. "And it happened five years ago today?"

Coop nodded. "Seventeenth of May, 2006. Not a date I'm likely to forget. You want another?"

Jo gave an absent-minded nod. She had read something about twins and not that long ago either. *Where? When?* Then it came to her. Her file, the list of names she'd sent Mavis. There had been twins mentioned. She even recalled being upset at how young they'd been, thinking how devastated the family must have felt. *What were their names? John? Judy?* They both began with a J. She remembered that much. She searched her mind. Jade and Jason Magill! That was it. But it couldn't be. Could it?

"Here you go." Coop plopped a drink in her lap.

Jo grabbed it and took a swift drink, trying to figure out a way to get the information she needed. "Do you have a picture of your family, Coop? I'd really like to see it, if you don't mind."

Coop looked at her for a moment, then reached into his pocket and took out his wallet. "I don't mind. Here you go."

The picture was frayed, creased from years of folding and unfolding. It showed a young woman with long black hair and tired eyes, holding two babies, one dressed in pink, the other in blue. Jo didn't dare look up. "They're gorgeous, Coop. What were their names?"

Coop took the photo from her, stroked his thumb over his children's faces and smiled. "Julie's family had a fondness for J's so we continued the tradition and called them Jade and Jason. You would have fitted right in."

Jo swallowed another mouthful of beer and wondered how on earth she was going to tell him.

CHAPTER TWENTY-FOUR

Guilt was a bastard of an emotion. It made Coop feel dirty, a cad of the worst order. The old-fashioned word had a nice ring to it — short, sharp, and a bit abrupt, just like he had been with Jo when she'd tried to explain about Jade and Jason. Coop lifted the phone and dialled the number from memory.

She had been so nice, so careful of his feelings, and he had acted offhand, dismissive of her concerns. Coop rubbed a hand over his face. Yeah, guilt was a bastard of an emotion, but it suited a bastard like him.

Just then, his call was answered. "What?"

The voice was cranky, as if the speaker had been woken from a deep sleep. Good, Coop thought spitefully. The man had no right to sleep easy.

"It's me."

"Yeah."

"You were right. She knows."

"Everything?"

"Well, obviously not everything or she wouldn't have been talking to me. But, other than that, yes, she has it all pegged."

"Damn!" There was no trace of sleep in the voice now. "She's going to spoil our plans."

Coop wasn't so sure. Yes, Jo telling all and sundry a killer was on the loose meant they'd have to step up their timetable. Not a bad idea in his book. It was already taking too long. He wanted this sorted — and fast.

"Spoil what?" he said. "There's nothing to spoil, if you ask me."

"I didn't ask you. Tell me what she said. I want to hear everything."

Coop felt like he was betraying a confidence, an emotion that didn't sit well with him. He didn't owe Jo Woods any favours, he consoled himself. He owed them all to his family.

"She spotted the same pattern we did. She hasn't gone as far back as we have, but it's only a matter of time. In fact, it might already be in the works, judging by some of the things she let slip. I've flagged the records, which will tell us immediately if she does."

"You can do that?"

"I can do anything I want. Isn't that why you hired me?"

"Hey, you begged to get in on this job, so don't pull the vestal virgin act on me now. How does she know so much? Who the fuck is helping her. Did she tell you that?"

"A Mavis Tidy. She works for Tim Sheppard, the chief fire officer in Lisburn."

"Damn! I've heard of her, a right old dragon. She's well placed in the CFO's office to get all the information Jo needs. I'll have to see if I can't find a way to throw a spanner in her works."

Coop agreed. They had to cut off the flow of information to Jo, stop her before she dug any deeper and drowned in her own nosiness.

"She say anything about that hoax call last night? Strange business."

"Not a lot. I think she's embarrassed about the whole thing."

There was a bark of laughter. "I bet she is. Bill Simmons is livid. I wonder if a word dropped in the right ear might push him over the edge, get her suspended, and out of our hair for a while? Suspension would take her bloody mind off this investigation of hers before she gets herself killed — or one of us," he added viciously.

The only worry Coop heard in the voice was for the speaker alone, and while he agreed with him in principle, he wasn't sure he liked his tactics. Definitely a man to be wary of. But then, when you supped with the devil, a bad taste in your mouth was the least you could expect.

*****

I knew I shouldn't gloat, that it was beneath me, but I was inordinately pleased at how well my plan to contain Jo had worked. Bill Simmons had been furious, was probably still stomping around his big house with its broken window. I wondered what punishment he had in store for Jo. Would he suspend her? That would keep her away from any more of *my* fires'.

"But it will also give her plenty of time to investigate your other freeings."

"She's doing that anyway." I refused to be discouraged. My plan had worked faultlessly. I was sorry, though, that Bill's grandchildren had been frightened.

"A necessary by-product," the voice said. *"They weren't hurt."*

"But they've already had so much pain in their young lives."

"Pain that you will ease — later. For now, you did what needed to be done. As usual, you didn't shirk your duties."

No, I hadn't. I wouldn't. My mission was too important to me.

"Speaking of your mission, why are you here? And during the day, too? It's much too risky"

I knew it was. Fortunately, there was no sign of the amateur. Two skulking strangers in daylight would be hard to miss.

"So, why chance it?"

I didn't know. I couldn't help myself. It was like Jo — or some part of her — called to me

"I know which part is calling to you."

I bristled at the lascivious tone. "I'm just doing my usual follow-up. She spied on me. I figured I'd return the favour."

"A follow-up? Is that what they call it now? More of your close surveillance?"

I ignored the voice, staring at the front door of the flats where Jo and her semi-naked neighbour had just disappeared. My jaw clenched and my hand unconsciously rubbed my stomach. She was supposed to be suffering, hiding in her flat, licking her wounds, not licking around the man downstairs. Acid gurgled, souring my stomach and my good mood.

We had the connection. *We* did! Not him. But she had shut me out and let that layabout in — into her arms, maybe even into her heart. Why? What did he have that I didn't?

"You have your mission. It should be enough."

"It is."

"Liar. Remember, you can't fool me," the voice said.

Acid and resentment knotted together. "I'm only interested in Jo and how she pertains to the mission."

"And what have you decided?"

I considered for a moment. I had discredited Jo with the boss and the rest of the firefighters. It was enough. She would be scrambling to save her reputation, too busy to focus on me or my mission.

"More like she'll be focusing on the man downstairs."

I didn't rise to the bait. "That too. The added distraction can only help our cause."

"Then there's no reason to linger. You have work to do."

Yes, I had work to do. I always had work to do. My mission was a greedy mistress. It left no room for any other woman.

Yet still I lingered.

CHAPTER TWENTY-FIVE

"We need more chairs — and plates. Oh man..." Wart wrung his hands, looking round in dismay. "Cutlery, too."

Jo and Dave exchanged exasperated glances. "Relax, Wart," Dave said for the umpteenth time. "Everything's in hand." He pointed to a large van driving into the courtyard behind them. "The guys are bringing in the last of the stuff now."

Wart wasn't to be placated. He eyed Jo's long-sleeved T-shirt. "You're going to boil in that. If you've no summer ones yet, I can lend you one of mine."

Jo examined Wart's navy T-shirt, the fire service logo straining over the heavily muscled chest and refused his offer with a smile. "Thanks, but I'll be fine."

Once again, the weather had confounded the weathermen's predictions, a radiant sun beaming from a cloudless sky. "That about it then?" she asked Dave as Wart headed off to check that the guys in the van hadn't forgotten anything. She did a quick check of the playing field. The tables were laid in a continuous line on either side of the pitch. They ended at the far goal where a huge bouncy castle was set up, stalls selling trinkets and candy floss visible behind it.

In the centre of the pitch stood four huge barbecues, flanked by two tables lined with meat trays, all prepped and ready for the feast. White tablecloths fluttered like trapped doves beneath a mountain of food, while brightly coloured ribbons and balloons danced in the light breeze.

"It looks great, Jo. Don't do a Wart on me, for Christ's sake."

Jo smiled and edged away, eager to be gone before the rest of Red Watch appeared. There was bound to be some good-natured ribbing after her fiasco at the boss's house, but she'd rather let them wait for their fun. Plus, she didn't want to get into a conversation with Dave about the killer phoning her. That was one "chat" she preferred to leave until later, and the later the better. "Oh look, there's Mary and Emily. I'd better go check on them."

Dave's grin told her he knew full well what she was up to. Over his shoulder, Jo spied Wart, geared up for another tirade. "Good luck." She patted Dave on the shoulder.

"For what?"

Jo pointed behind him. Dave turned and gave a resigned sigh, just as Jo made her escape.

*****

"Hi." Jo bent to embrace Mary, careful to make the hug as loose and non-threatening as possible. "I didn't think you'd come."

"If I'd known that, I might have chickened out," Mary said, smiling nervously.

"Then I'm doubly glad to see you. And you too, Miss Emily." Jo tickled the giggling child. "Come on. I'll introduce you to the other mothers." She led Mary to the middle of the field where the firefighters' wives and girlfriends were helping with the preparations for the barbecue.

It was a quiet frenzy. There had been talk of cancelling — out of respect for the Forbes family — but a few of the children attending today were from the local orphanage and no one had the heart to disappoint them.

Fran came to meet them, a shy smile on her face. "Hi." She introduced herself. "Oh, what a gorgeous baby!" She bent to the pram.

"Thank you." Mary let herself be led into the group of chattering women, looking nervous to be the centre of so much attention.

Reluctantly, Jo left her there. She could see the first buses drawing into the courtyard and knew her presence was required to ferry the children and their helpers to their assigned tables.

She'd had reservations about this picnic. When the guys had first mentioned it, she'd thought it patronising — look after the orphans once a year. *Whoopee! What about the other three hundred and sixty-four days?* However, judging by what she had seen and heard, she was starting to revise her opinion. Every firefighter knew each child by name. Further inquiry told her they all took time at least once a week to visit one or two of the children, acting in each case like a big brother.

If one of these guys was a killer, he is doing a damn fine job of masking it, she thought as she checked for any sign of Coop. She was worried about him. She had hit him with some pretty big stuff in their early morning chat, and he hadn't taken it well. He had been too calm, for one thing, like it hadn't sunk in. When it did, she didn't want him to be on his own.

A black mantle descended on her, clouding any joy she might have taken in the day. No matter how much she'd wanted to love this town and trust her colleagues, she couldn't afford to let her guard down or forget the real reason she was here. Relaxed and surrounded by such gaiety, there was a chance the killer — if he was here — would let something slip. She planned to be there if he did.

Hiding how uncomfortable that made her feel, Jo went to greet the kids.

*****

"You having fun?" she asked Mary later. The food had been served and she had a break before the clear-up needed to be done.

Mary nodded, face transformed. "Oh, Jo it's great. Everyone's so nice, and Emily's having a ball."

Emily was sitting in her pram cooing, drool trickling down cheeks swollen from teething.

"Here," Pat said, his huge hand with stubby fingers edged in dirt dabbed at the rosebud mouth.

Emily chortled and grabbed the hanky, not letting go.

"Oh, I'm so sorry. Here, let me..." Mary tried to tease the little fingers free.

Emily pouted, tears forming.

"Ach, leave her be," Pat said, relinquishing the tissue with an embarrassed laugh. He touched Mary's shoulder. "Honestly, it's fine."

Mary recoiled as if scalded. "Sorry, I..." Pat took a step backwards, face burning.

Jo decided to intervene. "Mary, this is Pat Meehan. He's a firefighter, like me." The last was unnecessary because Pat was wearing his brigade T-shirt. "Pat, this is my neighbour, Mary Quinn, and her gorgeous daughter, Emily."

The two went the same fiery shade of red, struck dumb. Emily had no such inhibitions, chortling merrily and blowing milky bubbles. She waved her newly acquired plaything at them both.

"W-would you like to see the clowns?" Pat asked, pointing to where a crowd was gathering. "I mean... Emily might like them."

Mary hesitated, glanced at Jo.

For a moment, Jo was reluctant to let her go, but one look at Pat's smitten face convinced her otherwise. If someone here was a cold-blooded killer, she'd bet her bottom dollar it wasn't the bashful ex-mechanic. She just hoped she wasn't betting with Mary's and Emily's lives.

CHAPTER TWENTY-SIX

An hour later, seated with the rest of Red Watch, Jo began to relax. The guys had had their fun. And, she admitted, their jokes on the price of double-glazing were amusing, if painfully so.

Her meeting with the boss and his wife, Marian, had also gone better than expected, although the invoice in her trouser pocket would hurt for some time to come. Yet, even that couldn't dampen her spirits. After years of inaction, things were finally starting to happen. The killer had shown his hand by phoning her, and the fact he'd called twice in the space of twenty-four hours meant she was doing something right.

"It's all going well, isn't it?" Fran said, face beaming. She settled into the empty chair next to Jo and fixed her long skirt over her bare legs.

"Yes, unless Wart spoils it all by having a coronary on us."

Both women laughed, watching Wart flap his hands at Flanders, his face a study of rigid determination. Their laughter masked the approaching footsteps and they both jumped when the voice spoke behind them.

"Hello, Jo."

Jo was rooted in place. *It couldn't be!*

"Cat got your tongue, little sister?"

Jo swivelled in her chair to meet a pair of familiar blue eyes. "Trisha?"

"In the flesh." A slender hand pushed the mane of red hair off creamy cheeks. "Aren't you glad to see me?"

Before Jo could answer, there was a rush of movement. Sinead, her six-year-old niece, and Adam, her five-year-old nephew, clambered onto her lap.

"Aunty Jo! Aunty Jo!"

Jo bent to nuzzle their necks, saddened to find they had lost the sweet baby smell she remembered. They'd grown too, their limbs awkward and ungainly on her knee.

"You didn't come see us." Her niece pouted. "It's been *ages*!"

"Yeah, ages," Adam chipped in. "Even when I fell and hurted myself, you didn't come. See..." He leapt off Jo's knee and pulled up his trouser leg to show a newly healed scar.

Jo kissed the microscopic spot. "Oh, Adam, what did you do to yourself?"

"Wasn't me." He kicked at the grass. "It was Josh. He pushed me first."

Jo tried not to laugh and hugged him close. "Oh, it's good to see you both." She smiled at her sister. "You too, Trisha."

Fran rose to give Trisha her chair. "Can I get you something to eat? A drink?" she asked, flustered, obviously sensing the tension between the pair.

"A drink would be nice," Trisha said, "It was pretty hot in the car."

"Oh, have you come far?" Fran grabbed a tumbler from a nearby table, filled it with juice and handed it to Trisha.

"Not far — Belfast — but an hour in the car with my darling children can seem like forever." She gave Fran an impish grin and held out her hand. "I'm Jo's sister, Patricia Feeley, but my friends call me Trisha."

"Sister?" Fran looked at Jo confused.

"Older, obviously," Jo said dryly.

"Oh. I..." Blushing, Fran waved her hands in the air, stepping backwards towards Dave and the others. "I didn't mean... Oh dear. I'll just... Let me get you something to eat, Trisha." She scurried away.

"That wasn't nice," Trish chided, making Jo feel all of fifteen again. "The poor woman was just being friendly." Then, on the same breath, "Why haven't you phoned?"

"Why haven't *you*?" Jo retaliated, enviously eying Trisha's slender legs, crossing now in a graceful arch. She knew she wasn't the only one to follow their progress or their stilted conversation.

"Because you changed your mobile number and didn't see fit to give me your new one."

Jo smothered a curse. "Sorry, but I've been busy. New job, new flat, new town, you know how it is. How did you know about the barbecue, anyway?" she asked as an afterthought.

"Mavis. And don't you dare sound off at her," Trisha said quickly. "She thought it might be a good place for us to meet."

"Neutral, you mean?" Jo ran a hand over Adam's hair, sad to see it had darkened from blonde to dirty fair.

"They've missed you, you know." Trisha said following the motion.

Jo's gaze flew to Sinead and the ache in her heart grew stronger.

"It's okay, Jo." Trisha's voice softened, "I understand. I finally understand. But they don't."

Jo stiffened. This wasn't the time or the place. *Damn Mavis to hell.*

"Hey, you gonna introduce us, Jo?" Flanders shifted his chair towards them, tilting it on two legs for a better look at Trisha.

Jo resisted the urge to kick the remaining chair legs from under him. Not looking at Trisha, she stood, the children dropping like monkeys from a tree. "Guys, this is my sister Trisha, and these two," she tickled the squirming children, "are my horrible niece and nephew, Sinead and Adam."

A flood of introductions followed. Tumilty was quick to take advantage. While the others were talking, he lifted his chair and set it next to Trisha. "Hiya, Trisha, I'm Jim and I'm depending on you to give us all the gossip on our Jo." He leaned closer. "In case you haven't noticed, she's been a little closemouthed where you're concerned."

Trisha laughed. "That sounds like Jo all right."

"Aunty Jo."

Jo tore her eyes away from the surreal sight of Tumilty and Trisha flirting and looked at her niece, nervously twisting the hem of her dress in one hand.

"Who's that girl?" Sinead asked, pointing to where Dave sat with his daughter, Jenny.

"Huh?" Jo couldn't keep her eyes off the child. She was so like... She put a brake on her heart. "That's Jenny Evans. Would you like to meet her?"

"Uh-huh."

Jo took Sinead's hand and led her towards Dave and his family. Adam followed behind them. "Hiya, Jenny." Jo dropped to her knees beside the child. "This is my niece, Sinead. She's the same age as you and doesn't know anyone here. Would you look after her for me?"

"Of course she will. Won't you, Jenny Wren?" Dave nudged the child forward. "You want her to look after the boy, too?" He reached out a hand and pulled Jo to her feet.

"Thanks, Dave," Jo said gratefully. "That would be great." She ignored the question in his eyes, hurrying back to Trisha before her sister decided to give Tumilty a blow-by-blow account of Jo's life.

Not a moment too soon. Tumilty had his chair angled towards Trisha, his bony shoulders twisted to exclude the rest of the group. If it had been anyone else, Jo might have been tempted to leave them to it, but suspecting what she did about Tumilty, she was honour-bound to save her sister. *Not that she'd know or thank me for it, if she did,* Jo thought mutinously. She plonked herself between the pair, but before she could speak, Fran appeared with a plate of tired looking sandwiches.

"I hope this is okay? It's all that's left." She offered Trisha the plate.

"It's more than okay. Thank you." Trisha took the plate, smiling in delight. "I'm hungry enough to eat a week-old kipper. You're Jo's partner's wife, aren't you?" She giggled. "That sounds such a mouthful. Can I call you Fran?"

Jo watched in amazement as Fran responded with a girlish laugh and the two began to chat like old friends. *Typical!* Trisha had done in seconds what it had taken her a month to do. Old inadequacies rose but she pummelled them into oblivion, telling herself she wasn't that girl anymore.

Dave appeared. "Jim, I need a hand."

"What's up, mate?" Tumilty rose reluctantly.

"Wart's gone into overload and Geoff's about to make mincemeat outta him." Dave winked at Jo behind Tumilty's back.

Jo hid a smile. Good old Dave to the rescue again. As they moved off, she mouthed a thank you before turning to Trisha. "Okay, I'll be the first to say it. I'm sorry, Trisha."

The laughing eyes stilled. "And you're not going to get angry at Mavis, are you?"

"Nope. I guess I owe her one, but if you tell her, I may have to kill you."

Trisha giggled, an infectious sound that drew smiles from those around them. Then she grew pensive, the light died from her eyes, and her face filled with remorse. "I'm sorry too, Jo. I've missed you something awful, especially this last while."

Jo knew she meant her divorce and regret hung heavy in her voice. "I'm sorry I wasn't there for you, Trisha."

The strained look left Trisha's face. "Hey, I was glad you weren't. That way I didn't have to listen to you saying 'I told you so.' She hesitated. "But it made me realise what it must have been like for you with Brian." Her eyes flickered to where Sinead was playing with Jenny. "It pains me too, you know."

"I know," Jo said, for the first time realising what had affected her had also affected her sister.

Trisha touched her hand. "You can't hide forever, Jo. Lucy's anniversary is coming up soon and I would like—"

"Who's Lucy?" Tumilty re-appeared, unnoticed, next to them, Dave and Geoff a step behind him.

Jo tried to warn Trisha, but she was too late.

"Lucy? Why she's Jo's daughter." Trish turned to Jo, a puzzled look on her face. "Don't tell me you didn't tell them?"

CHAPTER TWENTY-SEVEN

Mary had been enjoying herself so much that she almost forgot her real reason for attending the barbecue. In the silence surrounding Trisha's pronouncement, she was reminded of what she had to do. She looked around. Everyone was focused on Jo. No one was paying attention to her or Emily. It was the perfect opportunity.

She double-checked the small bag she'd packed — a few essential items, mostly Emily's. It would do until she was settled and could buy more. She tried not to think of her flat, the home she'd thought she'd found in Mourne Lough. It would only make her cry, and she'd done enough crying.

She scanned the area for any sign of Thomas, but all she saw were families laughing and having fun. Maybe he had given up? Maybe he... Mary cursed her optimism. *Have I learned nothing?* She gathered her belongings and pushed the pram towards the courtyard. Time to take her life back.

She gave what she hoped was a nonchalant look over her shoulder, searching for her husband. *Nothing.* Her heart pounded as she pushed the pram onwards, stopping every few paces, ostensibly to check on Emily, but, in reality, to see if Thomas was watching.

Once past the courtyard, it would be a short walk to the bus stop. She glanced at her watch: 4:30, right on time. The next bus was due at 4:35. The walk took three minutes, twenty-eight seconds. She'd timed it over and over again, walking at a normal pace. That meant she'd be in the open for one minute, thirty-two seconds while she waited for the bus. This was the danger point, but Mary had a plan.

There was a small flower stall in the town square, next to the bus stop. It opened every Saturday at eight thirty and closed at five o'clock on the dot. She had struck up a friendship with the owner, Fred. Her habit was to arrive just before he closed, whereupon Fred would give her the pick of the left-over flowers — at a reduced price, of course, to be rid of them.

She could while away the time until the bus was due, jump on as it pulled off. If Thomas were following her, he wouldn't suspect a thing until the last second, plus he would be on foot. She'd have time to spot him, get off at the nearest stop and hide until he passed.

It was a deeply flawed plan, Mary knew, but she also knew it was her only hope. She tried to act casual as she weaved her way towards the empty courtyard.

CHAPTER TWENTY-EIGHT

Back in the playing field, there was a stunned silence broken by an obviously shocked Dave.

"You have a daughter?"

Jo heard the hurt in his voice, saw the same emotion reflected in the faces around her. This was the second time she'd withheld something important from them. She wasn't sure they'd be so forgiving this time.

Trisha, when she realised what she'd done, looked ready to cry. "Oh, Jo, me and my big mouth."

"It's okay."

"I didn't know you wuz married?" Pat said, confused. He looked at the others, for the first time noticing Mary and Emily's absence. "I really didn't."

"None of us did, you dope." Flanders was puce, his chubby jowls straining with emotion. "She didn't bother to share that little tidbit with any of us."

Jo looked towards Dave, Geoff standing behind him, and tried to explain. "I was married, *had* a daughter Lucy." *Had!* Her mind stalled. Such a simple word, yet behind it sat more grief, more pain than she could voice. She made herself to go on. "They're both dead, killed in a fire seven years ago." She was proud at how easily the words came out.

"Oh my God, Jo." Dave moved to embrace her, hurt forgotten. Fran hovered by his side.

Jo looked over Dave's shoulder, caught Geoff's eye and tried to communicate how sorry she was. Geoff refused to return her gaze. Jo didn't blame him. Not long ago, he'd shared the painful memories of his son Gavin's death with her. He'd every right to expect the same kind of honesty in return.

The others rose in a flurry of commiserations. Yet, as each arm encircled her, their voices dripping sorrow, Jo couldn't help feel she'd made the biggest mistake of her life. Bigger than fighting with Brian that night, storming out, and leaving him and Lucy to the mercy of a monster. If she was right — and she no longer had any doubt she was — then one of the people hugging her may have murdered her family.

Trisha, sensing her distress, stood. "That's enough, folks."

She looked so fierce that Jo was reminded of Mrs R. She began to giggle. The giggle turned into a chortle, followed by side-splitting, stomach-aching laughter.

"What are you laughing at?" Trisha hissed.

"Nothing," Jo snorted, hiccupped. "I'll tell you later." She hiccupped again, giggled, tried to gain control. "You're staying with me, I presume?"

"If you'll have us?"

"'Course I will." Jo hid another hiccup behind a splayed hand. "In that case, you'll meet the woman herself." Laughter bubbled. "You're gonna love Mrs R, Trish." A second later reality struck. "Oh no." Jo slapped her head. "The floor."

"The what?"

"I was supposed to mop the floors," Jo said. She couldn't believe Mrs R's request had slipped her mind. The eagle was bound to check the minute she got home. Hysteria died as Jo prayed *my Liam* wouldn't bring his mum home until very late tomorrow.

CHAPTER TWENTY-NINE

Mary couldn't believe her luck. Everything was going smoothly. It looked like her plan might actually work.

She made it to the bus stop with plenty of time to spare. There was no sign of Thomas — or at least none she could see. Without making it obvious, she checked again, warning herself not to become too complacent. Thomas had a fondness for striking when she least expected it.

She approached Fred, the flower seller, with a smile pinned to her lips.

"Hello, poppet. I've some nice roses left — yellow, your favourite — if you've a mind to buy?"

This was their usual game. Mary pretended to be reluctant, he pretended to haggle, but her heart wasn't in it today. "They're looking a mite tired, Fred." She lifted a bunch studied them, inhaled their fragrance.

"Ach, they're as fresh now as the moment they were picked." Fred took off his peaked hat, scratched his head and pretended to glower. "But it's mighty warm out today and the missus has me warned — home early or the tea goes in the bin."

He said this every week, but judging by his girth, he hadn't missed many meals in his lifetime. Mary searched the street ahead for the bus.

"Mebbe we can do us a deal, Poppet — say, half price?"

"I don't know, Fred. They're pretty wilted. I don't think they're worth half price. Maybe not even quarter the price." She spied the tip of the blue and white bus coming down the main street. *Hurry up,* she begged it. *Hurry up!*

"A quarter the..." Fred spluttered, placing his hat firmly back on his thinning hair. "Sure, next you'll be wanting them for nothing." His old eyes were watchful as he followed her gaze. "You drive a hard bargain, poppet," he said as Mary turned and caught him staring at the bus. "You can have them for the price of a smile."

Mary's brow wrinkled. This wasn't in the script. But the bus was gaining fast and something in Fred's eyes told her he was aware of her plans and approved. He handed her the flowers packaged in a sheet of bright blue paper, and she reached over and kissed his leathery cheek. "Thanks, Fred."

"You're welcome, poppet. Now hurry up. You don't want to miss your ride, now do ya?" He smiled sadly.

Mary tucked the flowers into the hood of the pram and pulled the bag from the basket underneath to make the pram easier to fold. The bus shuddered to a stop beside her with a hiss of brakes as she slung it over her shoulder.

She chanced one more look to make sure the coast was clear and froze.

He was standing behind her.

"You going somewhere, Mary?"

CHAPTER THIRTY

Trisha settled the children into the spare room and backed out, meeting Jo in the hallway. "I can't take your bed," she objected, not for the first time. "Why don't you let me sleep on the sofa? I don't mind."

Jo handed her a glass of wine and led the way to the living room. "Do as you're told, Trisha. This is my house. Remember?"

"But..."

"Don't."

"Don't what?"

"Do the big sister thing, okay?" They'd made a tentative beginning, built a bridge to span the years of hurt. Jo prayed Trisha wouldn't dismantle it before it had time to reach the other side.

She didn't.

"Whatever you say." Trisha fortified herself with a good swig of red. "We could always share. It's not like we haven't done it before, is it?"

"You liked crisps, as I recall," Jo said, sitting beside her. "Those crumbs cut like the devil."

Trisha threw back her head and laughed. "You remember that?"

"Hard not to," Jo said with feeling.

"It's strange, isn't it," Trisha said topping up their glasses. She didn't meet Jo's eyes. "With mum and dad gone, it's like the thread holding us together has snapped. If we're going to do this, we have to do it ourselves, because we want to, not because we think it's expected of us." Her brow furrowed and she looked uncomfortable. "I have to ask you something, Jo. It's not just what happened to Brian and Lucy, is it? This distance between us... It happened a long time ago, didn't it?"

Jo nodded. "You were a hard act to follow, Trisha." Jo had spent her whole life trying to escape the shadow of her beautiful, perfect older sister. She'd never wanted a career, which hadn't gone down well with her parents. She had fallen into teaching while waiting for her ultimate goal, which was to be a wife and a mother. That was all she'd ever wanted to be.

"You were a good mother," Trisha said, as if she'd read Jo's mind. "Don't ever doubt it. Lucy couldn't have asked for better."

"Mother maybe, but wife..."

"Hey, motherhood is natural, being with a pig isn't."

Brian's infidelity reduced to swine struck Jo as funny, mainly because it was true. "And what of Paul?" she asked speaking of Trisha's ex. " Was he a pig or...?"

Trisha drained her glass, grabbed the bottle to refill it and found it empty. "Do you mind?"

"Knock yourself out. There's another bottle in the fridge."

"Pigs," Trisha said, continuing the conversation on her return, "are clean animals. Paul was never that. Not even close." She uncorked the bottle, her face tight and hard. "He was a worm. No, I'm doing worms a disservice." She filled her glass, held the bottle out to Jo. "He was a maggot, the dregs in your sink, the waste left over when all the good stuff is gone." She topped off Jo's glass and set the bottle on the table. "Pure filth is what he was." She played with her glass. "He touched them, you know." She began to cry. "Both of them. So what would you call him?"

"Oh, Trish." Jo wanted to comfort her sister, but Trisha's posture told her it wouldn't be welcome. "I didn't know."

"You would have, if you had been around. But oh no, you were too busy wallowing in your grief, thinking your life was the only one screwed up. Oh God!" Trisha held a hand to her mouth. "I'm sorry, Jo. That was uncalled for."

"No, you're right." For the first time, Jo realised how selfish she'd been. Yes, she had lost Lucy — her baby, the light of her life. She had lost Brian, too — not the love of her life but a man who, if he'd ever grown up, might have been the love of someone else's life. But Trisha had lost things, too. Trust, her children's innocence, and Jo had been oblivious, which made her a pretty crappy sister.

They drank their drinks in silence.

"I want my kids to know you," Trisha said at last. "I know the sight of Sinead must hurt, looking so much like Lucy and now with her the same age."

"It's okay, Trisha. I want the same thing."

"You do?" Trisha's voice was full of hope. "When I saw your face today... it was the first time I really understood how you must have felt. When you looked at Sinead, I put myself in your place." Her eyes filled. "You're a stronger person than I am."

"Nope. Just got a gorgeous niece and nephew who, with you for a mother, need all the help they can get," Jo retorted.

"Why you—"

Jo giggled. "Got you."

Trisha grew pensive. "Mavis told me what's going on. You sure, Jo?"

Jo was sick of people asking her that. "I'm sure."

"You really think someone is killing children?"

"Not think... know," Jo said firmly.

"I believe you."

"What?" It was the last thing Jo expected. "You do?"

"Yeah. At the start, I figured it was your grief making you see things, but Mavis told me about the records you asked her for. I have them with me. Hold on a mo." She went to the bedroom, returned with a thick file. "I took a peek, I hope you don't mind."

Jo didn't. She glanced inside the file. It looked like Mavis had gone beyond the call of duty. Some of the dates she saw went back twenty years or more. *Mavis, you're a star.*

"I couldn't believe there were so many. No way can they all be accidents."

Jo didn't let on how much Trisha's words meant to her. She closed the file. "What else did Mavis tell you?"

"That all the cases you asked her about were for kids from broken homes or where abuse was suspected."

"And you believe it, even if the pattern wasn't definite — cases like mine for instance where rows and infidelity were the common denominator, not abuse per se?"

"Yes. And you've convinced Mavis, too."

"I have?"

"Yup, though she'd rather have her tongue cut out with a rusty nail than tell you. She's worried about you."

Jo felt a surge of relief. Like a puppet with its wires cut, she fell back into the couch, her body limp. Finally, people believed her. "That's great news, Trisha. But Mavis might be right to worry." At Trisha's questioning look she added, "I think the killer knows I'm on to him. He's phoning me."

"What?"

Jo immediately regretted her words.

"Jesus Christ, Jo. Have you told the police?"

"No."

"Why not?"

"Because he's only phoned a couple of times, and, at least until now, no one would have believed me." She tried to make out it was no big deal. It didn't work.

"C'mon, Jo," Trisha ran a hand through her fiery hair. "This is serious stuff. You have to tell them."

"I will when I've more to go on." Jo finished her drink, not willing to get into it. She also wanted to read Mavis's file. "I'm ready for bed. You?"

"But, but—"

"Come on." Jo steered her sister towards the bedroom. "We can talk about it in the morning."

*****

Rage consumed me.

How I kept it concealed I'll never know, but I managed it — just. The voice in my head didn't help.

"She sure had you fooled. Bet you feel stupid no—"

"Not a word. Not one more Goddam word!" I told it.

The second I was alone I let the rage have its way. It swallowed me whole, engulfed me in a red mist that pulsed before my eyes.

I knew her.

All this time, the connection I felt was nothing more than a memory — and a bad one at that. I had discovered Jo's secret. Why this was so personal for her.

"You didn't actually discover it, Sherlock. It more or less fell into your lap. As detectives go, you're sadly lacki—"

"Shut up." I didn't need the voice to berate me. I was furious enough at myself. How easily I'd been duped. How stupid not to see what was right in front of me. Josephine Hamilton — or Woods, as she called herself now — my only failure, the one person to have escaped me. How could I have failed to recognise her? The voice was right. I was a bloody fool. How dare she mislead me this way?

"You let your infatuation with her blind you."

"Did not."

"What are you? Three years old? Of course, you did. You let your dick do your thinking. It's not your fault," the voice soothed. *"It's a natural, instinctive body response."*

I refused to be mollified. "I am above that. I am—"

"Who's there?" The stooped figure of the amateur arose from the darkness ahead.

"Now you've done it."

I cursed. Anger had made me careless.

Outlined for an instant in the fuzzy orange glow of the streetlights, the amateur was less impressive than I originally supposed — if such a thing were possible.

"Hello?" The amateur craned his head and stared myopically in my direction.

I cursed again, this time under my breath. I had a choice here, I decided, fade into the overgrowth, slip away, and nothing would change. The amateur would continue to stalk the girl in the downstairs flat and I would... I paused. I would *what*? Keep staring at Jo in those precious moments allowed me or at the blank windows of her flat, desperate for a glimpse of her? It wasn't enough anymore, not when I knew who she was and the damage she could wreak on my mission.

No. I needed to deal with Jo Woods, which meant I would have to up my schedule. The idea of rushing such a sacred duty was anathema to me, but I didn't have much choice — not now.

First though, I had to get rid of this blasted idiot, which brought up another instinctive body response — fight or flight?

"Who's there?" the voice asked again and this time I stepped forward.

"You really want to know?"

The idiot, not realising his peril, raised his hands, palms outwards as I appeared. "Hey, man, it's cool. I was just asking. You want me gone? I'm gone."

He didn't move. Emboldened by my silence, he dropped his hands. "You got woman problems, I can tell. I've seen you here, watching, just like me."

Just like him? God forbid. I slipped the knife from my pocket, let him advance. The red mist faded and a plan formed in my mind. Maybe the bastard would come in handy after all? I watched his movements. *Come to daddy. That's it. Keep walking. Keep talking 'cause you're signing your own death warrant, you fucking idiot.*

And he did.

"I'm checking on my bitch of a wife. She ran off — took my fucking kid with her."

He was getting braver. He stepped closer until we were mere inches apart. He stretched out a hand.

"The name's Thom—"

My blade sliced downwards, across his hand. Sharp and wicked, it met little resistance. I watched, disinterested, as his shocked gaze followed his severed digits to the ground. He stared at them as if he couldn't believe they had once belonged to him. The blood drained from his face.

Before he could cry out, I grabbed his injured hand and swivelled until my right arm was caught tightly against his neck, the knife nicking the soft skin of his throat. I stood behind him, as close as a lover, but he took no joy from it.

My mind, free from the red mist, worked with razor sharp clarity. I had two venues of pain to explore — the stump of his hand and his windpipe, which I could pierce or crush. Neither choice appealed. I had already inflicted the maximum damage to his hand. Anything else would be overkill, and crushing his windpipe would be noisy and time consuming. No, I had a better idea.

"How dare you call your wife a bitch," I said. I let go off his hand, let it drop, quick to trap his cry of pain behind my palm. The nerve ends, I knew, would be screaming in exquisite protest as blood rushed to the injured limb. I lowered the knife, trailed it over his belly. "Women deserve respect, especially the mother of your child."

I liked his compliance, the shiver he made as if he knew what I was about to do. I felt invincible, all-powerful. Events were no longer out of my control. I was in charge. *I* was.

"Up close and personal feels good, doesn't it?" the voice said, its words caressing my brain. *"Time to get your hands dirty."*

The idea had its appeal. I pulled the amateur closer. "Woman are the weaker sex," I told him. "They need us to protect them. *Us.*" Without warning, I stabbed upwards, tearing into the flabby stomach. "But you are such a big fucking man, aren't you? You get your kicks from bullying women, don't you?"

Even without my hand over his mouth, I doubted he would have been able to answer. His body tensed, wracked with screams that would never be freed. I twisted the knife harder. Soft tissue ripped, tore.

"Animals like you deserve to die," I whispered in his ear. Then I gutted him, like the animal he was.

CHAPTER THIRTY-ONE

Mary sat in her flat in a stunned silence. To have freedom so close then ripped away was cruel — a body blow — and yet... She stared at the man before her and had the strangest sensation it may have been the luckiest moment of her life.

The instant she had seen Pat Meehan standing behind her, offering a stumbling apology for being so inattentive, she'd spied Thomas, huddled in a shop doorway a few yards ahead.

With a composure she hadn't known she possessed, Mary had taken a deep breath, slipped the bag containing her meagre possessions off her shoulder and handed it to Pat as if it were the most natural thing in the world. Heart in overdrive, she steered the pram towards the playing fields and pretended not to see Thomas duck out of sight into the shop.

It was a tiny victory. She'd pay later for being with Pat, but that punishment would be minor compared to what Thomas would have done if he'd known she was running away again. Mary's skin prickled at the thought, itching like a colony of ants marching over it.

"I can help you, Mary," Pat said now, "protect you. Just say the word."

Mary wanted to believe him, wanted in the worst possible way. But she knew better. Men lied, said whatever it took to get what they wanted. Pat, as nice as he seemed, was no different. She worried her top lip. *How had he known?* It bothered her. The second they'd met, when Emily had stolen his hanky, Pat had known just by looking at her. *How? How did he know I'm running from someone, something? Am I that transparent?*

"I know it's scary, Mary, but all it takes is one step." Pat's plain, good-natured face was earnest.

"I'm not scared," Mary said, hating the pity she heard in his voice. Pity she could do without.

"It's okay if you are." Pat's large hands covered hers, dwarfing them. "But you have to stand up to him. No more running."

"Do you think I haven't tried?" Mary shook her hands free, hurt that he thought so little of her. "Look." She lifted her jumper to show ribs healed crooked, sticking from her gaunt frame like arthritic knuckles. "This is what happened the last time I stood up to Thomas." She lowered her top. "Even then, I told him that if he touched me again, I'd go straight to the police."

"What happened?"

"Let's just say that next time, I wasn't going to be the one hurt." Mary looked at the pram, where Emily lay fast asleep.

"You don't mean...?" Pat's ruddy face paled. "Dear Lord. The man's a monster."

"Yes." Mary was glad he understood. "Now you know why I can never escape him. He'll always find me, and Emily will be the one to pay. I can't let that happen. I *won't* let that happen."

"All you have to do is tell the police what you've told me. I promise you, Mary, they *can* help."

Mary no longer believed in promises. They were too fragile, broken too easily. Her moment of bravado was over, the rebellion lost before it had begun. Pat meant well, but he couldn't help her. The police couldn't help her. Thomas was a law unto himself. Yet Mary hesitated, drawn to Pat with his earnest eyes and gentle hands, and wished with all her heart that things could be different.

*****

Pat sensed he was losing her. "You don't need to do this alone, Mary." Emotion overwhelmed him. "I can help, if you'll let me." He tried to embrace her. "Don't!" Mary jerked backwards.

"Oh, God, sorry." Pat retreated. Her husband really had done a number on her. Anger flared, but he dampened it. Anger was the last thing Mary needed right now.

"I'm sorry," he said again. He kept his voice steady, non-threatening. "Just so you know, my help isn't conditional. There are no strings attached, if that's what you're worried about." He knew she needed to feel in control. "I want to help, but the decision is up to you."

Feeling protective was a new experience for Pat. The foster homes where he'd grown up weren't conducive to caring and sharing. They were more the "look out for number one and bugger everyone else" kind of places. It was every man for himself, survival of the toughest. His fearsome size meant he was left alone, which was a good thing, because at heart Pat was a gentle giant. And yet, as he stared at the beautiful, fragile face before him, Pat knew he would kill this Thomas guy if he ever laid a hand on Mary again.

"We'll take this at your speed, Mary, whatever you want." His mind was made up. He didn't care how long it took or how bad it became, he was staying right here by her side.

CHAPTER THIRTY-TWO

Jo woke to the sound of someone talking. She opened an eye and winced. *Damn!* She had forgotten how potent red wine could be. She took a moment to let the pain subside to a dull throbbing agony.

"No. No. No!"

Beside her in the bed, Trisha's voice grew in volume.

"Trisha?"

"Who is this? Stop it. Right now. You hear me? *Stop* it!"

Jo sat up. "What is it, Trisha? What's wrong?"

Trisha didn't answer. She held the phone from her ear and stared at it as if it were a snake about to strike.

"It's him, isn't it?" Jo didn't need confirmation. Wide awake, she grabbed the recorder from the side of the bed and switched it on. "Give me the phone."

Trisha relinquished the phone without a word.

"You tricked me!" Fury laced the voice. "Fool me once, shame on you. Fool me twice, shame on me. Be warned. You won't fool me a third time."

Jo's blood curdled. "What do you mean?"

"You know exactly what I mean. I free birds, little birds with no one to look after them," there was a pause, "like I did with Lucy."

The use of her daughter's name immobilised Jo. It was no longer a theory. This bastard had murdered her baby!

The whispery voice took advantage of her shock, basked in her silence. "It's a pity about your brother-in-law — a pervert, no less. Tsk, tsk. And Mary downstairs? Her husband is a bastard, in case you didn't know — likes to hurt her. I bet the kid will be next." The voice hardened. "I can't have that, can I?

168

Can you guess what I'm about to do, *Ms Woods*?" He emphasised the name.

Jo's sense of foreboding grew. She motioned to Trisha. "Get the kids," she mouthed.

Trisha didn't move. "He thought I was you," she said, the warmth leached from her voice. "He asked if I'd heard Lucy scream. He said he had, and it was the most blissful thing." Trisha's blue eyes were dazed.

Jo tried to block out the horror Trisha's words invoked. "Snap out of it, Trisha." She pressed the bottom of the phone tightly to her cheek so the caller wouldn't hear, grabbed her sister with her free hand and shook her. "Listen to me. You have to wake the kids. Get them out of the flat. Now!" she shouted when Trisha didn't move.

The look on Jo's face, coupled with the urgency in her voice, forced Trisha into action. Without another word, she ran from the bedroom.

Phone clutched to her ear, Jo jumped out of bed and attempted to put her clothes on one-handed.

"Pity Mrs Reilly's son is such a cheapskate, dontcha think?" the voice said. "Couldn't be bothered to replace his dear mother's faulty fireplace. Tsk tsk."

He was targeting the building. Her worst fears realized, Jo didn't waste time answering. She dropped the phone, pulled on the rest of her clothes and grabbed Mavis's file. In her haste, she knocked over the recorder. She watched in horror as it fell through the mangled cardboard box doubling as her bedside cabinet. No time to search for it. With a regretful glance, she rushed from the room and out of the flat.

"Trisha?" She raced down the stairs. She heard voices below her, Sinead and Adam crying and Trisha's soothing voice trying to comfort them. "Get them out," she yelled. "I'll wake the others."

She had no need to wake Coop. He appeared in his doorway, hair tousled. His eyes went from sleepy to alert in seconds.

"What's going on?" he asked as Trisha flew past him, shepherding her weeping children outside.

"Fire!" Jo leapt the last few stairs. "Get Mary and Emily."

Coop didn't ask questions. He dashed across the hall and hammered on Mary's door, yelling her name.

Please, please let us be in time, Jo prayed. Mary's flat was directly underneath Mrs R's. If the fire blew downwards...

The door finally opened. Mary appeared with Emily in her arms. "What are yo—"

"Out! You have to get out!" Jo grabbed Mary while Coop took charge of the baby. Pat Meehan materialized in the hallway behind them. Jo looked at him, surprised, but didn't stop. "Get out. For God's sake, Run!"

Pat needed no urging. Together they sprinted through the doorway, trying to put as much distance as they could between them and the flats.

Just in time. The block of flats exploded with a mighty *boom!* Glass and debris showered from the sky. For a second there was silence, then the sound of alarms and the sobbing, fearful cries of the children.

"God damn him to hell!" Half deafened by the explosion, Jo didn't realise she was shouting.

"It's okay, Jo. You're safe. We're all safe." Coop knelt next to her, his arms cradling her.

He didn't understand. Nobody understood. Through tear-filled eyes, Jo looked at the rubble that had once been her home. Upstairs, or where upstairs used to be, was the evidence she needed to prove her daughter had been murdered, that Emma and the Thompson boy, and God knew how many other children and their families had been murdered. And it was gone, destroyed, all because she had been too lazy to unpack. She pounded the ground with her fists. "No. No. *No!*"

"Jo, what is it?" Coop, face grubby and scored with tiny cuts from the shattered windows, held her tighter. "What's wrong?"

Jo couldn't tell him, couldn't speak.

*****

It was surprising how many people thronged the hospital corridors at three am. It was dark outside, and yet inside, the day appeared in full swing.

The emergency waiting room was filled with the usual Saturday night crowd in various stages of inebriation. Their complaints were many and mostly incoherent. Jo ignored them, disgusted by their self-pity and well aware that it was morons like these who caused most road accidents she attended. The nurses seemed of the same mind. Unless they were missing a limb, they were left to pickle in their own juices.

An hour into their wait, Adam fell asleep on Jo's knee while Sinead curled next to Trisha. Emily snuffled noisily, but Jo diagnosed teething rather than trauma from the explosion. Pat inadvertently solved that problem and Miss Emily was now the proud, part-time owner of one of his massive fingers. She chewed happily, eyelids drooping.

Mary, pale and tense, clutched the child to her chest. Pat watched, a worried look on his normally genial face. Remorse filled Jo. This was her fault. She'd been so busy appeasing the dead that she hadn't considered the danger to the living. It had been irresponsible of her to let Trisha and the children stay in her flat when she knew there was a maniac on the loose. She shifted in her seat, Mavis's file digging into her side. She pulled Adam closer. She could have lost him, lost them all because she'd wanted to play Miss bloody Marple.

"You want me to hold him for a while, give your arms a rest?" Coop asked.

"No, he's fine." Jo leaned her head against Adam's hair.

"This isn't your fault, Jo," he said, his voice soft.

"Tell that to them." Jo tilted her head towards the others. "They could have been killed — *you* could have been killed — all because I wanted revenge."

"Revenge?"

"You didn't do this just because of Lucy," Trisha said at her side. She kept her voice low, so as not to wake the sleeping children. "You were trying to help, to stop it happening again. We know that."

Did they? Jo looked at the worry lines etched on Trisha's once smooth brow and knew it would be a long time before Trisha — or any of them — would feel comfortable in her presence again.

"Lucy?" Coop asked, confused. "Who's Lucy?"

Jo thought she heard a sigh from Trisha, but before either of them could speak, there was a commotion at the door.

"Jay-sus, Mary, and Saint Joseph, Woods, you got a fecking thing for explosions?" Bill Simmons, larger than life and just as rumpled, glared at Jo from the doorway. Tumilty hovered at his side. A nurse tried to shush Bill, but he brushed her off. "Lucky you weren't all fecking killed." He stomped into the waiting room. "You okay, Meehan?"

"Yes, Boss." Pat disengaged his finger from Emily's mouth and jumped to attention. "We're just waiting to get the all-clear from the doctors."

Bill's eyes darkened as he took in the sleeping children and the adults with their bruised and cut faces, their tiredness clearly palpable. He motioned to the nurse. "I'd like a word with you, outside."

Whatever he said worked, for they were seen and pronounced fit to go home within minutes of the red-faced nurse re-appearing.

"Which would be nice, if we had a home to go home to," Coop said, running his hands through his hair in frustration. "And there's no chance of getting a hotel at this late hour."

"Marian says I'm to bring you all back with me," Bill said. "We've two free rooms, which will do the mothers and the little 'uns." He nodded to Mary and Trisha. "Woods, you can kip in the study."

"I'm staying with Mary," Pat said, moving closer to her, a determined look on his face.

Bill didn't argue. "You can double up with Woods. The study has two recliners. You've slept in far worse places, the pair of you." His gaze rested on Coop, momentarily stumped. "Er..."

"He can stay with me, Boss," Tumilty offered.

Jo eyed him, surprised. Tumilty wasn't known for his altruism. *What is he up to?* Currying favour with the boss? Or maybe he hoped to stick Coop with a bill for his nights' board and lodging? Nothing would surprise her where Tumilty was concerned. A movement caught her eye, gone before her brain processed the information, but the damage was done. Coop had signalled Tumilty, a quick, furtive gesture warning him to take his offer back.

All the breath left Jo's body. It couldn't be. *They know each other!* Stunned, she stared at Coop.

*****

Coop saw the dawning knowledge in Jo's eyes and knew it would do no good to explain — not tonight, anyway. Maybe tomorrow, when they'd all had a night's sleep.

He watched her face close down, the beautiful eyes harden, and he knew that it wasn't going to be that simple.

CHAPTER THIRTY-THREE

"Jo?"

"Go away." Jo didn't want to get up. She burrowed her head deeper into her pillow, but whoever was knocking on her bedroom door was insistent.

"Come on, Jo. Time to get up."

Jo twisted to see what time it was and moaned as every inch of her body screamed in complaint. "Oh wow." She and Trish must have really tied one on last night. How many bottles of wine had they drunk?

"Jo, you hear me?"

The voice on the outside was male and all too familiar. *What is Dave doing in my flat?* Memory returned with all the force of an explosion. *Great choice of words, Jo.* She hauled her aching ass out of bed and pulled on the dressing gown Fran had left for her. How many hours of sleep had she managed? Three? Four? Not much more, she guessed.

She had dug her heels in and refused to stay at Bill's house, which had gone down as well as a fart in a phone box. But her mind had been made up. No way would she endanger Bill or his grandkids, never mind her sister and her family — or Mary and Emily. Not again.

The argument had become heated for a time — not to say, colourful — but Jo had stood her ground. Dave, who had heard the news and sped to the hospital, had saved the day, offering Jo a bed at his house. The clincher was the fact his daughter Jenny was on a sleepover at a friend's house. By that time, Jo was dead on her feet and more than happy to give in.

"Jo, are you awake?" Dave knocked harder on the door. "Can you come downstairs? We need to talk."

Jo stifled another moan as she opened the door. "What time is it?"

"Eleven thirty. Fran's made brunch. How are you feeling?"

Jo knew he was asking about more than her physical well-being, but she didn't feel up to talking about Lucy or Brian. Not yet, maybe not ever. "Like I've just been trampled by a herd of eager shoppers on the first day of the sales." She kept her voice light, upbeat. "It is 'herd', isn't it?"

Dave answered in the same vein. "Dunno. Don't suppose it matters, especially if they're wearing heels."

"Guess not." Jo smelt bacon, the rich salty aroma reminding her she hadn't eaten since the barbecue. Her stomach growled as she entered the kitchen and she smiled at Fran, embarrassed by the noise. "Something smells fantastic, Fran. But you shouldn't have gone to so much trouble."

"You know me, Jo. It's no trouble. Come." Fran took her arm and led her to the table as if she were a decrepit relative. Only then did Jo realise they weren't alone.

The rest of Red Watch sat at the large table, mugs of coffee in front of them, well-scraped plates pushed to one side. The party had started without her. Self-conscious, she pulled the cord of her dressing gown tighter. "A welcome committee, how nice."

No one laughed. Something in their silence, something more than the pity she was expecting, shrivelled her appetite. "What's up, guys?"

"I told you," Dave said, sitting beside her, "we need to talk about last night." He dipped his head in apology. "I told them about the phone call you got the

176

other night, the one that sent you racing to the boss's house."

"Gee, thanks, Dave."

"Don't you think we have a right to know, Jo, or are you the only one allowed inside info?"

This, of course, was from Flanders, but even his vitriol was muted. She looked round the table at the grim faces. "Okay, what's going on?"

It was Geoff who answered. "They found a body in the flats."

Jo pushed her plate away, no longer hungry. A body? Dear Lord. Had Mrs R come home early from her son's house? "Who..." She licked her dry lips. "Who was it? Do you know?"

"Not yet, the body's pretty mangled, but we're guessing it's your killer. Everyone else is accounted for. Bastard has murdered his last kid." Pat's voice was devoid of sympathy.

Thinking of Mary and Emily, Jo realised, recalling his tenderness with them at the hospital the night before, which brought up another question. What had he been doing in Mary's flat so late at night? Interested as she was in the answer, it couldn't hold her attention. The killer — dead? Caught in his own trap? For a moment, a brief glorious moment, Jo felt a surge of hope, then reality stepped in. *No way.* This guy was too good, too professional to be caught that way.

"I'm guessing you received another one of your phone calls last night?" Bill said. "And that's how you got everyone out in time?"

Jo nodded, still trying to consider the ramifications of a body being found in the flats. *Who could it be?*

"Odd."

That got her attention. "What's odd about it?"

"I was speaking to Shaunessy this morning and he swears it was a faulty gas fireplace in your upstairs neighbour's flat. The fecking thing could've come out of the Ark, he said. But if you got a phone call, then it can't be that, can it?"

Jo couldn't tell by his tone whether he believed her over the evidence. His next words dispelled any hope she may have had.

"Mind you, not one of you was drugged, far as I or the hospital can tell, and there's no mention of any fecking roses. That's your guy's MO, isn't it?"

My guy. How nice. The only man in her life was a raving, homicidal manic. *Lucky me.*

Bill waited on her answer.

Jo nodded. He was right, until last night, that had indeed been the killer's MO. So, what changed? Why the adult victim this time? Why no drugging or roses? It didn't make sense.

"Maybe Pat being there threw him off?" Dave suggested. "You're not a regular visitor, are you, Pat?"

Pat blushed. "No. It was a... spur of the moment kinda thing."

Some good-natured ribbing followed, but Jo didn't join in. She tried to recall the killer's phone call for a hint to why he had changed tack. What had he said?

"It's a pity about your brother-in-law, a pervert, no less. And Mary downstairs, her husband is a bastard, in case you didn't know — likes to hurt her. I bet the kid will be next."

Trisha and Mary fitted the pattern, so why no roses, no drugging? And his final salvo: *"Can you guess what I'm about to do, Ms Woods?"* The emphasis on her maiden name hadn't registered last night in her haste to get everyone out, but now it was obvious. The phone call hadn't been about Sinead and Adam or even Emily. It had been about Lucy and her.

He hadn't known! It was a slap in the face to Jo. She'd hated this man with such intensity — had for a long time — and he hadn't known who she was. Now that he did, it was clear he was furious with her and, like a spurned lover, determined to have his revenge. The thought frightened and energised her at the same time. *Bring it on, you bastard. Bring it on!*

"But if it were a faulty fireplace, as Shaunessy suspects," Tumilty said, "then what was the stiff doing there?"

Jo glared at him, remembered the covert exchange between him and Coop last night. What they were up to? However, he'd brought up another good point. How had the killer known about Mrs R's fireplace? Or that her son had been too much of a — what had he called him? A *cheapskate* — to buy her another one?

Jo knew about the dodgy unit because Mrs R had shown it to her, but who else would she show it to? Her mind slipped to Angela Parsons and the firefighter she'd mentioned asking questions after the Forbes fire. Would Mrs R tell another firefighter? But why would she when she had already checked with Jo? No, the killer had found out some other way and if she could find that link, then maybe she would find the killer.

"Could have been a burglar — wrong place, wrong time?" Dave offered.

"Bit of a coincidence, dontcha think? Or else he's the unluckiest burglar ever," Micko chipped in. "Guy decides to rob the place and *bam!* At the exact same moment, it blows up."

"Stranger things have happened." Wart's face was morose.

"Well, speculation's not going to get us anywhere," Bill said, rising from the table. "Let's leave it to the experts, shall we? Now, don't you all have places to go?" He raised an eyebrow.

The table cleared, voices ringing out, thanking Fran for the food. Jo rose with them.

"Where do you think you're going, Woods?" Bill motioned her to sit. "What are the rest of you waiting for, directions?" He glared at the others until they left, even Dave, who didn't appear to find it at all odd to be ordered from his own kitchen. Then the boss spoke again.

"I want you to take a few days off."

"Really, Boss, that's not necessa—"

"It's not a suggestion."

"Oh."

"Neil Peterson on Green Watch offered to fill in. He's on his four off at the moment."

Offered or was coerced? Jo knew it would do no good to argue, not when the boss had that look in his eye, but she tried anyway. "I need to work, Boss. I'll go mad with nothing to do."

"You'll have plenty to do. Have you forgotten you've a new home to find? Never mind new furniture, clothes..."

Jo blushed, uncomfortable beneath his gaze in her borrowed night attire. "I can do that today. Sundays aren't what they used to be."

"Then go see your sister," Bill roared. "Spend some time with her and your niece and nephew, and stop giving me fecking grief. Now, before I go, you had a folder with you last night." He held out his hand. "I'd like to see it. It must have been important 'cause it's the only thing I'm told you took with you."

Jo was temporarily struck dumb. *Who told him about the folder? And why do I think he already knows what it contains?* "That file is personal, sir."

"I'll bet it is, Woods. But I'm gonna have to insist, seeing as it contains highly classified brigade information."

Damn! He knows. No way was Jo handing it over without reading it first. "I'm sorry, Boss, but—"

"Don't you think about 'butting' me, Woods. I want that fecking file and I want it *now!*"

Stalemate.

Jo considered the situation, wondered how far she could push it — and him. "I don't have it with me, Boss." It was the first thing that came to mind. When he opened his mouth to remonstrate, she added quickly, "But I can get it... this evening." That should give her enough time to get to a printer, copy it, and phone Mavis to warn her someone had turned them in.

Bill looked set to argue then thought better of it. He lifted his hat, set it over his slate-grey hair, preparing to leave. "See that you do, Woods. My house — five pm."

Jo knew she'd better produce the file at the appointed time or her days in the brigade would be numbered.

CHAPTER THIRTY-FOUR

If there was one thing Bill Simmons hated, it was being played for a fool. He couldn't fault the information. Jo's shocked expression when he'd asked for the file had told him that the man had known what he was talking about, but he couldn't get past the notion he was being led round by the nose.

And if there's one thing this great hooter of mine doesn't need, it's a fecking great ring through it.

What was he missing? One of his firefighters wanted Jo Woods suspended. Why? What possible benefit would the man gain? Bill flicked through the computer printouts, thrown so blithely at him the night before, and tried to ignore his repugnance of the man. It was tough. Sometimes you *could* judge a book by its cover.

"Feck it." He got up and poured himself a shot of whisky. Even Marian herself wouldn't begrudge him a smattering of the hard stuff today. But on the off chance she did, he downed the drink in one quick gulp. He was about to do another of his least favourite things — ask a favour — and for the second time in as many days. He chanced a look over his shoulder, then back at the bottle, his eyes hungry.

To hell with it. If any situation called for the elixir of life, this was it. He poured himself another generous shot, took it back to the table, and sat down.

Bill hadn't come up the brigade the easy way. He started as a callow youth of nineteen, cutting his teeth in a time when firefighters were called firemen. Back then, they were considered little more than glorified civil servants and treated just as badly. He played a part in changing that — he and a few others who were now "in the know" and also ideally placed to give him the information he needed. None of them traded on it, but that wasn't to say they couldn't.

Someone was pushing him in one direction, towards Jo Woods, and Bill wasn't a man who took kindly to being pushed. He opened his phone, flicked through the address book, and found a name he hadn't thought about in more years than he cared to remember. He paused, finished his drink, and dialled the number.

"Tim?"

"Well, I never, Bill Simmons, you old Irish reprobate, how the fuck are you?"

Bill grinned. Tim Sheppard never changed. How the guy had managed to become chief fire officer was beyond him. He was the least politically correct person Bill knew. Hopefully, that would work in his favour. "I'm grand, Tim, and you?"

There was a guffaw at that, followed by a hawking and spitting noise. "Don't tell me you're calling me on a weekend, and after all these years, just to see how I'm doing, because I won't believe it. What's on your mind?"

Maybe there was a reason he was CFO after all. Bill chose his words with care. "I need to run something by you, mate. You up for that?"

"Run away. Ha, get it? Run away?" There was a chortle down the phone, followed by another hawk and spit.

Bill wasn't in the mood for levity. "I've a guy in my station and I need some information on him." He gave Tim the name.

"Damn." The line went silent. When Tim spoke again, the humour was gone from his voice. "I wish you hadn't asked me about this, Bill."

"But I am." Bill wanted another drink. He was madder than a nest of wasps and wasn't about to be fobbed off. Obviously, Tim was well aware of the man in question. But in what capacity? Was the guy on the up and up, or was something rotten in Denmark, as his oversized snout suspected?

"For feck sake, Tim," he said, when the line remained silent. "If there's something going on at my fecking station, I need to know."

"Details, Bill. I want details. Why are you asking about this man? You tick the right boxes and you'll get the answers you need. If not..."

He had no need to spell it out. Bill didn't know what he'd stepped in, but he was all too familiar with the smell.

CHAPTER THIRTY-FIVE

Coop was going out of his mind.

He'd messed things up with Jo — he knew that — and was at a loss how to put it right or even if he wanted to. To make matters worse, Tumilty buggered off earlier that morning, telling him to stay indoors, and he hadn't seen hide nor hair of him since. As usual, Tumilty hadn't bothered to tell him where he was going or what he was up to.

Frustrated with his enforced inactivity, Coop passed the time arranging new digs. Being this close to Tumilty was getting right up his nose. His first priority, though, was new clothes. He grimaced, looking down at his outfit, courtesy of the much smaller Tumilty. The jeans refused to button at the waist and stopped mid-way up his calf. The borrowed shirt was no better, hovering above his navel, causing a draft every time he moved. He was the skinny, white version of the Incredible Hulk.

He clicked on his shopping cart and added his credit card details. There was a delivery slot free later that day. If the online retailer lived up to their end of the bargain, he'd be able to leave this bloody prison with his dignity intact.

Once done, Coop paced the flat, unable to settle. The minutes hobbled by. One o'clock struck and the hands inched onwards.

Tumilty appeared thirty minutes later. "Hi, honey, I'm home."

"Where the fuck have you been?"

"Why, sweetheart, I didn't realise you cared." Tumilty pushed past Coop, but not before looking him up and down, grinning at his attire. He made his way to the kitchen, opened the fridge, and took out two beers. "You want one, sweetie?"

Coop gritted his teeth and accepted the can.
"What happened?" he asked. "Did you see Jo?"

"Which do you want to know first? What
happened? Or if I saw Jo?"

"What happened, of course!"

"Of course." Tumilty flicked open his can. He
took a drink, Adam's apple bobbing. "Sit," he said,
when he came up for air. He waved Coop towards the
fake pine chairs in the corner. "You're making the
place look untidy." He plonked himself in the chair
nearest the fridge, forcing Coop to walk around him.

Coop did as he was told. Tumilty held the cards,
for now.

Tumilty seemed disappointed. "Simmons called
a meeting at Dave Evan's place, just as we thought
he would, but the bastard chased us out just as it
got interesting." He narrowed his fox-like eyes. "I
didn't hear what was said, but I'd bet a week's wages
Ms Woods is now officially on leave." He smiled his
feral grin. "Result!"

Elation and loathing vied within Coop. The plan
had worked. Jo was safe, out of harm's way. But he
knew how much her job meant to her. She wouldn't
take this lying down. He hid his ambivalence behind
a smile. "So, using Simmons worked?"

"Ach, Simmons is small fry, big enough to eat
Jo Woods for breakfast, but not even close to the top
of the food chain."

It sounded like the station commander hadn't
reacted the way Tumilty had wanted. The thought
gave Coop pleasure. Tumilty needed taking down a
peg or two, and from what he'd seen, Bill Simmons
was the man to do it. He hid his amusement behind
another question. "So why go to all this bother of
involving him then?"

"'Cause it got Woods off our back! Fucking
woman was a menace and," Tumilty made a point of
looking at his watch," right about now, I'm guessing

the old dragon helping her is getting her wings clipped." He sounded satisfied with his day's work.

Coop held his tongue, but he was tempted to tell Tumilty it wasn't just a dragon's wings he should be concerned about. The same with Jo. If he thought putting Jo on leave would stop her, then the guy wasn't half as clever as he imagined himself to be.

His face must have given him away because Tumilty rounded on him. "Hey, I've got the results we needed. I know what I'm doing. Seems to me you're the one sadly lacking in that department."

"What the fuck does that mean?"

"You're the hot-shot computer ace. You tell me."

At Coop's blank stare, Tumilty's smile returned. "You don't know, do you?" He shook his head, grinning. "You *really* don't know."

"Know what?" Coop said irritated. "For fuck's sake, Tumilty, what are you blathering about?"

Tumilty rose from the table without a word and returned with the laptop Coop had been using earlier. "Here." He plugged the machine in. While he waited for it to load, he emptied his beer and went to the fridge for another. "Ah." He opened the can with ceremony and took a drink.

Coop schooled his features, took a swig from his can, and prepared himself. He'd known this moment would come. He had outgrown his usefulness and would be neutralised, as effectively as Jo and the dragon had been. He wondered what form his neutralizing would take. He took another swig, steadied himself, and waited for the axe to fall.

Tumilty, in a reversal of his earlier eagerness, appeared in no hurry to share. He played with the cursor, scrolling up and down the pages, tutting at certain points, drinking at others. He finished the last dregs of his can and stood up.

"There you go. Enjoy. I might wander down to Murdock's, see if any of the lads are there. One of them is bound to know what's happening." He smiled, a cold, mocking smile. "I'd ask you to go with me, but I'm guessing you're gonna find this more interesting. Plus, you could get arrested showing that much flesh in public." With a last cheery wave, he left.

Coop hurried to the computer. Just as he sat down to read what Tumilty was so eager for him to see, he heard a voice from the doorway.

"Oh yeah, forgot to tell you. Seems Jo has been getting phone calls from our *friend*. Naughty boy, isn't he? Tra la."

Still reeling from that little snippet, Coop found the segment Tumilty had highlighted. It was a form, one he knew well. For a moment, he was confused. Why was Tumilty showing him a Fire Brigade Dwelling Fatalities form? He scanned the page.

Incident Number: 58999000
Date: 08.07.2004
Address: 16 Basil Street, Belfast
Details of Stop: major fire— dwelling— detached house—1 female casualty— rescued. 1 male fatality, aged 28. 1 child fatality, aged 6
Type Code: MF37
Age: 28 & 6
Condition: Fatal
Status: F

All normal Fire Brigade bullshit as far as he could tell, the same kind of bureaucratic nonsense he'd dealt with when Julie and the twins had died.

His eyes searched on, found an extra column.

Casualty Details

That was new. In all the reports he'd read, there had been no survivors. He skimmed the particulars.

> Josephine Townsend, (nee Woods), aged 25.

Jo! Coop lurched back, pushing the table from him in his agitation. "No." He shook his head. She would have told him, especially after he'd told her about Julie and the twins. "No way." She would have spoken up, shared. Wouldn't she?

Coop couldn't deny the proof of his own eyes. *Why didn't she tell me?* The answer was immediate, and hurtful. She didn't trust him. She couldn't, if she had hidden something of this magnitude from him.

Jesus! He didn't know her at all. A worse thought struck: *What else is she hiding?*

CHAPTER THIRTY-SIX

"Sorry, Jo. I thought everyone had left." Fran backed out of the kitchen, a faint blush staining her cheeks.

Jo shook off her encounter with Bill, the ultimatum he'd given her, and called Fran back. "It's your kitchen, Fran. Come on in." She rose and began to gather the dirty plates. "The guys are slobs whe—"

"Leave them." Fran entered the kitchen at a run and snatched the dishes from Jo's hands. "You're our guest. Guests don't do dishes."

"Hey, if you don't tell, I won't."

"Dave says visitors should never have to lift a finger."

"Dave's not here and I don't mind helping. In fact, I'd be glad of the distract—"

"No," Fran said, voice firm. "Thanks for the offer, but," she glanced over her shoulder, as if worried the etiquette police were watching, taking notes, "I am the hostess, and I'd prefer to do it myself."

The hostess? Fran sounded like Bree from *Desperate Housewives*. Although, come to think of it, with her well-tailored dresses, perfect make-up, hair, and rigid manners, she could be Bree's doppelganger. Jo hid a grin behind her hand, unwilling to hurt Fran's feelings. She struck Jo as a lonely woman — plenty of acquaintances but not many friends.

Jo was reminded of their first meeting, when Dave had brought her home for dinner. Fran's nervous enquiry about the Forbes's fire and her reluctance to let Dave know she was asking questions had made Jo think theirs wasn't the most open of marriages, something she was familiar with.

She'd felt a kinship with Fran, a desire to know more about her.

"Have you and Dave been married long?" she asked

Fran, happy to have Jo in the role of guest once more, halted her clean-up. "Eight years last month," she said proudly.

"Wow! That's great. So, you had Jenny, what? Two years later?"

"Yes, about that. Jo, I..." Fran rubbed at a non-existent spot on the cooker. "I didn't get a chance to say it yesterday, but I'm really sorry about your daughter. It must have been a terrible time for you."

Damn. So much for putting Fran at ease. Jo wished she were better at this small talk stuff. She tried to smooth things over with a quick, "Thank you," and brought the subject back to Jenny. "She's a lovely child, Fran. You must be proud of her."

"Oh, I am. We are," she corrected herself. "She's our whole world, especially with Dave and I having no other family of our own." Her voice tailed off and her eyes took on a faraway look. "I'd do *anything* for her," she said at last, her voice fierce.

Jo remembered the feeling. The second Lucy took her first breath, her maternal gene had kicked into life, bringing with it the knowledge she would, quite literally, be capable of killing anyone who dared hurt her precious child. "Is something wrong, Fran? Is Jenny sick? In trouble at school? If you need to talk..."

Fran twisted the dishcloth between her fingers and stared at Jo, as if assessing her. She must have passed muster because she gave a quick nod and sat down. "There is something. Maybe you can help."

"I'll do anything I can." Jo wondered what she'd let herself in for.

"It's Dave," Fran said. "He's a good man, but the pressures of work..." She clasped and unclasped her hands. "I understand. I know he doesn't tell me all the details, but I'm his wife. I hold him through the nightmares." She bit her lip.

Jo could relate. "A lot of us have them, Fran. They come with the job." She tried to sound reassuring.

"Yes, but with his past. God! I feel so disloyal saying this."

"Don't." Jo moved forward in her seat, intrigued. "Everyone needs to talk and I promise it won't go any further."

"I know it won't. And you don't know how good that feels." Fran grasped Jo's hand. "Honestly, at times I think I'm going mad, but—"

"That's that sorted." Dave entered the kitchen. "I've arranged with stores to send you some new gear," he told Jo. "They're gonna—" He stopped, gazed at the two women, noting the clasped hands. An odd expression crossed his face. "Am I interrupting something?"

"No, No!" Flustered, Fran stood. "We were... we were—"

"Discussing how Fran does her mushrooms," Jo lied, certain Fran wouldn't want Dave to know they were talking about him. "I must admit, I've never tasted nicer." She tried to catch Fran's eye to let her know they'd talk later, but Fran had her back turned, running water into the sink and washing dishes as if her life depended on it. The moment was gone.

Dave's eyes switched between his wife and Jo, but all he said was, "They're gonna send you the whole kit and caboodle tomorrow — dress, undress, work rig."

"Thanks, Dave. I appreciate it. One less thing to worry about."

"Lots to do, I guess?"

Jo tried not to think about the humongous task ahead. She had to find somewhere to live and replace everything she'd lost in the fire — phone, computer, clothes, toiletries. The list was endless. Yet all that was minor compared to finding a place to copy Mavis's file. Mourne Lough, like most small towns, closed down on Sundays. Plus, she had the meeting with the boss later. *Joy.* And in between doing all this, she had to figure out how to get Trisha and her kids out of harm's way — no mean feat, considering Trisha was almost as stubborn as she was.

Her face must have said it all, for Dave settled in the chair Fran had vacated. "What can I do?" He'd obviously given the matter a great deal of thought because he said, "I've arranged with Pat to take your car to a guy he knows. He'll replace the windows and give it a quick once-over. Should be back with you this evening, with any luck."

Jo had forgotten about her car. The blast would have shattered every piece of glass within a fifty-to-eighty-metre radius, which meant her neighbours were suffering, too; broken windowpanes, cracked window screens, maybe a destroyed car or two if the debris had been thrown far enough. They were the lucky ones, though. They still had homes to go to.

"Thanks, Dave. You're a mate."

"No problem. And it goes without saying that you can stay here as long as you need."

Jo appreciated the offer, but last night was a one-off. Jenny would be home from her sleepover soon and she had no intention of putting another child in danger.

Dave shifted in his chair and dropped his voice so Fran wouldn't overhear. "Tell me to mind my own beeswax, Jo, but is something going on between you and Tumilty? I couldn't help notice some friction between you earlier."

Jo wondered what Fran thought of their tête-à-tête, but she seemed oblivious, busy with her clean-up. She hesitated for a moment, but she needed advice, and a man's perspective wouldn't go amiss. She told Dave about her fledgling relationship with Coop, the trust they'd built when Coop had told her about his family. It was a relief to share.

Dave nodded sympathetically, his green eyes gentle, but when she recounted the episode in the hospital the night before, his gaze sharpened. "They know each other?"

"Looks like." Jo tried to appear nonchalant.

Dave put an arm around her shoulder. "Ah, Jo, men can be bastards. I should know. I'm one of them." He patted her back in an awkward, avuncular manner. "I'd say, trust your instincts. If this guy lied about knowing Tumilty, then what else is he lying about?"

It was what Jo feared. "Do you think he's involved in all this?" Her eyes begged him to say no, but Dave wasn't that kind of friend.

"Could be. From what you've told me, he appeared around the same time the fires started. Although," he scratched the stubble on his chin, "the guys think the body they've found is the killer. If they believe there is a killer at all, that is."

Trust Dave to give it to her straight. "Oh, there's a killer all right, Dave. Don't doubt it for a minute."

"Coffee, anyone?"

Jo didn't miss the annoyed look Dave threw Fran, and to cover it, she replied with more passion than she felt. "I'd *love* one, Fran, thanks." She knew better than to offer to help. She sat where she was and mulled over what Dave had said. All along she figured the killer was working alone. *What if he isn't? What if he has a partner?*

The killer might have been caught in his own trap, but was there a second killer out there? Watching, waiting for another chance to strike?

CHAPTER THIRTY-SEVEN

"You've no choice, Mary. You have to go to the police now." Pat paced the Simmons' kitchen

"Why?"

For such a tiny thing, she sure could be stubborn. "Haven't you heard a word I've said? They found a body and they think it's the guy who set fire to the flats. Thomas threatened you." He saw her flinch. "I'm sorry, Mary, but it's true, and it's gotta be said. What if Thomas went too far this time?"

Mary bent to check Emily, but she was sleeping peacefully. "He'd never go that far. Thomas would never hurt—"

"You? Emily? Come on, Mary. He's already hurt you and he's told you Emily is next." Pat's words were harsh, but his voice was gentle. "You have to consider it. Look at how many people could have been hurt, killed."

"I know. Don't you think I know?" Mary was struggling to hold back the tears. "Your friend, Jo in the upstairs flat... Her sister was there with her children. Oh, God!" She buried her face in her hands and wept.

Pat hated to see her upset, but needed her to understand. He could go to the police, but it would carry more weight coming from her, and it was something she had to do on her own — the first step to freeing herself from Thomas.

"It's the only way, Mary, can't you see that? You have to end it."

"I know." Mary knuckled the tears away and ran a hand across her nose, sniffed. Her elfin face was tense, her dark eyes nervous but resolute. She took his hand, held tight. "Will you come with me?"

Pat felt like the strongest man on Earth. "'Course I will." He'd phone Jake, get him to deliver Jo's car to Dave's house. Jo would understand.

"And when we're done," he said, "I want you and Emily to come home with me. No strings," he said when her eyes flared and she looked ready to bolt. "I've a spare room, big enough for the two of you and a garden Emily can play in. Not as big as this," he apologised, "but I don't think she'll complain." Mary remained silent.

"Please, Mary. We can take it one day at a time."

Mary produced a shy smile, and the pressure on his hand increased. "Okay. One day at a time."

Pat thought his heart would burst.

CHAPTER THIRTY-EIGHT

Jo ran her hands over the silk skirt of the dress she had borrowed from Fran and mourned the loss of her jeans. The last time she'd worn a dress, she had been standing in front of a priest, Brian at her side, vowing to be faithful to her forever. No wonder she was uncomfortable.

Fran not owning a pair of jeans hadn't come as any great surprise, but to have no trousers at all! Jo was still reeling from shock. She slipped the matching high heels off and massaged her aching toes. She was bare legged, having baulked at nylons. She was desperate, but not *that* desperate.

"Never could unerstan' why women wear those things." The taxi driver nodded to Jo's abandoned heels. "How 'n the hell do you walk in 'em?"

"With a lot of difficulty," Jo grumbled.

"You women and your fashion." A rueful headshake, followed a self-satisfied smirk. "Us men don't 'precciate it near enough."

Her stony look must have spoken volumes because he swallowed whatever he was about to say and turned on the radio. Soothing music filled the air and his hands beat a steady tattoo on the steering wheel.

As the car ate up the miles, Jo opened Mavis's file and began to read. She had plenty of time to familiarize herself with its contents.

Lisburn was a lot farther than she'd intended to travel given her time constraint but she had no choice. She was penniless, at least until the banks opened tomorrow. She'd lost her purse, chequebook, and credit card in the fire and the only place to lay her hands on cash was the last place she wanted to go.

Dave loaned her the money for the taxi and would have given her more, but she had refused.

"This will be fine."

"You'll need all sorts of... stuff." He blushed, unwilling to get into the intricacies of a woman's wardrobe. "The guys have started a collection. I can get you that to tide you over if it's just my money you don't want?"

Jo was touched. "Thanks, Dave. Seriously, thanks. But it's okay, I can get some money to keep me going."

She hoped her confidence wasn't misplaced.

*****

I admitted to a certain satisfaction as I watched the chaos unfold after my last foray. It was exhilarating being witness to such extreme, delicious emotions — the tears, the abject terror on the faces of those I'd displaced. Not very worthy of me, I supposed, but then again, most people wouldn't consider my task either worthy or delicious.

The revelation no longer bothered me. I had it within me to pity those less fortunate. I walked a righteous path — a divine mission sent from God on high, no less. He observed everything I did, observed and approved. Of that, I had no doubt.

"And would he approve of the joy you're taking from this little interlude?"

Unease fluttered and immediately I sobered. The voice was right. What was I thinking? Joy was not a word to be used in conjunction with this holy undertaking. I was but a vessel of His will.

"Plus, survivors mean failure and, more importantly, possible discovery."

I hadn't thought of that. A wave of fear coursed through me. Was that to be my punishment for becoming cocky?

I fell to my knees. "Forgive me, Lord. I am here but to serve." I bowed my head. Usually prayer relaxed me, but not today. My mind slipped back in time to my siblings — Marge, Serena, and baby Amy. My brain filled with memories of them, except everything was different, wrong. I was confused. They weren't thanking me for saving them. They were cursing me, screaming as flames licked their bodies, their precious faces tortured masks of agony.

A hellish nightmare come to life. I couldn't bear it. I pounded my fists against my forehead, knuckles making a hollow sound against the bone of my brow. The pain steadied me. I took a deep breath. Their screaming faces faded, to be replaced by the image of the last time I'd seen them, still and content on their beds, eyes closed, hands crossed over their chests, their beloved faces wiped clear of all pain and hurt.

This was how I liked to remember them. My hands relaxed, slid over my face in relief. All was once again as it should be. I took a deep breath. I had time to remedy my mistake. Everyone — or at least the few who believed in my existence — thought I'd died in the fire. I had a few days to cement my plans and finish my mission before I moved on, to once again fulfil His holy purpose somewhere else.

"That'a boy. Focus your mind. Decide what you have to do and follow through."

The voice's calming tone soothed me. My choices were clear. Emily would have to go, as would her mother, Mary. Marriage, after all, was for life. The delicious Trisha and her brats were also on my list, for the same reason. But at the top of my list was Jo Woods, who had escaped me not once, but twice. She was probably at the fire station right now, too much of a goody-two-shoes to put anyone else at risk.

"Wouldn't it be ironic if the fire station went up in flames?"

I smiled. Wouldn't it just. But first, I had another, more taxing problem.

Jo wasn't alone in her pursuit. Someone else was trying to ferret out my secrets, a complication I could do without. I'd no time to verify this assumption or, if truth were told, any inclination to do so, not when my time here was so short. I knew what I knew and they would be stopped. Little or no finesse would suffice.

Once again, I cursed my lack of control with the amateur. He would have made the perfect scapegoat. But I wasn't to be deterred. I had a day — two at the most — to finalise my plans. Plenty of time. After all, I was no lily-livered virgin. This wasn't my first time. And there was always the chance I'd come across another scapegoat, which would tie things up nice and neatly, wouldn't it?

CHAPTER THIRTY-NINE

Bill Simmons watched Pat and his new girl, Mary, walk down his front path, pushing the pram in front of them. They looked happy, normal, like any family out for an afternoon stroll, except they weren't. His hand tightened on the curtains.

"Ach, Bill, You can't be thinking Pat has anything to do with this, can you?" Marian laid a hand on his shoulder, her eyes following his gaze.

"Jay-sus, woman, there's no secrets where you're concerned, is there?"

"I would hope not." She gave him a mischievous smile, pulling him away from the window. "There has to be some benefit to being married."

"If it's benefits you're after, I can think of a few." Bill wriggled his eyebrows.

"Away wit ya." Marian slapped his generous behind and tried not to smile. "You're a wicked man."

"Aye, I am that." Bill followed her from the room, but his heart wasn't in their banter.

"You're really worried, aren't you?" Marian said, as they entered the kitchen. She switched on the kettle and took down two cups. She added coffee and, to Bill's delight, a hefty tot of forbidden whisky.

"I am." He didn't elaborate. There was no need. As she'd said, there were no secrets between them. "Much as I don't want to believe it, Woods may be right." He rested his elbows on the kitchen table. "There's a killer out there and there's every fecking chance it might be one of my firemen."

"Firefighters," Marian corrected, handing him his coffee.

"Whatever." Bill waved a hand, sniffed the brew. Marian hadn't stinted herself. He raised the cup. *God's own nectar.* He licked his lips. The idea of any dedicated firefighter taking a life instead of saving it abhorred him. It was incomprehensible.

He took another sip, savoured the warmth and the fiery thrill it left in his belly.

"So, what are you gonna do about it?" Marian asked, sitting beside him.

Bill knew going through brigade channels would take too long. He'd do it, of course, the second Jo gave him the file and he had something concrete to run with. Until then, he needed a quicker route. He savoured another mouthful of whisky.

"Third time's the charm, Marian." At her uncomprehending look he laughed. "Let's just say, I may need another nip before I'm done."

"Bob?"

Bill nodded. Robert "Bob" Anderson, Coroner for the Mourne area, was the next logical step to get answers. He held out his glass, looked hopeful.

Marian made a show of pouring him a small tot before firmly capping the bottle. "'Tis all you can do." She patted his hand and stood. "I need to see to our guests, I'll be upstairs if you need me." She dropped a kiss on his head.

After Marian left — taking the bottle with her, Bill noted — he took his time finishing his coffee.

Then, with a weary hand, he reached for the phone.

Normally he'd have no qualms calling Bob. They were old friends, had discussed cases before, many times. But after his disastrous call to Tim, Bill was wary. Who else was in the loop, the one he was so obviously out of? He respected Bob, hated to think he might put their friendship at risk by pressing him on the matter. Yet he didn't have a choice. He wished Marian hadn't taken the bottle with her.

He dialled the number.

"Anderson abode. We are reluctant to come to the phone — better things to do, don't you know. If you must, leave a message after the beep."

Before Bill could decide whether he was disappointed or not, he heard the phone lift.

"Hello?"

"Bob?"

"Simmons? They paying you overtime now? Damn it, man, you'll give the rest of us a bad name. What do you need?"

Bill laughed with relief. Whatever was going on, it obviously hadn't reached Bob's ears. "A favour, Bob, what else?"

"Bar tab on the nineteenth then?"

Bill groaned. The nineteenth was the bar at their local golf club and the tab could run from scary to downright terrifying, depending how badly you played. "I'll buy you a drink for every eagle you make. How's that?"

"Sounds fair. So, what do you want this time?"

Bill told him. He heard Bob flick through some papers. "DB — pulled out of a flat fire this morning?"

Dead Body. That's what they all came down to in the end, a hunk of meat. "That's the one."

"It's scheduled for first thing tomorrow. You can't wait?"

"No, I—"

"Save it for the nineteenth. You need this done? It's done."

Bill let out a sigh of relief, one he didn't know he was holding. "Thanks, Bob. I owe you one."

"Oh, you owe me more than one, as I will prove on Wednesday."

Bill set the phone back in its cradle and reached beneath the table to his secret stash. He'd have answers in a few hours. Not all, he was sure, but enough to put him ahead of the game, he hoped.

He refilled his glass, drank it in one go, then went to find Marian to fill her in.

CHAPTER FORTY

Jo reluctantly slipped on the high heels as the taxi pulled to a stop.

"You wan' me to wait?"

"Please." The man might be a chauvinistic bore, his entire repertoire consisting of, "I tole the little woman this," and "Me and the lads did that," but he was a familiar face and her way home if things went pear-shaped.

Jo checked her watch: 2:10. She didn't have much time, not if she wanted back in time for her meeting with the boss. She eyed the pristine front path, the matching immaculate house and garden and took a deep breath. *Here goes nothing.*

"Josephine?" Mavis Tidy, a puzzled look on her face, opened the door to her knock. "Is this about sending Patricia to the barbecue? Because if it is—"

"No, no, nothing to do with that. In fact, I owe you one, much as I hate to admit it."

"Owe me one? What a quaint... expression." Mavis fixed her glasses, noticed Jo's attire. "Oh, my goodness."

"Betcha never thought you'd see me in a skirt."

Mavis sniffed and ushered her in. "At least you look like a lady now."

Jo curbed the impulse to stick out her tongue. "I never realised a *lady* was defined by what she wore, rather than her actions."

"Don't be facetious, Josephine." Mavis stalked ahead, not looking back. "Can I offer you a beverage, tea, coffee?"

"Nothing, thank you." Jo was eager to get on. "I have to warn you—"

"That the CFO knows about your investigation. Oh, excuse me, *our* investigation. Yes, we had a conversation first thing this morning."

Jo's shoulders slumped. "I'm sorry I dragged you into this, Mavis." She had her reasons for doing it, good reasons, and if she lost her job, well, that was a price she was willing to pay, but the brigade was Mavis's life.

"Dragged me?" Mavis bristled. "I'll have you know no one has dragged me anywhere, *ever*. And I told the CFO that. You may be a hoyden, and your dress code, barring today, leaves a lot to be desired, but you are not and never have been a malingerer. Your concerns, much as I hate to admit it, are well founded and, I have to say, with my help, well substantiated."

Jo was amazed. "You told the CFO that?"

"I did." Mavis patted her bun. "And why not? It is the truth."

"Oh, to have been a fly on the wall. Way to go, Mavis." Jo hugged her, ignoring her protestation of displeasure and the muttered "forward actions of girls today." Mavis might act a tartar but she couldn't fool Jo. Her heart was a soft toffee centre.

"The thing is," Jo said, sitting down, "someone knows what we're doing. It's obvious they're watching us. They know our every move." It disturbed her more than she let on. Bad enough the killer had his sights on her, now another unknown was added to the mix. "They know about the help you've given me, the records we've pulled. They've even got to my station commander." Jo told Mavis about Bill Simmons' demands for the file. "We've a mole somewhere."

"Maybe it's time to stop, Josephine?"

"What?" Jo couldn't believe her ears. *How Could Mavis suggest I give up now?* Now, when things were finally starting to move? "We can't give up, Mavis. We're getting close. I can feel it."

"That's the problem. Maybe you're getting too close."

"Ah, you heard about the explosion. Good news travels fast."

Mavis nodded, face basilisk-like.

Jo's eyes narrowed. "You know what's going on, don't you?" When Mavis didn't deny it, Jo was gutted, betrayed. First Coop, now Mavis.

"You've done your bit, Josephine. Those who need to know have been alerted. They will handle it. It's time to stop before something terrible happens."

"Something terrible has already happened, Mavis, or hadn't you noticed?" But there was no bite to Jo's voice. Maybe it was meeting Trisha again, realising anew what she was doing affected the people who cared about her. And Mavis did care, Jo knew. It was obvious in the lack of response, the biting, acerbic wit she knew so well momentarily silenced.

"Let me tell you this," Mavis said before Jo could speak. "And this is the last thing you'll get from me. Jim Tumilty is not who you think he is."

"I already know that."

"No!" Mavis looked angry. "He's *not* what you think he is."

Jo knew Mavis was giving her a last gift and she tried to read behind the words. What did they mean? Tumilty was *not* the killer? Or Tumilty was *not* the person he pretended to be? The latter she believed, the former? The jury was still out on that one.

"I've read the file, Mavis, seen the whereabouts of all the men at the time of the fires. Tumilty's work history matches the timeline exactly. And it can't be a coincidence that the Forbes fire occurred weeks after he arrived in Mourne Lough. Is that what you mean?"

"I have told you all I can. The rest — if you are determined to follow this path — you will have to find out yourself." Mavis's mouth set in a stubborn line. "Now, I'm sure warning me wasn't your only reason for this visit?"

Jo knew to push her further would spell the end of their friendship, something she was no longer willing to do.

"It's not. Although, whether you believe me or not, it was my main concern."

Mavis inclined her head, eyes softening for a moment. It gave Jo the confidence to say what she had to next. "I need to know if you have the stuff I gave you?"

Mavis went to the huge sideboard and opened one of the drawers. "I prepared it after Tim phoned. I figured you might need it."

"Thanks." Jo took the file, steeled herself and opened it.

It was as she'd left it — death certificates, insurance payment notification, bank statements. Her heart stalled. In every form, on every page, she saw their names — Brian Oliver Hamilton, twenty-eight. Lucy Alice Hamilton, six — like they were still alive, still in this world, just not with her.

Seven years. *When will the pain end?*

She flipped to the end. Bank card and pin number and an unused chequebook and cheque card.

"Josephine." Mavis's voice lacked its usual brashness. "From what I'm told, you've made a new life for yourself in Mourne Lough, a good life with people who care for you. Don't let it slip away." She stood beside Jo, one hand touching her shoulder. "It's time for *you* to live."

"I know." Jo didn't look up. She closed the file, careful, deliberate. "And I will, the second this is done."

Mavis said no more. Head bowed, she moved away. "Will you at least consider buying a few skirts while you're shopping?"

Jo snorted, smiling at the diminutive woman. "Not even for you, Mavis. Not even for you."

And, with a last, loving glance, she left.

CHAPTER FORTY-ONE

Dressed in jeans and trainers, an exhausted but more relaxed Jo arrived back in Mourne Lough. The driver gathered her bags from the boot, handed them to her. "Thank you," Jo said. She paid him, adding a generous tip.

"No. *Thank you*." The driver winked at her.

Jo had the essentials necessary to keep her going for the next few days — a mobile she had yet to fill with numbers, clothes she could breathe in, and best of all, a solution to the Trisha problem. Her good mood increased when she saw her Fiat in Dave's driveway. *Way to go, Pat.*

Dave appeared, holding her car keys aloft. "Pat's friend dropped it off half an hour ago." He took her bags. "He did a good job. Don't you think?" Jo agreed. The car looked unscathed.

"Oh, and the boss called, sounded a bit miffed that you weren't here."

Jo looked at her watch: 5:05 pm. *Damn. I'm late.* "Can you take those in for me, Dave?" She nodded to the bags.

"Glad to." But Dave was talking to empty air. Jo had snagged the keys from his hand and was in her car, reversing down the drive.

*****

"You're late." Bill met her at the front door.

"Sorry, Boss, I had to—"

"Save the excuses. Do you have the file?"

Jo reached into her large shoulder bag. "Right here."

Bill snapped the file from her hand. "'Bout fecking time."

"Now, Bill, 'tis that any way to treat a guest?" Marian appeared behind him, smiling at Jo. "Lovely to see you again, Jo." She took her arm. "Come in and I'll make us all a nice cuppa."

Jo had no chance to demur. Behind her, she heard the boss grumble that "fecking guests were just another name for people you hadn't invited."

"Pay him no mind," Marian said, "He's an ole grump. Sit yourself down, Jo. Would you like tea or coffee?"

"Coffee, thanks."

"Coffee it is." Marian put on the kettle. "Bill, you want coffee?"

"Huh?" Bill entered the kitchen engrossed in the file.

"*Coffee!*" She shook the jar at him.

"Whatever." He lit a cigarette and continued reading.

Marian raised her eyes. "Men!"

Jo grinned. The Simmons appeared to have a good marriage, solid. It would have to be to take on three grandkids so late in life. From what she'd heard, their son Brendan worked away from home, which meant they were the main caregivers. That reminded her. "Thanks for putting my sister and her children up last night, Mrs Simmons."

"Ach, 'twas no problem. Glad to help and I've tole ya, it's Marian. Mrs Simmons is my mother-in-law. Nasty old bat," she said in an aside.

Jo burst out laughing. She couldn't help herself. Marian joined in.

"What's the joke?" Bill asked, not looking up.

"Nothing, dear." Marian winked at Jo. "Speaking of your sister... She's taken the kids to the park — our Sara and the twins, too. What a treasure. I got more done in this last hour than I have all day." She handed Jo her coffee. "I must warn you, though. Your sister and the little ones... They're a mite upset after talking to the police. The kids set their mum off. Till then, she was fine." Her Irish brogue softened. "Good thing that nice Mr Tumilty was here. He was grand with them, jus' grand. Had them smiling again in no time."

Jo felt foolish. She had forgotten the police would want to interview them, but obviously Tumilty hadn't. Bloody man never missed a trick. She ground her teeth. *What is he doing sniffing round my sister? And, more importantly, what is Trisha doing letting him?*

Marian misinterpreted her look. "Don't worry. They were fine when they left, looking forward to a day out. Now, I'm guessing you two want a moment alone?"

Want wouldn't have been the word Jo would have used, but the boss, more aware of their conversation than she realised, said, "That would be great, Marian."

To Jo's surprise, Marian bent to hug her as passed. "Don't worry, love," she said in her ear. "His bark's worse than his bite." With a last wink, she left, and the room lost its warmth.

"I'm guessing you no longer consider me a mass murderer?"

"Huh?" The abrupt change of topic left Jo bewildered. "Mass... Oh." She blushed. "The file?"

"Yeah, the feckin' file," Bill said dryly. He held up his work record, each year, each station, and location at the time of the suspect fires outlined in red.

"I can explain, Boss."

"What? That you believe your killer is a firema... fighter?" he corrected, lighting another cigarette from the stub of the first. "Or that you thought I was? Go on. I'd fecking *love* to hear your explanation."

With nothing else for it, Jo started at the beginning. Not with Brian and Lucy, who were only her beginning, but with the Thompson fire and the pattern she'd found when she'd delved deeper. "It was something you said, Boss," she threw his words back at him, "about it taking a mind greater than ours combined to fool not only us, but the SOCO guys, and a couple of coroners. It got me thinking."

Bill growled into his coffee and eyed the cupboard holding the whisky.

"You were right."

"'Least I'm good for something," he said, giving into temptation. He went to the cupboard. "You want some?" He held out the bottle.

Jo shook her head. "Only a firefighter could get away with this for so long. Don't you see? To fool Shaunessy and others like him, he has to have some kind of training."

"Mebbe." Bill poured a liberal amount of whisky into his glass.

Jo was beginning to understand this taciturn man. He hadn't dismissed her theory outright, which meant he was considering it. She left it for a moment and tried another tack. "The hoax call to your house."

Bills eyes grew stormy. "Yeah?"

"Didn't you wonder how I knew your grandkids were here? How I knew this was your address?"

"One of the guys could have told you."

"Your address, yes, but the fact your grandkids were staying with you? How many people knew that?"

Bill admitted there weren't many. "Brendan and the children only arrived a day or two before your hoax call, not enough time for the Mourne Lough gossip machine to spring into action. Okay, I'll give you the phone call, but," he sucked on his cigarette, "it could have been one of the guys yanking your chain. They like to feck with the newbies."

"An all-out fire call to your house, scaring your wife and grandkids?" Jo shook her head. "No way any of them would do that."

"Except the one who's the killer, of course. That is, if your theory's correct."

Jo's frustration grew. Every time she thought she was getting through to him, he turned the tables on her. The doorbell chimed. Trisha and the kids were back. She heard Marian greet them, the sound of laughing, chattering children in the hallway, then the sound of another, less welcome voice. *Tumilty.* A sense of urgency overtook her.

"If that file doesn't convince you, Boss, then I give up." She stood. "But believe this. When they get round to autopsying that DB from the flats, I'm betting they'll find the fire didn't kill him. When that happens, call me."

Bill's mouth opened to speak, but Jo didn't wait. She hurried from the kitchen, desperate to extricate her sister from the clutches of a man she feared could be a cold-hearted killer.

CHAPTER FORTY-TWO

"It's time for you to leave," Jo said to Trisha.

They were sitting on a low wall overlooking the beach, watching Sinead and Adam play in the sand below. Evening was drawing in, but it was still warm, the sun nestling against the mountain. "And I don't mean home. You need to go away, far way."

"Gee, thanks."

"I don't mean it that way. I was thinking a holiday. I—"

"Sinead! Adam!" Trisha called to the children, edging close to the water's edge. "That's far enough."

"They're fine, Trisha. Relax. Now, about this holi—"

"Don't you *dare* tell me to relax." Trisha's eyes blazed. "I've every right to be upset. My kids were almost blown up last night, and this morning? This morning they spent two hours talking to a bunch of policemen. Policemen, for Christ's sake. You know what that could do to them? Do you? Jesus! As if they haven't been through enough." At the reminder, her voice lost its fire and she started to cry, covering her face with her hands.

Jo wished she'd kept shouting. Shouting she could deal with. "I'm sorry you and the kids got caught up in this, Trisha. I wish—" She stopped. What could she say? That she wished Trisha hadn't come, that they hadn't made up? She couldn't. She had been without her big sister too long to ever wish that. Instead, she reached for Trisha's hand. "You've been through so much this year. A holiday would be good for you — for all of you."

"And I suppose you have a destination in mind?"

Jo relaxed. Sarcasm she could handle. "Yeah, I have as a matter of fact — Disney World in Florida."

"Florida!" Trisha almost fell off the wall in shock. "Are you mad? Do you know how much a trip like that costs?"

Jo fished in her pocket and pulled out an envelope. "£2,500, give or take a few quid. And that's with the kids going free. Here."

Stunned, Trisha took the envelope, opened it. "All-inclusive? Jesus, Jo, how on earth did you—?"

Jo tried not to think how long it had taken her to find an Internet café, never mind the mind-numbing hour scrolling through pages and pages of "deals" before she found one to suit. "I finally took your advice and used some of the insurance money.

Hey," she said when Trisha teared up again, "if this isn't a rainy day, then I don't know what is."

"Ah, Jo, I meant for you, for *your* rainy day. I can't take these." Trisha tried to hand the tickets back.

"Yes, you can." Jo folded her arms, a mutinous look on her face. "You and the kids deserve spoiling. And I want you as far as possible from all this." *And from Jim bloody Tumilty.* "Please," she said when Trisha looked set to argue, "let me do this. Anyway, the tickets are in your name, so if you don't take them, I may as well have flushed the money down the toilet."

"But the date on these... It's for tonight. We can't—"

"'Course you can. It's," Jo checked her watch, "not quite six now. That gives you just over five hours. I've a taxi ordered to take you to the boss's house for your things. An hour to Belfast gets you there by seven fifteen — thirty, at the latest — traffic's light this time of evening. The driver will wait while you pack. He doesn't mind how long. Your

house is five minutes from the airport. Trust me;
you'll make it with time to spare. "

"You've thought of everything." Trisha wiped her
nose, sniffed. "I don't know what to say, Jo."

"Yes, would be a good start."

"Then yes." Trisha threw her arms around Jo.
"Thank you. Thank you." She pulled back, joy fading.
"What about you? I don't want to leave you here
alone, especially since this guy seems fixated on
you."

"I'll be fine."

"Why don't you come with us? Please, Jo. I
couldn't bear it if anything happened to you."

"Much as I'd love to, Trisha, I can't — too much
to do," Jo said, keeping her voice light. "Bloody hell,
I've a new home to find, not to mention furniture and
all those knick-knacky things that go with it. Plus,
I've a job to get back to. I can't let the guys down."
She looked at her watch. "And your taxi will be here
any moment."

"You? Choosing knick-knacks?" Trisha snorted,
then grew sombre. "You're not going to rest until this
killer is either behind bars or dead, are you?"

Jo shrugged, not answering.

Trisha nodded. "Just as I thought. I worry that
the latter option is the only one that will bring you
any peace."

CHAPTER FORTY-THREE

"Are you psychic, Simmons?"

Bill, absorbed in the file in front of him, looked at the receiver, puzzled. For a moment, he didn't know who was on the other end. His brain finally caught up. "Bob?"

Robert Anderson, coroner for the Mourne area, said, "You're damn right. Is this your way of getting out of buying me a drink?"

"Now, Bob, would I do that?"

"Darn tooting."

Bill was in no mood to banter. "You gonna tell me what you found or are we gonna fecking dance around it all night?"

"Hey, I've seen you dance. Remember?" The voice sobered. "Okay, to business. The DB you asked me to check out? Well, guess what?"

"The fire didn't kill him."

"You got it in one."

"Then what did?"

"Twenty-two slashes, mostly to the abdomen, with a six-inch knife with a distinct serrated edge. Poor bugger was disembowelled. Nasty business. Oh, and he was also missing the fingers on his right hand. Happened close to time of death."

"You sure, Bob?"

"Naw, over thirty years as a coroner and I prefer to guess. More fun that way."

"Feck." Bill lit a cigarette. Woods was right all along. *Is she also correct about the killer being one of my men?*

"Charming. I do you a favour and all I get for my trouble is curses."

"Sorry, Bob. I wasn't cursing you."

"Then God help the person you were." Bob chuckled. "Glad I'm not on the receiving end. So, did I help?"

"More than you know, Bob," Bill said. "More than you'll ever fecking know."

CHAPTER FORTY-FOUR

Jo sat on the shore wall and watched Trisha's taxi move out of sight, Sinead and Adam waving from the back seat. They were safe, so why did she feel like crying? Annoyed, she pulled a newspaper from her pocket. If she didn't want to bed down in the station tonight, she needed to find somewhere to live.

She turned to the *Flats for Rent* section and scoured the rumpled pages. Nothing jumped out at her. They all looked the same, bland and impersonal. "Jeeze, girl, it's a flat," she told herself, "somewhere to rest your head. Pick one, any one." Since Lucy and Brian had died, there was no *home*, just spaces she occupied when she wasn't working. *So why am I stressing this?*

Mavis's words reverberated in her mind. *"You've made a new life for yourself in Mourne Lough, a good life with people who care for you. Don't let that slip away."* Jo stared out to sea, blind to the view. If only it were that simple. What Mavis, and Trisha, and everyone else failed to understand was that in order to have a new life, she had to lay the old one to rest.

"Firefighter Woods? Jo?"

Pulled from her reverie, Jo turned and saw Angela Parsons, Emma Forbes's next door neighbour, standing behind her. Blonde hair tied back in a neat knot, brown eyes nervous, she held tight to the arm of the man next to her.

"Hi, this is my husband, Mike. I don't know if you remember me or not?"

"Of course, I do." Jo folded the newspaper and held out a hand, first to Angela, then to her husband. "It's nice to meet you again. And you, Mike."

"Likewise," Mike Parsons said. He had a genial smile, which put Jo immediately at ease. A tall, muscular man he towered over his dainty wife.

"I'm sorry I didn't come over to you at the funeral," Jo said, "but—"

Angela waved off her apology. "You were busy, I understand. It was nice you were there... that so many came." Her voice faltered.

Her husband came to her rescue. "I hope you don't mind, Jo, but Marian Simmons told us about your... troubles, and thought we might be able to help — with accommodation, that is."

Troubles? What a quaint way to put it. This was no chance meeting. Marian had told the Parsons where to find her. Jo didn't know whether to be furious or grateful. "That's kind of you, Mike, but I have it sorted." Jo gestured to the paper. "Lots of flats available to rent. I shouldn't have a problem finding one to suit."

"You just... You don't strike me as a 'flat' kind of person, Jo," Angela Parsons' said. "Forgive me if I'm wrong but..." She looked at her husband for help.

"What my wife means to say, in her own, unique way, is that we have a property, fully furnished, you could move into right away. At a nominal rent," he added.

"It was my mother's," Angela said in a rush. "She died last year and I couldn't bear to sell it. I think you'll love it. Won't you at least come and take a look?"

Jo hadn't the heart to tell them she didn't want a house — and an old woman's house to boot. It sounded high-maintenance and she was a low-maintenance kinda girl. Then she looked at her paper with its bland, faceless ads and thought *what the hell? No harm going to look, is there?*

*****

Jo fell in love with the house the second she saw it. A once-single-story cottage, it had been added to over the years by someone with an unerring eye for detail. The original, not quite square windows were carried through to the later, upper addition. Even the brickwork was an exact match — the stone rough and seemingly hewn from the same quarry.

The front door was pillar-box red with two thick, black hinges, and there was a blast of heat when Angela pushed it open.

"She has the heat on twice a day," Mike Parsons said, curling an arm around his wife's waist. "She's here, cleaning it, every morning."

Angela made a moue with her lips. "I know it's silly, but I hate to think of it becoming dirty or cold. Mum was such a stickler." Her brown eyes were full of memories. "It was a happy house. I could never visualise anyone else living here, until now," she said, shyly.

Jo was flattered and could understand what Angela meant. Entering the hallway, she felt a welcoming presence, as if the ghosts of every past owner were bidding her enter. A strange sensation, ridiculous, and yet she felt immediately at home.

"I love it," she said. "It's perfect."

"You haven't seen it yet," Mike Parsons argued.

"I knew you would." Angela edged past Mike, a delighted look on her face. "I just knew you would."

And she did. Jo loved every nook and cranny, so much so she agreed to rent it on the spot, only then remembering she didn't have any money. Jo disregarded Brian and Lucy's life insurance pay-out. It was okay using those funds for Trisha and her children, but Jo still wanted no part of it.

Angela had waved off her apologies. "Bill Simmons has vouched for you. That's all the security we need. Pay us when you get things sorted at the bank."

CHAPTER FORTY-FIVE

Jo hurried back to Dave's to collect her stuff. She didn't have much. Thirty-two years old and all her worldly belongings fit into two plastic bags. *What does that say about me?*

When she returned to the cottage, she found a note from Angela, propped on the kitchen counter.

I didn't know which you preferred, so I got both.

A jar of coffee and a packet of tea stood on the counter, along with a pint of milk, some eggs, and a chicken casserole with instructions on how to use the large stove. There was a postscript at the bottom:

I put the water heater on. If you're anything like me, a bath will be the only thing you can think of.

Man, I knew there was a reason I liked that woman. Jo put the casserole on to heat and went to explore her new home.

*****

Later, stomach pleasantly full, Jo untied her hair and moaned in relief as it slipped free from her plait, making her scalp tingle. She moved upstairs to the spacious bathroom with its free-standing bath and shampooed her hair, twice. Then, and only then, did she run her bath.

She stepped into the water, lay back, and luxuriated in the steaming bubbles — courtesy of her shampoo — and added bubble bath to her mental shopping list. *Bliss.* Her muscles unknotted, turning her body to pulp. Steam, fragrant with the scent of apple shampoo, billowed upwards and she lost herself among the mist.

It was hard to imagine a day that had started so badly could end up this way — pleasant, enjoyable even. Trisha and her children were out of harm's way — her biggest concern — and she was no longer homeless. She had this glorious cottage to live in, somewhere no one knew about. Jo felt safe for the first time in a very long while and she intended to enjoy the respite.

She perused the file while she soaked, wondering anew who'd told the boss about it. She'd kept it hidden when he and Tumilty had showed up at the hospital, and before that, only four people, barring the children, could have seen it — Trisha, Mary, Pat, and Coop. Her sister had stayed in the boss's house, yet Jo couldn't believe Trisha would tell anyone about the file, not knowing what it contained. Although... she'd spent the day with Tumilty, seemed smitten by the man. Could she have let it slip to him last night?

Mary and Pat had also stayed at Bill's. Had either of them seen her with the file after the explosion? She doubted it. They'd both been too focused on Emily to notice or care about anything else.

Which left Coop.

After the subtle interaction she'd witnessed between him and Tumilty at the hospital, Jo reckoned he could be the culprit, either by telling the boss himself or telling Tumilty, who in turn rushed to tell the boss. Her stomach sank. Her theory of two killers at work no longer seemed far-fetched. *Are Coop and Tumilty in cahoots?*

She worked through the time sequence. If, as she surmised, the killer set fire to the flats because he discovered her relationship to Lucy, then Coop couldn't be involved. For starters, he hadn't been at the barbecue when Trish had mentioned Lucy. Secondly, she'd been with Coop when he'd told her about his family, stared into his eyes. No way to fake that kind of grief.

Grief does strange things and Tumilty could have told him about Lucy, good friends that they are. The thought disturbed Jo more than she cared to admit. Why hadn't Coop been at the barbecue? He'd angled for an invitation, said he was coming, so why hadn't he turned up? Was it possible he was setting the fire while they were enjoying themselves? Could he be that cold?

Which brought up another question... How did the killer know about Mrs R's faulty fireplace? Was the old dear so lonely that she had told the whole of Mourne Lough about it?

Frustrated at the roundabout direction her thoughts were taking, Jo turned back to the file. Mavis had excelled, expanding the search to similar fires over the last twenty years. She had also included both the work histories of all the firefighters in the Mourne Lough station and a psychologist's report on the killer. She read it now.

Based on the details provided, I would surmise the subject is in the thirties to early sixties range. Eighty per cent likelihood male, but female should not be ruled out. The subject's age has been estimated using the provided timeframe of relevant incidents within the last fifteen to twenty years.

It is highly probable this individual finds fire deeply significant and relates the fires directly to a personal incident, possibly a break-up in a relationship or the loss of a loved one through fire at an early period in their life. The use of fire might be construed as a cleansing of the victims — or the victim's soul. This would further suggest the perpetrator was subjected to some type of physical or sexual abuse in the past and views these acts as a form of *help* rather than a crime.

The ritualistic and somewhat risky act of leaving paper roses at the scene would appear to suggest a symbol of love and-or remorse. Usually, arson offences against persons are, more often than not, committed by females rather than males.

It seemed a lot of psychobabble to Jo, never quite getting to the point. There were a lot of "would appear to suggest", and "it is highly probable", but nothing concrete. "Eighty per cent likelihood male, but female should not be ruled out." Heck, she could have come up with that one, especially when they went on to say that arson offences were more often than not committed by females. But what had she expected? The killer's name, age, and home address written in nice, big black letters?

"Would have been nice." She straightened the soggy pages. The report continued in a similar vein.

In view of the care taken of the victims, it would appear the subject is of a sensitive nature and probably extremely loving towards those around them. It is possible the perpetrator has children or a deep, as yet unrealised, desire to procreate. This might have a tendency to make them over-protective. On the basis of prolific research of such subjects, it is likely this person is the perfect parent in all other respects and apt to be active in the community.

Yadda yadda yadda. Jo skipped a few lines.

> The subject is of above-average intelligence. This is based on the skill needed to carry out these murders undetected over a number of years and has obvious specific knowledge of fire starting and firefighting processes.

Vindication. Her suspicions confirmed in black and white. Jo was at once delighted and saddened. She concentrated on the few salient points she could gather, underlining them — subject likely to be late thirties to early sixties, above-average intelligence, might have lost a loved one in a fire, maybe religious, might have children or a desire to have them, perfect parent, and most likely active in the community.

Again, "maybe", "might", and "most likely", were not a lot to go on. The age and intelligence could be anyone. Religious? She couldn't think of anyone who stood out in that regard. A parent? That encompassed a good three quarters of guys in the station, and with the added "deep, as yet unrealised desire, to procreate", it could be anybody and his wife. Talk about covering all the bases.

The only information of any use was the psychologist's view that the killer might have lost a loved one in a fire. Jo felt a dull sensation in her chest. The evidence was stacking up against Coop.

In the interest of fair play, she checked the family histories Mavis had provided for the men in the station, to see if any of them fit the profile. They went alphabetically and she could discount quite a few on first pass using the psychologist's age criteria. She studied the rest.

Sean Abbot from Green Watch had lost his family pet, a dog, in a caravan fire when he had been twelve. She wondered if that counted, made a note, then moved on.

John Cassidy, also from Green Watch. Jo paused. The name seemed familiar. Her brow furrowed, then it came to her. The hoax call at Bill's house. John had been team leader, seemed a nice enough guy, but he'd lost two cousins in a disco fire back in 1998. His name went on her list.

She moved on. Phillip Cortez, White Watch... His fire link was less clear. His wife had torched his clothes, car, and a fishing boat he'd kept secret in a nasty divorce battle. Nevertheless, it could be classed as the loss of a loved one and it went on the list.

Geoff Davis. Jo's eyes moved past the name, stopped, shifted back. *Gavin Davis*. The name jumped out at her and she stared in disbelief. Geoff had mentioned his son had died in an accident. She'd assumed it had been a car crash. Why hadn't he told her Gavin had died in a fire at his boarding school, especially after he'd learned about Lucy? No wonder he'd looked at her so oddly at the barbecue.

The shocks didn't end there. Geoff wasn't the only one in Red Watch who fitted the profile, although there was one consolation. Jim Tumilty, her number one suspect, was still in the running. But Dave Evans and Pat Meehan? The idea of either one of them being involved was ludicrous, but Jo couldn't allow herself to be swayed.

Pat wasn't nicknamed "lap dog" for nothing. He was easily led, which would tie in nicely with there being two killers. Yet, she couldn't believe it of him. He was a big guy, could break a man in half with his bare hands, but he was a pussycat at heart. She remembered his tenderness with Mary and Emily. He cared for them and wouldn't put them at risk.

Might have children or a desire to have them. No, Jo refused to believe it. Not Pat. As for Dave, there was no word of any fires in his past. He was happily married, even if his marriage wasn't the most open, and he didn't seem overly religious.

Because Coop wasn't in the brigade, she had nothing on his whereabouts at the time of the earlier fires, but Geoff and the others... She scanned their work histories. They were all stationed close to each of the fires she'd tagged as suspect, and, she checked further, they'd also been within driving distance of the fires Mavis had earmarked.

"Which means nothing," she said, sliding up the bath. This was Ireland, after all — an island one hundred seventy-four miles at its widest point and three hundred and two miles long. Conceivably, anyone, north or south of the border, could have travelled to all the fires. However, Jo's training told her the planning, the detail involved in these murders, meant the killer had lived close by, close enough to strike up a friendship with the families and friendly enough to drug them without being noticed.

She went back to her list, searching for other suspects. In the end, she found twelve. There were two guys from Blue Watch — Bill Porter, who'd filled in for her the day she had visited the Forbes house, and Pete Murphy, whom she recalled vaguely from that first night in Murdock's. Three respectively from Green and White Watch, and four from Red Watch.

Having viable suspects didn't make her as happy as she thought it might.

The last two paragraphs of the report contained the most unambiguous wording:

> In conclusion, it is my belief the perpetrator transfers their emotions onto the victims, so they are, in essence, taking these drugs and finding peace elsewhere themselves.

They will not stop. Even taking into consideration their desire to be caught I suspect the subject will be more inclined to escalate this pattern of behaviour rather than desist. There is no final outcome to be sought, only a continuous rescuing of those they perceive require their intervention.

More inclined to escalate. Jo's bath no longer felt warm or soothing. Urgency seized her. She rose, grabbed a towel from the nearby rail, and hauled herself from the water.

CHAPTER FORTY-SIX

Jo woke early, feeling invigorated. There was none of that strange house complex she had become accustomed to over the years. Even with the revelations of the night before, she had fallen asleep the second her head hit the pillow and had slept dreamlessly all night.

While she made coffee and toast, she checked her mental list, ticking off the things she had to do. The bank was her first port of call. She'd cancelled her credit cards but needed to go in person to arrange a new chequebook and sort her rent payment to the Parsons. Changing her postal address also required her presence, which meant a quick stop at the post office. That still left her plenty of time to make her eleven thirty appointment at the police station.

Jo buttered her toast and took a bite, followed by a slug of coffee. The interview was a formality, she knew, but she was more comfortable on the other side of the table, working with the SOCO guys. After that, she had to collect her new kit at the station and let the boss know she was ready to come back to work. Jo chewed without savouring, forcing the bread past her windpipe with a swallow of coffee.

When all her chores were done, a bit of retail therapy was in order, she decided, and a sinfully expensive bottle of bubble bath was on the top of her list.

*****

Jo had no intention of visiting her old flat, but on her way to the station, she found herself taking a right, driving up the hill towards it. She gasped as the ruined apartment block came into view. It was a shell, the front façade missing, the inside a tangle of demolished metal and stone.

Surprisingly, the flats on either side had escaped with nothing more serious than broken windows and the odd bit of damaged guttering. *One less thing to feel guilty about.* She spied a familiar figure standing next to a gangly man with a pitted face and she pulled to a stop. "Mrs R." Jo got out of the car and embraced the old woman. "Am I happy to see you. I was so worried. I'm glad you're okay. "

Ethel Reilly rested her chin on Jo's shoulder, heavy, defeated. "Everything's gone." Her eyes stared at the destroyed building. "My things. Gone." Her voice wavered. "All gone."

Jo hugged her tighter. "I know." And she did. Some things were irreplaceable, like her last few mementoes of Lucy, scavenged from relatives and friends after her death. "And I'm so sorry. But they're only things, Mrs R. What's important is you're all right. That's all that matters."

"That's what I've been trying to tell her," the pockmarked man said.

At the sound of his voice, Ethel Reilly straightened and disengaged from Jo's hug. "Jo, I'd like you to meet my son, Liam. Liam, this is..." she swallowed "*was* my neighbour, Ms Woods."

"Call me Jo." Jo held out her hand.

"Nice to meet you, Jo." Liam Reilly shook her hand. "Cheer up, Mum." He put his arm around his mother's shoulder. "I've told you. You can come live with us. Janet has said more than once this weekend what a wonder you've been with the kids."

More like a cheap babysitter, Jo thought, seeing the desperation on Mrs R's face. "Don't worry, Mrs R." She tried to sound confident. "They'll rebuild the flats in no time and you'll soon be mopping the floors again."

The old woman didn't believe Jo, her eyes filling with tears. "I told you I saw someone skulking about. Why, oh why, didn't you believe me?"

Jo had no answer. She watched as Liam shepherded his mother towards his car, towards what she knew would become the old woman's prison. The killer, even if he didn't know it, had claimed another victim.

*****

By the time Jo arrived at the fire station, it was after one. She found Red Watch in the galley, eating their lunch — even Pat, who was supposed to be off duty.

"There she is. Had a nice lazy morning, Woods, while we've been slaving away here?"

Flanders' disposition hadn't improved over the weekend, Jo noticed. "Yeah, Don, got my nails done. You like 'em?" She held up her hands, nails in their usual, ragged condition. "And I'm thinking about getting my hair styled later."

The others laughed. They'd never seen Jo's hair any way other than in a plait.

"Very funny." Flanders bent his head to his lunch, ignoring her.

Jo sat next to Micko. "What did you do to yourself?" she asked, nodding to the plaster covering his eyebrow. "Don't tell me you've been doing handstands on the pool table again?"

"Daft bastard walked into a pole, eying up some blonde." Tumilty, on the other side of Micko, said. "He needs his eyesight tested, 'cause that 'blonde' was definitely male."

"Was not," Micko said. "You're just jealous, because she gave me her phone number."

"*His* phone, you mean," Wart said, "to call an ambulance. This bloody idiot," he hitched a thumb at Micko, "bled like a stuck pig."

Jo giggled. "Bet your wife loved that story, Micko."

She was glad the guys were acting normally. Even the bad-tempered Flanders was preferable to the pity she half-expected after Trisha's bombshell about Lucy and the loss of her home.

"Stores have your gear in," Dave said, getting up to put his dish in the sink. "How did the new digs go?"

"Great. But thanks again for putting me up. I owe you one. Maybe I can take you and Fran out for a meal, by way of thanks."

"No need. We're family here. You'd do the same for any one of us."

Jo knew she would, but even families said thank you on occasions. She would arrange it with Fran, she decided. She wanted another chance to speak to her anyway, seeing as their last conversation had been interrupted.

"Boss wants to see you," Geoff said. "Told me to send you up the second you got in, but can you hang on a minute?" He didn't wait for an answer, rising from the table, going to the cubby hole beside the door.

Jo followed him with her eyes. She wanted to ask him about his son, Gavin, but now didn't seem the time or the place.

Geoff came back to the table carrying an envelope. "We've had a bit of a whip round — the other watches, too — and we'd like you to have this." He held the envelope out to her.

Jo opened it, looked at the thick wad of money inside. "I don't know what to say, guys."

"Nothing to say." Pat's face flamed red. "As Dave said, we're family and we look after our own."

Jo struggled to clear her throat "Thank you. I guess the drinks are on me then. Murdock's. Six o'clock?"

"The money's meant to get you back on your feet, not off 'em. Bloody women!" Flanders said.

"So, you won't want a drink, Don?"

"That's not what I said." Flanders rose, hitching his trousers. He took his plate to the sink, throwing his next words over his shoulder. "You want to waste your money? Who am I to stop you."

Jo smiled. That was the Flanders she knew and hated, mercenary to the end. But she had no intention of spending the money on herself. She had a much better idea.

Once the spotlight moved off her and on to other matters, she motioned to Pat. "Can I have a word?"

"What's up?" Pat followed her from the galley.

"I want you to give this to Mary." Jo handed him the money.

"I can't take that," he said, upset. "We... we collected it for you,"

"I know you did, and I appreciate it, more than I can say. But I'm not hurting for cash at the moment, Pat. My bag wasn't in the flat," she lied. "I was able to go the bank this morning and take out what I needed."

Pat didn't look convinced.

"Honestly, I'm fine. And I think Mary needs this more than I do."

It was the wrong thing to say.

"I can look after Mary." Pat bristled. "She and Emily are with me now."

"I know you can, and they're lucky to have you." It was true. In the space of a few short days, Pat had changed. He was no longer Wart's lap dog — always following, never leading. Taking Mary and Emily under his wing had given him confidence, made a man out of him. She needed to use diplomacy.

"Don't you think Mary might appreciate some cash of her own, you know, for all those little female items?"

Pat blushed. "Oh, aye, I never thought."

"You would have." Jo patted his arm. "This is our little secret, okay?" She waited for his nod before pressing the money into his hand. "And good luck. Mary's a lovely girl and Emily is a sweetheart. Make sure you treat them well."

Pat's blush deepened and he smiled shyly. "Don't worry. I intend to."

Jo couldn't resist. She gave him a swift hug then hurried off to find the boss.

CHAPTER FORTY-SEVEN

Bill Simmons was a troubled man. He hadn't slept since his phone call with Bob Anderson. Instead, he'd spent the evening reading and rereading Jo's file. He had it with him now but couldn't bear to look at it.

Woods, damn her, had been right. There was a murderer in Mourne Lough, as the DB in the flat could attest. *But is she right about everything else?*

Normally, Bill wasn't a man to duck the tough questions, but on this occasion, he was finding it hard to get his head round the idea the murderer might be a fireman, and if the file was to be believed, had been killing for years.

"Jay-sus!" He slapped his desk. *How could this have been going on under our noses all this time?*

His door knocked. "Boss?" Jo hovered in the doorway.

"Come in and shut the fecking door." Jo did as he asked.

"Sit."

She sat, speaking in a rush. "I want to come back to work tomorrow, Boss. I've everything sorted — sister, digs—"

"You seen the police yet?"

"This morning." She grimaced. "Chief Constable O'Hare himself interviewed me, and you'll be glad to know he now considers me as crazy as you do."

"He might be changing his mind right about now," Bill said, lighting a cigarette, taking a draw.

"Boss?"

He pushed Bob's report towards her. "Read this."

Jo scanned it. "How did you get this so fast? I thought the autopsy wasn't scheduled until today."

"I called in a favour." Bill sucked on his cigarette, watched the smoke curling in the air.

"You called in a—" Jo threw the report on the desk. "You knew yesterday, didn't you, when I gave you the file?"

"Not the results, no, but that it was in the works, yeah."

"And you didn't tell me. You let me believe I was a basket case — that *you* thought I was a basket case." Her voice rose.

"Don't play the fecking martyr with me, Woods. If you'd clued me in at the beginning instead of playing your fecking Lone Ranger game, I might have been inclined to trust you."

Bill watched Jo struggle to contain her anger and was surprised when she managed it.

She took a deep breath then sat back deflated. "You're right, Boss. Whether you should have told me or not is immaterial now. I just want you to know I'm sorry. You don't know how much I wish I was wrong about all this."

"Then I'm your fairy fecking godmother, because you still might be."

"Huh?"

"The DB in the flats was murdered, no question about it, but that doesn't mean the others were." Bill stabbed his cigarette into the ashtray. "I've passed a copy of your file to Shaunessy. He'll check it with a fine-tooth comb, then we'll see."

"And until then?"

"We act as if nothing has happened."

"But—"

"I mean it, Woods. Not a fecking word. If you're right — and I'm admitting it's looking more and more likely by the minute — then we don't want to tip the bastard's hand. But if you're wrong..."

He didn't need to finish. If she was wrong and the guys found out, she would be causing all kinds of grief for both of them.

"Okay, we'll do it your way."

"Fecking right we will." Bill lit another cigarette.

"One thing, Boss."

"Yeah."

"You should take a hard look at Jim Tumilty."

"Why's that?"

Jo told him about her suspicions, leaving nothing out.

"I'll take it under advisement."

"But—"

"Who's the fecking boss here, Woods?"

"You are, Boss, but—"

Bill's brows rose. "There you go with those fecking 'buts' again Woods." He saw her colour rise, knew this time she wouldn't be able to hold back. He was right.

"What do you want from me? You say you believe me, then you pull this 'I'll take it under advisement,' shit. Tumilty was in all the right places at all the right times, and there's something not right about him. You're bound to have noticed." She shook her head. "I can't believe everyone is on Tumilty's side. What am I missing?"

Bill cursed under his breath. Feck Tim Sheppard anyway. CFO or not, he was a bollocks for swearing him to secrecy. "That's only half the pie, Woods. What about the psychologist's report? You think Tumilty matches that?"

"I don't know. All I know about Tumilty is what he's deigned to tell us, and I take most of that with a shovel of salt. The only way to see his personnel records is at brigade HQ, and only with a good reason. Maybe you could—"

"Speaking of the psychologist's report." Bill flipped open the file, pulling out the relevant page.

"Says here, and I'm paraphrasing, that the killer is over thirty, intelligent, and might have lost a loved one in a fire. Now, pardon me if I'm wrong, but that could just as easily describe you, couldn't it?" He saw his words strike home, the stunned look on her face, and felt the lowest of the low.

Jo recovered quickly. "Yes, I've been bereaved by a fire, and I guess I've been stationed in or near all the suspect fires, at least those in the last five years," she said, "but not the earlier ones. I wasn't in the brigade then."

Bill was ahead of her. "Nothing in here says this person was a firema... firefighter to begin with. Could be he, or *she*," he stressed, "decided to join the brigade to become more proficient."

When he saw the shattered look in Jo's eyes, Bills face softened. *Feck the political bullshit.* She had been hurt enough. He wouldn't put her through anymore. "Woods I—"

"It's okay, Boss. I understand." Jo stood. "Do you want my resignation?"

"No, I fecking don't want your—"

"Good. Then I'm back on duty tomorrow?"

Bill bit back a curse. *Bloody stubborn woman!* "Yeah. Go tell Peterson he's finally on his four-off. Now, get out of my fecking office."

*****

So, Jo was coming back. Much quicker than I anticipated, but not a problem. I was nothing, if not prepared.

"You're a right Boy Scout."

I wasn't sure the voice meant it as a compliment, but I choose to take it as such.

"Jo is my puppet. I pull the strings and she jumps."

"Ah, but lately she's been refusing to."

Yes, she had, damn her. "That's about to change."

"Let's hope so, for both our sakes."

I tuned the voice out as I mounted the steps to the front door and knocked. Everything would be okay. Government wheels moved slowly. Even if the autopsy on the amateur today showed he had been murdered, there was no way they could link it to me — not in time, anyway.

It was so far removed from my usual MO that the police would be scratching their heads for months to come. MO, after all, was the be-all-and-end-all to those guys. And yet, I had a nagging feeling I'd overlooked something, something important.

I greeted the elderly lady with half a mind, following her into the kitchen, even as I ran over the scene again. The knife was history. It lay at the bottom of the Lough, and I'd burned the bloodstained clothes I'd worn. There was nothing to tie me to the crime anymore. As for the mouse of a girl in the bottom flat? Fear was too well ingrained in her. No way would she go running to the police to provide an identity for her erstwhile husband.

As usual, everything was perfect. So why did I feel I had missed essential?

"Are you okay?"

The woman reminded me where I was. "I'm fine, Mrs Blake." I smiled, gave it my best effort. It worked. She smiled back, oblivious.

"It's lovely to have company," Mrs Blake said. "Tom and I don't get many visitors nowadays. And how fortunate that you arrived just in time to help with the oxygen delivery. It's awkward for one person to get the cylinder up those narrow stairs."

Fortunate was one word for it. Careful planning was another. I smiled modestly. Getting the tank positioned exactly where I wanted it was only one reason why I needed to get into the old man's room.

"Here." She held out a plate of sandwiches. "Take one. You firefighters do so much for the community. It's nice to be able to give something back for a change."

Oh, you'll give something back all right. I hid my excitement behind my smile as she shuffled back to her seat. I'd checked the rotation for tomorrow. Jo was down as BA wearer, which meant she would be first in to any fire, a dangerous position at the best of times.

Tomorrow wasn't going to be the best of times.

I had changed my MO once with the amateur. Now it was time to change it again. Mr and Mrs Blake could never be considered "little birds", but they were still caged, and they desired to be set free. I could see it in Mrs Blake's eyes as she spoke of her husband, confined to his bed in the upstairs room. The unbearable pain he suffered every day and the pain she felt watching him all but screamed from her face. The hopelessness in her voice, and his, when I'd seen him a few minutes ago, would break the hardest of hearts, and mine was far from hard.

"I think sometimes it's too soft," the voice said.

I knew it wasn't talking about the Blakes, knew it blamed me for going too easy on Jo. Well, no more. I couldn't afford to let her get any closer. It was now a fight for survival — mine — and I had no intention of losing.

I bit into the sandwich of dried bread with even drier ham, chewed it as if it were the finest nectar. I was passing time now. I'd gained all the information I needed. This would be the best *accident* ever. I'd also managed to deposit the drug in their milk, which Mrs. Blake had revealed they both took heated every night, to aid their sleep.

It was going to do that all right.

They were going to sleep straight into the afterlife.

As was Jo Woods. *Finally!*

CHAPTER FORTY-EIGHT

Jo met Red Watch in Murdock's to buy the thank-you drink she had promised. She'd had time to reflect on her meeting with the boss and had come to the conclusion that him considering her a suspect was no worse than her considering him, and the other firefighters, one. And Geoff not telling her how his son had died no longer seemed a sinister oversight. After all, she hadn't told anyone about Lucy until she had been compelled to do so.

Overall, considering its rocky start, the day had gone well and looked to be an even better night. Bill had shared the autopsy findings with the others, and the first hour or so was spent speculating on who the DB might be. Theories abounded.

Dave still maintained it was an unlucky burglar, while Wart suggested it could have been a squatter, taking advantage of Mrs R's absence. The idea it might have been Jo's killer was glossed over, too awful to contemplate, but she knew it was in the back of all their minds.

Micko, of course, put forth the unlikely scenario that it was Mrs R's toy boy, which lightened the atmosphere, leading to even more extravagant and unlikely scenarios. All in all, it was a good night, relaxed, and just what Jo needed. The only sour note occurred as they were leaving.

"You think that's bad," Dave said, in reply to one of Micko's quips about his kids. "My Jenny wanted to go down the street the other day — to meet her friends, if you don't mind. She's six."

Jo slapped him on the back. "Just wait, Dave. Soon it will be boys she wants to meet. That's when the real fun begins."

"What would you know?" Flanders, unsteady on his feet and bleary eyed, said. "After all, you're hardly the best person to offer advice on families. Tell us again. Where were you when your kid died?"

A shocked silence followed before Geoff ordered Flanders to apologise. He had, but the damage had been done.

*****

Jo was glad to get back to work the following morning. Leaving the cottage after another night of undisturbed sleep, she felt ready for any challenge — and that included Don Flanders.

This time it was Dave's turn to be late. He joined Jo in the compressor room, where she was charging the breathing apparatus cylinders, apologising to Ryan Parks, who had hung back.

"Bloody doctors," he said to Jo, when Ryan left. "Wait half an hour to see them, then you're in and out in five seconds. And for that, they get the big bucks." He helped Jo fill the BA cylinders.

"Hey, the big bucks aren't just for that, remember. They've spent years at school, learning the technique of how to speak to people so they don't understand a word you say. And don't get me started on their handwriting." Jo studied him. "What's up? You sound as pessimistic as Wart." She wondered if it had anything to do with Fran. She had called to see her yesterday, using the excuse of setting up a date for a thank-you meal, but had found Fran reluctant to talk.

"Hey, give me a break, I'm not that bad, am I?"

Jo laughed. "No, but you sure are easy to wind up."

"Why you..." Dave opened the cap of the cylinder he was holding. There was a hissing noise as he pointed it in her direction.

Jo held her hands up, backing off.

"To be honest, Jo," Dave said, his face turning grim, "I'm still ticked off with Flanders. He was well out of order last night. Fucking twat!"

It was unusual for Dave to curse, but Jo couldn't fault him. Flanders had been out of line.

"I can't help thinking it was my fault for bringing the subject up in the first place."

"Jeeze, now you really *do* sound like Wart. Forget it. Don Flanders could start a war in heaven without anyone's help."

She was glad to see Dave smile, but she had to admit Flanders' words, coming so quickly on top of the boss's dressing down, had stung.

"I don't know how you can forgive him so easily." Dave lifted the filled cylinders, attaching them to their brackets.

"One thing I've learned, Dave," Jo said, helping him, "is life's too short to worry about petty-minded people."

"Oh, I don't know, a swift kick to the nuts usually makes me feel a whole lot better. Now, what's next on the agenda?"

Jo punched his arm. "Duty room. A lecture on high rise fire-fighting — not that we'll need it much here, but you might for your next post." It saddened her to think of him leaving. Their loss was some lucky station's gain.

"Oh goody." Dave's face fell. "I can hardly wait."

Just then the alarm sounded. From overhead came the thud of running feet. "I guess you're gonna have to," Jo said as she ran to suit up.

CHAPTER FORTY-NINE

Jo knew the instant Geoff told them a call had gone out for a second pump that the fire must be bad.

"Persons reported," he said, reading the printout. "Elderly couple. Husband bedridden."

Not good news — husband unable to leave under his own steam and wife unlikely to leave his side.

Once again, Jo and Dave would be first in — Dave acting as team leader. Suited and masked, they checked their air as the fire engine screamed into the estate.

"How long till backup get here?" Jo asked Pat.

"Six minutes, tops," Pat said, readying the safety covering hose for Dave.

Six minutes. Jo looked towards the house. A lifetime. She jumped from the engine and handed Wart her BA Tally. As entry control officer, he would monitor her air.

Dave did the same. "Ready?" he asked Jo, voice muffled behind his facemask.

Jo gave him the thumbs up.

When they reached the front door, Jo kicked it open, crouching low as Dave sprayed the entry hall. Smoke billowed outwards, flames flashing inside, lapping at the staircase.

Jo and Dave shared a look. If they wanted to search upstairs, they had to do it now, before the staircase became impassable. With the husband bedridden, chances were that both he and the wife would be there.

While Dave dampened a path for her, Jo tapped the first stair with her foot. When it held, she stepped onto it, banging the stair above with her gloved hand. She repeated the process with the next step and the next, hugging the wall where it was safest. Flames licked around her, but insulated beneath her sturdy fire kit, she was impervious — a state of affairs she knew wouldn't last long if they didn't get a move on.

She quickened her pace, surprised to find most of the stairs intact. The flames feasted on the wooden banister to her right, not yet ready for the delights of the thicker, sturdier stairs. Jo didn't query their pickiness. In her job, she had learned never to look a gift horse in the mouth.

Geoff had filled them in on the layout, as relayed to him by a neighbour, before they'd entered. Three rooms upstairs — two bedrooms, front and back, and a bathroom at the end of the hall. Your basic two-up, two-down. Which was a good thing, Jo thought as the heat and smoke intensified. A room each was all they'd have time for.

She refused to speculate how they would get the bedridden gent out or how badly he might be affected by whatever ailed him. They would face that when the time came.

The last stair caught her unawares, making her stumble. She grabbed the banister, winced as heat filtered through her gloves. She regained her balance, Dave right behind her.

They both sank below the smoke, moving to their left. An old-fashioned mahogany door appeared in the darkness. Sturdy. It looked untouched by the fire.

Jo checked the back of the door. *Not too hot. Good.* Next, she tried the handle. *Unlocked.* She nodded to Dave and pushed the door open. Dave sent a pulse of water into the room and Jo shut the door.

Dave tapped her shoulder, motioned towards the staircase. Jo looked back, saw flames shimmer up the steps they'd so recently climbed. Dave tapped her again, gestured to himself, then to the bedroom on the right. Jo nodded. If there was any chance of finding the couple alive, they needed to split up.

She spoke into her skull mic. "Downstairs compromised. Coming out front bedroom window. Repeat, coming out front bedroom window."

"We'll be there," Geoff said, voice steady and calm. "Casualties?"

"Don't know yet." Jo opened the door and entered at a crouch.

The mahogany door might have blocked the flames, but it was no barrier against smoke. The room heaved, pitch black inside. To her right, Jo spied a worrying flicker of red close to the floor. Were the floorboards already alight? The fire downstairs was robust, but it shouldn't have moved upstairs this fast. She had no time to debate the issue. She groped for the bed. The room was a nightmare of unknown obstacles and dangers that she was unable to see.

Her mind flashed back to the Forbes fire, and Jo fought a surge of fear. *That was a one-off,* she told herself. *It won't happen again, and this time I have plenty of air.* She took a deep breath, heard the valves in her facemask click a regular tempo. Air filled her lungs. She calmed, concentrated on the known, rather than the unknown. The window, her escape hatch, lay directly opposite her position. If this were the old man's room, it would mimic a hospital room — a bed, a table, maybe a chair or two, nothing more.

Arms splayed, she moved forwards. Her knees made contact first, thumping off the edge of a metal bedstead.

Thank you, God.

Aware flames were encroaching on the room through the open doorway, Jo moved faster. She ran her hands up the bed, feet tapping the floor in front of her. Her boot touched something.

Leaving the bed for the moment, she groped to the side and found the curve of a wooden armrest followed by the outline of a body.

It was a woman, slumped in a chair beside the bed.

The wife.

She yelled for Dave, gloved hands checking the bird-like chest. She felt it rise and fall. "Okay, Mrs Blake, let's get you out of here." She shouted again for Dave.

The woman mumbled something that sounded like *Tom.*

"We'll get him," Jo promised, hoping it was one she could keep. She grabbed the woman under the arms and pulled her from the chair. Jo held her steady with one hand and checked the bed with the other. Beneath her searching fingers, she found the husband. "Tom!" She shook the withered frame.

The man didn't stir.

"I see him," she told the woman. "I'll come back for him. Don't you worry."

Jo was disorientated and confused by the smoke and she held her position, attempting to get her bearings. She had entered the room, marking off straight ahead from the doorway. The chair and the old woman had been to her right. Therefore, if she moved a step or two to her left then forwards, she should be on track to the window.

Praying she was right, Jo made sure her grip on the old lady was secure. Then, doing a reverse firefighter's shuffle, she tapped her way to where she hoped the window would be.

Her hip bumped the windowsill. She groped for the latch and pushed the window open. It moved, but only a fraction.

Damn! A window lock. She was ready to punch the glass out with her turnout gloves when she heard a voice beside her.

"I'll take her." Dave closed the branch on his hose, leaving it charged and dropped it to the floor, holding out his arms.

Jo handed the woman over, leaving her hands free to work on the lock. The design was similar to those in her old flat. You pulled the window closed, released the latch and voila. She did so. The window still refused to open.

"Jo!"

Dave's voice, while not panicked, was a decibel higher than usual.

Jo ripped off one of her bulky gloves, tested the latch with her bare fingers. Immediately, she spotted the problem. The latch was raised, prised out of its housing. She jiggled the catch, felt it give. *Result.* She swung the window open. "Go," she told Dave.

Pat was there to greet them. "Give her to me. What about the husband?"

"Going back to get him," Jo said, pulling on her glove. Dave grabbed the hose. The smoke was thicker now. The second crew downstairs, knocking the fire down, was generating more smoke and steam. She and Dave walked blind, hands outstretched, feet tapping.

Jo spotted a flash of orange, the spread growing, close to the floorboards at the head of the bed. Dave spotted it, too. They quickened their pace, the valves in Jo's facemask keeping time. *Click. Click. clickclickclick.*

Jo used the flames as a marker, followed them back to the bed. All she had to do was pick the old man up and they were outta there. Her radio crackled.

"Jo, Mr Blake's on oxygen."

Great, just great. Her nice safe room, filled with its noxious, killing smoke, had become a time bomb.

"Home help is with me now," Geoff said, voice terse. "Says the doctor put a new cylinder in yesterday."

This wasn't good. Not only did oxygen feed a fire, but one spark and the whole bloody cylinder would explode. To make matters worse, it looked like the oxygen tank was sitting next to the flames she'd spied. At that moment, Jo's hands touched flesh. The old man wasn't moving. She checked his chest. *Nothing.*

Usually, if there were any doubt, she would take the casualty out, but Geoff's call had changed everything. If the old man were dead, she should get her ass out of there. No sense having three corpses.

Yet, she hesitated. Jo knew from personal experience how much it meant to a loved one to see a relatively untouched body instead of a shrunken, blackened husk. Determined to at least try, she grabbed the old man, unhooked the oxygen mask covering his face and dragged him from the bed, hoping she wasn't doing him more harm than good.

With Dave moving ahead, escape was metres away. She wasted no time getting there.

Dave clambered out the window Then said, "Give him here."

Jo passed the man to him. Dave fumbled, checked to make sure he had a firm grasp. *Hurry up.* Jo wanted out of the house.

Finally, Dave was satisfied. "Got him."

Jo lifted one leg over the sill. "Coming down," she informed him as he descended with the casualty. She lifted her other leg and found she couldn't move. She tried not to panic. Her suit was caught in the jemmied clasp, that was all. Fire kits were heavy, cumbersome. She just needed to step back into the room, unhook herself and—

There was a whoosh as a lone flame ignited the oxygen cylinder, a short, sharp bite of agony as something ripped through her suit then, thankfully, everything went dark.

*****

Because I'd known what to expect and was ready for it, I was the only one who seemed to be enjoying the deafening silence left behind after the explosion.

"No way Jo Woods is walking away from this one."

I agreed with the voice, and it was hard to keep my satisfaction in check. My plan had worked perfectly, although, for a moment there, I thought she'd make it out in one piece. Thank goodness, I'd had the foresight to jemmy that window latch yesterday. Mr Blake had been so out of it that he wouldn't have noticed me doing a full striptease, never mind the few seconds it had taken my trusty knife to bend the housing so it would take precious minutes to escape. At the time, I was sure it was overkill, but now I was glad I was such a perfectionist. It had made all the difference.

"A job well done."

I heard pride in the voice and basked in it. My plan had worked. With one fell swoop, I had averted the risk of discovery and disposed of an adversary.

"Jesus Christ!" Geoff, our watch commander, was the first to react. "Did Jo get out?"

Deafened by the explosion, he didn't realise he was screaming. "Did Jo get out? Did she get out?"

He scanned the area, shocked eyes taking in the mass of debris littering the once-pristine garden.

"I don't know," I yelled, hiding my delight behind a panic-stricken look. "Jesus!" I shook my head as if in disbelief. "I didn't see."

I was proud of my performance. Maybe if I hadn't my mission to occupy me I could have used my skills on the stage. With a performance like this, I would have been fêted the world over. My grin this time was harder to conceal.

Suddenly, everyone was galvanised. Red Watch, as one, sprang into action, running towards the house, towards where they had last seen Jo. I ran with them, lifting debris, kicking it out of the way as we cleared a path and all the while I was rejoicing. It was over. It was finally over. I was safe. My mission was safe.

"Over here!"

The call stopped me in my tracks. Flanders, huge belly straining against his fire kit, stooped over a large piece of masonry, scrabbling frantically. I couldn't see what lay behind it, but his florid face was set and determined. I knew he'd found Jo.

The others rushed towards him, but I was reluctant to join them. My reluctance confused me. This was what I wanted — no, what I needed — in order to continue my mission, so why was I dragging my feet, unwilling to view the fruits of my labour?

"Because you are not a monster. You take no joy in death. It is a tool, like any other. One you wield with flair and skill. Only those most deserving — or those who try to disrupt your calling — are chosen."

The voice, as usual, was right, but still the strange emotion persisted. I had no time to evaluate it. Aware of how close I had come to discovery, it was more important than ever I be seen doing my bit. On legs that no longer felt steady, I rushed to join the others.

They had cleared the rubble, throwing it to one side. The body underneath was clearly visible. I stopped, more shocked than I imagined at the sight they uncovered. Jo lay unmoving, her body broken and bloody, and so unbelievably, deathly still.

I had been right. Jo wasn't walking away from this one.

CHAPTER FIFTY

Jo woke to find someone tearing at her facemask, cutting off her suit and the clothes underneath. In the deepest, darkest recess of her mind, she knew she couldn't let that happen.

Voices screamed her name, said it over and over until it became one long, confused word.

"Jo! Jo! Jojojojo!"

It was a scream she echoed in her own mind, only hers said, *No! No! No!*

She tried to stop the hands cutting at her clothes, unwrapping her shame. Shocked and winded from the fall, she couldn't make her arms work. She smelt burning, the sickening odour of melted skin and hair. It made her want to throw up.

Memory returned. The oxygen cylinder exploding, something biting into her skin... Falling... Falling...

It was *her* skin, *her* hair she smelt burning. Her nausea grew.

The harsh wail of a siren sounded in the distance, drowning out everything else. Then it was uncannily quiet.

Flat on her back, Jo looked up at the sky. It was so pretty — a perfect sky with one lone, perfect cloud. She couldn't feel anything and she knew that wasn't right. She'd fallen two storeys. Odds were she should be in a world of pain.

Where is everybody?

Then she could feel them around her, their presence. They were so quiet!

"Oh my God!" Flanders' voice shattered the silence.

What was wrong? Was someone still in the house? Jo tried to rise. Now it was Geoff's voice she heard, his gentle hand pushing her back.

"Lie still, Jo. You hear me? Lie still."

Oh God, it must be bad. She'd never heard that tone in his voice before. *Am I badly hurt? Am I... dying?*

The silence unnerved her. Jo made her hands move, whimpered at the pain in her neck. *Broken collarbone?* One by one she checked her limbs. All accounted for. Relief flooded her. She tried to lift her head off the ground, but the pain was too intense. She let it fall. "What are you guys trying to do, scare me half to death?" she said.

No one answered.

Her gaze slid to the side. Pat had his face buried in his helmet. She could see his shoulders heaving. Wart stood beside him, hands in his pocket. He took a step back as if afraid to face her.

"What?" Jo struggled to rise, but again pain defeated her. "Are they dead? Tell me," she begged. "Goddamn, did I just get blown out a window for nothing?"

A hand patted her arm. "They're fine. It's you we're more concerned about. You need to lie still."

"Why?" Jo said, bemused. She felt fine, sore, but fine. At least all her limbs were intact. "Dave?"

Dave came to her side. "We need you to stay down because..." He swallowed, eyes lowering.

Jo followed his gaze. Her jacket lay on the grass beside her, the tattered remains of her shirt on top of it, her bra the only thing covering her modesty. But it was the sight of her scars, mottled and ugly that made her feel most naked.

"We had to do CPR," he said, kneeling beside her. "You weren't breathing."

"Oh."

"That's why you wouldn't take my T-shirt at the barbecue?" Wart said. "And why you always wear long-sleeve tops."

Jo closed her eyes, pierced to the core. Geoff threw a blanket over her, his hand resting for a second on her shoulders. Flanders bent to tuck it around her.

Jo wanted to sink into the ground. *Flanders being nice? Has the world gone mad?*

Flanders avoided her eyes as Geoff asked the question they all wanted to ask. "Lucy?"

Jo nodded, tried not to cry, tried not to remember. It was impossible. That night was with her again, her own personal version of hell.

The acrid smell of smoke. Sparks crackling, spitting. Flames — burning, searing flames, licking greedily at her home, her body, her beautiful, precious child.

Pain.

Grief.

Desolation.

The tears came then, unbidden, unwelcome. They spilled down her cheeks and Jo cursed her weakness. She squeezed her eyes shut, trying to stem the flow.

"Ah, Jo." Dave wiped the tears away. He looked like he wanted to say more, but the paramedics arrived and he moved out of their way, out of view.

The paramedics worked quickly, professionally. One placed a foam collar around Jo's neck to keep her head immobile, while the other shone a light in her eyes, asking her questions to make sure there was no concussion. Geoff filled them in as they worked, explained what had happened and what treatment they had administered.

Jo let it all drift over her, kept her face blank, trying to hold in her emotions. But as she was lifted onto the stretcher and wheeled towards the waiting ambulance, she felt that resolve weaken and die as each member of her watch lined up, saluting her in silence as she passed.

CHAPTER FIFTY-ONE

Jo swam through a sea of clouds to wake. The minute she surfaced, pain attacked. It radiated outwards, growing, expanding. It went deeper than bone, deeper than the marrow of her soul, and it was all too familiar.

She had been in the fire that had taken Lucy. Flames had danced with exquisite agony on her skin and she had danced with them in an overwhelming desire to save her child.

"Lucy!" *I have to save Lucy. I have to—*

"Hold still," a voice said. Gentle hands held her steady. "You'll knock your drip out."

Jo opened her eyes to find Coop standing over her. "What the—?" Her tongue stuck to the roof of her mouth. She swallowed and gasped. It felt like shards of glass coated her throat.

"Hold on." Coop lifted a beaker filled with water, a plastic straw inside, and held it towards her. "Here you go."

Memory returned. She was in the present, the fight to save Lucy long over. Jo gritted her teeth against the stab of grief and attempted to lever herself upright. Pain multiplied, making her nauseous. She glared at Coop. She didn't want his help, didn't want him anywhere near her, yet she wanted the water more.

With ill grace, she allowed him to place a hand behind her head, tilt it to reach the straw. Lukewarm water had never tasted so good. She sucked greedily, felt it soothe her inflamed throat.

"What are you doing here?" she said, when she was done.

Coop ignored the question. "Jesus, Jo, you got a death wish or something?" He sounded angry.

"You make this sound like it was my fault." Jo blinked back tears, cursed her weakness.

"Well, three explosions in one week, either you're crap at your job or you were born under the unluckiest star ever."

Jo didn't correct him. A week or nine days, the time didn't matter. What did matter was he wasn't the only one to remark on her *thing* for explosions. The boss himself had mentioned it when he'd sprung them from the hospital Saturday night. The self-same hospital she now lay in.

Jo's tears dried as a horrible suspicion formed. If they were lucky, a firefighter saw maybe six explosions their entire career, depending where they were stationed, of course. A built-up area, with lots of factories, might have a higher count, as would more impoverished districts where *poor housekeeping* meant more than a brigade term. Yet here she was, in a salubrious area like Mourne Lough, experiencing three explosions in a little over a week.

Jo ran over the fires in her mind — the gas heater in the Forbes fire, Mrs R's faulty fireplace, and the oxygen tank in the old couple's house. All believable situations, yet all occurring when she was on BA duty — the first into any fire. Could it be a coincidence? Fear zinged up her spine, causing a strangled moan. She didn't believe in coincidences, especially when the killer had her phone number on speed dial.

"Take it easy, Jo," Coop said, mistaking her mewl of pain for physical. "You've a broken collarbone, a couple of crushed ribs, and a nasty gouge on your back, but seeing as you fell two storeys, I guess you could say you were pretty lucky."

Jo didn't feel lucky. Her mind was joining dots and she didn't like the picture they formed. Had the killer gone from taunting her to trying to kill her? On one hand, the idea pleased her. It meant he was worried she was getting too close. On the other hand, being targeted by a lunatic wasn't exactly on the top of her wish list.

Fear warred with satisfaction. Three brilliant, believable fires that, in any other circumstances, wouldn't occasion suspicion, reinforced her theory the killer was a firefighter. Who else knew that as BA wearer, she'd be first in, or have the expertise to set the fire so the oxygen cylinder would explode?

His partner, though, might be a kind, caring individual who visited her in the hospital in order to find out what she knew and maybe silence her if he got the chance. Her breath hitched. She didn't want to believe it, but it made sense.

"Are you okay?" Coop hovered. "Let me—"

"Get away from me." Jo flattened herself against the thin mattress, eyes searching the ward for help.

The curtains on the other beds were closed tightly — empty, for all she knew. She checked the hallway, hoping to see someone — anyone — passing. It, too, was deserted. Coop loomed closer. *Where the hell are the nurses? Doctors? The place is like a morgue.* The thought increased Jo's panic. Her fingers hunted for the nurses' call button. "What do you want?" She kept her eyes trained on Coop. "Wh... why are you here?"

"Why am I here?" Coop looked confused. "I'm keeping an eye on you," he said. "We all are, waiting for you to wake up. Guess I'm the lucky one, huh?"

"We?" Jo asked, desperate to keep him talking. *Where is the button?* Her fingers could move no farther. Her broken collarbone screamed in protest and she was pretty sure Coop would notice when she screamed, too. Frustrated, she let her arm relax back onto the bed.

"The guys from your watch — nice bunch, by the way," Coop said. "Your boss, too. Man, the nurses fawned over him. I'm guessing he's a well-known figure in these parts. Occupational hazard, huh? The lady with him, Marian, wasn't quite as impressed with their fawning, let me tell you." He smiled in remembrance. "Oh, and Mary Quinn, you know, who used to live across from me? She was here, too."

Jo was only half listening. She scanned the ward and corridor, praying for any sign of life. Finally, she spotted a nurse in the corridor outside. She signalled to her with a quick incline of her head, trying not to make it obvious. "How long have I been out?"

"Eighteen, nineteen hours. Fire happened yesterday around ten am. It's now," Coop looked at his watch, "five am Wednesday."

"Uh-huh." Jo wasn't listening. She tracked the nurse's progress, relief flooding her as she entered the ward and made her way towards Jo's bed. "Thanks for stopping by, Coop, but I'm fine now. No need for you to stay."

Coop recoiled as if he'd been struck. "If that's what you want."

"That's what I want." Jo refused to be swayed by his hangdog expression. She owed him nothing, she reminded herself. Killer's apprentice or not, he'd lied to her, kept his friendship with Tumilty a secret. Whatever was going on, he was in it, right up to his perfectly muscled neck.

"Nice to see you awake, Ms Woods." The nurse checked Jo's vitals, wrote something on the chart at the bottom of her bed. "My name's Barbara, but *you,*" she flicked a blonde curl, razor-green eyes sharpening on Coop, "can call me Barbie."

Oh sweet Lord. Jo watched as the nurse edged closer to Coop, batted her fake eyelashes and said, "Did you manage to sleep at all, Mr Cooper? He stayed up all night with you," she told Jo, not taking her eyes off Coop. "Wouldn't leave. Now that's dedication for you."

Dedication or hoping to finish his partner's work while I slept? Jo ground her teeth in frustration. Never mind coming to her aid, Barbie looked eager to help Coop with whatever he desired. A scary thought, seeing as the woman was ideally placed to provide the perfect, untraceable means.

She thought quickly. "The things people will do to collect five hundred quid." She threw Barbie what she hoped was a defeated look. "But I guess once a bookie, always a bookie." She sighed, hoped she hadn't overplayed her hand.

She hadn't.

"Well, really." The nurse impaled Coop with a frosty glare and flounced off.

"Thanks a bunch, Jo. Now she thinks I'm a total toe rag."

"Aren't you?"

"I stayed up with you all night. That's gotta earn me brownie points?"

His smile could have made a dent in the national debt, but Jo wasn't buying. "So you lied when you said the guys took turns. You're good at lying, Coop. Aren't you?"

He had the grace to look ashamed. "You mean Tumilty? I wanted to talk to you about him."

"Good, 'cause I'd really like to talk to you about him, too."

Coop shuffled his feet. "First off, let me say I didn't lie about the guys being here. They were, but they went home for some shut-eye before their shift tonight. And Mary had to get back to Emily. Everyone's been really concerned." He grabbed Jo's hand and held on. "Me included."

Man, he's good. He sounds like he means it.

When she didn't speak, Coop grew bolder, lifting a strand of her hair, playing with it. He let the lock slide through his fingers. "You should leave your hair loose more often."

Jo brushed his hand away. "It gets in the way at work. And don't change the subject."

"Hey, if you want me to go, I'll go." He went to stand.

"No." Jo made a decision she hoped she wouldn't regret. "Stay." From what Barbie had let slip, if Coop had wanted her dead, he could have done it at any point during the night. Plus, she was eager to know what dirt he had on Tumilty.

"Thanks, Jo. You don't—"

"Save it," she said, voice icy. "I want the truth, Coop. That's the price for staying. You willing to pay?"

In answer, Coop pulled his chair closer then took her hand. "I've been a fool, Jo."

Jo didn't disagree with him. Her brain felt fuzzy. She wasn't sure whether it was the medication or the pressure of his hand on hers, but her heart was doing strange things, too. What was it about this man that made her willing — eager even — to believe the lies dripping from his perfectly formed lips?

She didn't have the energy — or, if she were truthful — the desire to pull free, and she cursed herself. She was useless and couldn't hold a thought for more than a second. The stupid tears were back. She squeezed her eyes shut. She couldn't will them away, couldn't stop them. They kept coming.

"Oh, Jo." Coop traced her cheek with his thumb, wiping her tears. "Tumilty told me about your daughter, what you did."

At the mention of Lucy, Jo opened her eyes and tried to jerk her head free.

"Don't shut me out." Coop refused to let her go. "You know my story. You know how I got this." He rubbed the bump on his nose. "But if I'm honest, I'm glad that guy hit me." His face filled with shame. He lowered his head. "When I saw those flames... the heat... Jesus! I couldn't have done what you did. I wanted to, wanted more than anything in this world but I-I couldn't." The last was barely audible.

Jo ached to comfort him, but he had a lot more explaining to do. "What I did had nothing to do with bravery, Coop. It was panic — pure and utter panic." Jo was finding it hard to concentrate, her thoughts slipping into one another. "I didn't have anyone... to stop me. If I had... Well, who knows? At the end of the... day, neither of our actions... saved our babies, did they?"

Coop shook his head. "I guess not. Are you okay, Jo? You're slurring your words. Maybe I should get a nurse?"

"I'm fine. It's just the... morphine." Jo licked her lips. It felt like they were twice their normal size. Or maybe that was her tongue? She forged on. "I want... to know what's going on with you and... Tumilty? And I want the... truth."

"I guess that's the least you deserve." Coop cleared his throat. "But first, I want you to know that what happened between us — the kiss... kisses we shared — wasn't planned." His eyes fixed on Jo with an intensity that made her stomach join her heart in doing strange things. "I was attracted to you from the moment I met you." He said it simply, honestly. "You are an amazingly beautiful woman, Jo Woods, inside and out, and I would like to explore that further when this is over."

Jo didn't know whether to punch him or hug him and decided she didn't have the energy for either. "Depends on... what you tell me."

"I suppose that's fair." Coop took a deep breath, started to speak, and told her everything.

*****

It was impossible to act normal. My world had been knocked off its axis, taking my faith in my mission with it.

How could Jo still be alive?

It had to be divine intervention. There was no other explanation for her seemingly charmed life. Yet, if that were true, why would He intervene on her behalf — against *me*? For a moment, I wavered, doubted myself much as Abraham had when asked to sacrifice his beloved son. Surely, if my mission were righteous, Jo would be dead by now?

I waited, but the voice remained quiet. It had been strangely silent since the explosion. In its silence, I sensed condemnation. I didn't care. Good riddance to it. I could function just as well without it. The voice was a distraction. Plus, people were inclined to look askance at someone who talked to themselves, and I couldn't afford to attract attention at the moment.

Jo was still alive! And so were the Blakes. The whole operation had been an unmitigated disaster.

My stomach rebelled, disgorged acid in a painful, volcanic rush, and the nagging suspicion I'd missed something — something important — wasn't helping.

Tension grew within me. Were the two connected, Jo and this missing something?

A test, maybe? But if so, of what?

I had no answers. Neither had the voice. I was alone — confused, upset, and alone.

What more did I need to do? Hadn't I proven myself? All my years of toil, the birds I'd freed, did they count for nothing? And if it all meant nothing, what was left for me?

Nothing.

The notion paralysed me. Nothing was the abyss. That endless pit of bleakness and despair squatted in the corners of my mind, waiting to consume me as it had so many times before. Before the voice found me and showed me my calling.

I teetered on the brink, fought to keep my balance.

"You don't need the voice," I told myself. "You can handle this." I was used to being alone. I was no longer a scared child. I was a man — a man with a very important mission.

Reminded, I stiffened my spine. All was not yet lost, but it would be if I couldn't gain control of my emotion, if I succumbed to the darkness. Abraham had not failed when tested and neither would I.

I swallowed back the fear, pushed back the darkness, focusing on the light of my mission. I had to go to work tonight, preserve the image for a while longer. I took a deep breath, then another, calmed. I was on track. The Blake fire had raised no eyebrows. They'd classed it an accident. My only problem — if you could call it that — was the amateur. However, I had breathing space. He hadn't been identified yet and wouldn't be for a while.

Guys like the amateur chose their victims well. They preyed on the weak and vulnerable, brainwashed them into believing they deserved what they got. There would be no police reports, no fingerprints on record to connect the body to a name. It would be days, weeks, before they figured out who the amateur was and his relationship to the girl in the downstairs flat. Even when he was identified, there was no way to link him back to me. Still, it had been a stupid move, a decided lack of control, even if it had served to muddy the waters.

A thought struck. Was this why I was being tested? I was supposed to free the weak, the innocent, and the amateur could never be called that.

"See? I don't need you," I told the absent voice. I felt better, now that I understood. He was right to test me. I had failed Him — put my wants, my desires above His. Redemption was possible. I just needed to work harder to prove myself worthy of Him and the task He had given me.

I had time, I consoled myself. Not much, admittedly — not as much as I planned, which rankled. A few days, a week at most, and I would have been gone, no one any the wiser. Damn Jo Woods, anyway.

She'd had me off balance from the second I'd met her. She had been the reason I'd lost my temper with the amateur, the reason I was being tested now. Lucky for me her "killer" theory, while gaining popularity, wasn't yet officially sanctioned. I had time to finish my mission, slip away before anyone connected me to the fires. However, I needed to make sure Jo didn't follow me, which left me in a bit of a quandary. To make another attempt on her life would fast-track her "killer" theory, so I had to stop her without touching her.

How?

Her sister and kids would have been the perfect deterrent, but she'd sent them out of my reach — for now. Mary Quinn and her brat, though, might be an option. They came with the added bonus of making their hero, the lap dog, sit up and beg. Three for the price of one. I reined in my contempt, aware that in my search for redemption I must be above reproach, separated from such petty, worldly emotions.

There were always Bill's grandkids. Although, I was wary of involving one of the brigade's own. It would generate too much heat if I freed too close to home. Plus, I had played that card once before. I didn't think Jo would be fooled again.

I made myself a cup of tea and pondered the problem further. Jo was at her lowest ebb, hurting, both physically and mentally. I remembered the horror in her sister's voice when I spoke about Lucy. How much better it would have been if Jo had answered the phone first. A plan formed. Maybe prodding that wound would do the trick. I smiled as I sipped my tea. And I knew the perfect way to turn the knife.

CHAPTER FIFTY-TWO

Jo listened in silence while Coop talked, retelling his family's history, sharing his pain.

"I didn't know about your family that day," he said, "but I knew you understood. I'd never had that connection before. If I had..." He dropped his head. "Well, let's just say I might not have gone off the rails like I did."

"The dope?"

"Dope, drink... You name it, I tried it." He smiled, shamefaced. "I was in self-destruct mode — nothing mattered, nothing and no one, not even me."

Jo knew the feeling. Joining the fire brigade had been her salvation. It had given her a purpose, something other than her pain to focus on. She didn't like to think what would have become of her without it.

"You had no other family to lean on?" she asked softly.

"My parents, but they were working through their own grief. I didn't want to bother them with mine." Coop stopped and rubbed a hand over his face. "That's not true. If I'm honest, I didn't want to deal with their pain. My own was bad enough.

Sounds terrible, doesn't it?"

Jo shook her head. "Sounds all too familiar."

"You do the same?" Coop said, surprised.

"Oh yeah. In fact, if you had been at the barbecue, you would have heard my big sister, Trisha, tear a few strips off me for it." Which reminded Jo. "Why weren't you at the barbecue, Coop?"

"I had to—" Coop stopped and his eyes narrowed. "Jesus, Jo." He pushed back his chair then stood up. "You think I was setting the fire at the flats?"

Jo refused to be swayed by the hurt in his voice. "Hey, you more or less forced me to invite you, then you didn't bother to show up. What else was I to think?"

"I was working, Jo."

"Ah, now we're getting to it." Jo was angry, too, and her anger focused her thoughts. "You gonna fill me on this *work* of yours or shall we shout a bit more? I don't think the people downstairs can hear us?"

Coop looked around at the twitching curtains and the avid glances thrown in their direction. "Sorry." Embarrassed, he sat.

Jo's anger drained away. "I'm sorry, too. We've buried this stuff for so long that it's kinda hard to dig it up again, isn't it?"

"Understatement of the year," Coop said with a wry smile. "You know, until last Friday, I hadn't said my family's names out loud or talked about what happened to them. Not a word, nothing, since the day they died."

Jo reached for his hand, touched by the admission, then felt woozy. She kept her head still and hoped the room would stop spinning. Eventually her stomach settled. "Maybe it's time, Coop."

Coop stared at their clasped hands, hazel eyes hidden from her for a moment. When he raised them, they were clear, his face set. "Maybe it is." He squeezed her hand, held tight.

"As I said, I did everything I could to numb the pain, but nothing worked. Oh, it did for a while — an hour, sometimes two — or, if I was extremely lucky, a whole night would pass without remembering. But reality was always quick to rear its ugly head, usually first thing in the morning. And let me tell you, it was no fun coping with reality *and* a hangover at the same time." His laugh sounded hollow. "'The cold light of day,'" he said bitterly. "I never understood that saying before. Now I know it better than I want."

Jo remained silent. Coop needed to talk, needed to get this out of his system.

"Finally, I did what I had always done, I threw myself into my work."

At this Jo couldn't stay quiet. "What is your work, Coop?"

"Computers." He laughed at the surprise on her face. "Seems I'm a freaking genius where they're concerned. I can do things that haven't been invented yet — or so most people think." He winked.

His grin was infectious, relaxing the lines on his face and lightening the shadows under his eyes. Jo found herself smiling.

Coop leaned towards her, eyes boring into hers. Tiny flecks of amber appeared in his irises, glowing, as if lit by some internal fire. "You keep looking at me like that, Ms Woods, and I'm really gonna give these people something to talk about."

Heat stole through Jo's body. She dropped her eyes, unable to hold his gaze. "Don't change the subject."

Coop grinned. "I'll come back to that later. Now, where was I? Oh yeah, computers. Well, I talk to them like others do people." There was no embarrassment in his voice. He was stating a fact. "I like them. They don't lie. They do exactly what you ask — no arguments, no quibbling — and they never minded that my sole conversation was centred round fires and burned corpses.

"People want every little detail at the beginning, almost like they're feeding off your pain, but they soon become bored, move on to the next tragedy." He tilted his head. "You find that?"

Jo nodded, trying not to think about the probing, insensitive questions she'd been subjected to when Lucy and Brian had died. That had been the main reason she'd agreed to have skin grafts on her hands, to stop people from asking what happened. The other scars she kept as her penance for not having saved Lucy.

"Anyway," Coop cleared his throat, "in my 'chats', I found other fires, similar to the one that killed my family. I guess I'm no better than anyone else, because they fascinated me, all the gory details laid out for my instant perusal, a sadist's smorgasbord. Then I saw that someone else was interested in the same pages."

"Me?" Jo said, shocked. "You can do that? Follow my browser history?"

"Baby, I can do anything." Coop caressed her hand. "I flagged certain sites — more to confirm what I already knew — that someone was doing the same kind of 'chatting' I was. Then I saw the pattern you were following." His fingers stilled. "I didn't know whether you were a survivor or one of the many tragedy junkies I'd come across." He paused.

"What?" Jo caught his hesitation.

Coop looked uncomfortable. "Well, there was always the chance you might be the person I was looking for. An outside chance," he hastened to add.

Horrified, Jo tried to snatch her hand free, but Coop wouldn't let go. "Remember, I didn't know you then and I couldn't understand why — if you had so much information — you didn't go to the police with it. And, with you being a firefighter and all, I thought—"

"That I was ideally placed to set those fires myself?" Jo wasn't really angry. He had only done what she and, when she thought about it, the boss, had done — followed the clues and made two and two make five.

Coop looked relieved. "Yeah, but your emails to Mavis finally convinced me I was barking up the wrong tree."

"You read my emails?" Jo felt violated. "You can't do that. Isn't there a law or something against it?"

"More than one, probably."

Jo was dumbfounded by his cavalier attitude. "But... but, how did you get my password?" It was the first question that came to mind. But she had more. A *lot* more.

"Oh, an encryption thingy I use." He avoided her question with a blithe wave of his hand. "You know, I always wondered why you used the name 'Lucy'. I understand now. But really, Jo, you should add a few numbers and use lower and upper case letters. It makes it much harder to hack."

"Thanks," Jo said through clenched teeth. "I'll bear that in mind in future."

Coop hurried past the fire in her eyes. "It became clear the brigade was stonewalling you, not taking your fears seriously, so I took everything I had to the police."

"And I suppose they sat up and panted because you're a man and not a bereaved, illogical woman," Jo snapped.

"Not quite. They took me seriously when I hacked into their mainframe — showed them their salaries, home addresses..."

"You didn't."

"Hey, it worked." His eyes danced with merriment. "Not only did they take me seriously, but I was also offered a job to upgrade their security system."

Jo giggled. It made her feel dizzy again, and her broken ribs hurt, but she didn't care. It felt good to laugh. And yet, at the back of her mind lurked the thought *if Coop isn't the killer or the accomplice, then who is?*

CHAPTER FIFTY-THREE

Pat stared out the kitchen window. Mary sat on the summer seat by the tree, Emily lying on a blanket at her feet. She gazed into the distance, but he knew she didn't see the view, her mind focused inwards. He longed to comfort her, but she needed this time alone. No matter what Thomas had done, she'd loved him once, and he was, and always would be, Emily's father.

Pity he hadn't realised that sooner.

Pat was no stranger to the whims of the human mind. He knew the dead were often imbued with qualities they'd never possessed in life — all the hateful things they'd done erased until only the good remained. It riled him to think of Mary grieving for a hateful bastard like Thomas. His shoulders slumped. How could he compete with a newly sanitized ghost?

It was strange how differently they had reacted when the police had informed them early this morning that Thomas had been identified from his dental records. He'd felt relieved, like a weight had lifted from their lives. He'd expected Mary to feel the same way.

He watched as she bent to stroke Emily's hair, heart twisting in his chest. In a short space of time, Mary and her daughter had come to mean everything to him. He had spent his whole life searching for them, although he hadn't known it until he'd found them.

Family.

That was all he wanted, a family of his own to replace the one he'd lost. Now he was frightened he would lose this one, too. If he did? Well, he didn't know what he would do.

He had messed up, big time, and he knew it. After the police had left, he'd begun making plans, excited they could move forward with their life together. It had taken a while for her stillness, her silence, to register.

"What's up, Mary?"

"I can't believe you could be so insensitive."

"What? What have I done?" he had asked, baffled.

"Don't you understand anything, Pat? I've just lost my husband. Emily has lost her daddy. We need time to grieve. Talking about the future is the last thing on my mind right now. I don't want to think about tomorrow, never mind the future."

"But... But..."

"Don't say it," Mary said in a tone Pat had never heard in her voice before. "Don't you dare say what a bastard he was, Pat. Don't you dare."

Pat was amazed she could be so blinkered. "But he was."

Mary's face flushed, her voice thick with tears. "He's dead. Don't you understand, Pat? He's dead!"

"And good bloody riddance," Pat said under his breath, but not quietly enough.

"I need some fresh air." Mary had stormed past him. She'd lifted Emily from her pram, grabbed a blanket and made her way towards the summer seat. She had been sitting there ever since, staring into space.

Pat wasn't sure what to do next. Every time he opened his mouth, he managed to stick his bloody size elevens inside.

"Some knack you got there, Meehan," he scolded himself, chewing on a ragged fingernail. He tried to remember how he'd felt when he'd lost his first family, but he had been too young. The memories of the car accident and resulting fire were hazy, vague. They may as well have belonged to someone else for all the impact they'd had on his life — or his mind.

He did remember being scared, frightened of the grown-ups who towered above him, making decisions he had no part in. This memory spawned others. *Helplessness.* That's what he remembered most — an aching, constant helplessness like a hole in his chest that had never gone away. He pressed a hand to his chest as if the imaginary hole were real and found to his surprise that it no longer hurt. Mary and Emily had done the impossible, filled the aching, empty void.

The least he could do was return the favour. Pat went to the fridge. No matter what he felt about Thomas and the things he'd done, he had to give Mary space to grieve. However long it took, he would wait, because they were worth it.

He took out ham and coleslaw — not your typical breakfast, but he knew they were Mary's favourite — and made a stack of thick sandwiches. He poured two glasses of lemonade and heated a bottle of milk for Emily, added them and the plate of sandwiches to a tray.

If the way to man's heart was through his stomach, surely the same could be said for a woman? He took the tray outside, hoping he was right.

*****

Mary watched Pat approach, huge hands clutching a laden tray, a hesitant smile on his face. She knew he was there to apologise and she felt awful. He hadn't done anything wrong. She had lashed out simply because his relief at Thomas's death had mirrored her own emotions. What an epitaph, she thought sadly, patting the seat beside her for Pat to sit down, that the only feeling produced by Thomas's passing was relief to be free of his presence.

"I made your favourite," Pat said as he slipped into the seat next to her.

"I can see that. You sure you made enough?" Mary eyed the stack of sandwiches, trying not to smile.

"I was hoping... Well, I thought maybe I could join you?"

Without a word, Mary handed him a sandwich then laid Emily on the blanket and gave her the bottle of milk. She smiled as the child grasped the bottle in both hands and began to suck. She took a sandwich, bit into it. "Tastes great." She rested her head on Pat's shoulder.

*****

Seems men and women weren't so different, after all, Pat thought, putting an arm around Mary's shoulder, so happy he could barely speak.

CHAPTER FIFTY-FOUR

After Coop left, and with the aid of her morphine drip, Jo managed to sleep most of Wednesday, oblivious to the hustle and bustle around her. She rose out of her stupor at mealtimes but only because the nurses insisted she eat to keep her strength up. They stood over her, eyes watchful, as she picked at the unappetising fare.

The simple act of eating drained her and it wasn't long before she drifted back into Morpheus's arms. While she slept, her body used the time to heal.

Teatime Wednesday she woke with a pounding headache and feeling like a herd of elephants had stampeded over her in her sleep. Minor aches and pains, unnoticeable earlier, now vied for attention. She touched her cheek. It felt swollen, the skin abraded and rough to the touch — a result of her less than graceful swan dive from the Blakes' bedroom window.

The least of her worries, Jo decided as her nerve endings screamed in concert with the pulsing in her head. Even breathing was a new experience in agony.

She took slow, shallow breaths, focused on the sounds of the hospital. Voices rose and fell in the corridors, the distinctive rattle of metal trolleys trundling up the hallway to deliver dinner.

When she felt able, she hauled herself upright, grimacing. "Shit!" Sweat broke on her brow. Once upright, though, Jo found the pain in her chest eased, making it easier to breathe. She surveyed her little piece of hell. Sitting on the cabinet next to her bed was a huge bouquet of red roses. Hand trembling, she plucked the note nestling between the plump blooms.

Thinking of you and wishing you a speedy recovery,
Angela, Mike & Mike Jr

Relief rushed through her. What a lovely gesture, then a not-so-nice thought struck. *Were the flowers delivered to the ward or did the Parsons visit while I slept?* She liked the Parsons — she did — but now she knew someone was trying to kill her, the idea of anyone standing over her while she slept made Jo nervous.

No more morphine, she decided. She needed to be alert and awake at all times. So, after dinner, when the nurses appeared to dispense the medication, Jo motioned to one. She cursed under her breath as the flirtatious nurse, Barbie, stalked over.

"Yes?"

Jo ignored the look of haughty disdain. "Would it be possible to have some other kind of pain relief, Barbie?"

"The name's Barbara," the nurse snapped, disdain turned to surprise. "I can't give you anything on top of the morphine, Ms Woods. It's the strongest pain reliever we have."

"No, you misunderstand," Jo said. "I would prefer *not* to take morphine at all. Surely you have a tablet that will do just as well?"

"Nothing works *just as well*." Barbie sniffed. "But if you prefer milder medication, I'm sure I can oblige."

Something told Jo she wasn't about to get the strongest painkiller available, but she didn't care. She'd rather be in pain and awake than doped up and murdered. She watched Barbie confer with the doctor then tried not to quake when the woman returned with a not-so-nurse-like glint in her eye.

"Are you sure you want to do this? We're about to get you up and moving about. Now might not be the best time to lower your pain meds."

"I'm sure." Jo kept a smile pinned to her lips as Barbie whipped her cannula out then plonked two plain white tablets in her hand.

Jo downed the tablets, hoping she had misjudged the nurse's prejudice against gamblers — a prejudice she admitted that she had not only fostered but actively encouraged. God help her, because she would now be the one paying for it.

*****

The Spanish Inquisition was missing a member, Jo reckoned when Barbie finished torturing her and allowed her to return to bed. Even her fingernails hurt.

"A visitor... My kingdom for a visitor," she said. The rest of the evening passed with excruciating slowness. She cast envious eyes at the overflowing beds beside her, full of laughter and hushed chatter. One other patient appeared equally friendless — an old woman in the bed opposite her, no more than a ripple of bones under the thin white blanket, who slept constantly.

Jo averted her eyes from the pitiful sight. She'd settle for a magazine, a crossword — anything to distract her from thinking about the time she was wasting and what the killer might be up to while she was trapped in this damn hospital bed.

Her wish was granted, although not in the way she hoped.

"Hiya doll fa... er, Jo." The bulky figure edged through the ward door. "How you feeling?"

Jo stared in amazement. "Flanders?"

"In the flesh, speaking of which..." His eyes dropped to the flimsy blue hospital gown she was wearing. "Whooeee! This is the second time I've seen you undressed, sweet cheeks." He winked. "Mind if I sit down?"

Jo shook her head, too shocked to speak.

"Betcha you're wondering what I'm doing here?" Flanders settled his huge rear into the tiny plastic seat, fleshy jowls straining with the effort of holding his smile in place.

"You could say that." Jo recovered, clutching the hospital blanket to her chest, wishing it was Teflon coated. "What's up?"

"Nothing, I..." Flanders hunted in his pocket, pulled out a hanky and wiped his forehead. "I want... wanted to say I'm sorry...for what I said, that time... in Murdock's." His words tumbled over one another in his haste to get them out. "Even if I hadn't seen those scars of yours, I would have apologised first chance I got. I don't know what came over me." He dabbed his forehead again. "Sheila says it's envy. My wife," he explained, seeing Jo's uncomprehending look. "We never could have kids, you know — biggest tragedy of our lives." He ducked his head. "She says I'm inclined to resent people who do."

Jo felt a surge of pity but had to wonder if she would be feeling half as compassionate if she hadn't read Mavis's work history and knew Flanders couldn't possibly be the killer.

So much made sense now — Flanders' terrible anger over Steven Forbes's drunkenness and disregard for his family's safety, the deep-seated grief she'd seen in his eyes when he'd talked about being a Scout leader, and the strength of his response to what he perceived as her abandonment of Lucy.

"I know I can be a bit of a jerk," Flanders said. His gaze slid away from her face and Jo, aware of how much this was costing him, managed to bite her tongue. "I don't mean to be. I also know what it must have taken to put those scars there." He bobbed his head towards her chest. "You went in, didn't you?"

Now Jo was the one feeling uncomfortable. As she had told Coop, it hadn't been bravery that had made her run into her burning home. It was primal, an overpowering instinct to save her child, no matter the cost. Any parent would have done the same.

She tried to explain. "Flanders, I—"

He held up a hand. "I know what you're going to say. Anyone would do the same thing, right?" Jo nodded.

"Not true. Oh, the urge is there all right, but most," he rubbed his fleshy jowls, "well, they're the ones who put their kids in that situation in the first place." His voice rose to a falsetto: "'Off to the pub — sure they'll be okay for a few hours.'" Then it dropped, deeper, harsher. "'Bloody screaming kids, is a man never to get any peace?' We've both seen it, Jo. Those kinds of *parents* wouldn't save the bacon if it were burning in the pan."

Jo didn't answer. He was right.

"It's always baffled me why God chose to give children to people like that when... when..."

The chubby face twisted with grief and Jo didn't know how to comfort him.

"You would have made a great father, Don," she said at last, taking his hand, not quite believing they were having this conversation. "Any child would have been lucky to have you as their dad."

"Well, wasn't to be, was it." The hanky made a quick swipe over the piggy eyes, then disappeared. "But thanks for saying that, Jo. I don't deserve your kindness after all the things I've done."

"How about we start anew, from today?"

"You mean it?"

Jo pumped his hand. "It's nice to meet you, Don. My name's Jo."

Flanders grinned. "Good to meet you, doll face." He winked, but before Jo could react, he checked his watch. "Gotta go or I'll be late for my shift." His ruddy face darkened. "Before I forget, the boss wanted me to pass along a message."

Jo could tell by his tone this wasn't going to be good news. She braced herself.

"It's to do with the girl in your flats who's taken up with that jerk, Meehan." Flanders caught her eye, blushed. "I mean, Pat's girl, the one with the kid."

"What about them?" Jo's heart contracted. Had something happened to Mary, Emily?

"Boss told me in confidence that the DB they found in your flats was her husband. No loss to the world, as I understand it," he said. "Right bastard, by all accounts."

Jo smiled. Flanders might be trying to change but it would take time — a hell of a lot of time.

"He also gave me this." Flanders handed Jo a sealed envelope. "Love letter?" When Jo didn't open it, he said, "Go ahead. Don't mind me." But he didn't wait to see what the letter contained and he was smiling, the first genuine smile she'd seen on his face, as he left the ward.

Jo stared at the envelope. *Good news or bad? Should I open it or not? What the hell.* If Flanders could apologise and act like a human being, there was every chance for once in her life, this might be good news.

Taking a deep breath, she pushed her thumb under the fold and broke the seal.

CHAPTER FIFTY-FIVE

Jo was ruminating over the note Flanders had given her when her mobile rang. She grabbed it. The use of mobiles was forbidden in the hospital but she figured she wasn't near any high-tech machinery. She wouldn't stop someone's pacemaker by taking a phone call. Anyway, she felt cut off enough as it was.

"Hello?"

"How are the aches and pains?"

The voice needed no introduction. She had known, deep down, that the DB in the flats wasn't the killer, but the call was still a kick in the teeth. How had he got hold of her new number? He spoke again before she could ask.

"So sorry I *missed* you." He chuckled.

"You bastard!" Jo gripped the phone tighter. "Why don't you drop dead and save us all the trouble?"

"Hey, isn't that supposed to be my line?" More laughter.

"This is a big frigging joke to you, isn't it?"

"Far from it." The voice roughened. "In fact, I was phoning to tell you to stay out of my business. This is my final warning."

"Business? You mean murdering kids, destroying homes, and scaring the wits out of the community?" Jo said, thinking about Angela Parsons and Mrs R. "Or maybe you're talking about your feeble attempts to kill me?"

The killer didn't rise to the bait. "All of the above, Jo, and if you don't heed my words, I can promise you plenty more of the same. I'm almost done here, but if you don't back off, I will change my plans, stay a while longer, free more little birds."

The threat silenced Jo. Was he saying if she didn't stop her investigation he would kill more children, but if she did, he would leave Mourne Lough, go somewhere else, and start all over again? Jo's brain might not be working to its full capacity, but that sounded like a no-win situation to her.

"No witty comeback, Jo? Have you got it? Have you *finally* got it?" He didn't wait for an answer, slamming home his point. "You try and pursue this, make any more waves, and I swear to God I will kill every child in Mourne Lough."

"God? How can you mention his name in a sentence like that?" Jo asked, aghast by the threat.

"Easy. I have right and might on my side. I—" The voice stopped as if aware he was giving too much away. "Don't test me, Jo. You might have sent your sister and her kids out of harm's way, but they have to come home sooner or later."

"You touch them and I'll—"

"You'll what? Kill me?" Coarse laughter filtered down the line. "Wouldn't that make you as bad as me? See?" the voice said when she remained silent. "The line between what you consider good and evil isn't quite as cut and dried as you thought, is it?"

Jo refused to believe that, but the boiling rage inside her at the threat against her family told her she could kill this man as easily as swatting a fly.

"And again, no witty rejoinder. You disappoint me, Jo."

"You leave my family alone, you hear?" Jo trembled with anger and fear. "You touch one hair on their heads and I swear to God, I'll kill you myself." His snort of anger inflamed Jo. "You obviously don't know a lot about families or what I, or anyone for that matter, would do to keep them safe. And why should you?" she taunted. "You have nothing, no one, except your urge to kill. Does that keep you warm at night?"

"So sure of yourself, Jo, so smug. Would it surprise you to know I, too, had a family once — parents, siblings, the whole hog?" He paused, drew the seconds out. "I have a family now."

Jo knew she'd failed to contain her shock when the killer laughed.

"Let me guess... Psychologist report? Hmm... male, over thirty and under fifty, white, of above-average intelligence and probably hate my father or love my mother too much?" More laughter. "I've been doing this a long time, Jo — longer than you can imagine. Profiles? Reports? They are for ordinary mortals, not for extraordinary people, such as myself. I don't conform — never have, never will."

The shock of hearing his voice was wearing off and Jo blessed her decision to forego her morphine. She needed a clear head. His anger was making him careless. She knew he had a family, and he had been doing this for a long time, which was more than she had known a minute ago. She felt a spurt of satisfaction. Did he know how much he was giving away? She smiled. He wasn't as clever as he thought. He had an ego. She could use that. If she could get him talking, use his conceit, who knew what else he would let slip? She tried again.

"Tell me about your family."

"No. Why are you smiling? What are you up to?"

"Nothing, I—" Understanding dawned. A chill started at the top of her head, moved towards her feet. She tensed, afraid to move.

"You look good with your hair loose, Jo — gorgeous, especially with that delectable tinge of fear. It's almost as satisfying as freeing one of my little birds. Almost."

Jo's eyes shifted, searching the ward. He was here, watching her. *Where? How?* She dragged herself up in the bed, the motion causing pain to whip through her. Ignoring it, she scanned the room.

Visitors, arms full of flowers and hugs, came and went. Nurses flittered by, busy and oblivious. She saw no one with a mobile phone, but she could feel his eyes on her, crawling over her skin. She eyed the bed opposite her. The curtains were closed, a snore from inside told her the elderly patient was asleep. Could the killer be in there, hidden, ready to strike? She tried to control her panic. No, he wouldn't chance it. She would have seen him come in, wouldn't she? Desperate, she inched her hand towards the button to call the nurse.

"Don't!"

Jo froze.

"This is between you and me. If you call anyone, I won't tell you why I freed Lucy."

*****

I knew I had her by the quick flash of desire on her face. Desire, such a delicious emotion. I felt almost vampirish as I drank it in. I waited, drew out the agony. Finally, I said, "Don't look for help. Don't call anyone and I will tell you."

I knew the moment she gave in — knew it by the way her shoulders slumped and her hand dropped from the call button. Power tasted equally delicious.

Her voice, when she spoke, was smaller, eager. "Tell me."

I was glad to tell her. She was bending, but she wasn't broken — not yet.

"You were in a bad mood that day," I began. "In fact, you were so cross with your husband that you took it out on your daughter. You wouldn't let her eat the sweets in her party bag."

"How—?"

"You should have let her eat those sweets, Jo. It would have made it easier on her."

I could see the moment she understood, and I was glad I'd left this little tidbit until I was in a position to appreciate the look on her face. It was priceless.

A person really can fall apart, I noted, surprised and not a little turned on. It starts with the eyes. They widen until they can go no farther, then the mouth drops open and the neck muscles contract. It's like the skin sloughs off the facial bones, dropping until only a skeletal, screaming mask is left. Not a pretty sight — at least, not to the casual observer.

Now, I thought with satisfaction, *now* she was broken.

*****

"You drugged the sweets?" Jo's mind spun. She thought she had visited every horrendous possibility of what Lucy had gone through that night, but with the killer's words, she knew she had only skimmed the surface.

"Yes. Freeing my little birds is supposed to be painless — for them. No matter what you think of me, Jo, I am not a monster. Imagine my surprise when I found not a sleeping little bird, but a wide-awake, frightened little girl. It definitely added a certain... frisson to the whole experience — one, I might add, I particularly enjoyed."

"You bastard!" Jo couldn't believe how much she hated this man. Why, oh why, hadn't she let Lucy eat those sweets? Brian had drunk the wine Lucy brought back from the party, a gift from her friend's parents, she'd said. It hadn't struck her as odd at the time, just a nice gesture from one parent to another. How stupid she had been. How gullible.

*****

Her recovery was swifter than I anticipated, but no less enjoyable for that. I laughed. I still had the upper hand.

"Did you know you and your husband made Lucy's life a misery? Your petty squabbles, your arguments. She cried all the time, afraid her mommy and daddy were splitting up and thinking it was her fault. You did that, you and your precious Brian." I could hear my voice rising and I tried to control it. This was Jo's hell we were in, not mine. But the memories of my own parents fighting crowded my mind, making it hard to be objective.

"She was loved. She knew that. We would never have hurt her, even if we had spli—"

"Liar! She was hurt. She was hurting badly."

"How do you know so much?"

"Because I look, because I care, and because I was her a long time ago." Even now, I wanted Jo to understand, to share my pain, my frustration. "I lived through that shit. It tainted us."

"Us?"

"My sisters and I"

"And you... freed them?"

"Yes. I had to save them, to save them from the pain."

I didn't know why I was telling her this. Maybe it was the tone of her voice, the kindness and understanding I heard in it? Maybe this was why God had saved her? Maybe she was here to bear witness, to understand and help me in my task.

Her answer reinforced my belief.

"That must have hurt."

"It did." I began to cry. It was the stupidest thing. Stuffed into a tiny closet opposite her ward, phone pressed to my ear, I began to rock, sobbing like never before. "You can't imagine how much."

"How old were they?"

With her question, they were with me again, as they always would be. Marge was nodding, smiling, telling me it was okay to share.

"Amy was five. Serena, six. Marge..." I trembled on the name, "was seven."

"So young," Jo breathed down the phone.

I could no longer see her, my vision blocked by tears and the ghosts of my past. "Yes. I was the oldest, I looked after them."

"I know you did." Her voice was soft, compassionate. "And you freed them."

"Yes."

"How old were you?"

"I was—" Immediately I understood and her betrayal was worse than anything that had gone before. "You bitch! You're pumping me for information."

I couldn't believe I had fallen for it again. The tiny cupboard wasn't large enough to contain my anger. It spewed from me, angled towards the girl on the bed. If emotions could kill, I would have felled her in an instant, so strong was my hate. Gasping, choking, I wiped my eyes. "I was going to leave, cut my losses, but not now. Mourne Lough has a lot of little 'birds' waiting to be freed."

It was a lie, but she didn't know that.

"Their deaths will be on your head. Do you hear me, Jo?" I said, before I closed the handset. "Their deaths will be on *your* head!"

I saw her collapse on the bed, face ashen.

Good. Served her right. She should suffer, like I was suffering.

And suffer.

And suffer.

CHAPTER FIFTY-SIX

My stomach felt alive — and not in a good way. I burped, grimaced as a wave of acid lapped the back of my throat. Since my disastrous phone call to Jo yesterday, everything was unravelling.

I'd had the upper hand and still she'd bested me. Anger coiled amid the acid. I'd acted no better than the desperate, needy child I had once been, so eager for my father's approval that I would have said, done, anything for a loving look or a murmured "Good lad!"

Who was I kidding? I would have settled for not getting the crap beat out of me because the old man couldn't hold down a job. Oh, he'd couched it in religious terms. He was beating the devil out of us, like he was doing us a favour. We all knew the devil he was trying to beat. Alcohol had been his God *and* his demon, and no amount of beatings could have silenced the bottle's call. He'd prostituted the Lord's word for his own gain, and it had got him nowhere. Well, I amended, it had. I couldn't allow him to malign God and His sacred Word. In punishing Father, I had freed my siblings, and so discovered my own calling. Now it was being threatened.

Goddamn Jo Woods to hell. To quote our fearless leader, she was a "fecking" blight on my life.

How much had I given away in my misguided telephone conversation?

"Everything but my fucking name and the size of my underwear." I groaned. She had my sisters' names, their ages. A sure-fire way to trace me. I cursed my stupidity. When would I learn I was in this alone? I couldn't look for, or expect, help or understanding.

I had to stay positive. All the greats had been tested — Abraham ordered to kill his own child; Lot, saved because of his chaste spirit in the amoral land of Sodom and Gomorrah, yet fated to lose his wife. There were so many. Who was I to complain when my only adversary was but an annoying slip of a girl?

I recalled Jo's face when I'd mentioned her daughter. The pain and longing that transfused the normally impassive features, how it collapsed when I recounted how she had condemned Lucy to the living nightmare of my "freeing". I'd had her then. *Right in the palm of my fucking hand.* The thought calmed me as I slipped into my cot, mid-shift.

I subscribed to Locard's theory that a perpetrator will both bring something to a crime scene and leave something behind. I not only subscribed, but I had also refined the concept. I believed contact of any kind, physical or otherwise, left its mark. So, while I had transferred knowledge to Jo, she must, in return, have left some snippet for me. I just had to find it.

I reran our conversation, but nothing sprang to mind.

"Damn." I twisted in the narrow bunk, unable to get comfortable. The dorm was stuffy and I kicked off the top blanket, listening enviously to the snores of the others. I checked my watch: 1:00 am. My shift ended at nine. If I were to strike, it needed to be soon, before Jo returned to spoil my plans. Pain ate at the lining of my stomach. She had to have left me something.

Two hours later I found it. *"Scaring the wits out of the community!"* That's what Jo had said after I'd warned her off. She had meant more than the broken windows and mangled cars I created blowing up her flat. I could hear it in her voice. What had I missed?

I was almost asleep before it had come to me and, with it, the knowledge of what had been bugging me these last few days. I hadn't missed anything with the amateur. That had been my own inadequacies at work. No, it had been something that had happened earlier, at the start of my mission in Mourne Lough — my "follow up" visit after the Forbes fire.

There had been no need to hide my identity. After all, no one had known of my existence. I had been a wisp of smoke. When someone had noticed I was there, it had already been too late. I had become over-confident. Another reason for Him to test me

Going to the Parsons' house had shown my arrogance. Now I was to be shown humility. Jo Woods had done that by almost exposing my mission. But she had also, inadvertently, shown me the error of my ways — the only living witness to my deeds.

I cupped my hand beneath my cheek. Not too late to rectify that oversight, I decided as I slid into sleep.

No. Not too late at all.

*****

I woke early, showered and shaved long before the others crawled from their pits. I was energised. I knew exactly what I had to do and how to do it. Once more, all was right with my world.

My good mood took me through breakfast and to the end of my shift. I paraded off duty and was about to leave when I spotted the arson investigator, Shaunessy, making his way upstairs. Without thinking, I followed him, careful not to be seen, and I saw him enter Bill's office.

I moved closer, senses on full alert. Why was Shaunessy here? He'd given Bill his preliminary report on the Blake fire last night, and the official report wouldn't be ready for another few days. No reason for Shaunessy to return so soon unless... Anxiety gnawed my insides. Had he discovered something?

After a careful glance up the hallway to make sure I was alone, I pressed my ear to the door. From within I heard an unexpected voice greet the arson investigator, followed by Bill's more colourful hello. Indigestion re-surfaced, suspicion mingling with acid. Something was going on. The pain focused my mind and the tumblers clicked into place.

Of course! It was so clear now. The unexpected *guest* had to be a mole. There was no other explanation. He'd been sent to ferret out Mourne Lough's secrets, but whose secrets was he after? Jo's or mine? I gave no consideration to the other men in the station. Their biggest secret was who was shagging whose wife, and I already knew. I made it my business to know, which made me all the more furious that I had failed to spot the traitor in our midst.

And yet, I should have. It explained why Red Watch had an extra man on their team. But the idea was ludicrous. The DB had been my only mistake — well, apart from the one I was about to rectify. Until then, everything had been perfect.

But had it?

Uncertainty struck. Jo had made waves in Lisburn long before being turned out to pasture in Mourne Lough, and while the top brass didn't have the combined IQ of a herd of wildebeest, you make enough noise and someone is bound to listen, eventually.

A trickle of fear slithered up my spine as I considered the unthinkable. *They are on to me.* I refused to panic. I needed more information before... The sound of chairs scraping back and voices moving towards the door had me scurrying into the nearest room. I kept the door ajar and watched them leave, then I followed the threesome.

In the station car park, the trio piled into Shaunessy's car. I waited until it pulled out of sight before rushing to mine. I slipped into the traffic behind them, careful to keep a few cars between our vehicles.

When they turned left at the roundabout, I knew where they were going. It wasn't rocket science. Mourne Lough was a small town and this was a familiar route. I relaxed, allowed my speed to drop. My car fell farther behind.

When they reached the boss's house, I waited at the corner, out of sight, car idling. For the benefit of anyone passing, I took out my phone and proceeded to have a non-existent conversation. I watched the trio enter the house then waited a second or two in case they'd forgotten something before driving into a neighbouring garden on the opposite side of the road. I reversed up the driveway, coming to rest under the leafy shade of an old tree — a perfect vantage point with an unobstructed view of the boss's front door, yet far enough away and well enough camouflaged to be invisible to the casual observer. Even better, I knew the owners of the house worked in the city and wouldn't be home until late, if then. I had all the time in the world to wait and watch.

In the end, I didn't need nearly that much.

Seconds after I'd switched off the engine, Coop — Jo's new boyfriend — arrived, followed twenty minutes later by the tubby figure of the coroner, Bob Anderson.

I couldn't believe it. It looked like the unthinkable had happened. They were giving credence to Jo's theory. Confirmation arrived moments later with the arrival of Tim Sheppard, Chief Fire Officer for the area, accompanied by a high-ranking police officer, judging by the bells and whistles on his uniform. But the icing on the fucking cake was Jo's appearance soon after.

That she was included signed, sealed, and delivered my fate. My insides twisted but I breathed through the pain. Even if they believed Jo, there was no way to connect me to the "killings", as they called them, except for one thing — my mistake.

I started the engine, thankful my preparations were in hand. I checked and re-checked the plan as I drove away from the house. I couldn't afford any screw-ups this time, but it all seemed perfect.

Bill and the others could talk, discuss, and analyse until they turned blue in the face. In the end, they'd be too late to stop me.

CHAPTER FIFTY-SEVEN

Jo arrived at Bill's house, out of breath and out of patience. Rushing caused lightning bolts of pain to shoot through her body, but the boss's note hadn't left her much time. *Which was probably his intention*, she thought, furiously.

Jo was under no illusions. Bill's invitation to this meeting was a formality, a sop to his conscience. He would have been confident she'd be unable to attend.

He was almost right.

Luckily, a quick phone call, interspersed with a lot of begging, and a reluctant Angela Parsons had supplied her with fresh clothing and a lift to Mourne Lough. Jo paused in the driveway to catch her breath and tried not to remember the night she'd broken the boss's front window or the terror she'd experienced believing he and his family were in danger.

The clutch of cars in the driveway soured her mood further. Jo didn't know who was waiting inside, although she had her suspicions, but the choice of venue spoke volumes — well away from any prying eyes in the station. Regret settled heavily on her shoulders. It was okay formulating theories when they were abstract, but now they were tangible, moving closer to people she knew and cared about.

A strange sensation swept through her, and for a second, Jo mistook it for guilt. She shivered, the skin on the back of her neck prickling. An instinct as old as time made her spin around. *Someone is watching me.*

The road behind her appeared empty, but the feeling didn't go away. If anything, it grew stronger. She checked up and down the street, the parked cars on either side, but apart from a lone child playing with her dolls in a nearby garden, it all looked clear. Goosebumps erupted on her skin and her nerve ends tingled. *Is he here? Is the killer observing me, enjoying my fear?* She shivered again, still numbed by his latest revelation.

"*Did you know you and your husband made Lucy's life a misery? Your petty squabbles, your arguments. She cried all the time, afraid her mommy and daddy were splitting up and it was her fault.*"

Was it true? Had Lucy known, suffered? *Oh, my darling girl.* Jo fought the guilt. She couldn't let it consume her. If she did, *he* would win. But it was the memories that consumed her.

Lucy, gorgeous in her party dress, dancing into the kitchen, babbling about a clown at Jessica's party who was "the bestest ever"!

Brian snapping at the child, taking his anger and frustration out on their daughter, mollified when shown the gift of wine then pouring two glasses, even though Jo didn't want any. Taking a sip to avoid another confrontation, anxious to get Lucy out of the room before she did something to set Brian off again. Too late. Lucy, skipping with excitement, knocking into the table. Jo's glass wobbling, falling...

Jo didn't want to follow the memory, but it overpowered her, dragged her into its dark embrace.

Brian yelling, Lucy's crestfallen expression, the terrible, awful row after she'd put Lucy to bed, things said that could never be unsaid. Storming out, walking for a mile or so before dizziness struck, making for home, queasy, light-headed and, in the distance, an alarm blared.

Recognition, but not worry, until she turned the corner, saw her house, flames leaping from the windows.

Running. Trainers slapping on damp pavement, breath hissing between clenched teeth.
Too slow. Always too slow.

Even knowing she'd been drugged didn't make it easier. "What ifs" tortured Jo. What if she'd been quicker? What if both their glasses had broken when Lucy knocked the table or the wine bottle? No wine, no drug, which brought her full circle to the killer's coup de grâce.

"You should have let her eat those sweets, Jo. It would have made it easier on her."

Jo closed her eyes. "Oh Lucy, forgive me." She approached the front door, took a deep breath, and knocked.

CHAPTER FIFTY-EIGHT

Coop knew there must have been a time in his life when he'd experienced this degree of awkwardness and ineptitude. In his pimpled youth, perhaps, when self-confidence was at an all-time low? Try as he might, though, he couldn't recall a single instance.

He eyed Jo's boss, who reminded him of his old form teacher, a man who believed firmly in "Spare the rod and spoil the child." The memory didn't help his equilibrium a whole lot. Neither did the way Bill and his two companions huddled together at the top of the kitchen, heads bent, voices low. Coop didn't know what pissed him off more, the fact they made no attempt to include him in their conversation or that he cared.

You can hold your own with these professionals, he told himself. Hell, without him and his skill with a computer, they'd still be scratching their asses and writing Jo off as a head case.

Jo.

Coop's discomfort grew. *Will she show?* The others were confident she wouldn't, but he knew better. Part of him wanted to see her and yet... He clasped his hands together. He had a lot to make up for.

In the beginning, blinded by grief, he'd seen nothing wrong with using Jo. He hadn't cared about her feelings. He hadn't known her from Adam. He'd needed to know what she knew and if wheedling her into an intimacy she didn't want helped him, then so be it.

Then he'd met her.

Coop squirmed in his seat. The second he'd laid eyes on Jo, flustered from her encounter with Mary

Quinn, and later, drunk and kissable on the steps of their flats, everything had changed.

For him, not for her, he'd reminded himself, because at that point, she hadn't known what a bastard he was. Later, as he kept vigil by her bedside, he'd faced the truth. In those endless hours when time had slowed and fears had grown in volume, he'd admitted he cared for Jo, more than he wanted and definitely more than he needed.

Instantly, like a spurned lover, Julie had been with him, Jade and Jason close behind. With them had come a spurt of love so strong it had made him gasp. He tried to hold their faces, preserve their images in his mind. He didn't have years of memories to build on — only a few precious months and a father's determination never to forget.

Grief had crawled through him. A person should never face this level of pain twice in one lifetime. Yet there he'd been, sitting at Jo's bedside, bargaining with a God he didn't believe in to spare her and wondering if He did, whether he could ever forgive Him for not sparing his children.

He'd vowed if Jo woke up, he would confess all and damn the consequences. When she'd opened her eyes, he'd thought his prayers had been answered until he'd seen them flare with fear. Crushed, he'd watched her, even racked with pain, try to escape him.

Me!

The thought seared, because he knew he'd brought it on himself with his lies and half-truths. He hoped he'd done enough to convince her of his sincerity. Where they went from here, he didn't know, but he was willing to find out.

He slouched lower in his chair, trying not to draw attention to himself. It was hard with Bill's wife bustling around the kitchen, being so nice.

"You'll take something to eat, Mr Cooper?"

"Coop," he said for the third time. "Call me Coop."

Marian's smile enveloped her face, falling like sweet pastry over plump apple cheeks. "Here ya go." She heaped food on a plate, handing it to him. "You'll be wanting to keep your strength up."

For what? Coop wondered, but the food was delicious and conversation stilled as they ate, marking time until the others arrived.

The coroner, Bob Anderson, was the first to appear. With his sparkling blue eyes and genial smile, he quickly dispelled the uncomfortable atmosphere. "Mmm," he sniffed the air as he entered, "something smells good." A plump eyebrow edged hopefully in Marian's direction.

She laughed. "Subtle as a brick, you are, Bob Anderson." She prepared a plate for him.

"Ah, Marian, me darling," Bob said, wrapping his arms around her waist, "when are you going to leave the old reprobate and marry me? The bounder doesn't deserve you. Doesn't know what a pearl he has."

"Ach, away wit ya." Marian shook him off, but she was smiling.

"One wife not good enough for you, Anderson?" Bill growled. "You want to fecking steal mine, too."

"Steal? Sure 'tis you who must have stolen this wondrous woman," Bob said, mimicking Bill's soft Irish accent. "No way would she have gone willingly into your arms. Isn't that true, Marian, my love?" He winked at the woman. "Speaking of steal, though, you owe me a day at the nineteenth, Simmons."

"A day! What do you mean a fecking day?" Bill demanded, "We decided on a drink."

"A drink for each eagle," Bob corrected, "and, seeing as I managed to get one on every hole, I'm guessing a day ought to do it. Pity you weren't there to see it. 'Twas an awesome sight." He beamed, face innocent. "But I guess you were too busy in the aftermath of the Blake fire."

"Bill," Marian said, spying the warning signs and hoping to divert her husband from exploding, "that's the door. Can you get it? I need to put these in the oven."

"These" referred to a tray of sausage rolls that looked made from scratch, Coop noted.

"Gladly." Bill threw a disgusted look at Bob before stomping from the room.

"You're an awful man, Bob Anderson," Marian said when Bill left, but she was laughing. "Would you please stop winding him up."

"What did I do? I can't help it if I'm a golf god, can I?" Blue eyes twinkled in the angelic face.

Coop watched the byplay with amusement, glad to be diverted from his tangled thoughts. He looked up as Bill entered the room followed by two men.

The first wore the full brigade uniform. "Undressed", Coop thought it was called, which was odd to his mind. Apart from sounding like the wearer was naked, he would have assumed dress uniform would be a more apt description. But no, "undressed" in the fire brigade meant shirt, tie, jacket, shoes shined to a mirror finish, and trouser creases sharp enough to cut the unwary. *Go figure.*

The man towered over Bill, thick grey hair shorn to military precision, face clean-shaven and angular. Shaunessy and Tumilty stood to attention as he approached. He ignored them and walked towards Coop, hand outstretched. "Tim Sheppard, Chief Fire Office," he said in an accent as clipped as his hair. "You must be Mr Cooper?" He shook Coop's hand, motioned to the man behind him. "You know Chief Constable O'Hare, I presume?"

Coop nodded. He'd met the liaison officer when he'd first come to Mourne Lough, and once had been more than enough. He eyed the shorter man with distaste. Raven black hair, with a sheen that could only come from a bottle, lay slicked over the prominent forehead, attempting to hide the receding hairline. No such problem with his moustache that crawled over the fleshy upper lip like liver on a milk bottle. He reminded Coop of a bloated Adolf Hitler, a comparison which furthered his dislike of the man.

"Everything's done, Bill." Marian's chirpy voice broke the strained silence, "Just the sausage rolls to keep an eye on." She untied her apron and hung it on the back of the door. "I've a few errands to run, so you won't be disturbed for a while." She pressed a kiss to his cheek, and with a last cheery wave, was gone.

"Crew's all here, I see." Tim Sheppard rubbed his hand together and padded towards the laden table. "Let me get some of Marian's fine fare and we can begin."

"Shouldn't we wait for Jo?" Coop said.

"No need." O'Hare joined the CFO at the buffet table. He stroked a forefinger and thumb over his moustache. "Unlikely she'll attend." The two shared a smug grin.

Sanctimonious gits. Coop wanted to punch the pair of them and was debating doing just that, hopefully flattening the constable's moustache in the process, when the doorbell rang.

The others looked at each other in consternation, and Coop grinned. "Hmm, I wonder who that could be?"

He lifted a forkful of food, put it in his mouth, and waited for the fireworks to begin.

CHAPTER FIFTY-NINE

Jo, despite the pain, squared her shoulders as Bill ushered her into the kitchen, determined not to show any sign of weakness. The sight of the men looking comfortable and matey, ready to begin without her, hardened her resolve.

"Gentlemen." She smiled as they rose. They might not want her here, but good manners dictated they rise in her presence.

Coop rushed to pull a chair out for her. "Couldn't keep away, could you?" he said under his breath.

"And miss all the fun?" Jo wasn't surprised to see Coop there. It had been a shock when he'd told her he was working with the police and not just updating their mainframe — a shock, but a hell of a lot better than her original suspicion. Besides, it was nice to see at least one friendly face.

"Okay, gentlemen." She sat, folded her hands demurely in her lap and said, "Who's going to fill me in?"

Bill sent her a warning look, but all he said was, "Glad you could join us, Woods. Before we begin, let me introduce you to the rest of the gang.

Robert Anderson, Coroner." He nodded to his right. "Chief Fire Officer, Tim Sheppard," he said, indicating the man next to the coroner, "whom you already know."

Her old boss and Mavis's current one. Jo nodded. "Sir."

Bill worked his way down the table. "Shaunessy you've met, and Chief Constable O'Hare, who's leading this investigation and will take over in a minute."

"We've also met," O'Hare said curtly.

Jo inclined her head, trying not to remember the tense interview she'd endured with this man on Monday or his patronising behaviour towards her. Things had changed since then. They were, she reminded herself cynically, on the same side of the table this time.

Bill, as if aware of her thoughts, moved swiftly on. "I'm informed you already know Mr Cooper."

Jo shifted in her chair but didn't confirm his obvious suspicions.

"And lastly..." Bill's eyes inched past Coop and his voice took on a note of anticipation. "Jim Tumilty, firefighter extraordinaire, also known as Jim Healey, on loan to us from the Police Service of Northern Ireland." He looked disappointed when Jo didn't react.

Jo pushed to her feet. "Jim Healey, firefighter from 1999 to 2001 when he decided to join the police force, obviously found a job with a better pension plan." Her tone was tart. "But the perfect Trojan horse." She glared at the CFO.

"Couldn't put just anyone in. We needed someone with experience. Seemed like a good plan at the time." Tim Sheppard couldn't hold her gaze.

Jo rested her hands on the table, ignored the pain to lean forward until she was facing Tumilty. "I have to say, *Healey*, you played your part well — maybe too well."

Jim Healey's weasel face creased in agreement. "Me mother always said I should have been on the stage." He bowed theatrically.

"She was right. Maybe if you hadn't been such a good actor, we wouldn't have wasted so much time. And to make up a service record to match the dates of the murders was plain irresponsible!" Jo didn't attempt to hide her anger.

"Maybe, but the results speak for themselves. I've been on this case six weeks. Tell me again how long you've been tracking our killer?"

"Cut it out, Jim." Coop half rose from his seat, but one look from Jo held him back.

"Leave it," she said. There was no sense arguing. The powers-that-be had ignored her all these years and when they'd finally taken her seriously, they'd cut her out of the loop, preferring to work in secret. She knew she was here under sufferance, probably so she could be pumped for information, which was okay. She was happy to do some pumping of her own. "How about we pool information?" She conjured a smile. "See what we can come up with?"

Chief Constable O'Hare took that as his cue. He stood, dabbing his moustache with a napkin. "Good idea." He marched to the end of the kitchen, where a large flip board Jo hadn't noticed before stood. It was the same kind they used in the duty room for their lectures. It might well be the same one, for all she knew. O'Hare flicked it over.

"We've come up with list of thirty-eight names, all male, all with the knowledge and skill to set these fires. Eleven," he said, producing a blue marker from his pocket, "are firefighters stationed in Mourne Lough." He focused on Coop and Bob Anderson but couldn't control his satisfaction as he ticked them off one by one.

"From Red Watch: Geoff Davis, Pat Meehan, and Dave Evans. Bill Porter and Pete Murphy from Blue Watch." Two more ticks covered the board. "Then we have three from White Watch — Tony Sands, Phillip Cortez, and Michael Walsh." The blue marker continued its journey. "Another three from Green Watch: Conrad Peak, Sean Abbot, and John Cassidy." The blue pen halted. "Plus, we have two retired firefighters living in the designated areas.

Both have a grudge against the brigade, as well as the skill and opportunity to carry out these attacks."

He circled their names. "Alan Blake: retired in 2005, reluctantly." He slicked his finger over the glossed fringe, making sure it was in place. "Showed signs of early onset Alzheimer's, poor bugger. Not a great contender, but he bears watching. Simon Trainer is a different kettle of fish. He was disabled out in 2006 after a bad road accident — not job related. He wrote a few vitriolic letters to the brigade about making them pay for putting him on the scrap heap. He's worth a closer look."

"You can forget both of them," Jo said.

The policeman didn't like being interrupted. "And why would that be, Ms Woods?"

"Because the killer told me he murdered my daughter in 2004."

There was a shocked hiss at her pronouncement.

"When the feck did he admit that?" Bill demanded.

"The night he blew up my flat," Jo said, anticipating his next comment. "I didn't tell you because I had no proof. Everything went up in the fire and you did tell me to bring you only *evidence*."

Bill, looking furious, went to speak, but Coop jumped in. "So these guys wouldn't have any reason to murder anyone, not *before* their retirements?"

Jo shot him a grateful look. "Exactly. I'm assuming they had spotless records before then?"

Bill had no need of his notes. "Yeah, both exemplary officers. Wipe them," he told the Chief Constable.

Reluctantly, and with a furious glance at Jo, O'Hare did as he was told. "Okay," he said, "moving on. We've earmarked twenty-five arsonists in the time frame. Between death and prison time, twenty have been excluded. Of the five left, one appears to have turned his life around — married, a couple of kids, and a steady job." His voice, like his face, was sceptical. "The other four..." He turned to the board. "Two have left the country and are someone else's headache now, and the last two are teenagers. I guess we can count them out too, seeing as Ms Woods has redefined our time frame." He reached for the cloth, wiping the bottom third of the board.

There was a collective groan as the meaning of his actions became clear.

"Fuck! So, we *are* looking at a firefighter for this. We've trained the bugger and now he's killing people." Tim Sheppard looked harried. "Oh, this is not going to look good in our stats."

*****

I reached my destination, pulled the car to a stop and waved to the woman who came to greet me.

"Come on in. We've been waiting for you."

Not as much as I have for you, I thought. I lifted the doctored cake and locked the car door. Kids loved cake, as did hosts, especially nice ones like this woman and her husband who would find it rude not to take a taste.

And a taste was all that was needed.

I hid my thoughts behind a polite smile and followed my hostess up the path, letting her inane chatter wash over me. For a moment, it was as if I had stepped outside my body, able to watch from a distance as we progressed up the well-kept garden. I noticed, in a strange, detached kind of way, that I was sweating and my mouth was moving in answer to her questions. But inside my head there was only silence — a gentle, peaceful calm.

I liked the sensation, the way my emotions disengaged and the blasted acid in my stomach had finally stilled.

How come I'd never been able to do this before?

The question absorbed me as I stepped through the front door. Maybe it was the absentee voice. For so long it had filled the empty chambers of my mind. Keeping me sane, I'd thought, but maybe I'd been wrong? Maybe the voice was the madness and this, this calm peacefulness was the sanity I craved? Why had I waited? *Should have got rid of you long ago.* I didn't know why I was talking to the voice. Habit, I guessed. No longer. I was free, and with freedom came an intense sense of peace.

I greeted the man of the house with a respectful slap on the back and chucked the child he was carrying under the chin. "You have a lovely home," I said, as I was ushered towards the kitchen. "Here, a little something for you."

"Oh, you shouldn't have." The lady took the box, peeked inside. "Oh, fresh cream, our favourite."

The child, eyes aglow, begged for a piece. "Why don't we all have a slice?" I saw my mouth say. Hers moved in answer. I filtered the words. "Tea? I'd love a cup."

I sat, watched from afar as the cake was divided and delivered to four china plates. I even helped the child eat his, feeding him until his plate was scraped clean.

Knocking my own plate off the table was easily done. A flurry of apologies, an offer to clean up which was, as I expected, rebuffed. I sat again, smiled and nodded, spoke in all the right places, but inside I felt numb, like a part of me had died. Or maybe it had been reborn.

It was most peculiar.

CHAPTER SIXTY

Bill Simmons looked at the CFO as if he wanted to punch him. "Feck the stats, Tim. We've bigger problems." He slapped the table. "Much as I don't want it to be one of my men, I want this bastard caught more. Ideas anyone?"

Shaunessy spoke. "Jo, you're the closest we have to this guy. Anything you can tell us, anything at all?"

Jo stared at the names left on the board, stunned. Familiar names. Someone she knew, someone she had touched, was the bastard who'd murdered her baby. Her voice, when she spoke, was harsher than she intended. "He's trying to kill me."

She waited until the shocked babble of voices passed. "I'm only telling you this because so far we haven't been able to come up with *how* he's setting these fires and, more importantly, getting away with it. Maybe it's time to turn our attention to *why* he's doing it?"

"What a load of rubbish," Tim Sheppard said. "I don't believe in all this psychology hoo-ha. How's knowing why he's doing it going to help us catch him?"

"Knowing what makes him tick might get us a step closer to finding out who he is. For instance," Jo said, before the CFO could speak again, "he's never failed before, that we know of, and yet he's failed with me at least twice." She didn't mention his first failure, when she escaped but Lucy and Brian died.

"Twice?" Shaunessy pulled out a notebook, wanting details.

Jo hesitated. She thought she had come to terms with the idea that someone — a complete stranger, or so she thought until a few seconds ago

— wanted her dead, but at Shaunessy's question, she knew she hadn't. She had pushed it to the back of her mind and packed it away in a box, like she did everything else.

A wave of crippling fear washed over her. It caught her breath, drowned any reply she might have made. Sweat broke on her forehead, cooled and went chill. She felt sick. Around her, the room was silent, except for the sound of Shaunessy's pen tapping against his notebook and the frantic thudding of her heart. Jo's panic grew. Everyone was looking at her, waiting for an answer.

Just when she thought she was going to lose it, start bawling like a baby, a hand gripped her knee. It squeezed once, twice, then lay still, heavy and comforting on her thigh. Jo caught Coop's calm steady gaze and the fear receded. She took a deep breath, let it out slowly. "The first time I know of for sure, is the explosion at my flat." She heard only the faintest quiver in her voice and hoped no one else did. "He phoned to warn me."

Jo wasn't sure "warn" was the right word. She recalled the taunting voice on the phone, talking about her brother-in-law, speaking of things she hadn't known until a few hours before, when Trisha had confided in her. Then his lightning switch to Mary Quinn's husband — again telling her things she hadn't known. *Showing off or something else?* And his parting shot: *"You just guess what I'm about to do now."* A hint. Had he given her a chance? And if so, why, when he seemed desperate to kill her?

"And the second?" Shaunessy asked, oblivious to her thoughts.

"The Blake fire." Jo told him about the suspicious flame she'd seen next to the old couple's bed, close to the oxygen cylinder — a fire that shouldn't have been in that location at that precise moment in time.

Shaunessy wrote that down. "And why you, do you think?" he asked. "What is it about you, or what have you done to make him change his MO?"

It was a good question. The boss had asked her something similar when they'd gathered in Dave's kitchen. She hadn't known the answer then and she didn't know it now. Why had the killer turned his sights on her?

The only thing that made sense was if he knew she was on to him. *But how? What have I done to give the game away?* And suddenly she knew.

"The Forbes fire. He knew I was suspicious, that I'd linked him to the murder of my family. No, not my family," she corrected, "the other murders." It was true. The killer hadn't known about her connection to Lucy until after the barbecue.

"His first phone call to me was the morning of the Forbes's funeral." Had it only been a week ago? "He thought he'd got away with it all these years," she said, piecing it together in her mind, "considered himself invincible. To his mind, there was no chance of getting caught." Her smile verged on vicious. "Guess I disabused him of that notion."

"You guess? Without you, we'd never have known what was going on." Coop waited for the others to agree, but Shaunessy was the only one to acknowledge the truth of his words.

"Agreed. Without you, Jo, we'd still be in the dark. But you mentioned the Forbes fire raising your antenna. Why? And if, as you suspect, the killer was aware of your suspicions, how did he find out? Who did you tell?" He cocked his head. "It might help us narrow the field."

Reasonable questions, but Jo baulked at baring her soul to these men. In the end, though, she knew she had no choice.

She started with the roses she'd seen on Emma Forbes's bed, how they'd linked in her mind to the

Thompson fire and the paper roses she'd spied on the little boy the year before. Then, in a voice that wasn't as steady as she would have liked, she told them about Lucy and the seared blooms on her child's face — her last image before flames consumed her baby.

"I thought I'd imagined them. Later, between the drugs and the pain... well..." her mouth twisted, "for the longest time I figured they were part of my nightmares, until the Thompson fire. As for who I told..." She gave Shaunessy a sheepish look, remembering the night in the dorm when Flanders goaded her into saying more than she meant. "Everyone in Red Watch, basically."

"Not a lot of help, then," Tim Sheppard said.

Shaunessy ignored him, eyes sympathetic. "No, this is great, Jo. So far, we haven't been able to figure how this guy sets these fires. Clever bastard. Maybe, as you say, it's time to concentrate on the why, get into his head, and you're the best person to help us do that." His thin face came alive. "Tell me everything you remember about these 'accidents' of yours."

Jo took him at his word. She told him how it hadn't occurred to her she was under threat until Coop's comment about how many explosions she'd been involved in. "They've all been so plausible," she said, "even the Forbes's fire. Not that I think he was after me, not then, but it was such a textbook case. Don't you think?"

Shaunessy agreed. "Give me specifics."

"The jemmied latch in the Blake fire, for starters," she said. "And the flames near the oxygen cylinder I mentioned — flames that shouldn't have been there, not with the way the fire was going downstairs. It didn't make sense."

"A second point of origin." Shaunessy looked energised. "I knew it!" He said something to Bill. "What else?"

"The fire at my flats was set with Mrs R's faulty gas fireplace specifically in mind, but as to who knew about it...?"

Shaunessy jotted another note. "You told Bill you thought he drugged his victims, any idea why? With the stuff on the market today he could kill them and be done with it, no chance of discovery. Why go to so much trouble, have them asphyxiate in their sleep?"

Jo didn't let on how his words, coming so soon after the killer's revelation about Lucy, skewered her heart. "He doesn't see it as killing," she said, rerunning the conversations she'd had with the killer in her mind. "He says he's 'freeing his little birds'. As for the fires. I think fire is important to him — cleansing, like the profile says."

"Cleansing! What a load of codswallop." Tim Sheppard sprang to his feet, face rigid with disapproval. "And little birds. Is the man a fucking birdwatcher?"

Shaunessy again ignored him. "Cleansing. Interesting. The drug renders them unconscious and it's the smoke that kills, which means he doesn't feel responsible because their deaths aren't actually by his hand."

Finally, someone got it. "That's what I think," Jo said.

"Bob?" Shaunessy turned to the coroner.

Bob Anderson's eyes no longer sparkled. "It's possible. There are a few drugs, ones we wouldn't check for, not when carbon monoxide poisoning was so obviously the cause of death. Even if we did, some of them can be undetectable in the body from anything from two to six hours after ingestion, and seeing as these people were unconscious for hours, breathing in smoke..." He shook his head.

"So there's nothing to be gained by digging these people up?" Tim Sheppard said, determined to be heard.

"Not once they've been embalmed. Nothing useable to test, I'm afraid. If we get any new cases..." Bob shrugged. "It's possible our killer used something traceable, hoping we wouldn't look too closely, but I doubt it."

Shaunessy agreed. "He strikes me as a careful man, one who covers all his bases." He turned back to Jo. "While his reasons for setting these fires are important, I think the fires themselves are our best way to catch him. He'll have a signature, and that, more than anything, will tell us all we need to know. You have any thoughts on this second origin point?"

"Judging by how far the fire had developed, I figure it was set no later than two to three hours before we were called. Turn-out time was ten forty am, so... eight to eight thirty?"

Shaunessy agreed. "Does that take anyone off our list, Bill?"

Bill looked at his notes, rose, and took the marker from a reluctant O'Hare. He faced the board. "Peak, Abbot, and Cassidy from Green Watch were off duty, as were Sands, Cortez, and Walsh from White Watch." He drew a line through the six names. "Buggers were on a fecking stag do. Left Mourne Lough at four thirty am Tuesday morning to catch the early ferry to Scotland. Poor city probably never knew what fecking hit it." His smile didn't reach his eyes. "But they're all accounted for." He glanced at the list. "Then there were five."

Five. Jo stared at the remaining names, numb. Three were men from her watch.

"Blue Watch was on duty from six pm to nine am the night before," Shaunessy said, eyeing the list. "Were Porter and Murphy present their whole shift?"

Bill checked his notes, nodded. "Aye, both present and accounted for until they paraded off duty at nine am." His meaty face looked shrunken like a roast left in the oven too long.

O'Hare spotted his opening, grabbed the marker from Bill and elbowed him out of the way. "That leaves us with Geoff Davis, Dave Evans, and Pat Meehan. We've established this guy's been killing since 2004, so—"

"Earlier," Jo said. "In his last phone call, he told me he 'freed' his sisters — seven-year-old Marge, six-year-old Serena, and five-year-old Amy." She fought to keep her voice steady, remembered how the killer's voice had trembled as he spoke of his siblings, sounding almost human. "He said he was the eldest, but I'm guessing with the ages involved, he wasn't much older — eight, nine tops, when he set that first fire."

"Do you know how unusual that would be, Jo?" Shaunessy sounded sceptical. "Fire setters begin at an early age, but they start small, work their way up. It would be rare for someone so young to begin with killing people."

Jo knew the statistics." Rare, but not impossible. This guy, whether he conforms or not, started at an early age and he started as he meant to go on." She looked at the board. "What are the family backgrounds on these men?"

Tim Sheppard reached for the phone, bristling with importance. "If anyone can find out, Mavis can."

Minutes later, he thanked Mavis and holstered his phone. Not looking at anyone, he went to the board and crossed out one of the names.

"Seventeenth May, 2006, the Magill-Cooper fire, in Spain with his daughter and her family."

Jo glared at the CFO. Did the man have no feelings? An awkward silence followed. Under the table, Jo grasped Coop's hand, felt an answering squeeze, but Coop didn't look at her, his eyes locked on the board.

Two names left.

Jo stared at them, chilled, and knew that Tumilty/Healey, for all his bravado, felt the same.

"That can't be right," he said.

"They fit the profile." Tim Sheppard sat, looking no happier than the rest of them. "Both orphaned at an early age through fire. Both have the skill, plus opportunity." He made a temple with his hands. "Mavis did say one other thing, which fits with what you were saying, Woods." He consulted his notes. "A fire from 1982, five vics: two adults, three children. Not a lot of evidence, but enough of a question mark to make the coroner leave the case open." He dropped the punch line. "One survivor, male, ten years old."

"So, we have a name?" Shaunessy looked expectantly at the CFO.

"No. Kid ended up in a bunch of foster homes. We can track him until he hit eighteen. After that, the trail ends. He must have changed his name."

"Surely the brigade would have a record of that?" Coop sounded frustrated.

"Not necessarily. Not if they didn't volunteer the information themselves. A change of name is a legal document, you know."

"Jesus!" Coop rose out of his seat. "I don't believe this. Get me my computer. I'll find the bastard."

"Calm down, lad," Bill said, "we've narrowed it down to two suspects. That's bloody brilliant. Next we've gotta—"

"No need, Boss." The words were dragged from Jo. "I know who the killer is."

"What?"

Consternation filled the kitchen.

"Who?" they all chimed.

Jo shook her head. "I need to make a phone call first, check something." She opened her phone, scrolled to a familiar name. Fingers trembling, she hit dial and turned her back on the others so they wouldn't see the tears in her eyes.

CHAPTER SIXTY-ONE

The husband was the heaviest. I placed him last on couch, next to his wife and child and stood back. Almost perfect. I just needed to... I took his right arm and stretched it to curl around his wife's waist. But that left the boy out. I tugged the father's left hand from beneath his body, interlinked it with the mother's, settled both in the tiny grasp of their son so all three were linked.

Perfect.

It was almost done. I subdued my doubts and grieved the detachment I'd experienced earlier. It would have been easier if I could have maintained that disconnected feeling. This family didn't fit my criteria. They seemed like good parents, nice people. Then again, I knew first-hand how quickly that changed, how looks deceived.

They hadn't been tested yet, I told myself. If the husband lost his job, who was to say he wouldn't go off the rails? As for the wife? She could have an affair, split her family as surely as if she had taken an axe to them.

It happened.

Then where would their little bird be? No, he was better off this way, saved from the pain the world would inflict on him. But no matter how I tried to convince myself I was doing the right thing, I had a knot the size of a fist in my stomach. It churned the acid inside until I cried out in pain.

"It's not the acid. It's 'cause you know you're doing wrong."

Marge stood before me, hand on hip, sounding like a mother hen. I ignored her, brushing past the sleeping family I'd positioned in the conservatory next to the kitchen. The TV was on, a cartoon channel playing in the background. Husband and wife lay curled on the soft leather settee, little bird nestled between them. A happy family overcome by smoke watching TV. What could be more perfect?

"Them not dying at all," Marge said, eyes fierce. *"You're being really naughty."*

"Am not, Marge. I'm doing what I'm told. This little bird needs freed."

"Does not!" She stamped her foot. *"You're doing it 'cause you messed up."* She began to sing-song: *"Yooou messed uuuuppp. Yooou messed uuupppp!"*

"Shut up, Marge." I was angry, mainly because she was right. "I'm the boss here, *okay?*"

She shrank back, eyes sombre. *"You're just as bad as Daddy,"* she said and faded from sight.

"Just as bad as Daddy?" Her words stung. I was nothing like Daddy. *Am I?*

I hesitated. Was I doing the wrong thing for all the right reasons? I looked at the Parsons, at my carefully orchestrated scene. Were they like this in real life? Were they the family I had searched for all this time, who loved and cared for each other through thick and thin?

The acid in my stomach moved into my head. Pain sparked over synapses, spread like wildfire through the multitude of veins and capillaries in my brain. I gasped, breath hitching in my throat. I had to... I had to...

I no longer knew what I was supposed to do.

Stricken, I hovered in the doorway. "What should I do, Marge?"

I waited, but she didn't reappear. Without Marge or the voice, I was alone. Truly, frighteningly alone.

Bereft, I raised my eyes to the heavens. "Lord, what should I do?"

*****

When Jo put down the phone, everyone snapped to attention.

"Well?" Tim Sheppard demanded.

"We've got him," Jo said, her aches and pains numbed beneath the chill of what she'd learned.

"How?"

"A slip of the tongue and a Goddamn phone number." She couldn't believe it. All these years, all the twist and turns, and she'd caught the bastard because of a simple phone call. It would be funny if it weren't so tragic.

Conscious of everyone's eyes on her, she walked to the board and held out her hand for the marker. O'Hare relinquished it without a word. Jo drew a line under the last two names. Next to them she made two headings *Crime* and *Opportunity*. Beside the first name she wrote *Forbes fire — on shift*. She did the same with the second. "But we know our killer uses smoke as a weapon, so this fire could have been set hours before either of these guys came on shift."

"Lot of bloody good that does us then," the CFO said.

Jo continued writing. Below *Forbes fire* she wrote *Flat fire*, and beside the first name she added *With one of the victims*. She moved to the second name. *Not on scene, but knew about the faulty fireplace.* A niggle scratched at the back of her mind, too faint to grasp. *What is it? What am I missing?*

Frustrated, but aware the others were waiting, she continued. "That's where his first slip-up occurred." She wrote faster. *Blake fire: on shift, outside only. On scene, but late to work —* "A doctor's appointment his wife knows nothing about, which gives him plenty of time to set and watch the second fire take effect."

"No fecking way, Woods." Bill stood, but his voice lacked its usual confidence.

"Fran just confirmed it, Boss. Dave's entire family was killed in a house fire when he was ten years old." That's what Fran had been trying to tell her that day in the kitchen. *Why didn't I pay more attention?* And later, when she'd gone to see Fran to arrange a thank-you meal, she had known something was wrong. Why hadn't she pushed harder? So many opportunities missed. "She said he spent his early years in foster homes. That's why family, especially his little Jenny *Wren,* is so important to him."

"Oh bloody hell." Shaunessy caught on first. "Wren... bird — freeing his little birds."

Jo nodded. Nausea clawed her stomach and a blinding headache developed behind her eyes.

Dave — her friend, her confidante — had played them like the proverbial fiddle. She wondered how much Fran knew. She'd seemed oblivious, judging by their conversation. Fran had answered her questions, speech slurred and thick with tears but hadn't shown any interest into why Jo was asking about Dave, until the end.

"I told you he was having problems, Jo," she'd said as if that excused everything. "Is Dave in some kind of trouble?"

Trouble? Dave had gone past trouble, and then some, Jo had wanted to scream, but she hadn't. How could she blame Fran when she was guilty of the same blindness? They all were.

"And the slip of the tongue you mentioned?" O'Hare asked.

"After the flat fire, Dave suggested Pat's presence in Mary's flat put the killer off."

"I don't see—"

"Of course." Tumilty slapped his leg. "How did he know? He wasn't at the flats, supposedly, nor was he at the hospital, and by the time he arrived at your house, Boss, Pat and Mary were in bed. Yet he knew about it first thing the next day."

"Only way he could have known was if he had been there, watching us running for our lives," Jo said. She looked over at Bill and had no need to ask whether Dave had been stationed close to any of the fires. His stunned face gave her the answer.

"And the phone number? What did you mean by that?" Coop asked.

The enormity of her discovery was sinking in and Jo knew if she tried to speak she would burst into tears. She turned to the board and wrote *I only gave my new mobile number to one of these guys.*

She faced the table. "I should have realised sooner. How else could the killer get my number? I bloody well gave it to him." And that's when she realised what was niggling at her. It wasn't just her number she'd given the killer.

"Oh crap."

"What?" O'Hare demanded.

"There's a witness."

"A witness?" he said, "Who?"

Jo dropped the marker, lurched towards the door. "How could I have been so stupid?"

"Wait a goddamn fecking minute." Bill grabbed her arm. "What witness? What the bleeding hell are you talking about?"

Jo winced as pain travelled up her arm to her shoulder. "After the Forbes's fire, I interviewed their neighbours. I needed to see if it fitted my profile," she explained. "But I wasn't the only one. At first I thought Angela Parsons was talking about Tumilty." She cursed. "Then I forgot about it. Jesus! I forgot about it. Don't you understand?" She tugged Bill's sleeve. "Angela Parsons can ID Dave, and if he realises that then..."

She had no need to explain. The group, as one, leaped from their chairs and ran for the door.

*****

Vacillating in the doorway of the Parsons' den, I startled as my phone rang. The cheerful tune mocked my sombre mood, an affront to what was a solemn and, dare I say it, holy occasion.

I pulled the mobile from my pocket and checked the display, surprised to see Fran's name. Was this the answer? Sadness filled me. After everything, was this the way it would end?

Marge was back, smiling, nodding, telling me it was okay. She had such a sage, grown-up look on her face. Why had I never noticed before how much she looked like Mother? In a good way. Eyes glued to her face, I pressed the button to accept the call.

"Dave?"

Fran's voice was barely audible yet managed to carry a faint thread of anxiety. "Jo phoned. She sounded really upset and was asking a lot of questions about you." It was said in a rush. "I didn't know what to do. I hope it's okay. I told her about your family. You don't mind, do you?"

Did I? I no longer knew how I felt.

"Dave?"

When I didn't answer, her voice rose an octave. "What's going on, Dave?"

My eyes locked on Marge, taking strength from her presence. "Nothing for you to worry your pretty head about, Fran."

I smiled at Marge and she beamed back at me. *"You always knew this would happen, didn't you, Davy?"* she said.

I nodded. "I did. Deep down, I always knew."

"You've set the end in motion, haven't you?"

I thought about the drugged cocoa at my house, the mint flavoured one Fran and Jenny loved so much. I'd left it out for them, with a note. A doting husband and father looking after his girls. I nodded again, feeling like a guilty schoolboy. "I have."

"Clever, Davy." She winked. *"You're nothing like Daddy. I'm sorry I said that before."* Her face scrunched, as if ready to cry.

"Don't cry, Marge." I hated it when she cried.

"Am not!"

I laughed at her fierce look, my heart swelling with the joy of being with her again.

"Dave?" Fran's voice sounded confused. "Who's Marge? And why are you laughing?" She broke off to yawn. I could hear it down the line, long drawn out and sleepy sounding. "I'm so tired, Dave," she said after a moment.

"I know you are, darling." I ignored her questions. She would never understand, even if I wanted to explain. "Is my little Jenny Wren with you?"

"Yesh." Her voice slurred. "She's... right here... shound... asheep. I might... I might jus' join her."

Marge bounced from foot to foot. *"Hurry up, Davy. We're waiting for you."*

We? I looked around and there they were, my sisters — Serena, Amy, and Marge, together again. They laughed, waved, told me it was time — past time — for me to join them.

"You do that, my love," I told Fran, eyes locked on my siblings. "Don't worry. Everything's going to be all right."

The Parsons were forgotten in my need to get home. With my sisters at my side, I left the house in such a hurry that I didn't bother to close the front door.

"Everything's going to be all right." It was a mantra inside my head.

Everything's going to be all right.
Everything's going to be all right.

CHAPTER SIXTY-TWO

"I'll never forgive myself if we're too late," Jo said to Coop. They were in the back of Chief Constable O'Hare's car, holding on to the seats for dear life as he sped down the busy road. "Dammit. I should have picked up on the Parsons earlier."

"You weren't to know, Jo. You can't know everything. You're a hell of a woman, but Wonder Woman you ain't."

Jo refused to be comforted. "I should have listened to Angela, followed up on her visitor." She bit her lip. "What if we're too late?"

Coop put an arm around her shoulder. "We'll face that when, or if, it comes to it," he said, "but let's not give up hope yet, huh?"

Jo nodded, glad he was with her. The journey was taking forever. She peered past O'Hare and saw Shaunessy's car speeding out of sight, siren blaring. She growled in frustration. She should be with them, not following in the rear, relegated to the embarrassing status of civilian — and an injured one at that.

The boss and Shaunessy were more than capable of dealing with whatever they found, but the CFO wouldn't be a button's worth of help, she thought in disgust. A pencil pusher if ever she saw one. As for Tumilty, or Healey, as she should get used to calling him... He was the worst, a bloody has-been firefighter.

Jo stiffened in her seat at the reminder of Tumilty's duplicity. The action jarred her wounds and she reached into her pocket, pulling out the sheet of tablets she'd been given at the hospital. She popped two free from the foil and swallowed them dry.

O'Hare shouted instructions into his radio and she knew in the car ahead Shaunessy was doing the same. Bob Anderson strained forward in the front passenger seat, as if he could propel the car faster by the sheer dint of his will.

Jo knew how he felt. Tension coiled in her stomach. She prayed his services wouldn't be needed. "Can't this car go any faster?" she asked.

O'Hare didn't answer. Face set in grim determination, he sped after Shaunessy, flashing blue light clearing the traffic ahead. One or two motorists panicked, but he expertly steered past them, cursing their incompetence.

Jo was impressed. Not once had she seen him check his dreadful comb over, which, even from the back seat, she could see had fallen in a sad tangle over one eye. She reassessed her opinion of O'Hare. There might actually be a real copper underneath all that posturing.

She grabbed Coop's arm to steady herself as they squealed around a tight bend. Ahead, she saw her house. *Not far now.* Angela and her family lived a few metres up the road. She peered ahead as their house came into view, searching for signs of smoke.

Nothing.

"Can you see anything?" she asked Coop, hoping he had a better view.

"No," he said, voice terse.

Neither could Jo, but smoke and flames weren't her only concern. They still didn't know what drug Dave used, whether it was fatal or just debilitating. Even if they arrived before he'd had time to set the fire, there was always the chance they would be too late to save the family.

She had her belt unbuckled and was out of the car before it skidded to a halt. Forcing her body to move, Jo sprinted up the driveway, past the CFO barking orders into his car radio. Coop appeared at her side, Bob Anderson hard on their heels, cursing his bulk and wheezing loudly. Shaunessy, Tumilty and the boss were mere seconds ahead.

They arrived at the front door together. It swung open at Bill's touch, as if the last person out had been in too much of a rush to close it.

Jo wasn't sure if that was a good omen or not.

She rushed into the hallway, shouting Angela's name. No answer. The house remained silent.

"If you won't fecking stay in the car, then make yourself useful — check upstairs," Bill ordered Jo. "Go with her," he told Coop. "Keep an eye on her. Tum—" He frowned. "Healey, take the left. Shaunessy, with me." He headed towards the kitchen.

Jo sprinted upstairs, blocking pain from her mind. She hesitated at the top. She had never been in this part of the house and it took a moment to get her bearings. The hallway was L-shaped, doors to her left and right with a huge ornate window in between.

"Angela!"

She threw open the first door, looked around. It was a bathroom, tiled walls and floor. Huge, gorgeous, but empty. She didn't take the time to close the door, backing into the hallway, opening the next door.

"Mike. Angela."

Coop echoed their names as he checked the doors on the left-hand side while Jo focused on the right. Three doors in all — bathroom, bedroom, and an immense playroom. She took the last in at a glance. It had been divided to accommodate a toddler, with a huge jungle gym complete with plastic balls and safety matting. But at the far end, an even bigger child had been catered for. There was a pool table, dartboard and a low-slung couch with a small TV in the corner opposite. It looked like Mike Parsons was an overgrown kid at heart. If Jo hadn't been half out of her mind with worry, she would have smiled.

Coop finished checking the last room on his side. "Empty," he said.

Jo frowned. *Where on earth are the Parsons?*

*****

"Park it in the garage, not out on the street. Don't you know anything, Davy?"

Marge's voice sounded loud in my ear, but there was no censure to it. I'd enjoyed the ride from the Parsons' house with my siblings, wishing it could have lasted longer.

I steered the car into the garage and closed the outer door with the remote. "Will that do, bossy boots?"

Marge made a face and we both giggled. Serena and Amy looked happy, too, holding hands and jiggling up and down in the back seat.

My chest expanded. I loved them so much. They were the best sisters ever. I whistled as I got out of the car. I couldn't remember the last time I'd felt happier. "This way, munchkins." I motioned them forwards.

And everything changed.

Their smiles disappeared and they moved together, arms wrapped around one another.

"What's up?" I faltered on the step. "C'mon, Marge. Serena?" I looked between them, "Amy?"

They didn't move. *"This bit you have to do on your own, Davy,"* Marge said, face sad. *"Don't worry."* Her smile peeked through. *"We'll be waiting for you on the other side."*

The other side. It sounded like paradise and, like any paradise, too good to be true.

"You sure, Marge?" I asked, worried.

"'Course I am. Me, Serena, and Amy will be waiting right here for you." She drew a line on the floor with her foot and pulled the others behind it. *"Right here, okay?"*

I stared into her eyes, eyes as green and as clear as my own. There was no subterfuge in their depths, only love and the same desperate desire to be united that I felt.

"Right there?" I pointed to where her foot lay. "You promise, Marge?"

She nodded solemnly, marking a cross on her chest. The two younger ones mimicked the gesture. *"Right here, Davy. I promise. We'll be waiting for you, just as we have for the longest while. Now hurry up."*

I laughed and the sound echoed in the empty garage. "I'll be right back." It was only a few steps from here to the kitchen.

A few steps between me and my reward.

CHAPTER SIXTY-THREE

"Jo. Coop. Down here."

Jo and Coop flew down the stairs, halting in the hallway. "Boss?"

"In here."

They followed Bill's voice to the kitchen. Jo's heart pressed painfully against her chest with every step. *Were we too late?* The kitchen appeared empty, then she spied the boss's huge frame blocking the doorway to the conservatory.

"What?" She pushed past him, dreading what she would find but needing to know.

Shaunessy and Tumilty hovered over Bob Anderson, on his knees next to the family entwined on the couch, deathly still. A large TV spewed out something boisterous and childish, but Jo was oblivious, eyes focused on the Parsons.

"Are they...?"

"They're fine — sound asleep, as far as I can tell," Bob said. "Mind you, they might have a bit of headache when they wake." His eyes twinkled.

Jo felt weak with relief. "Thank God."

"I've called an ambulance. After all, we don't know what they've been given, but their vitals are fine — not that I know a lot about vitals." He winked. "That's one thing my patients don't usually have."

Relieved, Jo joined in the laughter while outside the sound of a familiar siren approached. Green Watch had made good time. Thankfully, they were no longer needed.

"You think the wife warned Evans?" Shaunessy asked.

"Sure looks that way," Bill said from the doorway. "He can't have got far, though. O'Hare is on his way to get more men. When he picks the fecker up, we can ask him."

Their smiles faded. It was inconceivable that Dave — their Dave — was the killer, but there could be no doubt now. They stood aside as the paramedics arrived. Bob barked orders, clearly enjoying himself.

"Let's get out of here," Coop said, "and let the professionals do their job."

Jo was happy to oblige. Her tablets were kicking in and she felt mellow and sleepy.

"All's well that ends well," Shaunessy said as they left the house. "Guess that's lucky three for us?"

"Huh?" Jo was only half listening, relishing the feel of Coop's arm around her waist and the forgotten sensation of having someone to lean on.

"You said he didn't make mistakes — that he'd only ever made two, both times with you," Shaunessy said, "Guess the bastard wasn't as clever as he thought."

The others laughed, but Jo didn't join in.

Something was wrong. She might not know Dave Evans as well as she'd imagined, but she knew this killer inside and out. There was no way he'd allow himself to be caught, or have his plans thwarted this way, not if he didn't want them to be.

Her stillness communicated itself to Coop. "What's up, Jo?"

Jo didn't hear him, her mind leaping ahead. Fleeing wasn't an option. Dave would know he'd be hunted until the day he died, which wouldn't fit his perception of himself. So what would he do if every avenue of escape was closed to him?

In that instant, she remembered Fran's slurred voice on the phone. A prickling sensation, similar to pins and needles, enveloped her body, painful, intense. What if it hadn't been tears she'd heard in Fran's voice?

The thought was too awful to contemplate.
He wouldn't.

But Jo knew he *would.* Cornered, Dave would make sure he had an escape plan. Not one she — or any sane person — would consider, but one that would make perfect sense to him.

"Oh, sweet Jesus." She wrenched free from Coop's arms. "It's not over."

"Huh?" Shaunessy, still on a high, laughed. "What do you mean it's not over? Of course, it is. We've got the bastard." His laughter died when he saw the look on Jo's face, and his voice lost its certainty. "Haven't we?"

Jo grabbed his arm. "Not yet. Get Green Watch," she ordered. "And we'll need your car." When he didn't move, she looked at Coop. "Trust me. We have to hurry."

One look at her face and Coop leaped into action. Propelling Shaunessy ahead of him, he said, "Better do as she says, mate."

*****

I pushed open the door from the garage and entered the kitchen — my pristine, state-of-the-art kitchen. It may as well have been a hovel for all the notice I took of it. My eyes, like my body, pulled to the cupboard above the kettle. I let out a breath of relief when I saw the jar of drinking chocolate inside.

"Thank you, Lord." I took a moment to bow my head, but eager to join my family a minute was all I allowed myself. No time to boil the kettle. I opened a drawer and grabbed a spoon.

The chocolate granules, neat and undiluted, were harsh and bitter on the tongue, even with the strong minty taste. I wasn't to be deterred. I took a second spoonful, mixed saliva with the loose grains, formed a paste and forced it down.

The pain in my stomach eased. Maybe I should have been taking minty cocoa powder all this time instead of the indigestion remedies from the chemist? I smiled, high on life, on the promise of resurrection and everlasting happiness with my family.

While my heart was light, my legs felt leaden. Had I taken too much? Would I have time to reach Fran and my Jenny Wren?

Fearful, eager, I left the kitchen and stepped into the labyrinth of a corridor. My vision blurred and my heart slowed until the beats between were no faster than my footsteps.

The stairs were miles away, mountainous and more than I could manage. I was angry with myself. It had to be perfect. I couldn't believe it wouldn't be, not after all my hard work.

The chandelier ahead blinded me and I rubbed my eyes and blinked. Ahead, far, far ahead, lay the staircase and the rooms above — to my right, the family room. I blinked again. Which would Fran have chosen? Upstairs or downstairs?

I tried to put myself in her place, Jenny sound asleep, her own fatigue overwhelming as the drug took effect. The same thing was happening to me.

"Marge?"

I called for my sister. I needed her help. But my voice had lost its volume, my limbs their strength. Through film-covered eyes, I stared towards the family room.

"Family room." I ran the word past my tongue. It sounded like a good place to die.

I staggered to the door, hands clawing the expensive wallpaper Fran insisted we buy. Strength failing, my heart slowed and my breathing laboured. Mount Everest had been conquered easier.

I reached the door. It took three goes before I caught the brass knob and was able to turn it. Relieved, I fell inside and saw an image similar to the one I'd left in the Parsons' house. Fran and Jenny lay on the couch, arms cradled around each other. All it needed was me to complete the picture.

I inched towards them, my perfect, beautiful family. I was right to make this as painless and as easy as possible for them. I wasn't a monster, no matter what Jo Woods and the others might think. I ached to join them, but I had one more chore left to do.

From a drawer in the table next to the couch, I took out a pen and a sheet of paper. I didn't have much time. The drug I'd used wasn't the same one I'd employed in my missions. This one, regardless of whether we were found or not, would do its job and do it well.

I wrote quickly, spared myself nothing. It took longer than I anticipated. Finally, I sealed the envelope and used the last of my strength to position myself between my wife and child. I breathed in their unique scent, cradled them close. In my head, throughout my body, I felt the somnolent beat of my heart. *Slowing. Slowing.* My next heartbeat landed with a painful thud.

"Have I done enough, Lord?"

The next beat was slower, agonisingly so.

"Have I, Lord?"

I had no need of an answer, not any longer. My family was safe. I was content. No more worrying about little birds, about what tomorrow would bring. Soon I would introduce Fran and Jenny to my first family. There was harmony in that. My first and last family meeting for the first time, meeting forever.

The next heartbeat didn't hurt nearly as much.

My eyes closed. I spared a thought for Jo. I wondered what she would think of me, what the world would think of me when I was gone. Would people understand what I was trying to do? Maybe I should have explained it better when I had the chance?

   Then it didn't matter.
   Nothing mattered.
   Anymore.

CHAPTER SIXTY-FOUR

Jo had a feeling of déjà vu and not in a good way. Their mad dash to Dave's house, reminiscent of the one they'd so recently undertaken to the Parsons', wasn't going to end well. She could feel it. Empathy, she discovered, could be a blessing or a curse.

With Green Watch forging ahead, clearing a path with their siren, they reached Dave's house in record time. There was no easy access this time. Front door, garage, and windows were locked tight. Cassidy, Green Watch team leader, took care of the front door and they raced inside. The house felt and smelt empty, dead.

"Stay here," Bill ordered, but Jo didn't listen. With Coop at her side, she joined the others in their search.

Once again she opened doors, dreading what she'd find inside. Jo had the nightmarish sensation she was fated to do this forever, a never-ending loop of doors and dead bodies. She sped down the hallway, checked rooms, thoughts of Fran and Jenny torturing her. They were too late. She could feel it.

"Oh, Jesus."

Coop's voice alerted her. Jo ran towards him, to a room close to the kitchen. She stepped inside and her nightmares came to life.

"Get the paramedics," she told Coop, rushing towards the waxen figures on the couch. "Hurry."

Her fingers trembled as they searched for any sign of life. She checked Jenny first, couldn't find a pulse but wasn't giving up. The sight of the child, floppy and still, awoke memories of Lucy, and she felt the same frantic rush she had then.

"You are *not* going to die." She dragged the child from the couch onto the hard, wooden floor. "Not this time, Dave, do you hear me? Not this time." She tilted the girl's head back and breathed into her mouth, once, twice, then clasped her fingers together and pushed on the tiny chest.

Where is everyone? Jo continued to work on Jenny, trying not to look at Fran and Dave, pale and lifeless above her. Guilt flared, but she knew Fran would want her to do this, to try to save her baby.

"Come on, Jenny. Come on, darling. Breathe for me. Breathe."

Footsteps sounded outside, boots slapping on wooden floors, raised voices in the hallway. Jo's arms grew tired, her broken collar bone screaming for attention. "Come on, Jenny. Come on."

It couldn't end this way. She wouldn't let it. She pushed past the pain, pressed harder on the thin chest, breathed into the unresponsive mouth, and knew it was useless.

"Noooooo!" She pounded on the child's chest with her closed fist. "Come back to me. Come back to me, Lucy."

"Ach, Jo." Strong arms lifted her, stroked her hair. "It's okay," Coop soothed. "It's not Lucy. It's okay."

But it wasn't okay. It would never be okay again.

CHAPTER SIXTY-FIVE

Even with so many police officers milling around, the house was eerily silent. Jo and Coop stood in the garden, watching with dazed eyes the ebb and flow of personnel. They didn't speak, struck dumb by the events of the last few hours.

"My guess is a massive overdose," Bob Anderson said. "Painless, but lethal. I'll be able to tell you more after the autopsy." He pressed a hand to Jo's shoulder, eyes full of sympathy. "Nothing you could have done, even if we'd got here sooner."

Just as Dave had planned. Jo felt a rush of hate so strong that her body trembled. Her fingers tightened around the note, crushing the paper until the words crumpled and blurred. It didn't matter. Every syllable, every rambling, self-serving, smug line of patronising crap was embedded in her brain.

Clever, Jo.

I knew you'd guess I'd attempt to free the Parsons, just as I knew you would be the one to find this note. I leave it for you and you alone.

We are linked, you and I, in a way that transcends all else — except maybe death. Everything I did, after discovering you were on to me, was to help you find answers, to find me.

So why didn't I follow through, kill the Parsons when I had the chance? One word — Marge. My sister came to me, reminded me of my true mission. Something else we have in common, Jo — ghosts.

Lucy was your ghost and you were mine. You haunted me, Jo — your scars, your grief... so strong, even after all these years. It made me doubt my mission, but then I realised the devil wears many guises — father, lover, mother, friend...

And we were friends. In another time, in another place... Who knows? There is evil all around us. It was my duty to free the innocent from it.

I did my duty to the best of my ability.

It was signed. *Your friend, Dave.* And there was a postscript:

I took Fran and my Jenny Wren with me because they would have been lost without me, forever tainted by what others saw as my "evil deeds".

I couldn't have that, now could I?

With the letter was a faded photograph, cracked and brittle with age. It showed four children, scrawny and knock-kneed, arms locked around each other. Dave and his siblings.

They looked sad, as if they had known what was going to happen to them. Jo felt pity for the abused and damaged boy Dave had once been — but not for the adult. It wasn't pity she felt for the man who had murdered her husband and child.

"I need to take those now." O'Hare, comb-over back in place, stood before her. He touched her hand. "I'll have copies made, if you want?"

Do I? Jo looked at the letter, traced the faces on the photograph, nodded once, and handed them over.

He took them without a word, slipped them into an evidence bag.

"Guess we're hitting lucky four." Shaunessy breezed past O'Hare. "I told you the bastard wasn't as clever as he thought." He did a double-punch with his fists. "Howzat!"

Howzat indeed. Jo watched the ambulance speed off with its precious cargo aboard, siren blaring. There was a modicum of satisfaction. Dave hadn't got everything he'd wanted. He hadn't got to take his wife and daughter with him. It had been close, though.

Fran regained consciousness long enough to tell them Jenny had a tummy bug that day that Bob reckoned saved both their lives. Prolonged bouts of vomiting had expelled the biggest portion of the drugged cocoa from Jenny's system. And Fran, busy tending her daughter, hadn't managed more than a sip of hers. They would need careful observation. After all, they still didn't know what they'd ingested, but Bob was cautiously optimistic.

Dave hadn't been as lucky.

Jo averted her eyes as his body was taken from the house.

"Come on," Coop said. "Nothing more we can do here."

Jo let him lead her to the waiting car. *Nothing more to be done?* Then why did she feel it wasn't over, that the book wasn't yet closed?

EPILOGUE

One year later

It was a cold July day; thick clouds loomed in the sky, promising rain, as Jo and Coop climbed the hill to the graveyard.

"You sure you're up to this?" Coop asked.

Jo avoided his real question. "It's steeper than I remember. That's all." She stopped, out of breath. "Or maybe I'm just older."

The last twelve months would have aged anyone. A full investigation was under way, sifting through twenty-nine years' worth of fires. Who knew what the final tally would be. Whatever the number, it would never reflect the true horror of Dave's crimes.

Jo and Coop had taken it upon themselves to visit all Dave's "little birds", or at least those they knew about. It was important to them to pay their respects, mark their passing in some way. Now they were nearing the end of their journey.

Yesterday they had travelled to Belfast, to a sprawling graveyard where Coop had a chance to say goodbye to his family, safe in the knowledge that they had been avenged and could rest in peace. It was a beautiful, peaceful site, much like the one here today.

Jo rubbed the stitch in her side and looked at her watch. "We should hurry. Pat and Mary will never forgive us if we're late for their wedding."

"I'm sure Trisha and Tumilty would be happy to fill in for us."

Jo pursed her lips, an angry flush appearing on her cheeks. "No way José. I'm the matron of honour and you," she poked him in the chest, "are second groomsman. Got it?"

Coop gave a quick salute. "Yes, ma'am." His face took on a mischievous look. "You gonna be matron of honour for Trisha when it's her turn?"

"When, to quote the boss, there's two fecking blue moons in the sky, I will." Jo had tried everything to thwart the couple — sending Trisha and her kids on holiday, warning Tumilty off when he'd attempted to contact them on their return, but it seemed love would find a way.

"Hold on a minute." Coop shaded his eyes and peered into the darkening sky. "Is that...? I think I see two moons, and be-jayus, they're looking kinda blue."

Jo laughed and reached for his hand, the weight of the wedding band on her finger still new and surprising. The last year, while hard, hadn't been all bad.

Coop squeezed her fingers. "You ready?" he asked as they reached the top of the hill.

"As I'll ever be."

Together, they walked to the graves. Jo paused at the first, said a quick prayer for Brian, then moved to the one next to it. The tiny headstone told the facts but not the life.

Lucy Hamilton, beloved daughter.
Born 11th January 1998—taken 8th July 2004.

Today was the eighth anniversary of that dreadful day. It had been eight long years since Jo last had last seen or touched her daughter. She knelt, awkward, ungainly, Coop at her side, and brushed a stray leaf from the grave. Her hand rested for a moment on the pink coral pebbles, Lucy's favourite colour. Visions of a candyfloss bedroom and a Barbie-pink nightdress flashed into her mind, both burning, melting to black.

Coop circled her waist with a strong hold and his presence steadied her. Jo banished the images, bowing her head. "Goodbye, my darling Lucy. I'll never forget you. *Never*," she vowed, as she placed the delicate posy of pink daisies in the granite centrepiece.

Feeling hypocritical, she uttered a long forgotten prayer from her childhood. In her most optimistic moments, she believed there was a heaven and Lucy was there, safe and free from harm. And maybe, just maybe, smiling down on them, giving them her blessing.

She wanted — *needed* — to believe that.

"Time to go, Jo. We've a wedding to attend."

"Give me a minute." Jo took the photograph of Dave and his sisters from her pocket. The original "little birds" — Marge, Serena, and Amy. Her fingers traced their faces. They had no one left to mourn them, but they would be safe here, forever remembered with her darling Lucy.

And Dave? Who will mourn him?

The answer was there before she could stop it. *I will.*

Jo flinched, but it was true. In her mind, Dave was three separate people — the tortured and abused child, the sadistic killer citing piety as his reason for killing, and the genial work colleague and friend she had come to love.

For that reason, she hadn't cut him out of the photograph. The four siblings stared at her one last time as she slid the picture beneath the pink coral, covered it until the faces were lost to sight.

She pressed a kiss to her fingertips and laid it gently against Lucy's headstone. "Sleep well, my darling."

Coop helped her to rise and Jo smiled at him through her tears. Lucy would always be in her heart — her first baby, never forgotten. She rested her hand on her swollen abdomen. She had another baby to think about now, another life to live, and she knew that Lucy, wherever she was, would understand and be happy for her.

Jo took Coop's hand and together they left the graveyard.

They didn't look back. They had no need, the book of their past was finally closed.

THE END

ABOUT THE AUTHOR

Cathy Cole is a novelist and award-winning short story writer and poet from Northern Ireland. Her first short story won a national award and was broadcast on local radio. Her next took second place in the University of Winchester "Reaching Out" competition. You'll also find her work in the 2009 and 2010 *A Writers' Christmas* – anthologies published for charity – and in Bridge House Publishing's *Crime After Crime* anthology, released December 2012

In 2018, Cathy's first ever attempt at a poem was accepted by the Community Arts Project for their anthology *Resonance*, and her second – a Haibun – published in *The Trees of Kilbroney* (Light 2000), has been nominated for the 2019 Pushcart Prize.

Cathy's debut novel *Where There's Smoke* was inspired by the bravery of firefighters everywhere, but especially by those who gave so much on 9-11. She draws directly upon her family's experience in the fire brigade in order to bring realism to her story and believes passionately that first responders are the true, underrated heroes of this world.

Cathy has just finished her next novel *The Hungry Ghost*, and is working hard on her third, titled *Legacy - The Beginning*, which she hopes will be the first in a series based in Belfast.

You can view her other published works on her website:**cathycoleauthorweb.wordpress.com** or contact her at **CathyCole1@outlook.com**

TITLES BY CATHY COLE

Available from **Amazon**

Where There's Smoke

Available from **Third Party Distributor**

"A Christmas Miracle" and "The Wicked Weed"
in *A Writer's Christmas*

Available from **Third Party Distributor**

"Mother Knows Best" in *Rascals of the Red
Barren Bar*

Available from **Bridge House**

"A Killer Week" in *Crime After Crime*

Available from **Third Party Distributor**

"Scar Tissue" in Trees of Kilbroney

TRADEMARKS ACKNOWLEDGEMENT

The author acknowledges the trademarked status and trademark owners of the following wordmarks mentioned in this work of fiction:

Babygro: Delta Galil Europe Limited *Barbie*: Mattel, Inc.
Bodyguard: Draeger Safety UK Ltd
Budweiser: Anheuser-Busch LLC
Cub Scouts; Boy Scout: Boy Scouts of America
Desperate Housewives: Disney Enterprises, Inc. / Splash Media Limited
Fiat: Fiat Group Marketing and Corporate Communication S.P.A.
Firestarter: written by Kim Deal, Anne Dudley, Keith Flint, Trevor Horn, Liam Howlett, J.J. Jeczalik, Gary Langan, Paul Morley
Keeping Up Appearances: The British Broadcasting Corporation
Miss Marple: Agatha Christie Limited
Psycho: Universal Pictures
Sherlock Holmes: written by Sir Arthur Conan Doyle
Teflon: The Chemours Company FC, LLC
The Incredible Hulk: Marvel Characters Inc
The Lone Ranger: Fran Striker, George W Trendel
Tweetie Pie: Warner Bros. Cartoons
Walt Disney World: Disney Enterprises, Inc
Waterford: WWRD Ireland IPCO LLC
Wonder Woman: DC Comics Partnership

42259188R00211

Printed in Poland
by Amazon Fulfillment
Poland Sp. z o.o., Wrocław